The Cusp of Everything

Everything

A Novel

by Laura Huntt Foti

The Cusp of Everything. Copyright © 2012 by Laura Huntt Foti, Prince Willow Publishing. All rights reserved.

www.cuspofeverything.com

Library of Congress Cataloging-in-Publication Data

Foti, Laura Huntt

The cusp of everything / Laura Hunt Foti–1st ed.

ISBN-13 978-0615628400
ISBN-10 0615628400

First Edition: May 2012

Dedication

To **Peter Mustich**, for valuable input and lifelong friendship.
I love you, but not that way.

To my wonderful son **Gregory James Cohen**. Keep reading!
It's not as old-fashioned as you think!

To my mother, **Paula Crandall**, for instilling my love of pop music.
Also for not strangling me a) during my teen years and
b) after reading this manuscript.
We don't say it often, but we know it's always true: I love you, Mom.

In memory of **James J. Foti, Gaynor Toye Jones** and **Kevin R. Devey**, whose lessons in three kinds of love—family, friend and romantic—will stay with me all my life.

CONTENTS

I've Got the Music In Me

The Cusp of Everything was written specifically to be a novel with a soundtrack, a literary manifestation of music's power to shape our experiences and memories. More than 200 songs run through the text, their titles underlined, setting a mood or providing context.

My intention was to allow readers using a Kindle Fire, iPad or other device with an internet connection to pull in a clip of each song on demand. So as you read about a gay disco circa 1975, you could get a sense of the music played at the time. If you liked a song, you could click to buy it.

While such music integration is not yet feasible, I hope you will play along to the extent currently possible by visiting cuspofeverything.com to hear songs featured in the book. Music defines *Cusp*'s era and characters.

- Laura Huntt Foti
May 2012
Los Angeles

1

ONE OF THESE NIGHTS

July Fourth 1975

With the windows down, I forget about my broken air conditioner, until I careen to a stop at the bottom of Old White Plains Road's rocky curves. That's when the heat thuds into my baby blue 1967 Oldsmobile, instantly gluing my hair to my neck. Crap, I forgot to bring a rubber band.

I turn up the music to keep my mind off the temperature. At traffic lights, my radio joins with others, all of us synchronized. If our songs clash, a punch or two of the radio buttons and I can find whatever they're playing. Tunes surge and fade with the heat and breeze. "Love Will Keep Us Together." "Philadelphia Freedom." Oh good, my current favorite, "One of These Nights."

Heading toward my summer job at Playland, I navigate barefoot, Kork-Ease sandals by the door, right foot toggling between accelerator and brake. Passing Hess Gas, I merge onto 95 North, then the leafy Playland Parkway in Rye, singing along to the radio the whole way, dropping my voice at red lights.

I'm in a great mood, which used to be rare but now happens regularly. After only a couple of weeks at Playland I feel like I'm on the cusp of everything. I sense a total shift in my life, my demons scattering, my desires about to be fulfilled, the promise of normalcy ahead. This feeling should last right up until I arrive back at my driveway. But that's hours away. For now I block out the thought of home and focus on my new life on the outside.

I might actually be a member of the cool crowd at Playland. I'm not sure, I've never been popular, but I think this must be what it's like. All I know is I feel completely different than I did before. The job is just a job, with rude customers and a humorless boss. But the people are brand new, and mostly guys. After years of wretchedly unfulfilled crushes, I'm suddenly being noticed. I've already had a brief fling with Jon, the guy who cleans the bathrooms. He smelled like ammonia and had a pimply back, but it's a start. One advantage to discovering his ultimate loathsomeness is that I don't miss him now that it's over, and I know that feeling is mutual.

It could be the fact that no one at Playland knows I was an unpopular loser in high school, or maybe it's the contact lenses. After a lifetime of glasses, I finally don't have to be defined by my frames: granny, librarian, four-eyes, nerd. I look in the mirror and actually like what I see. My long brown hair is split down the middle like everyone's yearbook photo. The braces are off and my skin is clear. I don't stand out as a loser, so hopefully that makes me a winner.

I pull into the employee lot, park and get out of the car. Without the wind on my face, it's steamy and gross. As bad as it is, though, I still have to add a layer. From the back seat I grab my freshly washed red-and-white striped uniform shirt. Slipping its stiff fabric over my favorite embroidered peasant top, I turn to look at the opposite end of the parking lot. Ugh. About two dozen yellow school buses sit like emptied, taunting jail cells. Most of Playland's patrons are not the local suburbanites who know how to behave in public. They're hooligans bused in every morning, I think from New York City detention centers in some kind of play-release program. Somehow I thought a holiday would be different, but apparently not.

Walking to the side entrance gate, I pin on my white plastic nametag. A seagull soars over the word "Playland" and a blue Dymo label reading "Karen" is stuck on underneath. The scent of cotton candy and garbage, with a touch of Jon's ammonia, fills my nose. I can hear the clatter of the Dragon Coaster on its wooden tracks, the screams of its riders, the endless loop of carnival music, almost drowned out by the roar of thousands of people yelling, whining and talking with their mouths full.

I enter the game area of Playland, a green-and-cream-painted row of animal-themed races and tests of "skill" owned by my employer, Funtime Inc. My next-door neighbor Patrick Dowd is manning Shoot

Out the Star, the most macho game in the row. BB riflemen must completely obliterate all traces of a red star on a white paper target to win a giant stuffed toy. Disputes break out all day as guys with girls wearing "I'm With Stupid" T-shirts insist the red is gone, despite evidence to the contrary. Working "The Star" takes an even firmer demeanor than average. Patrick doesn't really look tough enough, but so far he's managed to handle the conflicts.

"Hey," Patrick says, turning slightly but keeping an eye on his current shooter. Sweat drips out from under sideswept brown bangs and down his round, downy cheeks. "Welcome to hell." As if to reinforce his statement, a pack of pre-adolescents runs past screaming.

"Did you see all those buses?" I ask. "Looks like the entire city showed up!"

Patrick counts on his fingers: "Crowded, check. Inferno, check. Meaningless, repetitive work, check."

Over Patrick's shoulder, I see a short, balding, heavyset man inspecting the game booths. "Satan, check. Yep, it's hell. And I signed up for overtime!"

Folding down a fifth finger, Patrick notes, "Eternity, check."

I walk past him, asking, "Have you ever thought about another line of work, like motivational speaking?"

"Hey," he calls after me. "Hell is what you make it! Go grab some gusto!" He turns back to Shoot Out the Star, shooing away an acne-blasted teen trying to remove one of the dusty teddy bears from a hook where it's probably been skewered since the first lunar landing.

The heavyset man is Henry Drake, boss and fashion plate. He's one of the new people I'm *not* happy I met. He wears tight brown polyester pants with a slight flare at the bottom, a multicolored thin-striped shirt and a clashing red tie. On his left hand is a large brown wart, which he rubs distractedly with nicotine-stained fingers. The dark circles under his eyes match his pants almost perfectly. He creeps me out, but I have no choice: I have to pass him to get to the time clock behind his office.

"Good morning, Henry."

Henry looks at his watch. "Hello, Miss Walsh. How nice for you that you're not hung up on obeying authority figures. Very Sixties. Too bad it's the Seventies! Your game is the only one not ready!"

"But we don't open for half an hour! I'm early!"

"Do you see customers? Consider yourself late! What did you expect on a holiday?"

He turns and waddles away. I hurry to punch in behind the Pokerino parlor, where the prizes—cartons of stale cigarettes—line the shelves above the tired machines. I head to my boarded-up game, pull a key from my pocket, undo a padlock and roll up the peeling wooden shutters. My new home away from home: the Monkey Race, where players compete to make their monkey climb the tree fastest.

After clambering over the counter I turn on the lights and start setting up my ticket-taking system. Young kids immediately appear and ask how to play the game, while older kids make threatening comments implying I should let them play for free. I try to move quickly and keep them around so I'll have a full race of twelve people when it's all set up. I look over to see Henry glaring at me from the Rabbit Race across the way, where his pet Eric Thomas is attracting large audiences with a clever sales pitch involving word play on rabbits, bunnies, hares and hopping. Patrick, in the booth next door, has a long line of waiting gunmen.

Finally, in a voice barely louder than conversational, I call out, "OK, grab a spot! Four tickets or forty cents! Here we go!" This is the limit of my patter. I'm uncomfortable with the public speaking aspect of my job. Most of the time I operate quietly, turning up the volume only when Henry is nearby. On busy days, the games are usually jammed anyway. And this is the busiest day since I started here almost two weeks ago.

I move feverishly back and forth across the booth, taking fistfuls of damp ten-cent tickets and dimes and depositing them in a muslin bag and the ancient pewter cash register. I make change for dollars, wipe food scraps off the counter, try to remember to smile, step on the levers that release each player's wheel. Spin the wheel at just the right pace and the monkey climbs steadily. Get impatient and spin too fast and the monkey drops. First one to the top wins a prize worth bragging rights, but probably not even the forty-cent price of play: a tiny address book, a flocked plastic gorilla. Insider tip: wheel number eight can be made to go just a little faster than the others.

The time passes loudly and quickly. Trip, a stoner/floater who wears his name proudly, on his nametag and in his dilated pupils, arrives to relieve me for the mandatory thirty-minute lunch break. But by then it's almost twelve hours later and thirty minutes to closing time. I'm desperate for a bathroom, starving and almost out of prizes. Somehow Trip never got around to restocking; somehow my earlier breaks got bypassed. I'm annoyed but what the hell. Trip can close up.

The Cusp of Everything

I take off my striped shirt, stuff it under the counter and jump out of the Monkey Race. Lighting a long-craved Marlboro, I punch out, then race to the bathroom. I buy a hot dog and 7-Up and wander around the crowded park. Activity is even more frenzied since fireworks are about to begin. Families and groups of kids swarm the wide pathways, heading toward the beach, but I swim upstream toward the slow merry-go-round, where my friend Gwen hasn't yet shut down her ride.

Gwen and I have been partners in crime—literally—almost five years now. We started down the road to ruin freshman year by shoplifting together—once we stole six Kit Kats and a *Creem* magazine from a store in Scarsdale Village and took them to a spot by the Bronx River Parkway to devour: a thousand shared calories and the latest on Eric Clapton and the Who. It beat paying, so we got in the habit.

We got caught at Woolworth's in White Plains sophomore year with a purse overflowing with cheap makeup we planned to divvy up later. They took us in a police car to the dreary station where we had to sit for hours since neither set of parents was home. Gwen was fuming the whole time; I wept. The prison matron they left in charge of us said to me kindly, "I know I won't see you here again." Then she narrowed her eyes and growled at Gwen, "You'll be back."

That sucker-for-tears battleaxe was half right. Gwen did get caught again—but then so did I. I was hooked on "purchasing" (our code word for stealing) and kept right on going. Less than a year later, I was caught taking a plastic bracelet and a Mary Quant eye shadow kit from Lord & Taylor in Eastchester. In a windowless room in the basement, the store detective pointed at her desk and said, "You see there are no sharp objects here? That's because shoplifters have a tendency toward violence." Then she told me that I could never be a nurse because I had proven I couldn't be trusted around drugs.

I'm sure I'd make a terrible nurse, but having any career choice denied me at sixteen was pretty scary. Even scarier was when she told me since I didn't have a previous record they were going to let me go and my mother piped up, "What do you mean first offense? She and her friend were arrested for shoplifting last year!" Thanks, Mom. By the way, you're banned from visiting me in jail.

I always need money, so I stole for the savings. But Gwen's family has plenty. She just has poor money management skills. She spends every penny she gets and is always negotiating with her little brother to borrow at usury rates. She's hoping this summer at

Playland, her first job, will keep her in cigarettes, vodka, Kit Kat bars and <u>Bonnie Raitt</u> albums.

We're past stealing now, and on to trying to rack up some notches in our belts. We don't like the same guys, luckily. In fact, I don't think I've ever liked anyone she's ever been with and vice versa. We have a weird mix of competitiveness, disdain and jealousy. We never discuss it, but it comes out in comments about each other's usually poor choices.

Like me, Gwen struggles with her weight, but in her case weight has the upper hand. I always want to lose five pounds, preferably ten, but Gwen could probably stand to lose forty. Everyone, even her mother, is always telling her how much prettier she'd be if she lost weight. What a slap. At this point she doesn't even seem to care and has accepted heavy as her "style." I think the weight might even make her more self-confident, like she knows who she is and the hell with anyone who doesn't like her. She comes across as tough, maybe a little defensive—sort of an "I'll hurt you before you can hurt me" attitude. I'm more "Please like me!"

Finally Gwen chases away her last riders and closes up shop. She lights a Kool—she switched from Marlboros last year, after going out with one of the only black guys at Scarsdale High, an exchange student from Ethiopia. It pisses me off because now I can't bum cigarettes from her when I'm out. Menthol is just repulsive.

Together we walk through the throngs toward the beach, hopefully looking cool and jaded. Gwen flips her long blond hair and starts bitching. "I can't take much more of this shit. Today was like some awful combination of time passing quickly—'cause it's so busy —and dragging forever because I *hate* these people!"

"It's worse for me," I point out. "You mostly get little kids and their moms, and you don't even have to talk to them. I get assholes who think they're clever and are basically looking to either steal prizes or get laid."

"Hey, speaking of assholes who want to get laid, what happened to you last night? Who was that guy you left the Candlelight with?"

I shudder. "His name was Alex and he was a complete waste of time. Plus he had a two-door car, which is always a pain."

Shaking her head, Gwen says, "Sometimes I wonder why we bother."

"Because one of them might be 'the one'?" I ask.

"Please! If you're hoping to meet 'the one' at a one-night stand, all I can say is I know I'll never be a bridesmaid. Which is fine with me, by the way."

"Yeah, well, talking to guys in bars is more fun than an awkward dinner where you both discover you have nothing in common and try not to drop your bread in the fondue," I say. At least I think it is.

Gwen snorts. "You mean a *date?* How would you know what *that* would be like?"

"Hey, I read *Cosmo!*" I say. I sure do. I even keep the *Cosmo Bedside Astrologer* by my bedside.

Walking in silence among the mob, we pass the ice skating rink, site of birthday parties of yesteryear, toward the arcing swoosh that is Playland's small beach. Gwen sighs. "I thought graduating would be the start of something big, but this summer sure ain't cutting it. It's the same old crap as high school. I can't wait to get to college."

"Don't rub it in. You're getting out of Podunk and I'm still stuck at home. The only difference for me is that you won't be there. God, I hate my parents for getting divorced. How's it fair that my father gets to escape, but not me?"

Eric from the Rabbit Race comes running up behind us, forcing his way through the hordes. He's tall—basketball player tall—and hefty—football player hefty. He'd be cute, except for the crazy eyes and wild, wavy hair. Unlike us, who took off our striped shirts the first moment we could, Eric wears his whenever he's in Playland, like an off-duty cop who still wants the public to know they can rely on him. "Hey, gals—wait up!" he calls to us.

Gwen says to me, "'Gals.' Now that's how I like to think of us. Old-fashioned, with some bumpkin thrown in." I don't comment—she sounds so mean and I don't want to wound Eric, annoying as he can be.

"Aw, come on, give me a break," he complains, taking a deep drag from his cigarette. "Didn't I invite you to the most phenomenal party of the summer tomorrow night?"

"Now, how the hell do we know if it's 'phenomenal' if it hasn't happened yet?" Gwen asks snidely. I don't like Eric much, but I can't imagine being rude to him. Or anyone else, for that matter.

Eric exhales cigarette smoke loudly, his trademark. "It's a 1967 party! You dress in a 1967 costume and let it all hang out."

This makes no sense to me. I say to Eric, "In 1967 I was in fourth grade. Why would I want to relive *that?*"

"Hearken back to yesteryear! It was the Summer of Love!" Eric bellows, before breaking into a few notes of <u>"San Francisco (Be Sure to Wear Flowers in Your Hair)</u>." "You're not supposed to relive it like it really was for you, it's like a chance for you to be eighteen *and* have it be 1967."

"Yeah, yeah," says Gwen. "Very cosmic. Where is it again?"

"At my friend Mark Cassone's house, right behind mine. We can meet at my place."

I throw a quick look at Gwen. Do we want to encourage Eric by going to his house? She shrugs. I guess a party's a party. There will be guys there, even though one of them will be him.

"Where do you live?" I ask.

"Mamaroneck," he says, and all of a sudden he has a pen in his hand and he's writing his address on a crumpled napkin from his pocket. He smiles at me almost shyly and my heart sinks. I've caught him staring at me from his Rabbit Race. I know he has a crush on me and I feel guilty that this only makes me feel one overwhelming emotion: pity. It's for me as much as for Eric. Why him?

Gwen snatches Eric's address and starts to walk away quickly. "Hey, we have to duck into the *gals'* room for a minute. We'll catch up with you later." We run into the bathroom and hide behind the door until finally he checks his watch and scurries away, heading toward the sound of exploding fireworks. We come out and stroll to the edge of the boardwalk. There we gaze down at Rye Beach, packed with people, and up at the fireworks overhead.

I ask Gwen, "Why has this guy latched on to me? I don't want to hurt his feelings, but how could he possibly think I'm the one for him?"

"Well, you're always bitching about how you want a boyfriend."

"Yes, but a *cool* one! I want someone who rides a motorcycle and has good taste in music and wears cowboy boots and has a mustache and isn't looking to get high all the time."

"I think the Marlboro man is a bit out of your league. Plus the fact that he's a fictional character!" She points her cigarette at mine, which just happens to be a Marlboro. "An excellent salesman, though."

"I'm serious. The only thing I want by the end of the summer is to be in love."

"Karen, that's all you wanted by the end of high school, remember?"

"Yes, and thanks for reminding me! At least when I get to college

I can start from scratch with some *new* friends who won't constantly tell me what a loser I am."

"Oh, you're not a loser," Gwen says quickly. "I'm sorry, I didn't mean to hurt your feelings. You know I'm always making wisecracks." I shrug. It's true, she's always making wisecracks, but somehow they're easier to take when I'm not the subject.

We watch the fireworks bursting over Playland's small beach. "That's the Way of the World" by Earth Wind & Fire plays on a transistor radio held by the guy standing next to me. I fixate on the last lines about a child being born with a heart of gold, but the way of the world making his heart go cold. So true. I want to believe the world is good but all signs point to the contrary. I've been hoping that the end of high school means I won't have to feel angry and unloved and poor all the time, but even though my life is definitely improving, it seems like a long shot.

The fireworks are punctuated by oohs and aahs from the families below. The crowd is racially diverse in a way that's rare in Westchester. Some of the black customers act a little menacing but they don't really seem dangerous. And the kids are just adorable, like Michael Jackson of the Jackson 5. Sometimes they even seem to be dancing in formation. When I pointed this out to Eric, he told me I was racist but I don't see how it's racist to notice how cute little black kids are. He thinks he's so smart, with his scholarship to Georgetown and a vocabulary straight out of an SAT study guide.

2
DON'T YOU WANT SOMEBODY TO LOVE

The next evening, I put on a long white Indian gown I bought at Traprock Suite in Scarsdale. It's my favorite store, along with East of the Sun right up the street. I love Indian dresses, wore one almost every day of high school, when I wasn't wearing my perfectly decaying jeans. This one is fancier than the bedspread-style prints for school days and I love the way wearing it makes me feel. It has embroidery around the neck and wouldn't be out of place at one of those barefoot weddings on the beach I'm sure I'll never have.

Gwen was forced to go shopping with her mother so she's meeting me here at Eric's house in a part of Mamaroneck where I haven't been since Ruth and I used to come here for piano lessons. Driving over brought back a sickening memory of my last recital, when I blanked on the piece I hadn't practiced enough. I was the oldest one there, and the only one who choked. That was it for me and piano. Passing the Carvel stand where we used to beg Mom to let us stop for Brown Bonnets also brought on a major sense of déjà vu. We were really a family then. Not anymore.

The houses here are smallish and close together. It feels downscale compared to Scarsdale, more compressed, like you'd be more likely to hear families arguing through the open windows. Maybe that's because the front yards are smaller, or because everyone in Scarsdale has air conditioning so the windows are shut tight. Still, the big trees here make everything cool and leafy, and it smells like a summer night with lots of barbecuing going on. I'm parked in front of Eric's house waiting for Gwen. I can't go in alone. I hear a thumping beat from the party a block away but can't make out the song.

When Gwen finally arrives she's wearing exactly what she wears every other day: jeans and a loose peasant top. She didn't make any effort to look like it's 1967, which makes me feel extremely self-conscious about my gown. She doesn't even seem to notice what I'm wearing though; she's too pissed.

"I can't believe I had to waste all afternoon with her!" she gripes. "I only had time to wash my tits, pits and slits." I grimace but say nothing as we head up Eric's sagging porch steps to the front door.

Eric, shirtless and grizzly-like, greets us a little too warmly and clomps back up the narrow stairs in his Frankenstein boots to finish dressing in his own 1967 garb. His gargantuan hands and forearms are purple, and he informs us he's done his own tie-dying—just wait until we see his shirt! Reluctantly we follow, wiping his slobber off our cheeks and shuddering silently to each other at his broad hairy back. What a gorilla!

His bedroom blows us away: One and a half walls are lined with Parliament cigarette boxes; others are piled all over the floor, along with clothes, books and an array of other junk. It smells like an ashtray, not surprising since there are several lying around crammed with butts. As I would have predicted if I'd bothered to think about it, the bed is unmade. "Paint It, Black" wafts over, doubtless from Mark's house.

"Who's your decorator?" Gwen asks.

"Ha, ha," says Eric, exhaling smoke loudly and tossing another pack on the pile. "I'm a man with a vision."

"Your vision may be fine but I'm sure your lungs are shot," says Gwen. "This room would make my mother happy: it actually makes me want to quit smoking. Let's get out of here."

Eric looks hurt but doesn't defend his wallpaper. "No need to rush." He puts his cigarette on the edge of an overflowing ashtray, pulls on a shirt that looks like it's covered with purple vomit and ties a leather shoelace around his frizzy hair. "Haven't you ever heard of being fashionably late?" He returns the cigarette to his lips.

Gwen gives him a once-over and says, "In our case I think late is the best we can strive for."

I'm still trying to get a handle on what we're doing here. "I don't really get the idea of this party anyway. What's so special about 1967?"

"Mark is…different," Eric responds. "He saw this movie, _Riot on Sunset Strip_, about hippies in 1967, and it just cracked him up. He wanted to re-create it. And he's a huge fan of the Supremes, and they were still together back then. I guess you could say he's an anachronism."

"_You_ could say that, not me," Gwen says, rolling her eyes at Eric's advanced language. "And the _Supremes_? Who the hell listens to the Supremes?" I shake my head. Somehow the Supremes were not what popped into my mind when Eric mentioned 1967.

"I know, I know. It's quirky. He's sort of hard to describe."

Gwen looks at me. "Sounds easy to me: feeb."

"Oh well," I shrug, pretending I don't care that Gwen is already putting down the party and we haven't even gotten there yet. "It might be fun." Gwen, ever the cynic, rolls her eyes again, but I feel a little thrill about going to a party with new people. I seem to be on a roll lately; maybe they'll even like me.

We go downstairs, through a tiny kitchen, out the back door and across Eric's small yard. We climb over a low stone wall to Mark's house, swarming inside and out with people in Sixties clothes, including plenty of tie dye, but also plenty of jeans so Gwen won't feel out of place. But I do—I seem to be the only one in a dress, much less a gown. A huge replica of a joint hangs on a clothesline. Jefferson Airplane's "Somebody to Love" blares. Even though the party is outdoors, a cloud of smoke hangs over it.

We walk toward a dark-haired guy talking to a few girls, who quickly scatter when they see Eric—or at least it seems that way to me. "Hey Mark. I love what you've done with the place!" he says, turning to gesture at the giant joint. "Allow me to introduce you to Karen and Gwen. We toil together at the salt mines of Playland."

Gwen and I exchange a quick glance: Mark's no feeb! His black hair is thick and just the right length, near his chin. His dark eyes are friendly and I feel immediately at ease. He's tall and thin and interesting-looking. Mark greets us as Eric is grabbed by an Abbie Hoffman lookalike and dragged over to a group of people who apparently are willing to tolerate him.

"Hi, nice to meet you." Mark says to me, "Monkey Race, right?"

"Oh God, am I really identified by my Playland game?" I ask. This is not how I want Mark to think of me. Leon Russell's face in clown makeup from the cover of his _Carney_ album pops into my head.

"Sorry," Mark responds quickly. "It's just that Eric talks about you all the time, and he mentioned you work at the Monkey Race right across from him."

"That's OK. I'm not offended. Except by Eric talking about me all the time. *That's* a little unnerving."

"Well, I didn't mean *all* the time. He's also interested in Gentle Giant and the Mets. Just not as much." I laugh, and probably blush, as "Reflections" by the Supremes starts to play.

Gwen must feel ignored. She says, "You know, I think I've heard enough about Eric. I'm going to mingle," and walks off toward the house, past pockets of people laughing, smoking and drinking out of paper cups.

Mark calls after her, "Drinks are in the kitchen—just help yourself."

I wave in the general direction of the nearest speaker. "Supremes, right? Eric told me you're a big fan. I haven't thought about them in years."

"I can't explain it," Mark replies, his deep-set brown eyes crinkling. "But from the moment I saw them on the Ed Sullivan Show in 1964, I've been fascinated by them."

"Wow." I don't know what else to say to this. "What other music do you like?"

Mark looks at me blankly. "Umm…"

"Well, what radio station do you listen to?"

"I don't really listen to any single station. I just jump around to different stations, trying to find the Supremes, or Diana Ross." I know I'm staring, but I can't help it. "But I probably end up on WBLS most of the time."

"I never heard of that one. Does the S stand for Supremes?"

"Very funny. It plays R&B music. It's at 107.5."

"Oh."

"Don't you like R&B?"

"You know," I say, "I don't think I've ever even bought a record by a black artist—not even the Supremes. My mother has some singles, but that's it." My mother used to have an account at a store in Mamaroneck that put a copy aside for her of every new single released that week. She wouldn't buy all of them, but she wanted first dibs and she bought a lot. Over the years Ruth and I stacked them up on the record player and scratched them all to shreds. From "Lodi" by Creedence Clearwater Revival to "Stand!" by Sly and the Family

Stone, her tastes spanned pop music. Other mothers listened to pap like the Ray Conniff Singers, but at our house it was all Top 40 all the time. God, how we loved those songs.

"That's impossible. What about Marvin Gaye?"

I shake my head. "I like him, but I've never bought anything by him."

"Aretha Franklin? Diana Ross?" More headshaking. "What artists *do* you listen to?" he asks.

"Well, I love Jackson Browne, Steely Dan, the Eagles…"

"What about women? Carly Simon? Diana Ross?"

"You said her already," I point out. "You know, it's not that I don't like them, and I do have some of their records. I guess I just wouldn't name them as my favorites. Gee, I never thought about it like that. Am I musically sexist?" At that moment, the Supremes' "Love Is Here and Now You're Gone" starts to play.

Mark, amused, says, "I don't know you well enough to accuse you. But your taste does seem a little narrow."

Narrow, I think. At least I like more than one *group*.

As I'm trying to figure out a polite response, a beautiful dark-eyed girl with two long black braids and a beaded headband around her forehead bounds over. She looks like the most popular girl on an Indian reservation. Throwing her arms around Mark, she gives him a loud smacking kiss. "Great party!" she says, turning her head quickly to flick him on the cheek with her braids.

"Sophia!" Mark replies, laughing and giving her a little hug. "It is now! I was wondering when you were going to get here." Damn. Why are all the cute ones taken? He has such an expressive face. I bet he can raise one eyebrow. After hours in front of a mirror I've never made any progress. He's the perfect height—my head could tuck right under his chin. If he were holding me, that is, which is surely a long shot since he seems to be taken.

Before he has a chance to introduce me, the record gets stuck, playing "Love is here, love is here, love is here…"

Mark turns to me, says, "Excuse me, I think somebody passed out on the stereo," and heads into the house with Sophia by his side.

There's a scratching sound as the needle leaves "Love Is Here" and "Wouldn't It Be Nice" by the Beach Boys comes on. I look around and feel a little panicked—I don't know anyone here besides Eric and Gwen. I find myself almost relieved to see Eric downing drinks with some faux-hippies. They're standing under the giant joint.

The Cusp of Everything

I go over to him.

Eric flashes me a peace sign. "Hey, outta sight, man! It's Karen!" He doesn't bother telling me anyone else's name. "Want a drink?" He holds out a soggy paper cup and puts his arm around me.

Warily, I ask, "What is it?"

"I forget. Either a tequila sunrise or a 7&7. Maybe both."

I like both, but his lack of certainty gives me pause. "No, thanks."

Someone hands a joint to Eric, who grabs it enthusiastically and inhales the way he does a cigarette: deeply. To do this, he lets go of me, and I pretend to wave at someone and slip away. I survey the action. Gwen is flirting with a Bob Dylan (circa 1967) look-alike and Eric's trying to figure out where I've gone.

As another Beach Boys song, "Good Vibrations," plays, I feel relieved not only to have escaped from Eric, but also from having a joint passed to me. I've never felt comfortable holding a joint, always self-conscious, like I was probably doing it wrong. I'm not sure whether I avoid drugs because I can't afford them, or if I really don't like them. My few joints and acid experiences never left me craving more, and increasingly I'm thinking the whole thing is sort of stupid, not to mention an unnecessary expense. On the other hand, maybe if I were stoned I'd feel less self-conscious right now.

Mark comes over to me. "You don't look like you're having a very good time."

Mortified to be seen as a wallflower, I tell him, "Oh, I am. I just think maybe 1967 wasn't my era, you know?" We both look around: people are using the Summer of Love theme as an excuse to become over-the-top spoofs of hippies. There's a lot of Hey Man and Groovy in the air.

"I know what you mean. It's like watching _Riot on Sunset Strip_ all over again," he says. "That's the movie that inspired the party."

"I know, the Rabbit Race boy told me." We smile.

"Now that you mention it, what's a nice Monkey Girl like you doing with an animal like him?"

I am aghast. "What do you mean 'doing with'? We just work together."

"I hear it's a bit more than that."

"Oh? What do you hear?"

"Well, not to sound too high school, but I think he likes you."

I let out an unhappy sigh. Then, remembering that Mark is Eric's friend, I hurry to explain myself. "I mean, it's not that I don't like Eric. But he does drive me a little crazy. On one hand, he's like the teacher's pet at Playland; the boss just loves him because he's always bringing in the customers and his game makes more money than anybody else's. But he's sort of like that guy Eddie Haskell from _Leave It to Beaver_, you know? I mean, look at him."

We look. Eric is dancing to "Incense and Peppermints" like a big klutzy white guy, holding a drink in one hand and a joint in the other, probably crushing that section of Mark's lawn.

"You don't have to explain it to me. I've lived behind him my whole life. He means well, and he's sort of a genius, but a little goes a long way. For me, proximity is the best thing he's got going for him. Plus he somehow manages to attract good people."

Is this a compliment? I can't tell. "Yeah, well, thanks. I guess."

"No, really," Mark smiles. He has a nice smile. Small teeth, but straight. Is there something wrong with me that I immediately imagine kissing him? "You seem much more normal than I expected."

I smile back, not feeling too normal compared to him. He's so cute, so confident, so nice. Exactly the kind of non-Eric type I wish would like me. "You too."

After that, we go our separate ways, Mark being pulled into groups and extricating himself to solve problems related to music and spillage. I mingle a little, but in my quest to avoid Eric I end up talking to Mark yet again. As we discuss the Summer of Love vs. the summer of 1975 to the strains of the Kinks' "Waterloo Sunset," Gwen walks over with the Bob Dylan look-alike, apparently to say goodbye. When she sees me with Mark she gives me a look that says: "You guys are still talking—way to go!" I glance at Mark quickly to make sure he didn't see that, but it's hard to say one way or the other.

"Like wow!" exclaims Gwen, in true 1967 style. Her Dylan look-alike grabs Mark by the arm, leaning in to contribute, "And remember, man—the sun isn't yellow, it's chicken!" Mark recoils slightly.

I grab her by the arm. "Gwen, what are you doing?"

"Leaving. See you at work tomorrow. Bye!" She waves, walks down the sidewalk toward the front of the house and disappears. I've gone off with strangers myself, a series of one-night stands built on first names and rationalizations: At least he was cute. At least he bought me a drink. At least…I don't see anything to rationalize here. Worse, she's giving Mark the impression that we're slutty and, true as that might be, I don't want him thinking that about me.

"Who was that guy?" I ask Mark.

"A neighbor. His name's Bobby Little. He's a little crazy, but he's harmless."

"Crazy but harmless! Every girl's dream!" Jesus!

There's a noise by the back of the house and Mark and I head over to see what's going on. It turns out Eric has decided to take a nap in the garden. As the Beatles' "With a Little Help from My Friends" plays, Eric mumbles drunkenly. "It had a flower..."

I say to Mark, "They're dropping like flies."

"More like elephants," he replies. There's a puking sound. "Oh, God! Right in my mother's marigolds! This is the last time I give Bigfoot a chance to relive the Sixties. I must have been out of my mind."

"Well, maybe it works like fertilizer," I say. It's a weak joke and Mark conveys his review with a glance. "Sorry. Look, I'll help you clean up. I know my mother would kill me if she ever saw anything like this going on at my house."

"My parents are great. It's my friends I wonder about," Mark replies, trying to turn a groaning Eric with his foot. Eric eventually staggers to his feet and lumbers back toward his house like a wounded elk leaving the veldt to die in the underbrush.

The smell of vomit makes me nauseous but I feel compelled to offer assistance. "Well, I swore off shoveling puke after a bad experience at Girl Scout camp, but how about picking up cups and roaches?"

Mark smiles. "Thanks, that's nice of you." He's right, I'm nice. I'd rather just get the hell out of here, but I feel bad for him because his friends obviously aren't in clean-up mode. Even the pretty Sophia is only standing around chatting, holding a stack of paper cups like she's in the middle of helping. The party fades as word of "man down!" spreads. The stereo is shut off, right in the middle of Jim Morrison calling "Light My Fire." As the crowd dwindles and silence takes over the house and yard, I deposit the last of the debris in Mark's avocado and pine kitchen, tell him goodbye and drive home.

3
COULD IT BE MAGIC?

At work the next day, Eric is hung over and moving slowly at the Rabbit Race, but since it's a holiday weekend, he's swarmed with patrons anyway. With the oppressive heat wearing me down, I'm doing half-assed crowd control at the Monkey Race. Patrick's at Shoot Out the Star next door. Henry is glaring at everyone, aware that we're not focused on our work, that something happened that didn't include him but is now affecting him.

During a brief down time, Patrick bends his body around and into the Monkey Race. "Hey, what's up with our barker? I haven't heard a peep out of Eric today."

I lean out of my booth looking out for Henry. The coast is clear. I confide, "Too much partying last night. Last I saw him he was passed out in a flowerbed."

"Don't tell me you finally agreed to go out with him!"

"Well, yes, but only with my friend Gwen, and only to a party at his neighbor's house."

Patrick shakes his head. "You must have made his night. Too bad he wasn't awake to enjoy it!"

"Gee, does *everyone* know this guy's got the hots for me?" His line of shooters is getting restless and one looks like he's ready to aim at Patrick. I give him a head's up.

Turning back toward his booth he says, "Well, there was that skywriting, the full page ad in the newspaper…plus, of course the loving glances all day long."

I give a little anguished cry and return to my monkeys, a long stream of sweat running down my back. I stew about this conversation until Trip relieves me for break time, at which point I head straight to Shoot Out the Star.

"You know," I tell Patrick, "I just want to make it clear that there is *nothing* going on between me and loverboy over there."

Patrick, still working, responds, "Don't worry. I think too much of you to ever accept you with Henry's pet. Look, I can't talk now, but how about if we go out after work?"

I feel a sudden burst of elation. "That would be great." I have been flirting with Patrick in my own subtle way since the park opened. Of course, I'm not picky: I've been flirting with anyone who isn't Eric or Henry—speaking of which, there's Henry, approaching with a scowl. "Yikes, gotta run!" I rush off to the carousel and Gwen.

"Hey, you ready?"

Gwen growls, "Can you believe the idiot who's supposed to relieve me didn't show up today? If I can drag my sorry ass in after last night, *anyone* can. Burst appendix, right!"

"This cannot be happening! We have way too much to talk about for you not to have a break! Plus isn't it illegal or something?"

Gwen glares at me in that way she has. "Yeah, give me a dime to call William Kunstler. I'm sure he'd love to take on the case of the amusement park worker with a hangover who didn't get her break because her back-up was in emergency surgery. Look, I'm pissed off enough, don't wind me up more."

"Hey, your loss. Just because I've got a new beau…but you can hear about it later."

Gwen turns away from the ride. "You bitch. What are you talking about? Did you do the deed with Mark?"

"Oh, yeah. In fact it was a three-way with Eric. You know, he's not so bad once you get past the nicotine-stained fingers, and the fact that he can't hold his liquor."

"Come on, what happened? Wait, I think these kids are getting dizzy." She turns her attention to the carousel, stopping it so new riders can get on.

I watch mothers lift their young, excited children onto the brightly painted horses and buckle the leather straps. Then some get off the ride and start snapping Polaroids, while others climb onto a nearby horse and chatter away, telling their kids how much fun they're about to have.

Picking up where I left off, I tell Gwen, "Nothing happened with Mark. He's nice, but I think helping him clean up after his out-of-control friends is as bonded as we're going to get. And speaking of out of control..."

She turns back to me. "Don't tell me you disapprove. Just because *you* didn't meet anyone doesn't mean you can act more virginal-than-thou with me. And by the way, just because I left with someone doesn't mean he was worth leaving with. If that makes sense."

"It does to me, 'cause I saw him."

"Yeah, well, neither one of us ever will again. At least, not if there's a merciful God." She makes the sign of the cross.

I put my hands together in prayer. "Lord, deliver us from our one-night stands and lead us into the arms of someone worth screwing a second time." We both sing, "A-men!"

Gwen turns to the ride again. Under her voice she says, "Are all the little brats in place?" Rubbing her hands together, she sneers, "Hold on for the wild ride of your life, kiddies!"

She switches on the ride dramatically, as though it will send the children flying off their steeds. Instead, it begins to revolve leisurely, with appropriately paced calliope music. She turns back to me.

"So if it's not Mark, who's the man in your life today?"

"Patrick just asked me out for tonight."

"Who, Wyatt Earp from the gun game? Could this be the Marlboro Man you've been waiting for? And a real date—do I smell fondue?"

"I just think he feels left out because he found out I went to a party with Eric last night. Oh, guess what Mark calls Eric."

"Do I *look* like I'm in the mood for a guessing game?" The bags under her bloodshot eyes give me the answer.

"OK, OK. Bigfoot."

"Perfect. So you think Wyatt Earp is jealous of Bigfoot?"

"You know, when you put it that way it does sound crazy. Maybe he just wants to pick my brain and find out how he can get to *you*."

Gwen nods in approval. "Now *that* makes sense."

"Yeah, right. I'll see you later." I head back to the game area, memories of my miserable high school years dancing in my head. I was boy crazy all the way through but it never led to anything except some secretive groping and interest from the uninteresting, leaving us to trawl the bars at night looking for older men to test out our iffy charms. Nice of Gwen to assume it will always be that way for me.

* * *

That evening, Patrick and I take his brown 1975 Camaro, leaving my car in the Playland parking lot. We decide to go to Arthur Treacher's Fish & Chips nearby, where we sit together at a small Formica table. "Someone Saved My Life Tonight" by Elton John plays from a radio in the kitchen. It's from one of my current favorite albums. We both focus awkwardly on our food, unsure what to say to each other, babbling about the usual: Playland co-workers, pets, siblings, cars. The conversation dies out. I listen to the song change to Pilot's "Magic." I always notice what music is playing in the background, but usually if I bring it up no one knows what I'm talking about. I keep it to myself this time. Finally Patrick dips a piece of fried fish in tartar sauce and breaks the silence. "So how'd you end up at Playland?"

I take a sip of 7-Up. "Some guy my mother's dating had an in. I applied last summer and couldn't even get an interview."

"Your parents are divorced?"

Suddenly self-conscious, I try to play down the shame of my broken home. "Yeah, it's no big deal. Hey, it got me this job!"

"It'd be a big deal to me. I can't imagine my parents splitting up."

"Just imagine having to book an appointment every time you want to see your father, and watching your mother go through some kind of second adolescence. That's pretty much what it's like."

"Doesn't sound too great."

"Aah, it's not so bad. It's their business, not mine. I'll be gone soon enough." I'm trying to sound like it doesn't matter. How do I get off this subject?

"Well, I'm glad my parents took 'till death do us part' seriously. Even if it does mean they end up killing each other."

I laugh and look around the brightly lit restaurant. We're practically the only ones in here. "So how'd *you* end up at Funtime? This is your second year, right?"

"Yeah, round two for me."

"You must be some kind of masochist. I love it, but I'd never come back to Henry. I swear, that man is pure evil."

"Oh, he's not so terrible. He's actually the reason I *did* come back. I feel bad for him. Did you know he's just a couple years older than the rest of us? He works two jobs, to take care of his mother. After he leaves Playland, he works as a bartender at the Loyal Inn."

"Loyal Inn? What's that?"

"It's a bowling alley in Larchmont, near my house."

"Oh great, now I feel like a total creep."

"You? Never! I know he's not the nicest boss in the world, but it does explain him to a certain degree. I just think he's a lonely guy who doesn't fit into any particular group."

This could almost describe me, except for the "guy" part. "God, do you realize you're almost making me like Henry? You might be the nicest, most empathetic person on earth!"

"Yeah, well, unfortunately that's my only good quality!" We both laugh. Patrick continues. "You know, I've wanted to ask you out ever since Playland opened. But I figured A, Eric would kill me." Seeing my face, he quickly adds, "I know, I know, you don't feel the same way about him he does about you. And B, I thought you wouldn't be interested in a high school boy."

"What do you mean?"

"It means in September, when you're leaving for college, I'll be headed back to Salesian."

"What's Salesian?" I feel like I don't know anything.

"It's a boys' school in New Rochelle. A Catholic high school."

I make an unattractive snorting sound. "So what? I'll be in the next town over, living at home and commuting to SUNY Purchase. Barely any difference from last year, from what I can see. So we'll still be neighbors, at least."

"At least. And hopefully more than that."

"You're embarrassing me."

"Gee, I thought you'd be used to guys telling you they like you."

"Nope. Well, except for Eric, of course." I shudder.

Patrick leans in. "Well, let me be the second: I like you." We kiss tentatively, while <u>Barry Manilow's "Could It Be Magic"</u> plays in the kitchen. More magic. Maybe it's supposed to be a sign. Maybe this is the magic at last?

"So what do you want to be when you grow up?" Patrick asks after our kiss, "What's your major going to be?"

"Creative writing. I've always wanted to be a writer. I've even had a few articles published already."

"Wow, that's great. I have no idea what I want to do. Except kiss you again, that is." He does, and as <u>"Swearin' to God" by Frankie</u>

Valli begins, he asks, "Want to get out of here?"

I nod. We leave Arthur Treacher's and half our dinners and drive back to the now-deserted Playland lot, where Patrick parks next to my car, turns off his headlights and then his car.

We sit there under a streetlight, looking at each other. Patrick leans toward me, I move to meet him and we touch lips. But when he pulls me closer, the stick shift gets in the way.

"This isn't working. Do you want to get in the back?" Patrick asks.

I look over my bucket seat. "Well, it's not very big. Do you want to get in mine?" I know from experience there's plenty of room in my back seat. The difference tonight is that I know Patrick's last name.

Patrick looks over at my Oldsmobile Luxury Sedan, nicknamed "the boat." I know he loves his Camaro; he told me tonight how he worked so hard to save the money for it that his father finally couldn't stand watching him nod off during breakfast and kicked in the last five hundred dollars—at five percent interest. I bought my car for $300—or 200 hours of servitude—from a family I babysit for.

"Let's go," he says.

He jumps out and runs around to my side, opening my door and kissing me as I emerge from his low-slung car. We stagger together to my driver's side, where I unlock the door, open it and reach in to unlock the back door. Patrick nudges the front door closed with his shoulder and opens the back, his lips still suction-locked to mine, his tongue darting. He separates from me and guides me onto the leather back seat, bumping my shoulder, although I don't let on how much it hurts. He follows me in and shuts the door. The car is so wide that we can stretch out as if on a couch. And so we do, but not until I lean over the front seat and put the key in the ignition, turning on the radio. It's tuned to WBLS, which I switched to last night, after Mark mentioned it. Stevie Wonder is singing something about visions in his mind. I settle in happily.

We make out, Patrick's tongue gradually getting the message that darting is not what's called for. My own tongue finally lulls his into a slow dance, more circular than back and forth. He starts to follow my lead and slows it down. A couple of times our mouths make loud smacking sounds and he apologizes. We rub together rhythmically through eight songs, untold commercials, some deep-voiced deejay patter and the call letters that are an acronym for "Warmth, Beauty, Love and Sensitivity."

"Oh my God," I moan. "I can't take much more of this."

Patrick moves away from me quickly. "What, you don't like it?"

"Are you kidding? This is heaven!"

"Oh, so maybe you can take a little more?"

I laugh. Is he for real? "Maybe a little more! But it's getting late. I have to go pretty soon."

Patrick looks at his watch. "Yeah, me too. My mother's probably sitting in the kitchen waiting for a call from the hospital by now. My parents have conniptions when I'm late. But it was worth it!"

We sit up and straighten out our clothes, smiling at each other.

He leans in and kisses my forehead. "You're a good kisser."

"Thanks. So are you." Well, he's getting there. We kiss some more, then finally, reluctantly, part.

* * *

I drive home, navigating up a long, dark and rutted driveway. I imagine Patrick making this drive in his Camaro and shudder. How could I explain to him where I live? It's the dead end of Prince Willow Lane, the one stretch without a house number. We're in some vague Prince Willow Land at the end of the Lane, too messy to be defined in any traditional way.

The boat rocks from side to side as I try to avoid as many potholes and gravel spin-outs as possible. My mother found our house on a relocation scouting trip from Maryland when Dad took a new job up here. We owned a house in Rockville, but even after selling it couldn't afford to buy in Westchester County, probably one of the most expensive places in the country. So when a real estate agent asked my mother if she'd consider a unique rental, she wasn't only open but saw it as destiny: this sixteen-acre property with a run-down house was where we were meant to be.

It's officially in Mamaroneck, but is part of the supposedly elite Scarsdale School District. Mom is disdainful of a lot of the towns around here—New Rochelle, Mount Vernon, even other parts of Mamaroneck. I don't know what she has to be so snobby about, but she wanted Scarsdale schools, so here we are, renting. All my school friends live in Scarsdale and that's where I've mostly hung out since we got to New York nine years ago. I guess that's why I never heard of Loyal Inn or Salesian. I feel like I'm between different worlds, not a part of any place, and thinking about bringing Patrick here just reinforces that.

Mom's 1972 red Ford station wagon is parked next to the house. No sign of her boyfriend Stan's car, thank goodness. I can't stand that pompous geezer, and lately it seems like he's always around. Somehow she's not embarrassed by where we live. I pull in next to her, turn off my car and reflect. There's no moon tonight but even in pitch darkness I know how bad it is, can see it through Patrick's eyes.

The house is dilapidated, the driveway a disgrace. Yes, we have a ton of land to ourselves, plus we back up on Saxon Woods, a county park with a forest and streams. I used to think we were the luckiest family in town to have so much land and nature. I saw this place as our own private park, with deer and pheasant and chipmunks, plus the less appealing but still intriguing raccoons, snakes and rats. Unfortunately I no longer share Mom's continued enthusiasm for where we live. I'm older now and I know our living situation is freakish. Friends' parents refuse to take their expensive cars— Mercedes, Caddy, Volvo—up the quarter-mile driveway.

I'm parked beneath a dogwood tree, next to a patch of pachysandra. They're so reminiscent of my mother's beautiful childhood home in Washington that it seems almost a cruel hoax when you continue up the gravel walkway and climb the rickety steps to the battered wooden screen door, scarred with tape residue from seasons' worth of plastic sheeting. Then the front door itself, its window revealing the living room beyond, with its sagging, battered furniture. The thought of Patrick walking in that pathetic door seems even more impossible than his coming up the gut-wrenching driveway.

I rarely go in the front door. My room is in the attic, accessed from a staircase off the kitchen, so I go in the back door, through a small enclosed porch that houses our refrigerator, and then a second door to the rest of the kitchen.

The house is my comfort and my shame. I love its claw-footed bathtubs, old-fashioned wallpapers, glass doorknobs. I hate its sloping floors and the ancient stove that singed Dad's arm hair every time he lit the broiler. I love the giant rock in the front yard that probably dates back to the last ice age. I hate that our refrigerator is on an unheated porch that makes getting the milk a trip back in time to a new ice age on winter mornings. Most of all I hate that someday it will be gone. We're surely the final residents and our time is running out. It's like Dan Fogelberg's "Souvenirs" where he finds an unreconciled key to his childhood house, now torn down. Someday I expect to have a key like that myself. The property will be developed and we'll be out on our asses.

I get out of my car and enter via the always-unlocked back door. I turn on the light in the kitchen, then head back onto the porch to the ancient fridge. Gretchen comes running out to me, wagging her tail. Gretchen's a mini feather dachshund, half longhair, half shorthair. She lost the sight in one eye in a faceoff with a cat, so her good eye is enormous and her dead eye is shrunken. She's pretty strange-looking, not easily identifiable as a dachshund, maybe not even as a dog. I lean down to pet her while I gaze into the icebox. My mother comes into the kitchen, blinking at the glare, as I re-enter across from her. She's thin and attractive, I guess, but tousled-looking at the moment. Smiling groggily, she says, "Hi there. You're home early."

Annoyed, I reply, "It's 12:30."

"Oh, really? Well, what are you doing home so late?"

"I had a date. You're not the only one who can do that, you know."

"What are you so upset about? I was just making conversation."

"Yeah, right. You're just trying to get your bearings because you had no idea what time it is, and your shirt is on inside out. Looks like you had a date, too. Where's Ruth?"

Mom looks down at her shirt and her whole body snaps to, suddenly set and rigid. "Uh, I...I guess she's in bed."

"Still Stan? Or is there a new victim?"

"That's not fair. I'm a single woman, you know, just like you."

"Just like me? I just got out of high school! You have two children! Just because you got bored with family life doesn't mean we're going on a double date."

She definitely has her bearings now. "Oh, get off your high horse. I get to have a life, too, so accept it. It's called being liberated."

"Really? Well, I've got news for you. *I'm* liberated—you don't get to be. You're too late."

Got her with that one. She sputters. "What?"

"You missed out. You had kids instead. You don't get to liberate yourself from that."

Mom looks like she wants to strangle me and the feeling is mutual. "That's not your decision. You have no idea the sacrifices I've made for you kids, but now I need to think of myself."

"Yeah, *only* of yourself. Just so you know, *I'm* the teenager here, not you, OK? I don't want you waiting up for a mother-daughter chat, but Ruth's only twelve and she still needs you. It pisses me off that you think you can abdicate your responsibilities just to make up for lost time."

"I don't appreciate that kind of language, young lady," Mom snaps.

I'm honestly confused. "What? What language? 'Abdicate'?"

"You know what I mean. *Pissed.* That's a tacky word."

Is she for real? I snarl at her, "I was wrong. You *are* a mother. I'm going to bed." I start to leave the room, then turn. "I'm not going to run into some guy pulling up his pants, am I?"

"My, we are in a mood. Pre, during or post?" she asks, picking up Gretchen, who sleeps with her every night.

I look at her and shake my head. "It's not a monthly thing, it's *you.*" I head to bed, trying to block out images of bringing Patrick to meet my manhandled mother with sweet but already fading memories of the night's make-out session.

4
I THINK OF YOU

One morning about two weeks later, it's pouring and Playland is almost deserted except for its striped-shirt employees and a few hardy locals. I knew there wouldn't be much happening today so I snuck in a radio. Right now it's playing "When Will I Be Loved" by Linda Ronstadt. Luckily for me, I no longer have to ask myself that question. Patrick and I are in deep. Having a boyfriend is everything I ever wanted. It fills every second of my life: I am always aware of his presence in the world. Our world.

I sit on the wooden counter of the Monkey Race reading the paperback of _Jaws_. Patrick and I are going to see the movie this week, and I want to finish the book first. He's next door, straightening up Shoot Out the Star, plucking out old targets from between floorboards and frequently leaning around the corner to smile lovingly at me. From across the way, Eric glares. Sore loser.

Patrick makes kissing sounds. "Peek-a-boo! I'm crazy about you." I'm crazy about him, too. I think about him all the time. It's ecstasy to know that someone cares about me more than I even care about myself. Patrick and I spend every free minute together. Our breaks rarely coincide, but our cars are always the last to leave the parking lot after closing time.

I lean out of my booth to take his hand. "Hi, my darling!"

Kissing my fingers, Patrick says, "I never knew I could love rainy days so much."

"I know, I wish the rain would never end!"

"What are we going to do later?"

"Anything, as long as we're together."

"Well, that goes without saying. But my family's going out tonight, the weekly trip to Friendly's. And I'm officially excused because they think I have overtime! I feel like a creep for lying to them, but I want to do something special, how about you?"

"Whenever we're together it's special, Patrick."

"I love the way you say my name! Say it again."

"*Patrick.*"

"Mmm."

Henry comes up and startles us. "Hey, *Patrick* and *Karen.* You're wanted back here on earth. I don't pay you to watch your hormones percolate. Stay in your own booths. And turn off that radio!" He walks away. "Midnight Blue" by Melissa Manchester is playing. It's not one of my favorites, so I don't mind switching it off.

"God, how humiliating," I say. "Remind me again how sympathetic he is?"

"Well, I guess he just feels like he has to do his job. Which appears to be thwarting young love!"

"Never!"

"Hey, I met the guy who runs the Tunnel of Love. Want to go for a little boat ride later?"

"Oh, that sounds wonderful!"

We finagle so our breaks can coincide and walk hand in hand to the Tunnel of Love. It's just a couple of booths down from the Rabbit Race where Eric, seething, pretends to be engrossed in G.K. Chesterton's biography of Saint Thomas Aquinas, *The Dumb Ox.* He is such a show-off, as if anyone would be impressed by him. We joke that he's reading his own autobiography. *The Dumb Ox.* That's a good one. We cuddle and kiss as we float alone through the darkness, oblivious to the ride beyond our little boat. At the end we stagger off, blinking at the daylight.

Patrick escorts me the few feet back to the Monkey Race, saying, "Boy, I didn't want that ride to end. We just have to make it through a few more hours and then we can be alone together!"

"Our own private overtime, all right! I can't wait," I agree. We kiss and return to work.

* * *

The Cusp of Everything

As close to 6:00 as possible, I follow Patrick to the Dowd house in Larchmont. It's on a cul-de-sac and somehow not as large as I thought it would be. It looks a little run-down from the outside, its dark brown siding in need of a paint job and the small front yard overgrown. I'm not judging—after all, who am I to judge? I only care that his family is out since, other than in our cars, we've never been alone together.

"And now for the tour!" he says, leading me through the front door and steering me left. "This," he points out dramatically, "is the living room!"

We enter a space that redefines clutter. Rugs overlap rugs, and possibly carpeting, down at the Paleolithic level. There is so much furniture that we have to turn sideways just to make it through the room. The walls are covered with paintings from the top edges of the furniture all the way up to the ceiling. It's impossible to tell the color of the walls. Tabletops are mini cities of tchotchkes. The couches are barely visible through throw pillows. I look at him, speechless.

"I know. It's a little crazy. My mom loves garage sales. She's pretty sure there's a treasure in here, but she doesn't know what it is, so she just keeps everything. And keeps buying more."

"Wow." There isn't anything else to say.

He maneuvers his way to the stereo system at the far end of the room. "Want to hear my favorite record?"

"In here?"

"Sure."

I have never before felt claustrophobic but now I grasp the concept. I don't want to offend him, though. "Well, OK."

Patrick flips through a collection of about 50 albums sitting on a shelf under the stereo and selects one. I bet it will be romantic! He dumps out the black disc, places it on the turntable and moves the arm over to its edge. The needle hits the vinyl and a loud whistle blows. I flinch.

"It's the sound of a steam locomotive," Patrick informs me. When my father wants to make sure we're up, he blasts it through the house."

"Makes me appreciate my clock radio." I say, wincing. "And my father." The whistling continues, increasing in volume. "This is awful!"

"Really? I sort of like it. I mean, I wouldn't sit around listening to it but it's pretty cool."

"Mm hmm," I mumble, trying to sound like I agree. "So can I see the rest of the house?"

I guess Patrick is disappointed that the trains were not a hit, but he lifts the arm and turns off the stereo. We head into the kitchen, all knotty pine cabinets and metal-edged Formica counters, with cutesy wall hangings, potholders, dish towels and collectibles: spoons, thimbles and shot glasses.

I shake my head. "I've never seen anything like this."

"I know, every vacation we go on she brings back souvenirs. Our lives could probably be re-created just by looking at where this stuff came from," Patrick says looking around. "I never thought about it like that before, but it's true. Look, Niagara Falls." He picks up a shot glass. "Carlsbad Caverns." Another glass.

"You guys must get around," I remark.

"Well, not so much anymore," Patrick says, blowing some dust out of the Carlsbad Caverns.

Eager to skip the dining room and its likely teacup collection, I ask, "So where's your room?"

"Oh, you little devil. I should have known that's where you'd want to head."

For some reason this makes me feel put out. "Don't you?"

"Oh, of course! Sorry, I just figured a tour would make you more comfortable."

"Really?" At first I'm sure he must be kidding, but sincerity is written all over his moon face.

We go down the hall to Patrick's bedroom. "And this," he says, gesturing broadly, "is my bed." We look at the neatly made twin bed, with its racing flag spread. Patrick takes off his shoes and lies down, clothed. He reaches over and turns on the clock radio. It plays the vaguely operatic "I Think of You" by Renaissance.

I hesitate, then kick off my sandals and join him. He reaches for me and we tangle together, gazing into each others' eyes. We kiss, and feel our bodies relaxing into each other. We make out tenderly.

After a while Patrick rests his head on his hand and looks down at me. "A penny for your thoughts," he says.

Pressure! I was hoping I don't look too fat if my clothes end up coming off. I had planned to drop five pounds before this moment but now it's too late. Obviously I can't tell him this. Scrambling, I come up with, "I don't know if I could put them into words. Maybe euphoria?"

"I thought maybe you were thinking it's about time we went all the way. I know you're self-conscious about being more experienced than I am, but I want you to know that makes it even more exciting for me."

I sit up. "What do you mean 'more experienced'?"

"Well, Eric told me you aren't a virgin."

"How the hell would he know that?" I feel rage pulsing through my body.

"I don't know, he said something about Jon, the Bathroom Boy…" Patrick's voice fades when he sees my face. "I'm sorry, I should have known better than to listen to Eric."

I lie back and throw my arm across my eyes. "God."

Patrick pushes on. "Seriously, it doesn't bother me. You're almost a year older. You go to a co-ed school. You've had opportunities I never had. Maybe you've even been in love."

"No," I admit grudgingly. "I'm pretty sure love was never involved."

"Well, that's sort of sad!" Patrick says. "Don't you think it should be? Because I love you and I can't think of anything more wonderful than making love to you."

I struggle to respond. "I, I…"

Patrick shushes me. "You don't have to say anything. Although a moan of pleasure would be encouraging!" He fumbles with my clothing.

I find my voice. "Patrick, I love you, too." Did those words come out of my mouth? And why is "Listen to What the Man Said" by Wings playing? I'd rather say my first "I love you" to some meaningful soundtrack, not that dreck.

"I don't want you to say any more than that."

I don't. Instead I reach for his belt and start to open it. At that moment, he starts to pull my arm out of the sleeve of my T-shirt. This interrupts my efforts, and I end up removing my shirt myself and returning to his belt. It seems like he's considering trying to unhook my bra, but instead he reaches for the button of my jeans, blocking my view of his waist and again inhibiting my progress. I stop and wait for him to get me unzipped, then stand up and remove my Levis, leaving on my white cotton panties and sucking in my stomach. Instead of lying down again, I lean over and pull off his polo shirt. He is wearing an undershirt, which surprises me. I'm not sure whether to take that off as well, although it's sort of a turn-off. It reminds me of

40

my grandfather, which is not an image I want in my head right now. I hesitate, then figure what the hell, why get distracted from the main event. I kiss him and reach for his jeans. Luckily he removes his undershirt while I pull at his button and zipper.

"Here, I'll do it," he says. He leans back, raises his butt and pulls off his Wrangler jeans, revealing his own white briefs. Leaving his socks on, he pulls me to him and moves over so there is room for me on the small bed. In the process he bumps his head on the bedside table and lets out an "Ow!" but quickly recovers. He leans over me, pale, hairless and a little doughy, his face blissful. While I lie on my back, he kisses me slowly, starting at my mouth, moving down my neck and bra and kissing me on my sucked-in stomach before returning face-to-face.

"Are you ready?" he asks. "Because I am!"

Oh no, am I going to laugh because the radio is playing "Love Won't Let Me Wait"? That's too funny! But I don't want to break the mood so I just nod. Even though I've had sex before, this is the first time I have had it described as making love. It feels different. Our hearts are both pounding and our bodies glisten with a light coat of sweat. A faint locker room smell is in the air. Patrick pulls down my panties and I kick them off and maneuver myself underneath him. Suddenly realizing he still has on his underwear, he jumps to his feet and removes them. His penis springs out and I try to block the word "boing" from my head. He drops his Fruit of the Looms, grabs his pants from the floor and fumbles in the pockets until he locates a condom. Patrick is so responsible. Usually I have to raise the subject.

Finally, sheathed in latex, he glances down at my crotch, trying to get a sense of the logistics of the act he is about to perform for the first time. He straddles me and looks down again. Like me, he sees his penis suspended over a tangle of black pubic hair. Tentatively, he twists his body. I take him in my hand and guide him to me. He enters me slowly, gives one thrust and comes immediately, crying out and collapsing on top of me. I can't help it, I let out a little "Oof!" as he knocks the air out of me, but I recover quickly and embrace him.

Neither of us speaks. For a moment I'm afraid he might be crying but it's just a final spasm. He finally turns to look at me and rolls off to the side, hitting the bedside table again. A racecar lamp wobbles precariously. "Goddamn it!" he exclaims, rubbing his shoulder with one hand and grabbing for his lamp with the other.

I smile at him. "That was great," I say.

"No it wasn't," he admits. "It was too quick. But next time will be better. I know what I'm doing now."

I look at my watch. "When are your parents coming home?"

Patrick glances over at his clock radio, now playing <u>10cc's "I'm Not in Love."</u> It's about seven o'clock. "Oh crap, any minute! We need to get out of here!" He leaps off the bed, twisting his ankle and dropping to the floor in pain. "Ouch!"

I can't help it, I have to laugh. "Oh my God, I hope I don't end up having to take you to the hospital! You want your first time to be memorable but not this way!"

Limping across the floor, his rubberized penis flapping, Patrick insists he's fine. "We just need to get dressed and go. We should have parked around the corner. If my parents see our cars they'll know we're here."

"OK, but I need to use a bathroom." I've gathered up my clothes and am holding them in front of me in what I hope looks casual rather than camouflage-y. Despite what just happened, I don't want him to see me almost naked. I just can't stop worrying about my body.

"Oh, of course! Sorry, I should have thought of that. It's right down the hall." Patrick kisses my cheek and points me to the bathroom.

"Thanks," I say, backing out of the room. "And you might want to open a window, too." It's suffocatingly hot and smells like sex and B.O.

I wash up and get dressed in the messy, towel-strewn bathroom. I look in the mirror—my hair is tousled and I look sexy and pretty. I smile at my reflection. Returning to the bedroom, I find Patrick ready to go and looking sheepish. I give him a hug and he squeezes me hard. We leave the house in silence and drive off in our cars, he to park around the corner until "overtime" is done. I head home without the radio, instead replaying what just happened. We're officially in love now and it feels like I am flying.

* * *

The next day, Patrick and I walk through Playland with Gwen, through the crowds of families and surly teens. He and I have our arms around each other. Gwen says to me, "I'm so glad you were able to meet me during your break." I'm sure she's being sarcastic but I'm not going to give her the satisfaction of letting her think it matters to me. I've been the third wheel with her plenty of times.

Smiling at her, I say, "You know I wouldn't miss our time together."

Patrick leans around me and says to Gwen, "I hope you don't mind my tagging along. Karen and I hardly ever get to take breaks at the same time, but today was special."

This is the danger zone: I told Gwen last night that Patrick and I were in love and had finally gone all the way. Based on her reaction ("How many seconds did he last?") I'm pretty sure she doesn't want to hear any of that "special" talk. So I quickly interject. "Of course she doesn't. She's happy to have you along for some fresh perspective, right, Gwen?"

Gwen takes out a cigarette. "Just thrilled! Do you have a light, Patrick?"

Patrick says, "Oh, I don't smoke."

I give him a little squeeze. "He hasn't said anything, but I know he hates the smell of it. That's why I'm going to quit."

Disgustedly, Gwen says, "Your mother will be so proud."

Patrick stops and turns to me. "I didn't ask you to quit smoking!"

"No, but wouldn't you rather not kiss an ashtray?"

"An ashtray? I would never think of your perfect mouth that way!"

Gwen, still fumbling, finally finds matches in her purse. "So, no light. Don't worry, I got one."

I smile at Patrick. "You're so sweet."

"No, you are," he responds.

Gwen breaks away from us. "You know, I've gotta head over..."—she looks around—"this way to retch, I mean smoke, alone. Ta!"

She walks toward the beach, moving so quickly that her hair rustles in self-generated wind. Patrick, watching her, says, "Wow. She's pretty upset."

"Yeah," I reply. "Sorry, it's sort of a new situation for me. I didn't know she'd react like that. I probably should have been a little more sensitive."

"It's new to me too," Patrick says, pulling me close. "But it feels really good."

"Mmm," I hum as I kiss him. "It sure does."

* * *

The Cusp of Everything

Over the next month, Patrick and I spend every possible minute together. Sometimes I imagine him watching me in my private moments, marveling at my beauty and kindness, looking away when I yell at Ruth or go to the bathroom. We do our best to coordinate our breaks, although Henry doesn't make it easy. Funtime doesn't have enough floaters for multiple workers to take breaks simultaneously, and Henry prefers to assign them as he sees fit, not as "drooling teenagers" (his term) crave. Considering he's only twenty himself, you'd think he might be a little sympathetic. Hell, no. We only get a few breaks a week together, to wander the park, ride the Dragon Coaster, sit by the water.

Most of our time together is in the evening, after work, and on the occasional compatible day off. We eat at all the local fast food places, but also share an occasional special meal at a French restaurant. Once I ordered fondue, but it didn't measure up to the *Cosmo* propaganda, and besides, Patrick kept dropping his bread into the pot of cheese. We drop by to visit Henry, working the bar at the Loyal Inn, who seems almost like a normal person when he's not being a boss. We go to see the movie version of the Who's *Tommy* at the Elmsford Drive-In. I've been looking forward to it for months. But it's disappointing, maybe because the tinny, monaural sound from the speaker hanging off the window kills the whole point of a rock musical. We have better luck indoors, at *White Line Fever* and a re-release of *Billy Jack*. I wouldn't have chosen to see either one of those, but Patrick likes them.

Any dark space is our cue to start grabbing each other, but the backseat of the boat is where the real action happens, night after night. We're half-naked on a beach towel I keep stashed in the trunk and throw in the washing machine whenever I think of it. We don't make love all the time, but when we do he's always prepared with a rubber. Most of the time we just make out until our jaws hurt. He feels my A-cup breasts and I give him hand and blow jobs. I'm tempted to send Oldsmobile a letter thanking them for the spaciousness of their Luxury Sedan.

During this time I meet Patrick's family. Mrs. Dowd talks nonstop about how happy she is that Patrick has found someone wonderful like me. She invites me to family dinners, but I beg off, nervous about befriending my boyfriend's kooky mother, concerned that she might not like me so much once she gets to know me, and genuinely overscheduled with work. (I am still babysitting in addition to my Playland hours and I clean a house every Wednesday morning in Portchester where _Fear of Flying_ is on the bedside table and there's always a raging battle about whether the kids can get a dog.) The few times I go to Patrick's house, I have to navigate his mother's relentlessly upbeat chatter and her latest garage sale purchases.

When Patrick wants to pick me up at my house, I try to explain how weird my living situation is. He doesn't care, though. He doesn't even complain about the driveway, even though he has to practically hit a tree to avoid bottoming out in a pothole. It's like we're in a world where nothing is bad or wrong. Now that I have him, I can look at my life in a whole new way: interesting rather than tragic.

Whenever Patrick and I are apart, I think about him, even if I'm also thinking about something else. He is a constant presence, an awareness I have of him at all times. His very existence is like a love weight sitting on my heart. I know he feels my presence the same way I feel his. We're always connected, whether thinking about each other, on the phone, or talking to others about our powerful and unique love. We even write each other letters so that when we pick up the mail there will be a reminder, a manifestation of our love. We know we will always be together, that we have found our other halves.

5
SUMMER MADNESS

I'm a crappy babysitter these days. I'm so focused on Patrick and Playland, not to mention so bored with the kids and the parents, the bulging pantries and the hidden sex aids. I read the whole _Happy Hooker_ at the Finkels' house. At the back of the Bergers' bedroom closet shelf is a big brown Shopwell bag filled with dildos. One has a crank at the end so you can bend it to an angle, insert it (I assume) and rotate it. I guess it beats letting Mr. B put his in—he's gone most of the time anyway. He and Mrs. B were separated when I started with them three years ago and have since gotten back together and broken up again. So I guess that bag can come in handy.

The Steinbergs with the retarded son have a box of condoms in their medicine cabinet that date back at least a decade. Obviously they're not doing it anymore, and who can blame them? It took me awhile with the Guralniks, but even the Orthodox have their pornography—if you can call their one well-hidden book that. It's more of a how-to manual, with the woman in a wig and him with those little curls in front of his ears, acting out some positions, naked, pasty and determined-looking. I guess for them it's more about procreation than recreation, and with three daughters the pressure's on to find a new way of doing it. The Blicks installed a mirror over their bed that has turned it into their kids' trampoline and God knows what else. I try not to think about it. The idea of middle-aged people having sex is repulsive.

It's ironic that the parents trust me more after our years together.

Now is when they should be worrying. In the beginning I was on my best behavior and had the kids in bed on time with stories. Now I let them watch TV, stay up late, anything to buy me quiet time to talk on the phone, rifle through their drawers and scour the den for some decent music (something other than the ubiquitous "I Am Woman"). I investigate the fridge and cabinets for something sweet that won't be missed: a spoonful of marshmallow fluff, four Oreos, two Fun Size Milky Ways, a package of Pop Tarts, a Good Humor bar. Once, a frozen waffle was almost my undoing.

I'm up to $1.50 an hour from a starting point of 50 cents. I was only 13 then, and quickly got a raise to 75 cents, then $1.00. Getting to $1.50 involved serious negotiating, but I've learned to stand firm. I don't want to babysit anymore, so if they want me they have to pay the price. Besides, God knows they can all afford it. They buy whatever they want, have massive savings accounts for their little kids (I am obsessed with looking at the passbooks), get new cars all the time and just generally live in a way that feels both right and wrong, like what I should be striving for but forever out of reach.

* * *

One Sunday toward the end of August, I have a day off from Playland, but Mrs. Rossi calls and says she's on her knees begging. I can't turn down the money, so I walk over. Their new split-level is down my driveway and a block to the left, but it might as well be on another planet. I snuck in when it was a construction site a few years back. In what's now the backyard, they filled in a pond that used to be overflowing with tadpoles and then gigantic toads. That's pretty much where I think our property is headed. Pretty soon there won't be anywhere left to explore. Tough luck, toads.

I don't want to be here, so just on principle I don't pay any attention to the Rossi kids, even when Michael locks Ann out of the house. Finally she starts screaming and pounding on the door, so I do have to go let her in, but other than that I pretty much ignore them. I spend my time reading Arthur Hailey's Hotel from their minimal book collection. Luckily I just have to be there for a couple of hours, and I "earn" $5.00 for my trouble.

I'm home by early evening and draped over an easy chair in the den with Gretchen in my lap. The den must have once been a porch because it has two walls of windows. It's my favorite room in the house, even though its Colonial-theme slipcovers are embarrassingly queer. After all, this is where the communal TV and stereo console are. I'm playing the radio, the ubiquitous "Rhinestone Cowboy" by Glen Campbell, because I'm too lazy to get up and change the station whenever a song comes on I don't like.

Gwen and I are on the phone, smoking and grumbling. I'm bringing her up to date on my miserable life. "Yeah, my mother is up at the Nevele in the Catskills with her old fart 'boyfriend' and I get to stay home and be the mommy. I can't believe she expects me to kill my social life so *she* can sow some belated wild oats. I'm going to be eighteen at Thanksgiving. I'm starting *college!* I don't need this shit. I'll *never* get out of here. Why can't I go away like you?"

Gwen is sick of this line of complaining. "Stop bitching! Why do you want to leave town? You have Patrick, don't you?"

I rub Gretchen behind her ears, where she likes it. "Yeah, he *is* sweet. But for some reason I'm not feeling the same way I did. He seems a little…juvenile. I feel like the slut of the century next to him."

"I wonder why!" Gwen snorts in my ear. I can hear her shifting, like she's trying to get comfortable, since she must realize she's stuck with this line of conversation for the duration. "Let's face it, you guys celebrated a one-month anniversary. You're not used to having somebody last longer than one night."

"Fuck you. I could say the same thing about you!"

"Yeah," Gwen acknowledges, "but I don't consider that an insult. At least I know myself well enough not to get caught up in something I don't know how to get out of!"

"Who says I want to get out of anything? We're in love!"

"Yeah, sure you are. I can see all the telltale signs—like the fact that you're babysitting more so you don't have to see him all the time. Like the fact that you haven't stopped smoking."

"That's because I need the money and I'm an addict. It has nothing to do with him." I stub out my cigarette even though it still has a few puffs to go.

"Oh, face it: now that you've popped his cherry you know it's time to move on."

I gasp at this. Gretchen turns to look at me. "You're disgusting. And I am not like that! I still feel the same way most of the time. Just a little smothered every now and then."

"So what are you going to do?" Gwen sighs. I can tell I'm boring her.

"I have no idea. Maybe I should ask my mother for tips on how to ruin a perfectly good relationship."

"Why don't you shut up about your mother? You have your own life to screw up."

"I can't believe you're taking her side!"

Gwen sniffs in a way that sounds judgmental to me. "I'm not taking sides! I just think you'd be a lot better off if you didn't let her make you crazy."

"Yeah, well, that's easy for you to say. Your parents are still together."

"Right, and my mother just bought leopard-skin panties to get my father all hot. Then showed them to me! Gross! You hear that music in the background? That's her practicing a striptease to "The Hustle." And now she's decided she wants me to start calling her by her first name. I just pray when *I* turn forty I'll have a little dignity left."

"Forty! At this rate we'll be lucky to have any left by the time we're twenty!"

"Sad but true."

The radio has been playing commercials for what feels like forever. I put Gretchen down and go over to peer inside the stereo console and flip through the records. "Delilah." No one's played any of these for a long time. Sighing, I say, "Well, at least we'll have our wild oats out of our system. One thing's for sure, if I ever do get married, which I doubt I will, I won't cheat. I'll be so bored with sex by then I won't even be tempted." At that moment I come across "You Can't Always Get What You Want" in the stack. How appropriate.

"Ah, I don't blame anyone for cheating. You're getting sick of Patrick—imagine how sick you get of someone after *years!* You just need to look at things from another perspective. Maybe you could blackmail her."

"Since my parents are divorced, I think we can safely assume that blackmail wouldn't carry much weight."

"Maybe not, but I'm sure you can make her guilt work for you some way."

I come across Peggy Lee's "Is That All There Is?" in the stack of 45s. What fun I used to have hamming it up to that one. Oh, here's a whole stack of Ruth's old Burl Ives children's records. Man, it's like a time capsule in here and I'm not in the mood to reminisce. The hell with records. I head back to the chair and Gretchen immediately jumps back onto my lap. I light another cigarette.

"She's having too much fun to feel guilty. She went to the doctor last week and he called her 'a splendid animal.' " I make a gagging sound. It's sickening he would say this when she's so obviously past her prime, even more sickening that she was proud to tell me what he said. "And I swear, the way she's mooning around you'd think this grandpa she's seeing was Warren Beatty! His wife dropped dead and now he's thinking *he's* the one in heaven."

"How the hell do our mothers have better sex lives than we do? What kind of sick world do we live in?"

I hear a sound behind me and turn to see my father walk into the room with Ruth. It's unclear if he heard my last remark. I sit up. Gretchen jumps down, takes one look at Dad and heads down the hall. Mom got Gretchen without clearing it with him, and the two of them never made a real connection. Dad's not a dog person and Mom can't live without at least one.

"Hey, gotta go," I say to Gwen. "I'll talk to you later." I hang up the phone and get up, tossing my cigarette into a piece of foil I've shaped into an ashtray, ready to be balled up and stuffed in the trash when Mom gets home. I hug my father awkwardly. Ruth walks past us without saying hello and goes to her room.

"Hi, Dad."

He's looking older since he moved out, with more gray around his temples. Even his dark eyebrows have a few stray grays, and his formerly twinkling eyes look sad and tired. He's short, barely taller than my five-four, and seems even shorter than usual. He smiles weakly at me. "Hi, honey. I missed you when I picked up Ruth yesterday."

"I know, I missed you too. Today I was babysitting, but I've been working a crazy schedule at Playland. I'm earning a ton of money, though. Two-ten an hour!"

"Ruth tells me you have a boyfriend you met there. Anything serious?"

OK, this is embarrassing. Damn Ruth! "Well, a little. If you stick around, you can meet him. His name is Patrick."

"Patrick, eh. Irish?"

"Irish? I don't think so. He goes to Catholic school."

Dad makes a little humorless laugh that I'm not sure how to take. He looks around at his former house with a pained expression. "Sorry,

I'd like to stay but I've got a lot to do tonight." He pauses. "Be nice to Ruth. I think all this is hard on her."

"OK, Dad."

"And go easy on the smoking. You may think you can quit any time you want, but it's not so simple." Tell me something I don't know, I think. We hug again, still awkwardly, and he presses a twenty-dollar bill into my hand and leaves. I stick it in my pocket. Why is talking to Dad always so difficult these days? We go out about once a month, usually to a Broadway show of my choosing plus dinner, where his drink is always a vodka gimlet on the rocks. Each time, I prepare a mental list of topics to cover so we don't have those long uncomfortable silences: Grandma and Grandpa, something I submitted to *Seventeen* magazine, the pros and cons of nuclear power. He's an engineer and comfortable talking about technical stuff. I'm not, but if he's talking I don't have to.

"Ruth!" I call.

Ruth shuffles into the room. "What," she says flatly, not even a question.

"How was Dad's?"

"Fine. We played backgammon."

"How's he doing?"

"What do you mean?"

I hesitate, then reply, "Nothing. So do you want dinner?"

"We just ate. We went to McDonalds."

"Oh. Well, that's good because I don't know what there is to eat in the house anyway. Hey, Patrick's coming over tonight."

"Oh, big whoop," Ruth says, putting her hands on her hips and rolling her eyes.

"I'm just telling you so you don't bother us," I retort, annoyed. I put my hands on my hips too.

"Oh don't worry, I won't bother you and your stupid boyfriend." She turns and flounces out of the room. There's a knock on the door. I open it to find Patrick's beaming face.

"Hi," I say, still in a bad mood.

Patrick hugs me warmly. "Hi, honey. I missed you at work today. The Monkey Race just wasn't the same. The monkeys looked sad. I think I saw one crying."

"Oh, stop. I get one Sunday off all summer! Those needy simians will just have to lump it. So what'd I miss?"

"Zip. Henry was ranting because I swapped with Dave so I could leave early. But mostly it just felt empty without you."

"Henry is such a dip. He resents anyone who has a life outside Playland."

Ruth struts back into the living room, wearing baby doll pajamas. Sidling up to Patrick, she purrs, "Hi honey, I'm home!"

Jesus Christ! I yell, "Ruth! Get out of here! Go to bed!"

Ruth lifts her chin and says dismissively, "It's still light out, you *dip*. You're just jealous."

"Of what? A twelve year old? Why don't you get out of here and leave us alone?"

Swaying provocatively, Ruth says, "Why don't *you* leave *us* alone?"

I turn to Patrick. "Patrick, I am so sorry. Lolita here has obviously lost it."

He smiles. "That's OK. I'm flattered."

Ruth grins victoriously and says to me, "See? He's flattered."

"Oh, wonderful." I glare at Patrick. "That was helpful."

Patrick is at a loss. "I'm sorry. I just meant it doesn't bother me."

"Well it bothers me!" I order Ruth, "Go to your room right now, or you are in so much trouble!"

Ruth knows she has the upper hand. "No-o-o-o. You can't make me."

Patrick is trying unsuccessfully not to let on how amused he is, but I don't see any humor in the situation. I grab his hand. "Let's get out of here." Turning angrily to Ruth I growl, "Goodbye, brat." I head for the front door, Patrick in tow. He looks back. I don't.

Outside, on the gravel parking area, sit three cars: Patrick's brown Camaro, Mom's red Ford station wagon and my blue boat. Patrick and I get into the backseat of the boat. I reach around to lock all the doors, just in case Ruth keeps pushing it. I put the key in the ignition and turn the radio on. Kool & the Gang's "Summer Madness" plays, but I'm not in the mood for WBLS's warmth, beauty love or, especially, sensitivity. I change the station and bring up "How Sweet It Is (To Be Loved By You)" from James Taylor's new album. No, not the message I want. I switch again. Ah, "Sweet Emotion" by Aerosmith. I lean back and say, "I can't believe that. I think my whole family is insane."

"Oh, come on," Patrick tries to calm me down. "She was just trying to get attention."

"Really. I didn't realize you were planning on being a psych major someday," I snap.

"Come on, you're not being fair. She's just a kid."

"She's just ruining my life. We can't even go out because of her."

"Gee, you mean we're stuck here in the backseat of this big old boat with nothing to do? What a rotten break!"

Softening, I smile at him. "God, I'm sorry I'm such a bitch. I just hate my family so much right now. Except my father. I just feel sorry for him."

"Me, too, because he doesn't get to see you that much."

"Cut it out. You don't have to cheer me up."

"I'm not trying to cheer you up. I feel sorry for anyone who doesn't get to spend a lot of time with you. I feel sorry for myself because I had to go almost a whole day. Heck, I even feel sorry for the monkeys!" He pulls me toward him and kisses me. The windows begin to steam up as we slide down into our familiar embrace. I try to match Patrick's enthusiasm but things feel too muddled. I resent my stupid family situation and I find Patrick's lack of awareness of my bad mood to be just plain maddening. Why the hell would he even want to be with me when I'm being such a bitch? I give him a quick blow job, claim a headache and cut our time short. When I head back in, I go straight to my room without talking to that twerp Ruth.

6

THE SOLID TIME OF CHANGE

A few days later I'm lying on my bed flipping through *Cosmo* and listening to WBLS on the radio. They're doing a special on "The Philly Sound." It turns out that a lot of the music I like on BLS, like <u>the O'Jays</u> and <u>the Spinners</u>, is made with the same group of musicians, called MFSB (Mother Father Sister Brother). Their own song <u>"TSOP"</u> <u>("The Sound of Philadelphia")</u> was a big hit last year even though it didn't make my radar back then. <u>Harold Melvin and the Blue Notes</u> also come from Philadelphia, but they have their own musicians including Teddy Pendergrass who has a great voice.

"Karen! Telephone!" Ruth yells up the kitchen stairs.

"Who is it?" I yell back.

"Not telling," she says, and I hear her throw down the receiver and walk away.

Damn her. When Ruthie was younger she was my doting minion. Now she's an evil force working against me. I stomp down the stairs and pick up the receiver she's left lying on the floor. "Hello?"

"Karen! It's me!" comes the voice of Craig, my friend who has been away all summer, banished by his parents to a kibbutz in Israel to make him a real man.

"Craig!" I screech in response. Craig and I were bus friends the last two years of high school—we sat together every day and shared our life stories. His are pretty damn interesting, especially compared to mine, which I guess is why he always did most of the talking. He can be a pain in the ass, but he's lots of fun. "When did you get back?"

"Yesterday," he says. "I didn't think I'd make it! You can't imagine what it's like there. I had to get up before sunrise every day and work like a dog! It was always like 100 degrees. And the food!" He makes an extended retching sound. "I knew my parents hated me and now I have proof."

"You poor thing! But I bet you got a great tan." The perfect tan is my holy grail, but my work schedule gives me so little beach time that I might as well be sleeping all day in a coffin.

"Of course, I look fabulous, that was never in question. I'm telling you, I had to beat them off with a stick over there. See for yourself! Let's get together tonight. On the late side since my parents told me I have to unpack from my trip before I can go out. Plus they want me to start putting stuff together for Syracuse. Which is ridiculous because I don't leave until Thursday."

Craig is a first-class procrastinator, so I can understand why his parents want him to start now. I stretch the phone cord out onto the refrigerator porch to do an inspection. "Well, I'd love to see you but I have to go to a party tonight." Eric is having a gathering, and to keep the peace I have agreed to go, even though Patrick couldn't get the night off.

"Do you need a date?" Craig asks flirtatiously. I can almost hear him batting his long eyelashes. But I know he's just being cute—we had our moment, or what would have been our moment, a couple of years ago.

"As a matter of fact, I do," I say, settling for the cottage cheese container and heading back into the kitchen for a spoon. "My boyfriend has to work tonight and I was dreading going alone." I don't mention that I'm mostly going because I figure Mark will be there. I like WBLS and all, but part of my listening is homework for the next time I see Mark. I'm excited that he might be there tonight.

"Really! Your *boy*friend! Sounds like you had a busy summer. Tell me everything!" Craig sounds excited for me, but I'm not in the mood to describe Patrick or what seem to be my shifting feelings for him.

"Well, I tell you what. Let's go to the party together and I can catch you up on the way."

"Deal. What time does it start?"

"Seven o'clock," I say.

"Seven! No way will I be ready by then. I was thinking nine?"

"You know," I say, "I sort of want to go early and get it over with. It's being given by a guy from work I don't like much, but he pressured me into going. I wanted Gwen to go with me but she can't stand him."

"Why, what's wrong with him?" Craig asks.

"Oh, he's not so terrible," I answer, mentally running through a checklist of Eric's many flaws. "Just a little overly intellectual." Somehow I don't want to badmouth him to Craig. Unlike Gwen, I have some deep-seated need to be well-mannered—or at least to come across that way. Sometimes I cringe when I hear the things she says.

"Intellectual! That sure doesn't sound like my kind of party," Craig laughs, "but tell me where it is and I'll meet you there as soon as I can."

"Hold on," I say, heading for the stairs, "let me get the address. It's in Mamaroneck." I dangle the receiver over the back of a kitchen chair, run up the stairs, grab Eric's address off my desk and practically slide down the stairs to get back to the phone. I give Craig the address and he promises to be there at nine o'clock. Knowing him, I'm sure he won't be, but I'll give him the benefit of the doubt. We just have to have time to catch up after a summer apart!

Since I'll have to stay at Eric's at least until nine, I delay leaving my house, using the time to throw on a little extra eye makeup and change my shirt a couple of times. I don't have any cleavage, but some tops make that more obvious than others. Not that I'm trying to seduce anyone. After all, I have a boyfriend. So why do I feel so excited to see Mark again?

***

Around eight o'clock I stand on the wide front porch of Eric's old-fashioned house. It was a hot day but it's cooled off and I suddenly sense the end of summer as I ring the doorbell. I'm ushered in by a pretty blonde girl who introduces herself as Kim, a friend of Eric's. There's just a small group, and I only recognize Eric and Mark. It looks like I'm the only one here from Funtime except for the host. I think I might start to hyperventilate.

Everyone is gathered in the den where a massive painting—dark, with a quasi-religious theme—dominates an entire wall. It is so large that, even though it is sitting on the floor, it's leaning slightly so its top edge doesn't graze the ceiling. America's "A Horse With No Name" is playing. I think there is only one note in that song. It kills all the energy in the room. The twenty-watt light bulbs don't help either. It's dark and everyone is drinking. Eric is already inebriated—the term he would probably use to avoid saying he's drunk. When he sees me he calls out, "Quick, everybody put your clothes back on! Miss Priss is here!"

I look around. What the hell? "Miss Priss? I do hope you don't mean me, Bigfoot."

Eric, holding up his glass, imitates me. "Oh I *do* hope you don't mean *me*, Miss Dainty Feet."

I'm not sure how to react in this room full of strangers—presumably Eric sympathizers. "Gee, thanks for inviting me to your party, Eric. I didn't realize it was going to be Bring Your Own Insult." I throw a desperate look at Mark, who immediately gets up and comes over to me. He looks adorable in a black t-shirt and perfectly fitting jeans. Now that I see him again I notice he's not conventionally handsome. Something about his face is compelling, though. Maybe it's his mouth: wide but with thin lips. Maybe it's his deepset almond eyes. I don't know, but I'd like to look more closely.

"Well, *I'm* happy to see you," he says. He whispers as he steers me away from Eric, "I can't believe you called him that!" Louder, he says, "So where's your girlfriend—I can't remember her name." We sit down on the couch.

Eric sneers, "Don't you mean where's her *boyfriend?* She and her next-door neighbor at Playland have quite a thing going. Where is dear, *young* Patrick?"

OK, this is embarrassing, but I'm just going to deal with it. I say, "He's working. At the last minute Henry asked him to fill in…"

"…and he's such a nice guy he couldn't say no, even if it means missing my party," Eric finishes.

Now I'm pissed. "Yeah, hard to believe he'd be willing to pass this up."

Eric leans in close and I smell beer on his breath. "You know, Patrick is not the nice guy you think he is."

Pulling away from him I respond, "Oh? And are you who I think *you* are, Eric?"

"No. He snorts derisively. "To know me is to love me and you obviously haven't figured that out."

What an ass. "I guess I'm just wrong about everyone," I say.

"Let's say unobservant—that sounds better than wrong," he says, like he's doing me some big favor.

Another partygoer, to break the tension, gets up and crosses the room to the now-silent stereo. "So! How about we put on another record. What does everyone want to hear?"

Eric hurries after him. "I'll do it! My parents don't like anyone touching the stereo." He starts fiddling around with the console. I get up and leave the room and Mark follows me into the kitchen. After the sound of a needle scraping across a record, "All Around My Hat" by Steeleye Span begins to play from the middle.

Mark shakes his head. "What the hell did you do to him?"

I rifle through the booze on the counter looking for something to pour, and something to pour it into. "Nothing! I thought he was just this mildly annoying guy who used to have a crush on me but realized it wasn't going to happen."

"Try deranged lunatic who can't stand rejection. With terrible taste in music, I might add. What is this shit?"

Chuckling as I pour some vodka into a glass, I say, "Well, I realize he's drunk, but this is bullshit. He invites me over, and the minute get here he starts insulting me in front of total strangers. I want to leave but I'm afraid he might come after me with a gun."

"Don't worry, he won't get far without a car." This is pretty funny, since Eric is famous for bumming rides home from Playland every day. I laugh and Mark smiles at me.

"I know," I say as I pour in some orange juice. "Is he the only person you know who doesn't drive? Why is that?"

"He likes to criticize when he drives. It's more fun when someone else is at the wheel." We chuckle some more.

I offer to make Mark a drink and he chooses a Coke. This makes me feel sort of like an alky as I down a screwdriver, but what the hell. Liquid courage, as Gwen would say. He lights my cigarette and one of his own as I bring up the Philly Sound, hoping he doesn't figure out that I started listening to WBLS at his suggestion. But he's so happy to talk about any music other than what we're listening to I doubt he recalls that I'm the one who never owned a record by a black artist. From the other room I hear Black Sabbath's *Master of Reality* album playing. Funny, I wouldn't have thought my taste in music would overlap with Eric's one bit, but I have this one too.

Suddenly I remember Craig and look at my watch. It's about 8:30. I tell Mark someone's meeting me here, but feel compelled to make sure he understands that there's nothing between us.

"Craig's a friend from high school. He leaves for college this week and we haven't seen each other all summer—he's been stuck on a kibbutz," I explain.

"What's a kibbutz?" asks Mark. I forgot that Mamaroneck is not Scarsdale.

"A kibbutz? Well, I'm not exactly clear on the details but from what I understand it's like a Jewish work camp thing in Israel. Mostly farm work in the blazing sun, according to him."

"Sounds like a horrible way to spend a summer to me!" Mark seems shocked by the concept.

"Yeah, it's not Playland, that's for sure," I answer, taking a swig.

Eric lunges into the room. "Hey, Karen. I'm sorry," he says, towering over me like he's hanging off a beanstalk. "I don't know why I behaved so atrociously. You must think me a jerk."

I look at him stone-faced. "Eric, it didn't affect my feelings for you one bit."

"Well, everybody's been telling me what a jerk I was. I want you to have a good time tonight. Come on back in and let's start over."

I look at Mark who shrugs. I turn to Eric and say, "Oh, all right."

The three of us go back to the den. Eric introduces me to some of the other guests while _Close to the Edge_ by _Yes_, one of my all-time least-favorite bands, plays. We're standing around talking and smoking when Eric suddenly races over to some girl apparently named Cheryl.

"Cheryl! Get away from that painting! You're going to destroy it!"

Cheryl looks at him, confused. "What are you talking about? I wasn't even near it."

Eric says accusingly, "Hey, I have eyes! I saw you leaning on it."

Mark steps in. "Eric, it's an optical illusion—it's the painting that's leaning."

In a fury, Eric turns on Mark. "You stay out of this! You always have to make some crack about this piece. Ever since my parents brought it back from Italy."

"No, only since you decided it was an unsigned Leonardo da Vinci."

"What are you, some kind of art critic?"

Mark glances at the painting. "Art, interior decorating, cleanliness—pick one. That thing is an affront any way you look at it."

As Eric sputters, Mark and I spontaneously decide to leave together. I can't even explain it, we just exchange a glance and run for the door. Mark turns up the stereo so Yes is blasting as we run down the steps.

7
FEELINGS

We end up at the Mamaroneck Inn on Post Road, where Ambrosia's "Holdin' On to Yesterday" plays on the mini jukebox at our Formica table. I paid a dime to hear it. I find it haunting, even in a brightly lit and bustling diner. The odor of overheated coffee is intense, but that doesn't bother me. I can't stand the taste of tea so I'll take coffee even if it's old and sludgy. Which it is.

After we've settled in, Mark lights my cigarette, then his own. He's tall and seems comfortable in his skin, striking a match efficiently and reaching across the table gracefully. I exhale my first puff, smile at him and say, "You know, you rescued me. I didn't know anyone else there. Except Bigfoot of course."

Mark shakes his head, then pushes back his hair from his face. "I can't believe you call him that! That's the same name I made up for him when we were kids."

"I know, it's perfect!" I tell him. "It's what you called him at your party when he passed out in the flower bed."

"Oh, right. Well, I'm glad to share it with you and the world. And I'm glad we let him have it."

"I thought you guys were friends!"

Mark makes a harrumphing sound. "Please! I'm a tolerant neighbor, nothing more."

Suddenly I remember Craig. "Oh my God! I have to call my friend and make sure he doesn't go to Eric's. I'll have him meet us here instead, OK?"

"Yeah, sure," Mark says, looking down at his coffee cup. I wonder if he's disappointed the two of us won't be alone. I am, but I'm also looking forward to seeing Craig. I crush out my half-smoked Marlboro, slide out my side of the booth and head for the payphone by the door. As expected, Craig hasn't pulled himself together, but he promises to leave immediately. I make a quick pit stop and head back to the table, where Mark is flipping through the jukebox.

"He should be here in about fifteen, twenty minutes," I say, sliding back in as gracefully as possible. "I hope that's OK. I want to see him but I don't want to go to his place—his parents are crazy."

"They'd have to be, to send him to a work farm as a graduation gift," Mark responds, turning away from the jukebox without picking anything. "Poor guy!"

"Well, don't feel too sorry for him. You'll see when you meet him: Craig has a way of winning people over." Knowing Craig, I'm sure he got others to bale his hay, or whatever his chores were, and feel honored that he let them. I know I did his homework a few times along the way, not that I can remember why.

"He sounds interesting," Mark says.

"He is," I confirm. "He's sort of nerdy looking, but he's funny. I'm sure he'll regale us with tales of life on a kibbutz."

"Well, I do like to be regaled," Mark says. He takes a final drink of coffee, finishing his cup. "So, tell me about your boyfriend. I've seen you at two parties and he hasn't been with you either time."

I can feel myself blushing a little as I struggle to come up with a reply. I'm sure he must be asking because he wants to know how serious it is between me and Patrick. How do I play this one? Oh, who am I kidding—I'm incapable of anything except an honest answer. "Well, we weren't seeing each other yet when I came to your party. And tonight he had to work."

"Ah. What's he like, this…what's his name?"

"Patrick. He's…dependable? I don't know how to describe him. He's just really nice and very dependable." I check my watch. "In fact, he's probably calling my house right now because he will have just gotten home from Playland."

"Oh. Do you want to go call him?" Mark asks, turning away from me to look for our waitress. We're out of coffee, not that she cares since we didn't order any food.

"Call him? Oh, no, that's OK. I'll see him tomorrow at work." I sigh.

Mark turns back to look at me. "Trouble in paradise?"

How the hell did he figure that out from one little sigh? And what do I say now? I don't even know the answer to that question. Tentatively I offer, "No, not trouble. I just think maybe we're winding down." Did I just say that out loud? Jesus, it must be true. We're not going to be together any more. I feel my stomach lurch.

"Well, at least you had a summer romance," he says brightly. "Not such a bad way to spend a summer!"

"Oh, God," I say. "A summer romance, and it's almost Labor Day. Now what?" Mark maybe?

"I don't know," Mark says. "I guess love doesn't always go the way you want it to. Take you not liking Eric. You see cartoons with Cupid shooting arrows and think it's funny, but getting shot by a stray arrow makes as much sense as any other explanation for having the wrong person think you're the right one."

Just then the waitress walks by, looking straight ahead like she's determined to avoid us. "Excuse me!" Mark calls out, almost musically. Reluctantly she looks our way and he points to our coffee cups. She glances at them and keeps walking.

I say, "Don't you sound jaded. How come?"

"Oh, I don't know. My keen observation of human nature? Personally, I don't have any juicy tales of love gone bad. But from what I've seen, they're the rule, not the exception."

"It does seem like the odds are against true love," I agree. "All I ever wanted was a boyfriend. Now I have one, and at first it was so great. But now...I guess I can't believe in love either."

"You sound pretty caustic yourself," Mark says.

"Caustic! I like that word. Yeah, I guess I'm becoming caustic. How can I not? I've waited my whole life to have someone nice feel like the sun rises and sets on me, and all it makes me feel is suffocated."

"Wow, and of course you don't want to dump him and break his heart, knowing how he feels about you."

"Of course I don't want to break his heart! I feel like a creep, like I was only interested until I got to know him and now I'm bored." I realize I've said too much. "I'm sorry, I don't even know why I'm telling you this."

Mark frames his chin with his hands. "I have an understanding face. You can't help yourself."

Relieved that he's making a joke, I agree. "You're right." Eager to change the subject I quickly add, "So come on, tell me some horrible thing you're going through and we'll be even." The waitress returns, sloshes some coffee into our empty mugs and quickly moves on.

Mark reaches for the sugar and says, "Sorry to disappoint you, but I'm pretty angst-free this week."

I take it that means single, which is a relief. "Just my luck," I reply, grabbing a Sweet & Lo. "And I think we've exhausted Eric as a topic."

"Let's hope." There's a pause while we recalibrate, try to figure out what to talk about next. A middle-aged couple sits down in the booth next to ours, already arguing about what time they need to get home to relieve the babysitter, who luckily is not me.

"Wait, listen to this," Mark suddenly says. He starts flipping through the pages of our jukebox, deposits a dime and pushes some buttons. John Denver's "Thank God I'm a Country Boy" starts up. Good Lord, it's the live version, with hooting and clapping! Would it be rude to cover my ears?

"Wow," I say. I may have to reconsider Mark as someone I can hang out with.

"God no, that's not it," he rushes to reassure me. "Hopefully it'll be next." We both shake our heads at the awfulness of what we're hearing. I look around, trying to figure out what goober picked this atrocity.

When it finally ends, some wistful piano music starts. "Bye baby, see you around," comes the unmistakable voice of Diana Ross. I should have known.

"'Remember Me' from the *Surrender* album," he informs me. We listen. The song is about a breakup, and Diana is saying goodbye and asking to be remembered as a good thing. I don't know what to say. I'm all for finding messages in songs, but I'm not comfortable sharing any more about what's going on between me and Patrick when I have a crush on Mark. I sit there dumbly. Where's Craig? Shouldn't he be here by now?

"The one part I don't get," he says as the jukebox goes quiet, "is why she'd want to be remembered as a big balloon."

This breaks the tension, thank God. I'm not clear what message I'm supposed to be getting here. In a way it feels like he's a friend offering advice, but maybe he's telling me it's time to move on...to him. I look closely at him as he flips through the jukebox. Unsure of how to act I just say, "Great song, but let's talk about something else.

How about school? I can't wait to start college. That will be something new. Although not new enough, because I'll still be living at home."

"Really? Me too! Where are you going?"

"SUNY Purchase. You?"

"Iona. I'll be a sophomore."

"You know, I thought you seemed older."

Mark, putting his hand to his head, says, "Must be this fluorescent lighting. I'm not turning gray, am I?"

"Oh my God, you just reminded me of Craig!" I say. "He was convinced he was going bald last year and kept pulling back his hair and asking if I thought his hairline was receding. You guys!"

Mark chuckles. "I was kidding. If I'm going gray at 19, just kill me and save me a lot of misery. Same with bald, by the way." He shudders. "So," he continues, "you'll be living nearby when school starts. All my friends go to school out of town. My closest friend Sophia leaves tomorrow to go back to Skidmore."

Sophia. I remember her. The pretty one. Interesting that he called her a friend rather than a girlfriend. Maybe there's hope! At least I have geography working in my favor. "My best friend's going to B.U. tomorrow. I'd *love* to go away to school, but my timing sucks because my parents just got divorced. I'm lucky we can scrape together enough for tuition. So please tell me commuting isn't so bad."

"Well, it's OK. A little suburban, if you know what I mean." He looks around the diner, with its suburbanites, and sighs. "This will be my last year in Westchester. I'm planning to transfer to NYU to get into the city."

"Oh, God, that sounds great," I agree, rolling my empty Sweet & Lo packet into a tight little cylinder. "I'm dying to live in New York. I just love everything about it. NYU was my first choice for college, but my mother thought it would be unsafe. The big, bad city, you know."

"I know, that's the appeal!" Mark says.

"Right!" I say. "Plus it's more expensive than SUNY. But I'd want to live there. I'm not happy about commuting this year."

"Commuting's not great," Mark confirms, "but it's not a mark of failure. And since we'll both be around, why don't we stay in touch?"

"Sure," I say. I like Mark's company and definitely want to see where we might be heading.

"And I want to know what happens with your boyfriend, now that the thrill is gone."

I feel myself blushing again. "I didn't say it was gone. I'm just confused."

"Well then, maybe we could get together and play some records, help you figure it all out."

"More Supremes?" I ask. What I'm really thinking is: Did he just ask me out?

"That wasn't the Supremes," he informs me, sounding hurt.

"Sorry, Diana Ross." Jeez, I wouldn't be offended if he left off Neil Young from a CSNY credit.

Just then Craig swoops in, in a cloud of Jovan Musk. He looks tan and hunky—definitely not the Craig I remember! His hair is blond and fluffy, not brown and greasy. He has the same full lips and long lashes, but somehow they look different because he doesn't have as much of a baby face anymore. He was always a little chubby, but he's lost the baby fat as well. He's wearing a beige velour workout shirt that must be hotter than hell and he's exchanged his former droopy drawers for skintight jeans. I can't believe this is the same person I pushed away a year ago when he tried to kiss me, feeling sort of sorry for him. How can one summer make such a difference?

"So is this the hot hangout these days?" he asks, sliding in next to me. He gives me a wet kiss, then reaches across me and starts flipping through the jukebox.

Mark and I both seem to have gone mute. He's staring at Craig, probably wondering about my definition of "nerdy looking," while I try to come to grips with this handsome alien. Finally I say, "Craig, this is my friend Mark Cassone. Mark, Craig Landon." They shake hands and give each other a quick once-over, then Craig turns back to the jukebox.

"Hey, do you have a dime?" he asks. I dig one out of my wallet for him. He pushes some buttons and "Feelings" by Morris Albert comes on. What is he thinking? He's going to embarrass me in front of Mark! I try to catch Mark's eye to let him know I am not in favor of this selection, but he's looking at Craig. I look at him too.

"You look different," I say.

"I am," Craig replies briefly, holding my gaze.

"No, I mean really different. Like transformed. What the hell happened to you over there?"

Craig shrugs. "It's sort of hard to explain." He calls the waitress over and orders a cheeseburger platter with fries and a milkshake. As she leaves the table, probably feeling victorious at squeezing more than a couple of coffees out of us, he pulls down the zipper on his top. His chest hair is as meager as ever, and he's wearing a gold chain with a Hebrew *chai* charm.

"Nice necklace," I say, since he obviously wants us to notice it. "Souvenir from Israel?"

"Yeah," Craig says, reaching up to touch it. "My roommate Seth gave it to me."

"He gave you a gold necklace?" I ask, surprised. "What for?"

Craig looks amused. "He said he just wanted me to remember him."

Mark asks, "Like a big balloon?" He and I look at each other and crack up. We're sharing a moment! Craig glances at us like we're crazy.

I ask Craig, "So what was it like? Mark doesn't know what a kibbutz is and come to think of it I'm not too clear on it either."

Chuckling, Craig says, "Well, it's like a military base that's also a farm. There are fruit trees that always seem to need picking and smelly animals and endless work and never a minute to yourself." He shakes his head. "My roommate and I never had any time alone."

"Sounds like you guys really hit it off," Mark says.

"Yeah," Craig says. "I got lucky." He chuckles again.

I tell Craig, "Wow, it's great you got along so well. What did you guys have in common?"

"Trust me, you don't want to know," he answers. Then he turns to Mark and winks. "Well, you might." Mark just looks at him, expressionless.

The waitress brings Craig's platter. As she walks away he turns to Mark. "So," he says, picking up a French fry. "What's your story?"

"Me?" Mark says. "Just hanging out, taking it all in."

"Yeah," Craig says, popping the fry into his mouth, putting his hand on his chin and leaning forward across the table. "I can tell you're the quiet type."

Mark shakes his head. "I'm not any 'type'."

This is awkward. I don't know what the hell came over Craig but it almost seems like he's coming on to Mark. I'm starting to feel like I don't exist. Grabbing a fry off Craig's plate I try to bring some normalcy to the conversation. "Mark goes to Iona but we're both planning to transfer to NYU next year."

"Hmm," Craig says. He looks at Mark again, an intense, blink-free stare that starts to verge on the rude. Finally he asks, "What's your major?"

There's a pause, like Mark forgot his major. "Communications," he finally croaks, then coughs. "Yours?"

"Undeclared," Craig says, his gaze breaking away and dropping toward his cheeseburger. He lifts off the top bun and starts pounding on the Heinz bottle to cover the burger with ketchup. "Anyways, to get back to the kibbutz, not that I ever will again..."

"Forget the kibbutz," I say, determined to steer the conversation away from Craig's crazy innuendo. I can't tell what Mark is thinking. All I know is he can't be too impressed with the friends of mine he's met so far. "When are you leaving for Syracuse again?"

"I leave Thursday," Craig says, bits of food falling out of his mouth as he talks.

"I got accepted to Syracuse last year," Mark says. "I almost went. They have a great Communications department."

"Really?" I ask, surprised. "What made you decide not to go?"

Mark shrugs. "I just didn't feel like moving up there so far from civilization. New York City is where I belong. But I'm sure you'll love it," he says to Craig. "At least it'll be better than a kibbutz!"

Craig, finishing up his food, nods. "I'm sure I will too," he mumbles, his mouth filled with bread and meat. I forgot how appalling his table manners are. Even assuming this is his first cheeseburger in two months, that's no excuse for this display. He picks up his milkshake with one hand and turns his other wrist to check his watch. Gee, are we boring him?

"Hey," he says, once his mouth is relatively empty, "I know we haven't had a lot of time together but I have to go visit someone else tonight so I need to run." He looks around for the waitress, sees her and waves. She heads over, probably hoping for an order of lemon meringue pie. "Check, please," Craig says.

She flips through the pages of her pad, totals it up, places it on our table, says a quick "thanks" and walks off.

Craig turns to me. "Sorry, I haven't had a chance to trade in my shekels for dollars. Can you get this?"

I want to ask him "Are you kidding me?" But with Mark sitting there I need to keep it light. I bite my tongue and pull out my wallet. "I only have a five," I tell him. "That's why I only ordered coffee," I add, hoping it doesn't sound too accusing, yet that it makes my point.

"I can chip in," Mark says, pulling out a five of his own and putting it on the check.

"Thanks," Craig says, smiling at him. Where's my thanks?

Disgruntled, I throw my five on top of Mark's.

"Let's go," I say, and the three of us head out, past a table playing the Jackson 5's "Dancing Machine." Mark takes the money and the check and pays at the register, returning to throw the change on the table for a tip. I can't believe my hard-earned money went to keep rich kid Craig fed. I'll try not to resent it too much.

Out in the parking lot, Mark and I are parked next to each other, with Craig's father's black Lincoln across from us. We stand together by his car to say our goodbyes, but I don't want to let him go without figuring out what's going on with him. I ask, "Craig, can I talk to you for a minute?"

Mark looks at Craig, then me, and says, "I'm going to head home. Goodnight. It was a pleasure meeting you." He extends his hand to shake Craig's, but Craig reaches out both arms and grabs him around the waist.

"Great meeting you too," he says, his mouth right by the side of Mark's head. For a minute I'm afraid he's going to kiss him on the cheek or lick his ear. I don't know what to expect at this point.

Mark detaches from the hug and turns quickly toward his car. He gets in and drives off without even turning on his headlights. That hug has to have been uncomfortable for him—it sure was for me.

"What was that all about?" I ask Craig, now that we're alone.

"What was what all about?" he replies, in a way that tells me he knows exactly what I meant.

"Why were you acting so weird? Have you lost your mind?"

"Not at all," he replies, leaning on his car door. "I finally found it. I finally know who I am, and it all makes sense. Karen, I'm gay."

Gay? Gay as in queer? Homosexual? Gay as in all those insinuations about his roommate weren't an act? How in the hell could that be possible? Craig was always obsessing about girls: did I think this one was pretty? Did that one just give him "the look" and if so, should he go over and talk to her? I don't know what to say. I just gape at him.

"Say something," he laughs.

"Like what?" I ask. "'How's Liberace?' How can you suddenly be gay?"

"It's not sudden," Craig replies. "I think it's always been there, I just didn't understand it. But now I do."

"Well, that makes one of us. I don't understand how you leave on a trip one way and come back another. That roommate of yours must be quite the salesman." Why do I feel so upset?

He laughs again and opens his car door. "It doesn't work like that. Listen, you'll just have to trust me on this. It's real. It's true. But I have to run. I'm meeting a friend of Seth's in White Plains and I'm late."

"Seth? Who's Seth?" I feel completely thrown off, like I don't even know Craig anymore.

"Seth! My roommate from Israel. He lives in Chicago, but he has a friend who lives here he wants me to meet. I have to get going, but I want to see you and Mark again before I leave on Thursday. Why don't you come over to my house tomorrow afternoon? You can watch me pack for Syracuse." He gets into the car.

"Gee, what an honor," I say. "I'm sure Mark can't wait to see you packing your underwear after the show you just put on."

"I'm sure he can handle it," Craig replies. He closes his door, then turns the key and puts down the electric window. "Ask him if he wants to come."

I back away from the car and give him a little wave. I mean it to look dismissive but he gives me a big smile as he waves back. How infuriating.

* * *

The next day I call Mark. I'm all ready to apologize for Craig and his atrocious behavior, but he stops me.

"I liked your friend Craig," he says. "I can definitely say I've never met anyone like him before." I'm sure that's true. I never met anyone like him before, and I already knew him!

"Yeah, well, I think there's something you should know about Craig," I say. "He told me last night after you left that he's gay."

Mark's silent. "Are you there?" I ask.

"I'm here. I can't say I'm surprised, but on the other hand I am. Maybe more that he told you than that he is."

"I know what you mean. He made it pretty obvious—I've never seen him act that way before, so sorry about that."

"You don't have to apologize for your friend," Mark says firmly. "He was just being who he is."

"I guess," I say, sort of surprised by how open-minded Mark is. I was almost expecting the word "fag" to come up. Gwen used that term when I told her about Craig's announcement right before I called Mark. She claimed to be unsurprised, but that may have just been an act. Mark obviously accepts people for who they are. I feel even more drawn to him, plus a little guilty that I was embarrassed by my own friend. "I just never knew I had a gay friend," I tell him.

"Well, they're not all like Liberace," Mark says. "How would you have known?" yes, Liberace, the universal gay stereotype. He's the only homosexual I'm aware of, so they can't be that common. I get the message: Mark's won't hold Craig against me.

"Anyway," I continue, "he wants us to come over to his house today. He's getting ready to leave so we can't go out but we can watch him pack. Doesn't that sound like fun?"

"Sounds fine to me," Mark says, surprising me again. Is it possible he just wants to be with me, regardless of what we do together? I feel a little tingly just thinking that.

Logistically, the best way to go is for Mark to meet at my house. I'd rather meet him at Craig's, but since he practically has to pass my house to get there I might as well accept the inevitable. I try to gird him, warning about the driveway and telling him my place is sort of eccentric, but all the preparation in the world doesn't help when his low-slung Pontiac Bonneville scrapes the entire quarter mile of rutted road leading to my tumbledown shack. He manages to get to the house, but from his freaked-out expression, I know in my heart it will be the last time he makes that drive. He doesn't want to leave his car at my place, just to get the hell of out there. Without his even coming inside we get in his car and head back down the driveway, shaking and scraping the whole way, until we hit the smooth pavement of the *real* Prince Willow Lane. How humiliating.

We're a little late to Craig's but still he's not ready for us. His younger sister Shelly opens the front door to let us in and we feel the cool blast of central air. She tells us her brother's in the bathroom blow drying his hair.

I take Mark to Craig's modern, sparkling clean kitchen since no one's allowed in the living room. "Just a Little Bit of You" by Michael Jackson is coming from a clock radio on the counter. It's pretty bad and I go over and turn it down. The kitchen has a center island where we sit on tall chairs, a refrigerator with a freezer door that dispenses ice and water, and a microwave oven. A couple of my babysitting families have microwave ovens, but Mom says they irradiate food and are only for people who are too lazy and impatient to do things the right way. This from a woman who buys all her vegetables in frozen bricks. I get a couple of cans of Tab and Fresca out of the fridge for me and Mark. He says he doesn't drink diet soda, but that's all there is.

The Cusp of Everything

We sit at the island drinking and looking around. Craig's house is on a hill and the back of the house is higher off the ground than the front. There's a sliding glass door in the kitchen to a deck with a wooden staircase down to the sloping backyard. It's a pretty view, but not so great to have a hill for a yard. I am always finding flaws with my friends' houses, maybe so I'm forced not to be jealous or to want what I can't have. But really, I wouldn't want Craig's house. It's completely covered in high-pile wall-to-wall carpet, except for the kitchen which looks like indoor-outdoor carpeting. I like wood floors, like Gwen has, but her house is on a busy road and the bedrooms are small.

Finally, hair gleaming, Craig makes his entrance, to the radio softly playing "Bad Luck (Part 1)" by Harold Melvin and the Blue Notes. He's wearing itty bitty shorts and no shirt, like he just got out of the shower. "Hey," he says, heading straight for Mark and giving him a hug. On what seems to be second thought, he gives me one too, but since he's practically undressed it feels weird. Mark is very cool and quiet about the whole thing but he has to be grossed out.

Grabbing a Fresca of his own, Craig takes us back to his room, down a long dark hallway where we have to be very quiet (the carpeting helps). His mother never comes out of her room and no light is allowed in. I was introduced to her once, standing by her bedside. She was propped up on pillows, pale and weak, and wasn't much at making conversation. Craig says there's nothing physically wrong with her, she's just overwhelmed by life. Apparently even the microwave oven doesn't help lighten her burden. Craig's real father died in a plane crash when Craig was six years old. His mom remarried and his stepfather adopted him, then they had Shelly. Even though it's been more than twelve years since the crash, his mother still acts like she just got the news. She's in there now—I can hear Rosemary Clooney singing "Hey There" —but not taking visitors, which is fine with me.

Craig's room looks like an office with a bed. The furniture is mahogany, the drapes heavy and drawn. It's all very dark and formal— the exact opposite of Craig, but then he didn't pick it out. I think his father (actually stepfather) was trying to make a point: get serious. Somehow the mess strewn everywhere repudiates that point. We step over towels and socks on the floor and gingerly reposition piles of clothes on the desk chair (Mark) and bed (me) so we can sit down. Craig turns on the stereo and drops the needle. "How Long (Betcha Got a Chick on the Side)" by the Pointer Sisters starts to play. He throws himself diagonally across the bed, on top of the piles next to me, with a deep groan.

"I haven't even finished unpacking from Israel and already I have to figure out what I need for the next three months," he complains.

I try to be positive. "One thing's for sure: the weather will be different."

"Probably the roommate situation too," Mark adds.

Craig lifts himself up and gives Mark a look. He must be wondering whether I told Mark he's gay, and if Mark's being a smartass. But he doesn't say anything, just lies back down. He grabs his crotch and makes an adjustment. Jesus, is he hanging out of those shorts, aimed right at Mark? I try to shoot Craig a warning glance, but his eyes are closed. I peek over at Mark and he does seem to be looking at Craig with a somewhat stunned expression. I give Craig a sharp jab in the ribs. "Hey, pull yourself together. Shouldn't you be packing?"

"Ouch!" He staggers to his feet. "Leave me alone. I have a plan. Two days of mentally evaluating the right attire for my future life and one day of throwing it into a suitcase."

"Well, I wouldn't want to throw off such an elaborate schedule," I say. "Do you need any help with that mental part?"

"Yeah," Mark says. "Like will you be doing any horseback riding? Tennis? Ballroom dancing? Hanging out at the malt shop?"

"You're a funny one," Craig says to Mark, shaking his silky hair. "No, none of those. Any other ideas?" He sits down at the end of the bed, facing Mark and blocking my view of him. Once again I find myself feeling left out. I scramble for something to contribute.

"Attending classes? Studying in the library? Dining in the cafeteria? Sleeping in a semi-private dorm room?" I suggest. Not the most creative, but all things I wish I could be doing at NYU.

Craig twists around to scowl at me. "Party pooper." I feel chastised and a little hurt.

"I think her list is more accurate than mine," Mark says kindly, moving his chair sideways so we can see each other. He smiles at me, then turns back to Craig. "You probably don't need anything too exotic. And given Syracuse winters, I'd emphasize sweaters and coats."

"Yeah, you got that right," Craig agrees, getting to his feet and going over to his open closet door. "I have a bunch of sweaters I can take." He gazes into the cluttered closet, then turns around to face us and puts his hands on his hips. "I don't want to think of sweaters in August. Let's forget this and get out of here."

"Where can we go with you dressed like that?" I ask. I still can't believe he's wearing what look like gym shorts from eighth grade.

"I didn't mean go out, I just meant leave my room," he says. "Forget about the packing." And so we do. It's back to the kitchen where <u>ABBA</u>'s "<u>Waterloo</u>" plays quietly. Craig takes a fruit bowl from the refrigerator and puts it on the island, grabbing a banana for himself. He peels and eats it in slow motion bending his head over it and even moving it up and down so we get the point. Mark, holding a peach, watches him. I cringe and take an apple, eating it down to the core while we discuss when Craig might come home from school (probably not until Thanksgiving), what his roommate might be like (hopefully not a nerd) and what classes he'll be taking (mostly Science). He asks Mark again what he's studying at Iona (still Communications) and if he has any advice for an incoming freshman (talk to as many people as possible as early as possible). The whole gay thing doesn't come up, but is unmistakably in the air, thanks in part to the banana show. I have to insert myself into the conversation and feel left out and sorry I came. I hurry us out the door after about an hour, claiming a babysitting job.

That night Craig calls to tell me how much he liked Mark, how sweet and interesting he is. "He's got a great look and not a bad body either," he points out. "I'd do him. Don't let that one get away."

"I'm trying," I reply. "It might help if he didn't think my friends were wack jobs. What was that show with the banana?"

"Just a little practice for my new life," he laughs. "I like to get a rise out of people." There doesn't seem to be anywhere to go from there, so we say our goodbyes and promise to write each other.

8
WHY CAN'T WE BE FRIENDS?

And suddenly it's Labor Day. I stand at the railing with Patrick looking out over Rye Beach at sunset. I clutch the rail with both hands; he has an arm around me.

He pushes aside my hair and kisses my ear. "I can't believe the best summer of my whole life is ending. Do you realize next Saturday is our two-month anniversary? Let's do something special to celebrate."

"Well, there's a party tonight for the end of Playland," I say, not looking at him.

"That's not what I mean."

"Yeah, but it should be fun anyway." I finally turn to face him and ask, "What do you think? Want to go?"

"Sure, but what about next Saturday?" he persists. "Don't you want to plan something?"

"Yeah, OK. I just don't want to think about it right now. I guess I'm just feeling wistful about the end of summer. "

"I know. I feel the same way." He gives me a smile and a squeeze. "But I'm excited about how our relationship will change once it's not just a 'summer romance.' "

" 'A summer romance'?" I flinch, stunned that he's used the same phrase Mark did.

"I know, it sounds so casual. What we have is so much deeper."

I drop my eyes and turn away. "Oh, Patrick. I don't know. It just seems so complicated."

"Complicated? Loving you is the easiest thing I've ever done." He turns me toward him and kisses me. I return the kiss, but pull away quickly.

"Hey," I say, "I need to make a pit stop on the way back to my monkeys. Meet you back there?"

Patrick makes an exaggerated sigh. "These short breaks are driving me crazy!"

"Well, today's the last day. I'll be there in a few minutes." I try to fake a sincere smile, take off and am immediately lost in the crowd of Labor Day park visitors. I rush over to the merry-go-round to find Gwen. She's biting her nails with a deep-in-concentration look and gives a little start when she sees me.

"Hey, what are you doing here? Where's your shadow, Donny Osmond? And they call it puppy love…"

"Very funny," I say, grabbing her arm desperately. "Look, I don't have time for banter."

Gwen narrows her eyes at me. "I'm not bantering, I'm sniping," she says. "What's up?" She's definitely not the sympathetic type, but she's all I've got and I need help.

"I think I'm falling out of love," I confess. "In fact, I think I already have."

She gives a little laugh. "Well for God's sake, it's been a whole summer. He's not *that* interesting!"

Why does she have to be so mean? "Please, you've got to help me. I look at him and I feel nothing. Except that he seems so *young.*"

She stares at me like I'm an idiot. "God, it takes you a long time to notice the obvious. Shit, he's in *high school!*"

"Oh, don't be such a snob—three months ago, you were too," I retort.

"Yeah, but I wasn't a clueless virgin." She turns back to the merry-go-round and works the controls.

I cover my face with my hands. "Oh God, what am I going to do? He doesn't even seem to notice anything's changed! He's driving me crazy: even when I act like a total bitch he treats me like I'm this perfect princess!"

Gwen turns back toward me and looks like she's actually trying to come up with a solution. Cocking her head she asks, "Well, what have you told him?"

"Nothing in words. I was sort of hoping he'd pick up on it."

"You mean like Kreskin?"

"No," I respond, exasperated again. "I mean like a sensitive, loving boyfriend."

"You're asking a lot from someone you don't even care about."

"I *do* care about him—that's the problem. I don't want to hurt him, but I just don't love him anymore. But how can I tell him that when I see in his face how much he loves me?"

"I don't know. You're into uncharted territory—no one's ever felt about me the way he feels about you. It's sickening." She rolls her eyes.

"You're a big help."

Gwen glances over at the merry-go-round again. "Look, I'm sorry I can't give you the quick fix for your problem. Let's face it, you're going to break his heart, destroy his life, render him distrustful of all women. But look at the bright side—he'll always remember you!"

I turn to walk away. "Thanks for nothing." Looking at my watch, I head back to the Monkey Race. Just a few more hours to go.

* * *

At the nearest bar, a crowd of Playland staffers gathers, some still in their red-and-white shirts. Drink orders are placed: "A Golden Cadillac." "Sloe Gin Fizz." "White Russian." "Screwdriver." "Rum & Tab." From the jukebox, where I am naturally standing, comes "Why Can't We Be Friends?" by War. I didn't pick it, I swear. I don't even like it, especially now.

Gwen walks over to me. "Where's poor Patrick?"

Despondent, I reply, "Getting us drinks. If he doesn't get proofed, that is."

"So what have you decided?"

"I'm not capable of making a decision. I just feel sick. After praying for a boyfriend for years, and having my dream finally come true, here I am, worse off than before."

Gwen snorts. "How are you worse off? You broke the one-night-stand curse!"

"I know, I know. But now I see I'm incapable of having a normal relationship with a nice guy who cares about me. "I *am* my mother, and I can't stand her!"

"Oh, you are not," she says abruptly. "Look, it took her eighteen years to dump your dear old dad. If you don't want to be like her, why don't you just fake it? Who knows, maybe one day you'll like him again."

"No chance. It's dead. I can't even look him in the eye. I just can't believe he doesn't know it. I can't believe I'm going to have to say those words to him."

"Which words did you have in mind?"

"None! I'm speechless!" I grab Gwen's arm. "Please don't leave me. I don't want to be alone with him. I'm afraid I'll have sex with him out of pity."

"Pity, shmitty. I'm sure the virgin will take it any way he can get it!"

"Would you stop calling him that?" I growl. "It's not even accurate anymore."

"Close enough," she says. The song switches to "Games People Play." Jesus, is there no relief?

Patrick returns with two tequila sunrises. "Hey, Gwen."

"Hi, Patrick."

Trying to make conversation he says, "Can you believe the summer's over already?"

Gwen, flippantly, replies, "Yeah, it's a 'pity,' isn't it."

Patrick puts his arm around me. "In some ways, but in others it's time to move on."

"Yup. And sometimes the best we can hope for is a lovely parting gift." I glare at her. "Well, I know it's time for *me* to move on." She walks away.

Patrick looks after her. "You know, I just can't shake the feeling that Gwen doesn't like me."

I tell him, "Don't take it personally. She's my best friend, and sometimes I don't even think she likes *me*. It's part of what she probably thinks of as her 'charm'."

Patrick gazes lovingly at me. "Well, everyone can't be as sweet as you!" I cringe.

People mill around, saying hello and bumping into us. Eric is on hand, studiously avoiding looking at us. Someone yells out a toast to the summer of '75 and we all drink, at which point Patrick says, "Hey, let's get out of here. We have each other—we don't need these drunks!"

Not anxious to leave, I try to buy some time. "OK, just let me finish my drink." Then, realizing how that sounds I say, "I mean, oh, the hell with it." I notice that "Jive Talkin'" is on the jukebox, and that perfectly summarizes how fake I feel standing here with Patrick like nothing has changed. I down my drink, then put the glass on a table where two people sit making out. Poor schmucks.

We end up in the back seat of my car, once again parked next to Patrick's Camaro in the deserted Playland parking lot. For a change, my radio is off. We kiss. Patrick rubs up against me. My eyes are open and I try to interrupt the proceedings.

"Patrick."

"Mmmmm.

"Patrick, stop."

Stopping, he asks, "What, honey?"

"Patrick, I don't know how to bring this up…"

"Oh, it's up all right!"

"No, you don't understand. I need you to slow down."

"Oh, I'm sorry! Are you sore?"

"Sore? No! No, I'm not sore." How can he ask me that? We haven't "made love" for at least a week. "It's just that I've been thinking about ending at Playland and going to school and I think I need some time alone to get it together."

Still pressed up against me he asks my neck, "What do you mean 'get it together'?"

I sit rigidly and answer straight ahead. "I don't know what I mean. But I'm feeling sort of freaked out by everything. I mean, I'm starting college! That's a big deal and I think I need to throw myself into it 100%."

Patrick shifts, lifts himself up above me a little. "I am completely supportive of that! I want to be there for you every step of the way."

"I know you do," I say, lifting myself up too, so we're sitting rather than reclining. I wish I could lift his hand off my thigh; it feels like it's burning a hole through my jeans. "But you have your own stuff to deal with. You're going to be a senior and that means tons of extra work…"

Patrick lifts his hand off my thigh and gently touches my face, as if to shush me. "Don't worry, we'll have plenty of time to be together."

I shake my head. "I'm not so sure."

He grabs my hands. "My beautiful Karen, you know we'll be together forever!"

I can't meet his eyes. I can't help it, I pull my hands away from his as I say, "I guess I'm not so sure about that either."

"What do you mean?" he asks, with an edge of desperation. "We love each other!" I still can't look at him.

"I know, Patrick, but I'm sort of starting to see that I love you like a friend. A really close friend..."

"I think we're a little more than friends at this point!" he says, recoiling. Oh God, this is like a nightmare! As hard as it is to push ahead, I know I have to.

"We are, but I'm saying we need to step back and maybe just take a break, just be friends again for a while. You know, just until we get settled into school and stuff."

Patrick's voice sounds wobbly as he tells me, "I know you don't mean that. Everything will be so much easier with someone who loves you to talk to every night and kiss every possible moment." Tentatively he moves closer and I know he wants to reach for me. I can't give him any encouragement.

"Oh, Patrick. You're not making this easy. You're making it much harder! I need you to understand that I need for us just to be friends right now. I need some breathing room."

He sinks back on the seat. After a long pause, during which we listen to each other breathe, Patrick says, a little shakily, "I don't know what to say. I didn't realize I was preventing you from breathing."

Well, obviously I can breathe! He just listened to me do it for about five minutes. "You're not, you just...it's not anything you've done. It's me, not you. I've changed. I don't know what I'm feeling any more. I don't know how to describe it any more than that. I'm so sorry."

Patrick looks bereft. "You need space. I don't know what that means. Being apart? I don't want that." He pauses but I don't respond. I can't. "Are you sure it's not something I'm doing wrong that I can change?"

"No, nothing like that," I say miserably. How can I tell him to grow up?

"Because if I made a mistake, I want to correct it. I don't want to disappoint you." Receiving no response, he makes one last effort to stop the inevitable wave that's crashing over him. "I still feel the same way about you," he tells me.

I *don't* feel the same way, which I have just made obvious, but I'm not so far gone that I can tell him that flat out. I just sit there. Finally he asks, "Can I at least have a goodnight kiss?"

I lean over and give him a quick peck. "I'm so sorry."

Patrick pauses, then opens the car door. "Goodnight," he croaks.

I whisper, "Bye."

Patrick closes the door to my car and gets into his. I shrink down on the back seat of my car and wait until I hear him drive away. Then I open the door and get out. I stand in the parking lot and look up at the moonless sky. I feel like everything has shifted, like I will remember this moment forever. I feel alone, but also a great sense of lightness, like I am a single star hovering in the night. I open the front door and get into the driver's seat. I rest my head briefly on the steering wheel, then sit back, exhale, get a cigarette out of my purse and light it using the car's lighter. I start the engine. "Miracles" by Jefferson Starship plays on the radio: If only I believed what Patrick believed, we'd get by. But the only miracle I believe in is that I made it through that conversation. As I leave the parking lot, my red tail lights match the glow of the cigarette from my arm held out the window.

* * *

Late the next morning, I stagger into the kitchen in a ratty old nightgown. Mom is sitting at the table drinking a cup of reconstituted orange juice (one can of concentrate to three cans of water, store brand) and staring into space. Gretchen is by the stove eating from her dish on the floor.

Mom smiles at me. "So Playland's over. That must feel good."

I sit down, fold my arms on the table and lay my head on top of them. "Fantastic." The sarcasm is hard to miss.

She continues. "I just meant you have a couple of days off before you start college. I know you'll miss the social life, but you'll have a whole new one at SUNY."

"I'd better. I'm going to need it."

"Why? What happened?"

I don't look up. "Nothing," I say.

"It doesn't look like nothing. You look like you've been hit by a truck."

"I don't want to talk about it."

Resigned, she says, "Fine. I'm not trying to pry. But I do feel like talking about what's going on with me. I *need* to talk about it. Stan and I broke up."

This gets my attention. I even raise my head slightly. Intrigued, I ask, "What?"

"He said he wanted to get married and I just couldn't. I know it's a big sacrifice for him. His kids are grown. He doesn't need that kind of aggravation again."

"Gee, thanks!"

"Oh, don't be so sensitive. Believe me, no one in their right mind would sign on to live with a teenager. You used to be such a nice girl, and now you're a self-absorbed, hate-spewing beast!" I don't have the strength to argue. Who knows, she may even be right. She goes on, "I don't want to get married, or at least not to him. Once was enough for marrying the wrong man."

I sit up and glare at her. "And again I say, gee, thanks! I'm the spawn of an incompatible couple! I'm so glad we're having this chat. It's doing wonders for my self-esteem."

She ignores my comment. "I just took back my maiden name! I'm feeling like I know who I am for the first time in my life and I don't *want* another name!" Mom starts to cry and Gretchen looks her way. I can't believe I haven't noticed how dirty the floor is, not just around Gretchen's bowl. Mom sure has let the place go. "I don't know what to do!" she continues. "I should be thrilled that someone wants to marry me. I'm forty-one! I may never get another offer! I wouldn't have to worry about money or what happens when they finally condemn this house. He's smart and kind and not Catholic...I thought he would make everything easier, not harder." She scoops up Gretchen and buries her face in the dog's soft brown fur.

I'm stunned first by hearing her own up to her true age for the first time ever, but equally that her life is paralleling mine. I fumble for words. "I don't know what to say. I thought having someone love you made things easier, too. You're telling me it doesn't?"

"Not always. What's wrong with me that I can't just feel good about making the leap? I was having such a great time, it felt right, but I know in my gut that marrying him is wrong."

"How? How do you know that?"

"I don't know how I know, I just do. I didn't listen to my gut when I married your father and that was a terrible mistake." She grabs me by the shoulders. I can't remember the last time she touched me and it feels weird. "Trust your instincts! Even the nicest person in the world may not be the right person for you."

"So you're saying to hold out for someone not as nice? What are you saying?"

She drops her hands from my shoulders, giving up on me. "It's like you're deliberately misunderstanding me! I'm saying just because you think someone is nice, or good to you, doesn't mean you owe him your soul. If you don't feel it here"—she puts both hands over her heart—"then it doesn't matter how wonderful he is. You have to let him go to save yourself." She pauses. "And him, too, I guess."

"Although that's obviously a secondary consideration."

She looks at me, probably asking herself how it can be that I am her daughter. "You know, you think you have all the answers. Give yourself a few years. Then you'll know how little you know."

That gets me. "I don't know anything! I'm as confused as you are. I broke up with Patrick last night. Although I'm not sure he even knows that's what happened. I told him I needed a break but I just couldn't tell him I feel nothing when I look at him." I start to cry. "What's wrong with me? Why can't I make the leap either? Is it genetic? Did you do this to me?"

My mother shakes her head. "I don't know whether to hug you or smack you!" After what I assume is a brief internal debate, she leans over and embraces me, but my arms remain limp at my side. She's not really a hugger and this just feels wrong.

She leans back and holds me at arm's length. "Karen, life is a series of mistakes. But you owe it to yourself to learn from them. Without mistakes, you'd be lulled into a false sense of invulnerability. Mistakes show us who we are by how we respond to them. If we keep making the same ones over and over—as I'd be doing if I marry Stan—then we've given up control of our own lives. If we learn from them and work hard to stay true to who we are, we'll grow and maybe even make fewer mistakes as we get older." She lets go of me.

"But what about when your mistakes affect other people's lives?" I moan. "How do you deal with that? How do you apologize? I wish I didn't have to hurt Patrick! And I'm sure you're hurting Stan too." I don't mention how terribly she's hurt Dad, but I'm hoping she'll pick it up from the guilt that's in the air. "It would kill me if I had to think I was that kind of person, someone who would lead him on and then dump him."

Mom shakes her head. "Good intentions are worthless. It's not what you wish you had done, or know you should do. It's what you *do* that makes you who you are. Everyone wants to be good and kind and make decisions that don't hurt anyone! But very few actually do. Most of us delude ourselves into thinking we're good people by trying to justify actions that in our gut we know are wrong. But if we're not doing what we know is right, then we're not living honestly."

"I know now that the right thing for me is not to be with Patrick. I just wish I could have seen that before I got involved. Gwen thinks I'm going to scar him for life."

"The heart is more resilient than you or Gwen know. You'll find out. Things always work out for the best, even if it doesn't feel that way at the time. It's hard to be wrong about someone you thought was right for you, believe me. But better to admit you're wrong than to pretend it's right."

"I wish I could pretend."

She puts her hand on the same thigh Patrick touched for the final time last night. "Trust me, you don't. Be glad you're the kind of person who chooses honesty. It's better in the long run."

"Better for you, too?"

"I have to believe it is."

I think about that, and my brain hurts. It feels hypocritical to sit there like I am going to take advice from her. Her damn power of positive thinking has betrayed me one too many times. She talks a good game, but she's done nothing but make mistakes with her life, so why should I trust anything she says? On the other hand, she's sort of making sense. She's no dummy, after all, and maybe I can learn from her vast experience with making mistakes.

Finally I say, "I've had all the honesty I can take for one day. I need to go back to bed." I came down to get something to eat, but I no longer feel like it. I leave Mom sitting at the table.

I head back up to my room, my sanctuary. Mom acts like she knows it all, but she's screwed up her life pretty well. Her advice on men is to play hard to get, but also make them think they're the strongest, smartest and handsomest. Assuming I even *could* simultaneously ignore and fawn over someone, why would I want to? Having a boyfriend shouldn't mean giving up who I am or acting like a big phony. I can pay my own way, drive my own car. I don't think she's ever driven when there was a man in the car.

I know she doesn't have any answers for me. She's been looking to religion and that hasn't helped her one bit. Her parents were Christian Scientist and Methodist but couldn't agree on either of those so brought her up Episcopalian. Since leaving their home, she's been on some crazy Protestant journey from Unitarian to Congregationalist, Lutheran to Presbyterian and everything in between, always convinced this time she's found the right one, always disappointed at the end.

Now she's gone Methodist, not just her mother's but Stan's church of choice. I guess it's time for another change.

God, I don't want to think about her anymore.

I throw myself on my bed. My room is my haven. I painted it bright orange a few years ago and now when my grandmother visits, she refuses to sleep in it, saying it's so loud it keeps her up. My vanity table and an old trunk are covered with brightly flowered Con-Tact Paper, and peace signs and posters decorate the walls and sloped ceiling: _Butch Cassidy and the Sundance Kid_, Led Zeppelin, a satirical flag poster from _Mad Magazine_. It's looking a little dated, but I don't feel like redecorating other than moving the furniture. I do that every six months or so; for now, my two twin beds are tucked under each side of the sloped ceiling.

I'm trying not to think about the situation I've created. It's easy not to think about Mom's situation; in fact, I probably won't give it another thought. That's her own problem and has no bearing on my life. Stan is an old, retired dud anyway and she's better off without him. Yet the sight of her crying keeps coming back to me. It reminds me of when I was fifteen and my grandfather, her father, died and she couldn't stop crying. Of course, this geezer isn't as significant a loss, but still. I should probably be more sympathetic. Why am I not more sympathetic? Why am I such a bitch to her and Ruth?

Maybe I'm just taking after her. She's not exactly a role model in the empathy department. One afternoon when I was a freshman in high school, I was walking up the driveway from the bus and a bird came swooping down. It kept trying to attack me while I screamed and ran and covered my head with my backpack. I raced inside to tell Mom, who told me it was probably a mother bird protecting her nest. I asked her if she would take me to the bus stop the next morning and pick me up in the afternoon so I didn't have to risk getting my eyes pecked out. She refused, and sure enough, the bird swooped down on me both ways. Yet when I got home the second day she _still_ said I was on my own. She didn't believe me when I told her how scared I was— "Of a bird? That's ridiculous!"—and how relentless Mama Bird was. If we had a sidewalk in this wacked-out hellhole we call home, I would have stomped up and down it, stepping on all the cracks. The bird attacks lasted only a few days, but my anger at the lack of protection from my own Mama Bird will fester forever.

Now that I think about it, it pisses me off that Mom expects me to take her advice. Besides being wrong about most things—playing with dolls makes girls weak and dependent, sleeping with a pillow causes bad posture, shrinks are for self-indulgent narcissists and gargling with salt water cures everything—she expects me to buy into whatever she says. In this case, her advice is irrelevant because I've already made my own decision about Patrick and acted on it, but I do feel somewhat validated by what she said. Although that probably means I've done exactly the wrong thing.

9

WHATEVER GETS YOU THRU THE NIGHT

When school starts later that week, I immediately break out in hives. Luckily it's not on my face, but my hands look like they might need to be amputated. The term "creeping crud" keeps popping into my head. So I'm even more self-conscious than usual and basically don't talk to anyone when I'm out in public. I'm dying to call Mark, but no way would I let him see me like this. I can feel the potential for a swirling flush right down the depression drain.

The weird thing is that Gretchen has some kind of parasite living in her and we both have to go to the doctor at the same time. As bad as mine is, at least it's not hers, which is some disgusting worm that keeps poking out of a hole in her stomach. It makes me want to puke. Whatever they have to do to cure her is worse than my ointment, and luckily Mom takes her to the vet and handles it. I ask her to spare me the details. I love Gretchen, but seeing her taken over by an alien creature freaks me out.

I like most of my classes, but it all feels somewhat futile. I want to be a writer, but everything's already been written. Stars? Bare branches against a winter sky? The mysteries of love? All covered. Really, what's left to say? The stars look like they always have, someday the bare branches will sprout new leaves and love sucks. I have no new insights to offer. But I'd better come up with something for my Creative Writing class. I'm already thinking I need to dig out last year's papers and see if there's anything I can recycle.

I don't care about school, I care about life. Yes, I want to learn stuff, but I yearn to be in the world, to feel deeply, love and be loved, for real this time. There are different degrees of wanting, and the academic comes in lower than the real life. I just can't get myself to care about my classes.

As if feelings of academic futility aren't bad enough, I also feel very alone and invisible. I don't know anyone at school and can't figure out how to change that. As a commuter, I'm only here part-time, while it seems like everyone else is part of the SUNY family, probably having pillow fights and getting high together, pairing off and building layers of history I'll never be a part of.

I am incapable of starting a conversation with a stranger, so I go through every day by myself, sometimes without even saying a word. Mark's advice to Craig sticks in my head—talk to lots of people as early as possible–but once the first few weeks go by and I haven't spoken to anyone, it feels like it's too late. I have become a loser again.

I come home and cry while doing my homework. I play _Goodbye Yellow Brick Road_ because it was one of the bright spots of high school. I play _Captain Fantastic and the Brown Dirt Cowboy_ and cry because Patrick had it on a cassette in his car. He bought it when I told him a song from it was playing at Arthur Treacher's during our first date. I shouldn't play it because it reminds me of how happy I used to be. Or maybe I just thought I was, I have no idea. If I was, that almost makes it worse because my happiness was based on something that wasn't real, that didn't last. Nothing ever does. Nothing. More tears.

I have to keep reminding myself that this too shall pass. At least, I hope it shall. I'm getting more and more convinced my Playland "popularity" was a one-time fluke. I am constitutionally incapable of starting up a conversation with a stranger, and at SUNY everyone is a stranger and seems destined to remain so. I hate myself.

To make matters worse, Patrick keeps writing and calling. On the first day of school I came home to a ten-page letter going on and on about what he thinks went wrong and how he hopes we really will stay friends. I know I have to answer it but also that I can't.

He's had long talks with my mother and Ruth, who I'm sure have told him how miserable I am and kept his hopes up that I'll come crawling back. He probably even took the creeping crud as good news: now no one else will want me and I'll have to turn to him! I have mostly managed to avoid being around when the calls come in. Good thing, since neither of my loving family members is willing to lie for me, not even a simple "she's not home" when I'm sitting right there making desperate arm motions.

Since the one time I tried it my very obvious sign language was ignored, I had to take the phone that was passed to me by a smirking Ruth and talk to the poor guy. He wanted to tell me he was on the yearbook committee, which I guess he thought would impress me. But his main reason for calling, other than to remind me that he was still around, was to pump me for reasons I didn't want to see him anymore. In the name of self-improvement, he essentially begged me to explain what he had done to drive me away so he could be sure not to do it again. Well, continuing to call for more than a month after a breakup is probably at the top of the list, but I didn't tell him that. I didn't tell him much of anything, especially about my intense loneliness. After all, since I probably caused his I'm not in a position to seek his sympathy for my own. Even though I know I'd get it.

With Playland income over, I have to ramp up the babysitting again. I even do some "light housekeeping" for a couple of Scarsdale mothers who don't like to vacuum or set up their own coffeemakers. One of them has a husband who calls in sick to work almost every week on the morning of his wife's regular tennis game so he can flash me, suggest I give him a blow job and invite me to accompany him on his next business trip. They have two adopted children under the age of three and reinforce my impression of marriage as a hypocritical disaster.

The other husband is some kind of sex therapist with a pronounced stutter. He must work behind a one-way mirror since there's no way he could ever communicate with patients. He asks me if I want to make some extra money typing up a research paper he wrote. It's more than 50 handwritten pages about m-m-m-masturbation. I type it on Mom's IBM Selectric, with her hanging over my shoulder the whole time, giggling and gasping and pointing out my typos. When I give it back to the creepy guy he asks me, "Did you l-l-l-like it?" Seriously, what's to like about solo sex with footnotes? But at 50 cents a page I can put up with a lot. I give him a Mona Lisa smile and attempt a wink. Gross.

I'll do anything for money since it costs almost $10 just to fill my tank. It's typical: the gas crisis started the month before I turned 16 and prices jumped to more than 50 cents a gallon. Watergate was going on around the same time, which also helped kill my faith in society in general.

Gas isn't even my biggest expense. The boat requires constant repairs: a new water pump ($80). Tires ($20 each for retreads!). Some things break and I don't even consider fixing them, like the power window on the front passenger door. The heat was on for about a week last summer and refused to go off, but I just learned to live with it and it finally stopped. Other things, like the transmission and the oil pan, I have no choice but to repair. I'm a slave to my car and have to find money where I can.

The Blicks hire me to teach their live-in Guatemalan housekeeper English. I was an honors Spanish student in high school and love teaching it. I'm a few lessons into phonics when Mrs. Blick walks in on me and goes bananas. Apparently I'm not supposed to teach her basics, just have her memorize key terms she should know, like cook dinner, clean toilet, wash floor. This depresses the hell out of me since I liked seeing Yesenia make progress. The progress stops pretty much at the moment I switch from phonics to toilets and Mrs. Blick finally cancels my service since Yesenia is "too stupido" to learn. I hold my tongue and don't tell her that the feminine form is "estúpida."

* * *

By early October, I'm feeling completely alone. I exchange letters with friends from high school who are all off living in dorms, but I haven't made any new friends at school and I'm not in touch with anyone from Playland except Gwen, who is more than 200 miles away. Playland seems like a distant memory even though it just ended a month ago.

I decide to have my own phone line installed in my room. It's about $15 a month, and hardly anyone ever calls me, but when they do I don't want to have to sit in the kitchen and talk with an audience. Besides, my social life might pick up (I think hopefully…). The cord on the kitchen phone is long enough for me to go about halfway up the stairs to my room, but I picture the two of them lurking at the bottom just trying to catch a word or phrase.

I send everyone I know a letter with my new number, primarily to avoid doing homework. Now I don't have to answer the regular number, so there's no chance I'll ever pick up to Patrick's voice. I refuse to give Ruth my number because I know she'll give it to him if she gets the chance. I lord it over her that I have the only touchtone in the house and they still have to dial the old-fashioned way. Hell, I have the only car with power windows—three out of four anyway—

and air conditioning (when it works, which is usually in the winter). I'll probably have the first color TV too, which I won't let them watch.

Cleaning up my room one day, I find a scrap of paper with Mark's phone number on it. I was sort of hoping he'd have called me by now, but hell, I'm not proud. Besides, all that crap Mom advises about the guy should call first is just leftover BS from the Fifties. I liked him, he's nearby, and I need someone to talk to since all my friends left town and I haven't made any new ones. From the new phone in my room, I dial his number.

"Hi, it's Karen, remember me?"

Luckily he not only remembers, he seems happy to hear from me. "Of course!" he says. "I didn't know your last name and couldn't figure out how to get in touch with you without going through Eric. I'm sure he'll never speak to me again, so I guess I owe you!"

"Oh, I'm sure I'll never hear from him again either," I say. It's true. I burned that bridge every which way I could. Eric must be back at Georgetown now, moving on with his Karen-less life.

"So how have you been?" Mark asks.

"Well, fine, just a little down," I reply. I move the phone off my desk and onto the bed and lie down next to it, settling in. "My best friend left for B.U. a month ago and I can't afford those long-distance heart-to-hearts. School's not so great—I just don't relate to the artsy crowd. Plus my mother is annoying the crap out of me. And every time I turn around I have to shell out for another car repair."

"Wow, any other complaints? No wait, let me guess—you broke up with that guy you were seeing."

Yikes, I'm coming across as a miserable wretch. I need to shut up about how my life sucks and figure out how to paint my singleness as an opportunity for him. "Your psychic powers are most impressive. Yeah, I know you were going to help me figure it all out, but I sort of felt I had to deal with it myself. Anyway, the worst is over now."

"Mm. So now what—any new victims on the horizon?"

Appalled, I say, "Oh, thanks a lot!"

"I didn't mean it to sound that way," Mark says quickly. "I just meant are you seeing anyone else?"

OK, that's a better question. Maybe he just wants to know if he should make a move. But that word "victim" reverberates in my brain. I need to show him I'm worth getting to know. "No, there's no one else. I've been trying to concentrate on school. I've *got* to transfer out of here next year, and I won't be able to if my grades aren't decent."

"Yeah, I know what you mean. Hey, I could use a little break from my own rigorous studies." This sounds sarcastic. Somehow I picture him sitting on the floor of his bedroom surrounded by Supremes records. He asks me, "Want to go to the diner, that place we went to the night we escaped from Eric's?"

"Sure, that would be great. I'll come by your house in about a half hour." This is the closest I've gotten to a date since Playland ended. My heart fluttering, I hang up and change into my favorite outfit: a navy blue plaid flannel shirt from the Army-Navy store, a long brown skirt and my fake Frye boots from Kinney Shoes. Yelling a quick goodbye, I head out the door. It's about a 15-minute drive to Mark's house in Mamaroneck, partially retracing my old route to Playland and reminding me guiltily of Eric and Patrick. I disappointed both of them in different ways, and even though it wasn't completely my fault I wasn't who they thought, it still makes me feel bad to think about either one of them. So I won't.

I climb the stairs to Mark's house. I haven't gone in the front before and it feels more formal. I ring the bell. The door opens to a dark-haired woman about my mother's age and a beautiful speckled white dog with brown ears. The woman greets me warmly. "Hi, you must be Karen. I'm Loretta, Mark's mother."

Loretta. I have never called a mother by her first name so I'm thrown. I don't even think I can do it! I stammer, "Hi, Mrs…hi. N-n-nice to meet you." Instantly I am reminded of m-m-m-masturbation. Yikes, I have to get that image out of my mind!

Loretta introduces me to the dog, an English Setter named Tara. The two of them escort me through the small but immaculate living and dining room into the kitchen, familiar from the 1967 party way back at the beginning of summer. As we walk I can hear "Ain't No Mountain High Enough" playing faintly from somewhere. "Mark's down in his room." She indicates what looks like a door to the basement.

"OK, uh, thanks." This seems a little strange, but I open the door and go down the steps. At the bottom is a small bedroom with a poster promoting the Supremes Live at Lincoln Center hanging over the bed. It feels thrilling to be entering a guy's room, his private space, although a little creepy too since it's dark and no one's here.

I call out, "Mark?"

From the next room comes a voice. "In here." Off goes "Ain't No Mountain High Enough" and on goes John Lennon's "Whatever

Gets You Thru the Night" as he switches from a record to the radio.

Entering what appears to be a den, I can't help but gasp. "Wow. Is this your room?" One wall features a large aquarium and birdcage, another shelves holding a stereo system and a bunch of albums and 45s. That's where Mark is standing, smiling warmly at me. My heart gives a little bump. Yup, he's still got it. I'm glad he knows it's over between me and Patrick.

"This is my *suite*," he says. "It used to be a garage but I turned it into my bedroom and a den."

"It's amazing. And it's weird you're sort of in the basement. I have the attic at my house."

"Well, I'm sure you have a better view than this." He moves aside a small curtain at the top of a door and points out the window to a car in the driveway just outside.

I laugh. "Yeah, at least I have trees."

"Agh, who needs a view?" Mark says, letting go of the curtain and pointing to a leather recliner. I sit down and put my purse on the floor next to me. "To me, all that matters is privacy. I had to get away from my brothers upstairs."

"For me, my sister. She's only twelve and she drives me crazy. With my parents splitting up I end up having to watch her a lot more than I'd like." Jesus, am I going to tell him my whole life story in the first five minutes? I guess I have been starved for someone to talk to! I'd better switch the focus to him. "What about you? Are your brothers older or younger?"

Mark sits down in a big old easy chair across from me, directly under the shelf holding the stereo. "One older, one younger, and they're both still home. I wouldn't say they drive me crazy, but they do annoy the snot out of me. I need my own space and this is as much as I could get."

Looking around I say, "It's a great set-up. It's so interesting in here! Sort of like a zoo!" I get up and go over to the fish tank and birdcage. Somehow I can't imagine having any pet other than a dog. Imagine the work it takes to feed and clean everything!

"Well, we don't have to go anywhere. Are you hungry?"

I head back to my chair. "No, and to tell you the truth I'd rather not spend any money anyway. It's hard enough to earn it now that Playland is over."

"Money's tight for me too. I work in small appliances at Korvettes in Portchester and it doesn't exactly bring in the big bucks."

"Well, it's got to be better than babysitting. I have to work a half hour just to afford a pack of cigarettes!" Speaking of cigarettes, I pull out my pack of Marlboros. Mark reaches for his Kents. I remember noticing the last time we were together that he smokes the same brand as Dad.

For some reason, as I flick my Bic, I say, "I'm thinking of switching to Marlboro Lights."

Mark, striking a match, says, "I tried Merits for awhile but I almost burst a lung trying to suck in some actual smoke. What's the point?"

"Right," I agree. "That happened to me with Carltons. What a waste of tobacco! Assuming there's even any tobacco in there. So what's the story with the bird?"

"He's a parrot I've had for a couple of years. He only says one line, the stubborn son of a bitch." He walks over to the cage and addresses the bird. "Hello!"

The bird responds, "Your mother sucks cocks in hell!"

My mouth falls open. "What was that!?"

"Your mother sucks cocks in hell!" the bird squawks again.

Mark explains, "It's from _The Exorcist_. My friends and I had just seen the movie when I got him and we thought it would be hysterical."

"Well, I guess it beats 'Polly want a cracker'!"

As if in response, the bird repeats, "Your mother sucks cocks in hell!"

Mark grimaces. "Yeah, well, I'm sort of sorry I didn't teach him anything else when I had the chance. Now he's not interested in learning anything new." The bird acts insulted, turning his back on us.

I can relate to the bird with the one-track mind. "Same with me. I just can't handle the whole studying thing. I open a book and get an instant urge to make a sandwich. Or a phone call. Anything not to study. That's why I'm here!"

Mark says, "Studying isn't really my thing either. Yes, I need to be 'educated' but I wish there was an easier way than locking yourself up for hours with a bunch of books."

"I know, it's just the vision of myself as an unemployed, ignorant dropout that keeps me going—plus the need to keep my grades up so I can make the move into the city next year."

"Right, NYU."

"Right." There's a pause as we take each other in.

"So," he says, breaking the silence. "What happened with the boyfriend?"

I don't want to tell him how I broke up with Patrick because it makes me sound like a creep, so I skip ahead. "He's still calling. He wants to make plans for my eighteenth birthday, which is more than a month away. He wants me to tell him what he did wrong so he doesn't make the same mistake again. I tell him he didn't do anything wrong, but I can't tell him the truth."

"What's the truth? What did he do wrong?"

"Truly, nothing, but it felt like he loved me too much. Is that possible? Do you know what I mean?"

"No idea. Who wouldn't want to be adored?"

"I know, it sounds great, but it's really a lot of pressure. You know, to be adorable. And to adore him as much as he adored me. I did at first, but then it just seemed like he loved me way over the top and I couldn't keep up. Then there's the guilt: he loves me, so why can't I love him?"

Mark assumes a pensive look. "Ah."

"I don't know why he keeps calling! I tried to make it clear when we broke up that I didn't feel the same way anymore."

"You didn't give him that 'let's be friends' speech, did you?"

"Not only did I give it, but I knew even as I was giving it that I didn't want to be his friend. It just sounded better than 'Now that I know you, I see how wrong you are for me.' I just didn't know what I wanted, but still, I felt like a terrible person."

Mark shakes his head. "Poor slob," he says, then quickly adds, "Him, not you."

"Well, that's a relief," I say, but I certainly don't feel relieved. I feel like I just blew my chance with Mark. I've practically warned him to steer clear of my callous and careless ways! Why the hell am I telling him all this? I want to win him over, not drive him away! What do I say now, to get back on track?

"Hey," he says, getting up and walking over to the stereo, which has a framed photo of Diana Ross sitting next to it. "Have you heard from your friend Craig? How does he like Syracuse?"

"As a matter of fact I got a letter from him yesterday," I say, relieved to have the subject changed, but wary since Craig's flirtatious treatment of Mark hangs over the conversation. "I still haven't quite gotten over him deciding he's gay, but knowing Craig it's just a phase he's going through. All he said was that he's planning to go into psychology and taking classes in genetics. And that they're having a lot of drug busts and it feels like there won't be enough kids to keep the place open!"

"That's pretty funny. What about the roommate situation?"

"I don't think he mentioned it." At that point the parrot is heard from again: "Your mother sucks cocks in hell!"

I go over to the cage. "How does that bird know so much about my mother?"

Mark laughs, and the bird again turns his back on us.

* * *

Once we have bonded over our frustration about our siblings and our shared goal of moving to New York City, Mark and I become inseparable. It's my nature to need a constant companion. Before Gwen it was Dorothy; we passed notes between every class in ninth grade, sometimes traveling two floors and a building away to deliver those pathetic updates on who looked at us in Math class or what the popular girls were wearing, or what bitches our mothers were being. In eighth grade, it was Rachel, but we went our separate ways in high school and she could usually be found in the student smoking lounge while I preferred to smoke outside.

But those were best friends. I don't want Mark to be my best friend, even though so far it feels like that's where we're headed. With everyone else I know scattered throughout the Northeast, I need him, but preferably as a romance. He doesn't feel like a boyfriend yet, but I think it's headed in that direction. I don't let on that I have a crush on him, because I want him to be the one to make the first move. I guess some of Mom's lessons wormed there way in. Anyway, we talk on the phone daily, meet at the diner or at Cook's on Boston Post Road at least a couple of times a week. Cook's is a family restaurant where you get your food at the counter and can sit as long as you like. In the back they have games, like Skee Ball and pinball machines.

We visit each other's houses, but since his vintage Bonneville can't handle my stupid driveway I tend to go to his place. He's only been over a couple of times, leaving his car at the mailbox and making the long walk, while I can't even count how many times I've been at his place. We listen to records, usually the Supremes. He confessed that he had help programming the music at the 1967 party—pretty much any records other than the Supremes were supplied by friends!

I'm being indoctrinated, and I do like the music but it's not exactly realistic. Take "I'm Livin' in Shame." Apparently Diana Ross's "Mama" is an embarrassment who dresses in rags and eats her food right out of a pot, with her hands. Diana ran away to college and told everyone her mother had died, so imagine the guilt when Mama dropped dead while baking bread. Whew! The fact is, Diana and the rest never went to college, instead attending Motown's "charm school" to learn how to associate with royalty. Oh well, the song is dumb, but at least it's catchy.

Post-Diana Supremes songs didn't get the same traction as the earlier repertoire, but "Up the Ladder to the Roof," "Stoned Love" and "Nathan Jones" are as good as anything done with her. At S.U. (Supremes University) I learn about all the different iterations of "The Girls," from the revolving door of lead singers to those relegated to singing oohs and doing handclaps. It's like trying to care about football. If only it was football.

Mark buys *Billboard*, an expensive ($1.50) magazine for the music industry, when he knows there will be something about a new Supremes release—an ad or a chart appearance. I never miss an issue of *Rolling Stone*, and cut out its reviews to slide into my album covers. I love flipping through his carefully preserved issues of *Billboard* . Wouldn't either one be a fun place to work? I'd love it! They probably listen to music all day, get to meet the groups and know all the inside stories.

I used to fantasize about working at *Glamour* or *Mademoiselle*, but the hell with them, with their pushing of blue nail polish and white lipstick and using orange juice cans for rollers. I bet they're staffed by women obsessed with makeup and clothes. I'd much rather talk about music all day. Music is in my blood. Songs are tied to experiences for me, and I know when songs came out and where I was when I first heard them. "I'd Wait a Million Years" by the Grass Roots? 1969, driving to my piano lesson. "No Time" by the Guess Who? 1970, part of an annoying conversation with Josh Steinberg on the school bus, who turned it into an Abbott and Costello routine by asking me "Guess who does this song?" I decide working at *Billboard* will be my career goal.

Sitting for hours on end at Harbor Island, I end up with a dead battery from keeping the radio on while Mark and I talk. Once, in front of his house, listening to "Nights in White Satin," parked under a beautiful oak tree, we talk about how big it will be in twenty years. I get an image in my mind of us sitting there twenty years from now. I wonder, will we still be together then? Finally more than friends? Heck, I don't really care about twenty years from now—I want it to happen now!

There have been a few times when it seemed like he was going to lean over and kiss me, but so far it hasn't happened. I am almost as close to him as I have ever been to a girlfriend, yet it feels different because he's a guy. It's confusing. After just a couple of months together I find myself yearning to be with him, wanting to hear his stories, knowing he'll want to hear mine, that he'll have just the right perspective on my problems with money, school and my family. Yes, that's fulfilling in its way. If he was a girlfriend, it would be enough. But because he's not, I can't help but hope we go in a new direction. I've only had one other platonic male friend, Craig, and even he made a pass at me. I would definitely like to have Mark as a boyfriend, but it's scary to think about making the transition. Based on my track record, I guess for now platonic is safer. Meanwhile, time passes.

We watch _All My Children_ together. Like me, he remembers when Chuck married a pregnant Tara to give her baby a name because Philip, the real father, had been lost in Vietnam, although he did ultimately come back and boy was that awkward. Mark even named his English setter after Tara on the show.

We go to Burger King, where Mark insists on making them honor their "have it your way" pledge by forcing me to stand around for ten minutes waiting for a burger with no onions or pickles. He doesn't like any pulp in his orange juice, either (he calls it "bits"), and he takes his coffee with lots of milk and sugar. We sit and talk at Florence Park near his house. We go to Stamford to see Diana Ross in the movie _Mahogany_, which is pretty lame but still makes me cry.

I visit him at Korvettes and check out the record department next to small appliances. Mark's always sneaking over and rearranging the records to give Diana Ross and the Supremes more prominent placement. Sometimes we go to the Steak & Brew next door, where one night there is an embarrassing scene when I lose a contact lens and have to crawl around on the floor in the dark looking for it. I meet the rest of his family, including his older brother Dean and younger brother Chris. Dean is really handsome, in a Marlboro Man kind of way, and very charming, but he feels very out of my league, plus a little messy what with my crush on Mark and all. Chris is just a kid. Most importantly, together we fill out NYU transfer applications.

The Cusp of Everything

One night in November, having talked until the sun is about to come up, we decide to take a drive to Rye Beach next to Playland; of course it's deserted. Also freezing. Mark has a blanket in his trunk so we wrap up together and watch the puny waves hit the narrow shore. Hey, it's not Jones Beach but it's close, at least geographically. As we sit and talk, I block out the memories of the summer that keep pushing their way in, as well as the feeling that being wrapped up in a blanket with a guy should be more romantic than it is. I can't help but think my dumping of Patrick serves as a cautionary tale for him, that he's concerned if we make the leap I might lose interest in him, and that would destroy our friendship. Yet I can't reassure him, because how would I even bring it up? We talk about everything but "us."

We are both dead tired but also somehow energized by the intense conversation plus the coffee we made at his place and brought with us in an old plaid thermos. I think we both feel like we are explaining things not just to each other but to ourselves. I say things out loud that I've never even realized I thought or understood. And I think he is doing the same. We talk about philosophy (because we are here, there is no way we ever could not have existed) religion (brainwashing for those who don't want to think for themselves), family (the ultimate love-hate relationship), school (we're both crossing our fingers for NYU) and relationships (mostly in the abstract since neither of us has ever been in a long-term, fully functional relationship). But we both seem to want the same things from love, and this stirs something in me again. I'm surprised when I lean close on our blanket and Mark doesn't reach for me. It sure felt like a moment, but maybe he's not ready yet.

As we leave the beach, the sun is rising over Playland and the Long Island Sound, a golden glow that makes it look magical. The car radio plays a dramatic remake of Stevie Wonder's "I Believe (When I Fall in Love It Will Be Forever)" by Art Garfunkel that makes me want to cry but doesn't seem to affect Mark at all. I wonder if my senses have become more attuned through lack of sleep. I haven't pulled too many all-nighters but they tend to make me feel somewhat drugged.

Music has always been an important part of my life, and now, like him, I find myself constantly changing radio stations looking for a meaningful song. Unlike him, this can be something other than the Supremes or Diana Ross, although I must admit I have become very attached to "Ain't No Mountain High Enough," and always get a little thrill when I come across it. The holy grail is to catch the <u>six-minute version</u> from the very beginning, not easy to do. I've seen him do it psychically, though, and it's pretty impressive. With me, finding something good feels random, but with him it feels telepathic, like he sent some deejay a mind message.

10
YOU HAVEN'T DONE NOTHIN'

It's Thanksgiving, which means that I've made it through most of my first semester at SUNY Purchase. I have found a quasi-groove: I drive to school in the morning, park as close as I can to wherever my last class is going to be, walk to my first class with my head down and stay that way until I get to leave again. I avoid the cafeteria, where my loneliness would be on display. Instead, I get my food from vending machines or, if I've planned ahead, from my backpack. I don't even feel like I'm in school. It's like I'm going to a job every day, clocking in, working the assembly line in silence. I talk to virtually no one, including my teachers. I'm sure none of them have any idea who I am, which seems appropriate since I'm not so sure myself. What I do know is that this school is not the place for me. Mentally I have already moved on.

The funny thing is that it's the same for Mark. I spent a day at Iona with him last month and he doesn't know anyone on his campus either. Turns out he's painfully shy, but you'd never know it if you see him in his natural habitat, like when I met him at his party. It's weird how he seems so confident with me and his friends, but he can't even call a movie theater and ask them what time the movie is showing. He gets all tongue-tied and begs me to do it. I'm not crazy about talking to strangers either, but I'm better than he is. Both of us are fine in small situations where we've been introduced to someone, but terrible in unfamiliar settings with people we don't know. I tend to cling to one familiar face all night or, if I don't know anyone, the nearest dog.

But despite being like me in some ways, Mark is an amazing person and I'm grateful he's in my life. His parents are so nice and like me too, while Mom doesn't express interest in anyone who's not taking her out to dinner and turning her shirt inside out. Gross! I wish I could be with Mark tonight instead of here in this asylum.

I can hear Mom in the kitchen preparing Thanksgiving dinner. She took me to a brilliant concert last week, <u>Vladimir Horowitz</u> at Carnegie Hall. It was like we had a time-out from who we really are. Sure, we ate dinner at a hot dog stand and sat in five-dollar seats in the nosebleed section, but it still felt special. I'm not a big classical music buff, but you'd have to be deaf or unconscious not to realize there's something other-worldly about Vladimir Horowitz. I will remember that performance for the rest of my life.

For the first time in I don't know how long, Mom and I had a great time together. She said the day brought back memories of going to concerts with her parents, back in Washington in the '40s. She didn't seem wistful about it, but I think if I'd grown up rich it would be hard to adjust to pinching pennies. Sadly, I'll never know for sure.

Anyway, the time-out is now over and Mom and I are back to our usual sparring. She's cooking Thanksgiving dinner and I'm upstairs inhaling the scent of turkey and listening to side two of <u>Stevie Wonder's <i>Fulfillingness' First Finale</i></u> for the third time today. My excuse for not helping has been that I'm doing homework, but I spend more time studying album covers than school books. It's partially laziness (or, as Stevie would put it, <u>"You Haven't Done Nothin',"</u>) and partially avoiding preparing for something that just seems fated to turn into a catastrophe.

Mom yells up my stairs for about the fifth time, "Karen!"

I yell back, "What?" As if I don't know.

"I'm not doing Thanksgiving dinner by myself! Get down here and make these beans!"

I go down to the kitchen reluctantly. Bits of Mom's pageboy are stabbing out from her head and she looks deranged. Food covers every flat surface, from the table to the washing machine and dryer. The dish drain is on the floor, presumably to create some counter space. All four burners on our ancient stove are flaming at top speed. Gretchen is poised to gobble up any scraps that hit the floor. It looks like hell to me and I don't want to spend even a minute in here.

"Can't you get Ruth to do it?" I whine. "I have to write a paper about someone with vast historical perspective. Oh, that reminds me, are you free later for an interview?"

"Oh, you are missing your calling. You should be taking comedy classes! I sent Ruth to set the table and clean her room. So here you go." She shoves a paper bag overflowing with string beans at me.

"What am I supposed to do with these things?" I hold the bag out as though it smells.

"You're supposed to participate!" Mom cries, her eyes so wide it's like they're migrating to the sides of her head. "This is for a family dinner and your father is coming." She glances up at the wall clock. It's hanging over our ancient radio, playing "Born to Run." Its intensity perfectly matches Mom's urgent pace around the kitchen, plus it underscores how I was born to run from this deathtrap. Bruce hits it on the head: I've got to get out while I'm young.

Mom gives a little shudder when she sees the time and barks at me, "He should be here any minute, so get to work!"

"Don't remind me," I respond, forcing myself to gaze into the bag of beans leisurely, just to show I will not let her determine my behavior or reactions. Ever since she broke up with Stan she's been around way too much and trying way too hard to be a part of my life and Ruthie's. She throws herself into whatever she's doing—in this case making Thanksgiving dinner—to a maniacal degree. She dumped Dad, so why is she trying to impress him? What is she trying to prove?

I can't help but share my disapproval. "You two haven't spoken three words to each other since he moved out other than 'Where's my check?' This has disaster written all over it."

Mom purses her lips and glares at me like she's going to take the bait, but instead turns back to the stove and says, "Well, Ruth wanted the family together so we're just going to have to get through it."

"Good thing she didn't want a pony." God, I'm pretty good at this bitch thing.

Mom flashes me a fierce look. "Will you just wash the damn beans and break off the ends?"

"Ooh, you said the D word!" I taunt.

Infuriated, she opens the oven door to check the turkey and bangs it closed just as Dad walks in the kitchen door to the mellow and ironic strains of "Who Loves You" by the 4 Seasons.

As he takes off his windbreaker and surveys the dinner preparations, Mom calls out with false cheer, "Hello there! Happy Thanksgiving!" She reaches up to pat down her wild hair, probably a reflex. I remember when we still lived in Maryland, she used to apply bright red lipstick every day before Dad got home from work. Man, have times changed. She reaches up and turns off the radio; music was always her thing, not his.

Dad is less phony than Mom and doesn't even pretend he's happy to be here. "Hmph, hello," he says. He looks right past her to me. "Hi, honey. Are you ready for adulthood tomorrow? How should we celebrate the big 18?"

"I was thinking maybe a movie," I say. "There are some good ones out now."

"Whatever you want," he says. Since the divorce, I've seen so many Broadway shows and movies that often it's hard to find something new. "But let's bring Ruth with us, OK? Where is she?"

"I don't know," I respond. "Apparently she doesn't have to help at all. I have to do everything."

Turning on me, Mom practically yells, *"Everything?* You haven't done *anything!"* I force myself not to stick out my tongue at her. How dare she try to deny me my martyrdom! "Oh, just stop." She grabs the bag of beans away from me. "I'll do this. You go get Ruth."

Success! She finally gave up on asking me to sweep because I willfully flung dirt all over the place, and now I have proven my uselessness yet again. Maybe she'll finally leave me alone! I flee the kitchen. As I turn the corner into the living room I hear her say, "Just to get it out of the way, do you have a check for me?" There's a slight crumpling sound. Deciding to stop and listen, I lean against the upright piano that no one's played in at least two years.

Mom says, "Thanks." She sighs. "I don't know what to do with Karen. She's nasty all the time and doesn't want to do anything to help around the house." What a tattle-tale!

"That's a shame," Dad says, in a flat tone that doesn't sound too empathetic.

"Yes, it is a shame. I think you should have a talk with her."

"You want me to tell her to help you more? Sorry, that's not going to happen."

"You're still her parent too, Mike. That means more than taking her out to dinner and a show every now and then."

"Yes, it *should* mean being around while she grows up. But you saw to it that I don't get to do that."

"Count your blessings! Ninety percent of the time she's just insufferable. And she's horrible to Ruth."

"Did it ever occur to you she might be angry about the divorce?"

"Don't you think I know that? But do I have to pay the price forever?"

"As a matter of fact, yes. Yes, you do. We all do," he responds with bitter enunciation.

"Oh, don't be so melodramatic." I can tell she is turning away from him as she says this.

Ruth comes walking into the living room where I am suddenly sorry to be eavesdropping. I grab her by the hand and take her into the kitchen. "Here we are," I say loudly, in case they were going to ramp it up some more. They never fought in front of us and I'm grateful they spared us this ugliness. "Can we help?" I ask sweetly. It sounds like I'm being sarcastic, and part of me is, but another part is just trying to shut down a nightmare in the making.

Mom holds my gaze for a second, then starts banging around and asking for platters. Ruthie and I hustle while Dad heads to the dining room, lighting up a cigarette as he leaves the room. I wish I could do the same. The three of us work in silence, Ruth and I shoveling food onto platters while Mom carefully takes the turkey out of the oven and balances the pan on the lip of the sink. "Clear a spot!" she says.

I grab a couple of filled platters off the washing machine and turn purposefully, almost running into Dad, crashing back into the kitchen. He demands, "What happened to the liquor cabinet? Do you seriously expect me to get through tonight without a drink?"

The three of us stand paralyzed. Ruth and I turn our heads slightly toward Mom and catch each other's eyes as if sharing a prayer that her answer calms him down. Surely she remembers his nightly Jim Beam. Just because she doesn't drink could she be so insensitive as not to plan for him?

"Oh, Mike," she says, apologetically. "I'm so sorry, I got rid of all the alcohol after you moved. It never even crossed my mind." Uh oh. She looks down at the pan with the turkey in it, still half-resting on the sink. "But there's a beautiful turkey, and mashed potatoes and gravy, and apple pie for dessert, your favorite." Glancing at me she adds, "I'm afraid we don't have any string beans but I made candied sweet potatoes."

Dad's holding his arms slightly out from his sides. He looks like he can't decide whether to grab her by the throat or clutch his heart and drop to the floor. His cigarette ash dangles dangerously. I put my platters back down, grab a small bowl out of the dish drain on the floor and hold it out to him with a weak smile. "Here, Dad. You need to flick." He grabs the bowl without looking at me, stubs out his cigarette in it, shoves it back and shoots a look at Mom. He exits the kitchen, well, the word "soberly" pops into my mind.

Mom, Ruth and I exhale, then Mom nods at the platters and I pick them up again and carry them to the table, which is set with the rarely seen good china and real crystal. Somehow I have a feeling we won't do the traditional running our fingers around the rim to make beautiful music together.

Ruth brings in the rolls and butter. Dad is seated in his once-usual spot at the head, obviously still seething. She puts down her food and squeezes between Mom's chair and the wall of books to her spot on the far side of the table. The room is just a little too small for the dining table from our Maryland house; if Mom and Dad are both seated she has to crawl underneath to get to her chair.

Mom enters and places the turkey in front of Dad with a little "ta da!" that feels very wrong under the circumstances, then takes her seat across from him. "Who wants to say grace?" she asks cheerfully, like it's 1965 and the last ten years—never mind the last ten minutes—didn't happen. Grace! When's the last time anyone said grace in this house? I'm tempted to jump up and shout, "Good food, good meat, good God let's eat!" but restrain myself. I look across the table at Ruth but she isn't volunteering and I can't bring myself to look at Dad.

"Fine," Mom says, "I'll do it. Please, oh Lord, bless this table and all who sit around it. Bless..." She hesitates, as if considering getting specific, then cops out with the prefab "Bless this food to your use and us to thy loving service. In Jesus' name, amen." What a relief.

Dad picks up the carving knife and gives it a long, meaningful look. Or maybe I'm just reading into things. Finally he picks up the big fork and starts to carve the turkey. I must admit, everything smells delicious, but do I dare say that or would it sound like taking Mom's side? While I ponder, Ruth pipes up, "Mmm, it smells so good!"

"Thanks, honey! Mom responds immediately. "And Ruth, you did a beautiful job setting the table." Ruth smiles and looks at Dad, carving in silence, his perfectly placed glass of water sparkling and pallid in front of him. Mom adds, "I have an idea! Let's go around the table and each say something we're thankful for. Ruth, why don't you start?"

Oh, Jesus. Couldn't she stick to the weather? Anything but this! I dread what Dad will say and start trying to come up with something positive for when it's my turn.

"I'm thankful to have my family back together," Ruth says, reaching over to touch Dad's sleeve. He pauses his carving and gives her a small smile, his thin lips barely moving. Is it his turn now, or Mom's? She jumps in.

"Well, I'm thankful that we made it to another Thanksgiving, and that we're all healthy." Dad puts down the fork and raises his hand to his mouth, letting out a deep, phlegmy, unhealthy-sounding cough. Wow, not a good sign. The pressure's on me to keep things moving and ignore his attempt to contradict Mom.

"I'm thankful that I made it out of high school," I say, making it up as I go along. "And that Ruth is my sister," I add, feeling suddenly magnanimous. "Um…" I seem to have run out of ideas. I'm certainly not thankful we're together so I won't say that. But if I stop talking it's Dad's turn and I picture him crashing this little thank-fest back to earth fast. "I'm thankful for the food that looks so good, and that I didn't have to make the beans," I add, a small sop to my mother and as close as I plan to get to an acknowledgement of all her work. She should never have allowed this debacle to happen, so I'm not going to praise her for catering it well.

It's Dad's turn now and slowly Ruth and I face toward him, hoping for the best. He has amassed a pile of turkey and looking up from it he says, "Who wants white and who wants dark?" Wielding his big fork, he picks up a plate.

"Can I have a little of each?" I answer quickly, hoping this change of subject will bypass anything Dad might have to say on the subject of thankfulness. But no such luck.

"Mike, aren't you going to say what you're thankful for?" Mom goads. What the hell is wrong with her?

He glares at Mom. "Other than my two girls, I can't think of a thing."

She gives an exasperated sigh. "That's great. Poor you."

Dad puts down the knife (thank goodness) and fork and says, "You can't leave it alone, can you Paula? You just don't get it."

"Oh, I get it. I get that you love to feel sorry for yourself, and you never miss a chance to blame me for everything." Her voice is getting louder.

Dad escalates it further, snarling. "And you, you're so blameless."

Ruth pleads, "Mommy, Daddy, please don't fight."

Mom says, "I don't know what I was thinking, agreeing to this."

"You!" growls Dad. "I must have been out of my mind." He grips the edges of the turkey platter like he is going to fling it across the table, then closes his eyes and exhales deeply. Slowly his eyelids raise. He gives chilling glance at Mom, then a brief headshake. At that moment his face collapses in sadness like he lifted his foot off the mood accelerator. I can almost picture the cleft in his chin with a tear running down it even though for that to happen he'd have to shift his head around like a game of Labyrinth, where the marble always falls in a hole.

In a voice that sounds an octave lower than before Dad says, "Sorry, kids. This wasn't such a good idea. I'll come by tomorrow and we'll go to the movies for Karen's birthday."

Ruth howls as if in pain. "No! I want to have Thanksgiving as a family!" She jumps out of her seat and throws her arms around Dad. He looks like he's going to cry for a second as he picks her up. He hugs her close, even though she's too big for that, her legs banging into the arms of his chair.

I cannot believe this is happening. How can I be related to these crazy people? Feeling like I want to scream, instead I blurt out, "Ruth, I'm sorry, but we're not a real family any more. But a movie is a great idea! I want to see _One Flew Over the Cuckoo's Nest_. That's a documentary about us."

My mother, enraged, yells, "That is _it!_"

Dad tries to put Ruth down but she continues to cling to him. "I'm going," he says calmly. "Ruth, I'm sorry we were fighting. I know you wanted to have a family Thanksgiving but it's not possible. I do love you very much and I'll be back tomorrow." She won't let go of him and he's having trouble unwedging himself from his armchair, with its three-inch clearance from the wall.

Poor Dad. All his life he's played by the rules and now the rules have changed and he doesn't know how to adapt. "Why don't you walk me outside and we can say goodbye there?" he says softly to Ruth. She nods, her head still buried moistly in his chest. Poor Ruth, too. She isn't benefitting from changing rules either.

Dad says goodbye to me and heads out of the dining room stooped under Ruth's weight. By accident he half kicks, half steps on Gretchen, who had been hoping for some dinner droppings. She lets out a shriek and takes off.

Mom and I are alone at the table. She looks stunned, her mouth hanging open, even though she brought on what didn't _have_ to be inevitable. She infuriates me and all I want to do is spell out her failings to her. Standing up, I snap, "If you were trying to make us happy that you got divorced, you succeeded."

She turns to me in a fury. "Not another word out of you."

I hear my phone line ringing and take off running through the kitchen and up the stairs. Despite my anger, I feel a brief flash of pity for Mom, still sitting there surrounded by all her culinary efforts, but quickly I revert. She's the architect of what I know will be a traumatic memory for us all.

The air feels different up here, clearer, less polluted by dysfunction. I grab the phone. "Hello?" It's Craig! I can't believe he remembered my birthday! He wants to take me dancing at a club on Central Avenue. That sounds so grown up! Of course, I will officially be an adult, so I guess that's appropriate. I ask if I can bring Mark and he asks if he's made a move on me. "No, not yet," I reply, "but I think there's something there." I change the subject quickly. "I am so excited to see you! I can't wait to hear about school and everything." We agree to meet at 10:00. I hang up and immediately dial Mark.

His mother answers the phone. "Hi, Loretta," I say excitedly. "It's Karen. Happy Thanksgiving!"

"Hi, Karen," she replies. "Happy Thanksgiving to you too. You caught us in the middle of dinner."

Of course I did! I forgot that not everyone's dinner ended in five minutes. I apologize and ask if she could have Mark give me a call when it's over, but she's already getting him. There's a brief pause and then he picks up.

"Hello?" he says.

"Hey, sorry to call during dinner. Mine sort of got blown out."

"We've got the aunts and uncles here," he says. "What happened?"

"Ah, forget it, we can talk about it later. I was just wondering if you wanted to go with me tonight to see Craig. He's home from Syracuse and wants me to meet him at a club for my birthday, but I don't want to go alone."

"A club? Where? What kind of club?"

"I don't know what it is, but at least it's not Cook's! It's on Central Avenue in Yonkers."

He chuckles and after a brief logistical discussion agrees to pick me up at the end of my driveway about 9:30. I hang up and start pawing through my closet for something to wear to a club. This won't be easy since I have never been to a club. I'm pretty sure Indian print dresses and cowgirl boots are not the right uniform. I pick out a blouse and skirt, put on my worn and unseasonal Kork-Ease sandals over royal blue pantyhose and choose a big, bulky blue sweater rather than a frumpy winter coat. I put on makeup and fix my hair. Since there weren't going to be any family photos documenting this Thanksgiving, I hadn't done a damn thing to make myself look good, but obviously if I am going out in public that won't work. I even use my hot rollers to get that sexy ringlet look.

I'm ready with an hour to spare, but I'm too mad at Mom to help her clean up from our disastrous dinner, and she's too mad at me to even ask. I lie on my bed like a corpse and try to drown out the sounds of her banging around the kitchen to *Quadrophenia*, my favorite album from high school. There are a couple of skips permanently etched not just in the vinyl but in my mind—I can't imagine the songs without them. "The cracks between the paving stones/…flowing veins." I know what's missing ("like rivers of") from reading the lyrics, since I can't remember a time when that skip wasn't there.

* * *

At 9:20 I sneak downstairs, through the now-dark kitchen and refrigerator porch, then out into the cold night air. I don't want to talk to Mom, not because I care whether she knows I'm leaving. I don't tell her my comings and goings anymore—I stopped right after graduation and she never even mentioned the change. Maybe she wants me to be independent, maybe she doesn't even notice when I'm gone. Either way, I like the freedom, even though sometimes I still have to hold myself back from asking her permission to go out.

It's a relief to be leaving the funny farm, but the way I treated Mom starts nagging at me. She really killed herself making Thanksgiving dinner. I guess her intentions were good, but as she's told me repeatedly, good intentions aren't enough. Tonight sure proved that. And Dad didn't exactly act mature. I don't want to blame him instead of her, that's not the answer. They're just so mismatched, it's hard to believe they ever got together to begin with, much less stayed together for eighteen years.

As I trudge down the driveway, trying not to trip over potholes and rocks, the realization overtakes me like that dream where you find yourself naked in school: I've made a terrible mistake. How can I have been so nasty and unhelpful? How could I not have realized how hard tonight was on both of them, instead of just thinking about myself?

It's weird how I suddenly see things from her perspective. She was trying to make Ruth happy, trying to make a dinner that Dad would enjoy (minus the booze, which was a pretty big oversight), trying to give everyone what they wanted. And there I was, helping to ensure a disaster, then laying all the responsibility on her. Hell, it wasn't her idea! I feel like throwing up.

It's such a relief to put these thoughts out of my mind when Mark pulls up in his Bonneville that I almost lean over and kiss him. I restrain myself, though. He's not the touchy-feely type. In his dress pants and sport coat it looks like he came straight from Thanksgiving dinner. He even smells nice. Different and nice.

"Are you wearing cologne?" I ask.

"Yeah, I thought I'd splash on a little Pierre Cardin," he replies sheepishly. How strange. I thought we both agreed cologne is a dumb concept. "You know," he adds, "to kill the Thanksgiving smells."

"Hmm," I respond. Could he be wearing cologne to impress Craig? No, that's not possible. It must be something else. Maybe he's trying to impress me. Maybe I should take the cue and start wearing cologne myself.

As we turn right onto Old White Plains Road he asks, "How long is Craig in town?"

"I have no idea," I say. "Probably just through the weekend."

Mark doesn't respond. The subject changes to Thanksgiving and I describe my hellish scene, while he paints a picture of a big, loving Italian family around a table extended with two leaves and a couple of card tables in the living room. The contrast is remarkable and I feel a twinge of jealousy. I wish I could have been at his house instead of mine.

Before long, we're on Central Avenue. "OK," I tell him, "we're getting close. It's called The Sting. He said it was by a bowling alley."

Mark points. "There—Brunswick. It must be that one." Next door is a long, low, white building with no signage except the word STING spelled out in square letters in what looks like black tape along one side. We pull into the parking lot next to it. The sound of throbbing bass comes from inside.

"Are you sure this place is for real?" he asks.

"Well, it exists. That's as real as I know."

"Well, I'm definitely up for something new," Mark says. "Let's go."

The place looks tacky but we hope for the best. We pay $3 each to a guy in an overcoat trying to stay warm at the door and go inside. It's cavernous, dark and deafeningly loud. Both our eyes and ears have to adjust before we can get a handle on the place. The horns and keyboards of "Dreaming a Dream" by Crown Heights Affair blast. I see a giant bar on the right, a dance floor straight ahead, crowds moving through the space laughing and talking. Dozens of men are crammed on the dance floor under rapidly changing lights.

We survey the scene. "Holy shit," Mark exhales.

Holy shit—I couldn't have said it better. In fact, I couldn't have come up with even that much. I am speechless. Gaping, I look around. Men. It's all men in here. They're dancing together! Minutes pass as I try to take it in and figure out whether to run for the door or burst into tears. Gwen and I have bitched for years about trying to find a guy, and it turns out *this* is where they all are!

"What the hell is this?" I finally choke out.

Mark sounds stunned too, as he says, "I believe it's what's known as a gay bar!"

Just then, Craig struts over. He looks even hotter than last time, with his feathery hair, big brown eyes and full mouth. Tight pants accentuate a large bulge and an unbuttoned shirt highlights his still-sparse chest hair. "Hi there," he says, oblivious to—or maybe just ignoring—our shock. He gives us each a long hug and a short kiss. "Glad you could make it! I was just about to get back on the floor." He grabs my hand. "Do you know how to do the Bus Stop?" His feet are already moving to "(Are You Ready) Do The Bus Stop."

"Are you kidding?" I say, pulling away. "I don't dance! Who dances?"

"We do!" Craig says, and before I can tell him how I feel about being in this bizarre Sting place, he drags me off. I grab Mark's arm—no way am I going out there without him. On the dance floor, it's way too loud for real conversation, so I just give in and try to get my thoughts together while Craig teaches us the step. He yells over the music that the Hustle is passé and the Bus Stop is the hot new thing. I place my purse on the floor where I can keep an eye on it and try to focus as the song changes to the Intruders' "I'll Always Love My Mama."

The Bus Stop is a line dance, like the Alley Cat we did long ago in Social Dance class. Everybody does it all in a row, like male Rockettes (plus one female). The steps are basic, even for a distracted klutz like me, and before long Craig is leading the entire dance floor—dozens of men in open-necked shirts and gold chains, plus a few like Mark in suit jackets. I feel like I'm in a movie, but not a good one.

Craig's an excellent dancer, loose and comfortable. I never stop counting in my head, even though the steps are basic and repetitive. Mark's pretty wooden, too, but at least he's trying. Finally, as "I Love Music" by the O'Jays starts to play, the three of us head to the bar. I'm feeling a little more comfortable, although I can't imagine why.

Craig says, "Let's wait here a minute. Someone will buy us drinks. I'm a little short this week, but it is your birthday, after all."

I'm touched, and decide to hold off on grilling him about the Sting and gay life and how the hell this is all happening. Frankly, I'm afraid I might get a little hysterical. Instead I say, "I can't believe you remembered my birthday!"

"Well, it's always around Thanksgiving, so that helps. Guess I lucked out this year and hit the actual day!"

I look at my watch. "Well, you're off by an hour or so. But who's counting?"

Craig asks, "What time is it?" and looks at his own watch, then laughs and holds out his wrist. The face says "Time to Fuck." I stare at him and shake my head. Mark stands between us, looking around like he can't believe what he's seeing. Unable to stand it anymore, I ask Craig, "Who are these guys? It looks like a Parents Without Partners meeting, only all the women on earth have been wiped out."

Craig, smiling, glances around, then at me. "Except you, the most beautiful woman here." I give him a disgusted look; I am clearly the *only* woman here. Since flattery isn't winning him any points, he answers my question, waving his arm to take in the room. "They're regular guys. This is what Westchester really is. It's not just doctors and housewives and SATs and getting into Ivy League colleges. It's closet cases and guys who are happy to finally be who they are."

"Guys who like other guys." It feel like he's lying, despite the supporting evidence dancing and laughing and brushing the hair out of each other's eyes to the strains of Cameo's "Find My Way."

"It happens," Craig shrugs.

A handsome guy walks up and says to Craig, "Buy you a drink?"

Craig smiles. "I'm with friends." He points to me and Mark.

The beautiful stranger says, "Your friends are my friends." Is he batting his eyelashes? Turning to Mark he asks, "What would you like?"

Mark speaks for the first time since I dragged him onto the dance floor. "I'll have a Coke, thanks."

I say, "I'll have a 7&7," even though no one has asked me.

Craig, flirtatiously, says, "Black Russian. Oh, and it's my friend's eighteenth birthday." He points to me.

The beautiful stranger talks to the bartender and distributes the drinks. As we raise our glasses, several bartenders gather behind the bar, the volume of the disco music is lowered, and the bartenders gather and sing "Happy Birthday" with complex harmonies. The beautiful stranger bows and tells me, "Courtesy of the Vienna Gays' Choir. Happy birthday."

I am overcome with extremely mixed emotions. "Thank you," is all I can come up with.

We drink and watch the dancers, then the beautiful stranger takes Craig by the hand and moves him toward the dance floor. They dance to an overly caffeinated disco version of "Baby Face." I turn to Mark, sipping his Coke, his eyes moving like he's watching a tennis match.

"You're awfully quiet. Is this freaking you out?"

"Uh, no. Just taking it all in. I never knew places like this existed. At least not in my own backyard."

"Me either." Boy is that an understatement. "Craig's finding himself, I guess."

"Oh, Craig's OK. He knows how to enjoy life. I admire that."

"Yeah, I guess you could put it like that. He definitely knows how to have fun." We, along with at least half the others, watch him on the dance floor, where he moves gracefully and seductively. I wonder what this place is. It's nothing like what I pictured when I heard the word "club." It's not glamorous in any way—more like a converted warehouse. I say, "It sure is a whole different world in here. Interesting that he knew someone would come along and buy us drinks."

"That guy didn't buy *us* drinks, he bought *Craig* drinks. We were just along for the ride."

"Good point," I acknowledge. I look around. "Hey, where'd they go?"

Mark scans the room. "Yeah, they're definitely gone."

"Wow, that was fast! Do you think he's coming back?"

"I have no idea. He's your friend, what do you think?"

"I have no idea either! This sure as hell is not the Craig I knew in high school!"

"Well, people change," Mark says.

Another understatement. I shrug. "I guess." We scan the club for Craig, but there's no sign of him. "Don't you feel a little funny here?" I ask. "Because I sure do."

I'm OK, but if you want to go, that's fine with me." I almost melt at this. What a guy, willing to do what makes me happy.

"OK, let's go then," I say. "I can call him tomorrow." We finish our drinks and head for the door. The Ohio Players' "Love Rollercoaster" is blasting. I hate that song. Pockets of guys are making out, drinking and talking, although I must admit it's the making out that catches my eye. I feel like I've entered an alternate universe where everything is off. I'm used to not being noticed, but never at this level. I feel a little nauseous.

Just before the door we pass a poster: The Sting is having a New Year's Eve party with a Diana Ross impersonator and a $10 cover charge. I stop and point it out to Mark. "Hey, look: Diana Ross! What are you doing New Year's Eve?"

Mark, laughing, says, "Sounds like fun to me!" Wait, did I just make plans to come back here again? I seriously think there's something wrong with me. But on the other hand I have a date with Mark for New Year's Eve! How can that be bad? We exit to the sounds of the Jackson 5's "Forever Came Today." It's a remake of a Diana Ross and the Supremes song. The fact that I know this concerns me. What is happening to my life?

11
OUR DAY WILL COME

Gwen is home from school this Thanksgiving-birthday weekend too, but her parents are taking her and her brother Hugh to New Jersey to spend time with their grandmother. Granny's health is failing and my take is that they want to position themselves as the caring family members. While this could work out great for Gwen in the long run, it deprives me of my other best friend, the one whose biting perspective on all of this I could use right about now.

Friday I turn eighteen, legal drinking age, not that I waited for that milestone. Dad returns, picking up me and Ruth with a honk rather than the disastrous coming-inside approach. Mom made herself scarce today—probably so she wouldn't have to encounter Dad again—but he doesn't know that. She told me this morning that she blames me for yesterday even more than she blames Dad, and I told her she may be right. She didn't know how to take that, probably thought I was BS-ing her. I wanted to explain that I was honestly acknowledging my role in yesterday's disaster, but I just couldn't bring myself to go that far. I know I drive her crazy but I can't seem to help myself. Even when I try to be nice, something she does sets me off again.

As much as I want to see *Cuckoo's Nest*, I have to agree with Dad that it's not the best choice for Ruth. So instead we go to _The Sunshine Boys_ with George Burns and Walter Matthau. Dad and I saw the play on Broadway with Jack Gilford, the Cracker Jacks guy, during one of our monthly outings, and it's pretty funny.

The Cusp of Everything

After the movie we go to dinner at Howard Johnson's on Central Avenue, not far from The Sting, which naturally I don't mention. We don't talk about Thanksgiving either. Or dating. Conversation with your parents is a minefield once they get divorced. But no matter what the topic is, I can't stop thinking about The Sting. It has opened my eyes to a whole world I never knew existed. While I scarf down fried clams and buttercrunch ice cream and Ruth tells some long-winded story about a friend of hers who just got a new kitten, I probe my past for signs of Craig's gayness.

I remember one day when he came over and we went for a walk through the fields behind our house. He told me that his grandmother had a tattoo, which I found hysterically funny. He got mad and said it wasn't like she was a tattooed lady in the circus. The tattoo was a number and had been given to her in a concentration camp in Poland. I had no idea what he was talking about. He tried to explain it but it sounded so impossible I thought he was just making it up. He was always overly dramatic and a chronic exaggerator. Since then I have learned that he was telling the truth and feel like an idiot for laughing. But at the time we just moved on. Craig changed the subject, then, out of the blue, he grabbed me and tried to suck face. I pushed him away. Later we went upstairs so I could show him my new bedspreads from the Montgomery Ward catalog, but Dad got furious that I had a boy in my room and made him go home. Would a gay guy behave like this? I don't see any sign here.

There was one other time Craig made a play for me, and it's tied in with the frozen waffle fiasco I mentioned earlier. I was babysitting at the Finkels' and he wanted to come over. Of course I'm not allowed to have guests, but the Finkels are pretty predictable and always come back around the time they say they will. I told Craig when to come over so the kids would be asleep, and not to ring the doorbell. He showed up right on the dot and I opened the door to the Binaca Blast. He must have knocked and then put the drops on his tongue, mistakenly thinking he would be using it on me. Well, I refused to sit with him on the couch and instead suggested we get something to eat. Going through the kitchen I couldn't find *anything*. I finally came up with frozen waffles and put a couple in the toaster.

While we were standing there waiting for them to pop up, I heard the garage door opening. The Finkels were home early! I pushed Craig into the dining room and out the back door. He made some horrible, overly dramatic noise as I closed the door, but luckily Mrs. Finkel didn't hear. She had a friend with her since they had gone out to dinner with another couple. She told me the husbands were in the car and would drive me home. I just stood there, like I was nailed to the kitchen floor. She asked if everything was all right and I had no choice: I had to tell her about the waffles. She walked over to the toaster, grabbed the just-popped-up waffles and put them in my hand. They were blistering hot and I couldn't hold them without half-tossing them into the air. She didn't even offer me a paper towel. She was so thrown by my cooking that she didn't even ask about her son's bowel movements, her favorite subject.

As we pulled out of the driveway, me clutching the waffles, Mr. Finkel's friend commented on a bicycle lying under a streetlight in the landscaped island that divides the street. "These kids have no respect for their things!" he said. He obviously figured it belonged to someone who abandoned it hours earlier, rather than the lustful teen who now found himself waffle-less in the Finkels' backyard.

Craig called later to tell me that when I pushed him out the back door, he dropped about ten feet to the ground. I knew the Finkels were adding onto their house, but I hadn't realized they'd removed the back steps. That dramatic sound was him plummeting into a construction site. It took a while before he could even stand up, and then he was too sore to ride his bike home. He had to walk it, slowly. It occurs to me now that he might have decided that night that girls just aren't worth the trouble.

* * *

Around noon on the Saturday of Thanksgiving weekend, Mark and I sit at the Mamaroneck Inn, nursing coffees and waiting for Craig to arrive. We select Joni Mitchell's "Help Me" from the tableside jukebox even though I've always felt her voice seems a little screechy on some of the high notes. He presents me with a leather-bound journal for my birthday, a thoughtful gift but somehow not what I would have expected to mark my eighteenth birthday by someone who is becoming so important in my life. He also doesn't give me a card, so there's no handwriting to analyze or message to decode. Oh well, he obviously put some thought into it. I promise to write something meaningful in it and put it in my purse.

The subject turns to finals and the end of the semester, due in a couple of weeks for us both. Suddenly I'm aware of a change in the restaurant's energy and, sure enough, Craig has made an entrance. I wish I could figure out what happened to him between high school and now, because he has an aura around him that I could use a little of myself. No one looks up when I walk into a diner.

He plops himself down next to me, shakes his head slowly so his hair ruffles around his ears, then makes a little moué like he's kissing us. "Hello, Fred and Ginger," he says. "Were you waiting long?"

"For a change, no," I say. Mark adds, "We just got here ourselves."

I shoot him a look; I don't want to let Craig off the hook for being late. I say pointedly, "Based on last night, I wasn't sure when you might be waking up. Or where, for that matter."

"Oh, just another night out with the boys," Craig smirks. "Nothing special."

"Yeah, right," I say. "Nothing special, except the end of everything I ever assumed I knew about the world."

Craig laughs. "You're so provincial. If *Yonkers* has a gay disco, you know it's a new world. Better get used to it."

Is it my imagination, or did the mention of a gay disco generate a murmur, spreading outward like the ripples in a pond? If only I could get Craig to keep his voice down, but I know from experience there's no chance of that.

"Yeah," Mark jumps in. "It does seem a little surprising that place is here in Westchester."

"Oh, that's nothing," Craig replies. "You should see the places in the city! The Sting is a dump by comparison."

"What are they like?" Mark asks.

"Hot, muscular guys," Craig answers, leaning in.

"Oh, interesting," says Mark. He doesn't lean in, but he doesn't back away either. He's not going to let Craig intimidate him.

"Interested?"

"I said 'interesting' not 'interested'," Mark smiles.

"Is it that large a step from interesting to interested?" Craig asks seductively. "I think you'd like it. I should take you with me some time."

"Interesting," Mark says, inscrutably.

"Interested?" Craig laughs. Mark just smiles. I've had about enough of this ridiculous banter. What the hell is Craig trying to prove? I resent that he's making me feel like a third wheel. I should be the hub since I'm the one who's friends with both of them!

118

"What about me?" I ask, trying not to show how left out I feel.

Craig glances sideways at me like he just remembered my presence. "Sorry, boys only."

"Straight boys?" I ask. Surely he can't think Mark is anything like him.

"Straight, gay, whatever. Anybody can be had."

What bullshit. "You sound awfully sure of yourself," I say. I find Craig's straightforward approach to his gayness annoying. It feels fake to me, like something he's trying on after not getting any traction with girls in high school. Plus what seems like his attempt to recruit Mark pisses me off. He just shrugs and flips through the jukebox, drops in a dime and plays "Our Day Will Come" by Frankie Valli. Talk of gay discos fades, thank God.

When the check comes it turns out that jukebox dime was all the money Craig had, not that it stopped him from ordering a roast beef sandwich and Coke. Yet again Mark and I split the bill, even though we only had coffee. I'm starting to feel like a patsy.

I suggest we go see _One Flew Over the Cuckoo's Nest_ together and Craig and Mark both agree. It's only playing in the city so Craig volunteers to drive us in his father's Lincoln, I guess to make up for not having enough money to buy his own sandwich—assuming he even cares. I call the back seat so I can have the closest thing to a limousine experience I will have had since Rachel's chauffeur drove us into the city when I was still at Quaker Ridge School. That was probably in eighth grade when she and I were still best friends.

Rachel is Craig's neighbor and the richest person I know, even though we're not in touch any more. They both live in a newish development called Murdock Woods that backs up on Winged Foot Golf Club. Some of the houses in my neighborhood, on the paper route I had in high school, back up on the other side of Winged Foot and I used to wander through a backyard and lie on the grass occasionally. It's so short and soft and even though I couldn't care less about golf I can appreciate living on the edge of loveliness. In fact, the edge is close enough for me, since I wouldn't want to be like most of the people around here anyway. I wouldn't mind being rich, but I wouldn't spend my money the way these people do, like on white carpeting and Gucci purses covered with logos. It would just be nice not to have to worry about affording college or dinner or whether I can buy enough gas to last through the week.

The houses in Murdock Woods were probably carved out of an

actual former woods, and all the trees there now are as new as the houses. I'm sure someday the fields and trees around my house will be destroyed too, to make more cookie cutter behemoths. Unlike my house, which was permeated with the smell of a dead animal for what seemed like weeks last year, those in Murdock Woods still have that new house smell. No one uses even half the space, like the guest rooms, playrooms and, especially, the enormous fenced-off living rooms. After all, white carpeting doesn't lend itself to foot traffic.

I drove Mark to the diner but I can leave my car here as long as I need to. The three of us pile into Craig's father's Lincoln and get out of town. We switch radio stations, arguing over which songs are worth listening to. Craig prefers what I think of as novelty disco, like Carol Douglas' "Doctor's Orders." He even likes the dreadful "Fly, Robin, Fly," the "Horse with No Name" of dance music. Mark locates the tail end of "You Can't Hurry Love" but no six-minute "Ain't No Mountain High Enough."

We laugh the whole way, whether singing along or at stories Craig tells about his life at Syracuse. He lives in a colossal dorm called Brewster, like a high-rise with an upper age limit. It sounds like he is the unofficial Dean of Gay Affairs. I wouldn't have thought there would be so much gay activity, but then I wouldn't have thought about it, period. Mark and I ask him a bunch of questions and he regales us with descriptions of macho dorm parties involving bongs and Neil Young, transitioning to "special looks" and a party of two with Johnny Mathis music. Personally, I have always found his vibrato unbearable, but that's not the point. The point is that at college people get to discover who they really are, as well as find others who are just like them. This does not mirror my own college experience, but I have great hope for the future. I think the dorm aspect must be key. And a bigger school gives you more of a chance that there is someone there like you.

Even though *Cuckoo's Nest* is playing in a huge theater, we still end up in practically the last row. Mark and I not only have to pay for Craig's ticket, we have to pay to park his car. This is starting to get annoying. Mark and I both work hard and can barely keep ourselves in necessities. But we both seem to come to the same conclusion without even discussing it: just pay up and forget it. At least his father's car had a full gas tank.

We wait on line for ages, talking to people and just generally acting goofy. Somehow Mark and I find ourselves becoming more like the outgoing Craig. We're witty and charming, too. We feel like real New Yorkers. And the movie is brilliant; it has us buzzing afterwards. They start calling me Nurse Ratched and I respond by threatening to lobotomize them both. We talk about it the whole drive back to the Mamaroneck Inn. Craig offers to drop Mark at his house so I head home and crash.

Sunday I call Craig to wish him a safe trip back to Syracuse. I can hear Neil Sedaka's annoying "Bad Blood" in the background as he says hello, and it immediately puts me in a bad mood. My mood gets worse as Craig tells me that he and Mark went back into the Mamaroneck Inn to hang out together after I left last night. I'm sure he couldn't wait until I drove away and he had Mark to himself! Probably stuck him with another check, too.

"Then we spent more than an hour sitting in my car outside Mark's house," he tells me, sounding like he's bragging. "We had a great talk."

I can just see them sitting under *our* oak tree, Craig talking poor Mark's ear off about the hot guys at gay clubs in the city. No way will I give him the satisfaction of asking about *that* conversation. "Really? That's nice," I say. "Mark's a great guy."

"He sure is," Craig says. "He's got an interesting look. He's pretty hot."

"I know," I say. "I'm the one who likes him, remember?" Fucking Craig.

"Yeah, well, you're not the only one. *I* like him, and he can be had. If you know what I mean."

This pisses me off. "Jesus, Craig!" I snort. "Give it up! You can't have everyone, you know." I'm sure Mark expressed no interest in Craig and his horndog ways. I feel guilty for ever leaving them alone together.

"That's what you think," Craig responds with an annoying flirtatious tone.

"That's what I know," I say firmly. "I have to go. I just called to wish you a safe trip back. So goodbye."

"OK, if that's the way you feel about it. Bye. Guess I'll see you next time."

"Guess so." I am such a wimp.

After I hang up from Craig, I call Mark. I know he respects Craig for being so up front about being gay, but we'll see how he feels when the gayness is directed at him.

"You won't believe the conversation I just had!" I tell him.

"What? With who?"

"I hope you don't mind my telling you this, but Craig says he thinks you're hot!" I make a gagging sound. "I am so sorry I put you in that position."

"What position?" he asks.

"You know, having a guy with a crush on you. God, I hope he didn't come on too strong last night."

Mark laughs and says, "No, we had a great talk. Didn't he tell you?"

"Yeah, he said you guys talked for an hour," I say. "Although I don't think he mentioned what you were talking about." Now that I think about it, what the hell did they talk about for an hour?

"Just the usual, you know: school, parents, that kind of thing," Mark says, then changes the subject to plans for us to get together tomorrow. That's fine, I don't really want to know what Craig might have said. Whatever it was, at least Mark didn't get grossed out. He's certainly more live-and-let-live than I am.

I still haven't seen Gwen, who was only home for a few hours between visiting her grandmother and leaving for LaGuardia for to fly back to Boston. I've been dying to see her and bring her up to date on the recent developments in my life. We'd planned to go somewhere and hang out, but somehow end up just talking on the phone. At least it's not long distance.

I try to describe the Sting and how Craig has changed since we were all in high school. She never liked Craig much, and says she isn't interested in hearing about any faggots, especially him. It surprises me she isn't even intrigued by The Sting. If someone told me a flying saucer filled with aliens had landed next to the local bowling alley, I think I'd want to go and take a look. Not Gwen. The denizens of The Sting serve no purpose in her universe. In fact, she actually suggests Mark might be gay, since he didn't want to turn and run as soon as he got inside, like she would have.

I stand up for Mark. "He's not gay. I mean, he's nothing like Craig. I could see he was uncomfortable in the Sting; he barely said a word. It was like he was in shock. We both were."

"Mm hmm," she replies. "I'm sure he was. Has he made a move on you?"

"No," I answer, resenting her implication. "He's pretty shy. I had to grab my chance for a date on New Year's Eve."

"Really! What are you guys doing?"

"The Sting is having a big thing with a Diana Ross impersonator. You know how he likes the Supremes, and Diana Ross too." Saying it makes me feel a little queasy. It sounds so gay!

Gwen snorts. "You're going back to that place? On New Year's Eve? To see a guy in drag? And you're still thinking he might make a pass? You must be kidding."

"No," I say, but suddenly I'm thrown. When she puts it that way, it does sound weird. Maybe Mark was a little too eager to go back. Maybe he wasn't grossed out enough. But maybe he's just more open than she is. Maybe he wasn't repulsed when I told him Craig likes him. Oh God, why did I tell him Craig likes him? Shit, I don't know what to think any more. It's all so confusing. I stutter a little as I try to explain. "It was my idea. He's only going because I asked him. I mean, we have a date for New Year's Eve!"

Gwen scoffs. "Some date. Sounds to me like Mark's riding on the Gay Express and Craig is about to punch his ticket."

"Stop it!" I say. "You don't know what you're talking about! You weren't there, you have no concept of what it's like. He was as shocked as I was. But we got past the gay part and just had fun. The music was great and we even danced." I don't mention that it was line dancing with a bunch of guys. Or that last night he hung out with Craig after they ditched me…I mean after I went home. Oh God, now I'm questioning everything!

"Look, Karen, I don't want to burst your bubble. Maybe he likes you so much that he's willing to revisit Sodom and Gomorrah just to dance with you. But I think you're kidding yourself. Shit, it wouldn't be the first time. I mean seriously, who the hell cares about Diana Ross and the Supremes? Maybe you just need to put the pieces together and get your head out of the sand."

God, why am I friends with her again? She *says* she doesn't want to burst my bubble but she does it pretty consistently. I know she's wrong. She must be. "Look, I think I know Mark pretty well at this point, and there's nothing gay about him. Craig—he's another story. But Mark is just normal." Why does it feel like I'm trying to convince myself as well as her?

I tell Gwen I don't want to talk about Mark anymore and ask about college. She's been burning through the Men of Boston, as a pictorial in *Viva* might describe them. They're mostly black, her preference since high school. In fact, she tells me she can't imagine a black faggot, and what a waste that would be—so much more of a loss to our team than a wimpy white guy like Craig. I don't bother telling her Craig's not that wimpy anymore.

Her grades aren't great, but her social life is, especially compared to mine. I start to panic that Gwen and I might be drifting apart, and with Mark as my only backup, that means I have made it to adulthood without the ability to surround myself with people who know and love me. Those who know me generally lose interest in me. This is terrifying.

12

HE'S MY MAN

With Christmas coming, I ramp up the babysitting to earn some extra cash. For my family bargain gifts are fine, but I want to get Mark something special. Since Craig left town, things between me and Mark have been back on track. He never brought Craig up again, and I certainly haven't. I can't even believe I listened to Craig and Gwen when they said Mark might be gay. I would definitely know. We hang out almost daily and there's nothing queer about him. I feel like he really understands and cares about me, more than Gwen, in a way. He's certainly less of a downer, less judgmental. When I talk about my crazy home life, he totally gets it and always takes my side.

I think and think about what to get him. In some ways he's a better friend than my supposed best friend, but that's not enough; I want to take it to the next level. So it needs to be something unique and wonderful. Finally it comes to me. He's taught me about the various iterations of the Supremes, so I'll document them in a gift that will blow his mind.

The original Supremes were Diana Ross, Mary Wilson and Florence Ballard ("Flo"). First Cindy Birdsong replaced Flo, then Diana Ross struck out on her own and was replaced by Jean Terrell, then Lynda Laurence replaced Cindy. Finally, and most recently, both Jean and Lynda departed, and have been replaced by a returning Cindy and a new lead singer, Scherrie Payne. Their most recent album, *The Supremes*, opens with "He's My Man." It would be a great song for the

125

Sting, but sadly for Mark, Supremes records don't get any attention these days.

Anyway, with all my Supes knowledge, I go to a jewelry store in White Plains, pick out a lighter and have the evolving Supremes' initials engraved on it:

D M F
D M C
J M C
J M L
S M C

I'm sure Mark will know instantly what the initials stand for, even if no one else on earth would. How I can remember this level of Supremes detail when the periodic table remains a complete mystery despite years of study?

When we sit down the day before Christmas in Mark's personal den to exchange gifts he opens the box and stares at the lighter. There is a brief pause while he takes it in, then, "Oh my God!"

"What?" I ask innocently.

"I can't believe this! Did you have it made? What a stupid question. Of course you had it made! It's incredible!" He gets up and gives me a hug. "It's the greatest gift I've ever received." He gazes at it with something approaching rapture. "I love that you have Mary always in the middle. That's so perfect."

I feel all tingly. I have given the greatest gift ever! I got it absolutely right! And every time he lights up, he'll be reminded of me and my thoughtfulness. What could be better? Oh wait, I know! His gift to me!

Mark hands me a box from a jewelry store in White Plains, Aspasia. I love their stuff. I've never mentioned this to Mark, so the fact that he picked that store out of all others says something. He is totally on my wavelength. And he bought me jewelry! I pull off the ribbon and open the box. It's a necklace, with hishi beads, onyx and turquoise. No guy has ever given me jewelry before and it feels profoundly meaningful.

"I love it," I say. My hands are even shaking a little as I take it out of the box. Mark helps me fasten it around my neck.

He says, "I looked at everything in the store. I had to get something very elegant. Very you."

The Cusp of Everything

He thinks I'm elegant! Maybe the necklace is a reflection of a new me, an emerging elegant me. More than ever before, I feel like his girlfriend as I tell him, "It's great" and lean into him for a hug. He hugs me back, but it's brief because he takes me by the shoulders and looks at the necklace appraisingly. "You know, I don't think I like it as much as I did when I saw it in the store. Do you think I should take it back?"

I'm a little thrown. "Take it back? Of course not! This is the first real piece of jewelry anyone has ever given me, except a silver charm bracelet my father got me for my confirmation."

"I'm just saying now that I see it on, I think it's too casual. I mean, it's not something you would wear on New Year's Eve."

I stand on tiptoes to see my neckline in a small oval mirror hanging on the wall. Mark is probably eight or nine inches taller than I am, so the mirror is prime height for viewing the top of my head. He tilts it a little bit and I consider.

"Well, you're right that it's casual—elegantly casual. But as far as New Year's Eve is concerned, I don't know what I'm going to do. I literally have nothing to wear. Jewelry is the least of my problems." It's true. I've been through not only my own closet but my mother's, to no avail. Worse, I'm out of money so I can't exactly splurge. At the Sting, I won't even look as sexy as the guys dressed as guys, never mind the guys dressed as women! I'm pretty upset about it.

"I know," Mark responds. "What do you wear to a club on the biggest night of the year? I have a jacket I was going to wear but I was modeling it for Loretta and Dean came in and called it a fur chubby. I'm not sure I'll ever feel the same way about it again."

"Don't pay any attention to him! Brothers get off on causing pain. Let me see it."

Mark goes to the other room and gets the jacket out of his closet. It's dark green and black horizontally striped wool, in a windbreaker style, about waist-long, and zips up the front. If Joe's description wasn't ringing in my ears, I would probably like it. But now that I've heard it, I have to admit that it looks like something an overly blow-dried character on "All My Children" might wear. I sit mutely.

"Your silence says it all," Mark tells me.

"I just wish you hadn't poisoned it with Dean's comment."

"I know, he hit the nail on the head, didn't he? I spent $79 for this atrocity and now I don't think I can be seen in public in it!"

"Oh, it's not that bad," I reassure him. "I just think it's more of an outdoor thing, not a jacket you'd wear inside a club."

We've been listening to the Supremes' _Love Child_ album, but as side one ends I make a preemptive move to block the playing of side two. Enough Supremes, already. "Let's put on a something else," I suggest, going over to the stereo. "What do you want to hear?"

"I just bought _Love to Love You Baby_ by Donna Summer," Mark says. "You know, the orgasm song?"

Know it? It's everywhere. Outraged parents are calling into radio stations whenever it plays. "Of course I know it. I can't believe you bought that!"

"I know, it's sort of sick but it's great. And the album version lasts a whole side!"

"Like 'In-a-Gadda-da-Vida!'" I say. I think I'd rather listen to a half hour drum solo than a half hour of orgasms, unless it's going to cause Mark to make a pass at me, which would be nice but somehow still doesn't seem imminent. Still, he wants to play me the orgasm song—maybe it's a message?

We sit mostly in silence through about the first half of the full-side "Love to Love You Baby." I twirl my new necklace around my neck and stare at the ceiling, just like during real sex, waiting for Mark to make his move. I can't think of anything to say that wouldn't turn him off, like: Is she for real? I know I've never made sounds like that. I may ask Gwen the next time we talk, though, whether she gets so loud, or experiences such ecstasy. I know I sure don't.

Mark gets up and goes over to the stereo, listening intently and not looking at me. Every now and then he turns it down and comments on the use of the high hat, the strength of the underlying bass line or the chorus of women's voices that comes in at the end. Somehow he manages not to mention the moaning. Finally, since he's not using the song as a way to jump me, I get a little aggravated and ask him to turn it down. He does immediately and I start talking about clothes to change the subject from the orgasmic song. "You know, I wasn't kidding, I don't know what to wear on New Year's Eve. I'm sort of panicked about it."

"Really?" he asks.

"Are you kidding? I've never been to anything like this! Everything I have looks sickening to me. I know I have to buy something but I have no idea what, and no money to buy it. Any suggestions?"

"I'm not exactly an expert on women's clothes," Mark says. "But it does seem like your budget is the biggest problem. How much money do you have to spend?"

"After Christmas? I may get some cash from my father but I'm sure it won't be more than $50. I do have a couple hundred in the bank, but I think my car has an oil leak so I'm not in a position to blow money on a dress I'll probably only wear once. It would cost at least $50." I twist the necklace some more, and Mark looks at my neck.

"Well, here's a suggestion. But you have to give me your totally honest reaction."

"Of course! I'm a Sagittarius. I don't know how to be any other way."

"Do you *love* the necklace?" he asks, drawing out the word "love."

I reach for it again. "What do you mean? Of course I love it— you gave it to me!"

"Right, but is it something that you would have picked for yourself?"

I hesitate. I don't want to hurt his feelings, and I think I see where he's going with this. Finally I say, "No, probably not, but that doesn't mean I don't love it."

"That doesn't sound like it's the perfect gift the way yours was." He hasn't put down the lighter since he opened it.

"That's silly. I know you put a lot of thought into it."

"I did, but I have to say, it doesn't look like you," he says.

"It doesn't? In what way?" But I sort of know what he means.

"I don't know, I think maybe it's too hippie-ish or artsy-fartsy, not elegant enough. But if you want to return it, you can. I know it's rude to talk about money, but if you return it, you'll get $50. Then you'd have enough money for a dress."

I don't know what to say. He spent $50 on me! That's twice what I spent on him, including engraving! He just gave me the only piece of jewelry I've ever received from a man. I don't want to take it back! But I'm starting to see a solution to my Sting problem. Yes, swap the necklace for some cash and get a dress to die for. That's the only way. "I think you might be right," I tell him. Then I give him a big hug and he hugs me back. So there, I say internally to Gwen.

* * *

A couple of days later, Mark and I meet in White Plains to find me a dress. He sold his cursing parrot to a local pet shop, World of Finny Friends, and used the $75 proceeds to buy himself a new outfit for The Sting. Now it's my turn for a makeover. We exit Aspasia and walk down the crowded sidewalk, refund cash in hand.

"You know, I did love the necklace. It was a great gift, thank you," I say. "And I'm glad you weren't offended that I returned it."

"Of course not—it was my idea! You want to look great on New Year's Eve."

"Yeah, after all I'll have to compete with drag queens! I'm already feeling inadequate."

"Don't worry about that," Mark reassures me, as we search for a store. "You've got something they'll never have."

"Hmm, I think it's the other way around," I say. He laughs.

We come to a boutique called Chops. Mark asks me, "Want to try this one?"

"Sure, why not? I'm not sure what I'm looking for but I guess I'll know it when I see it."

We enter the store and a saleswoman comes up to us. "May I help you?"

Mark tells her, "We're looking for a New Year's Eve dress." He adds, "For her."

The saleswoman smiles warmly. "Great!" Turning to me she asks, "Do you know what you want?"

"No," I respond. "I just want it to be great."

"I think I have just the thing," the saleswoman says.

She does. It is a floor-length dress made of slinky black polyester with a halter top that's decorated with a semi-circle of feathers: white, brown, black, speckled. Its glamour is enhanced by a matching cape, closed at the neck by a rhinestone clip. The dress is fitted, but the cape, like a young girl's party dress, is swirly. So even though I'm self-conscious about my stomach in such a slinky number, I can just wrap up in the cape. The length will need to be dealt with, but Gwen's grandmother, a seamstress, is visiting from New Jersey and can probably handle alterations. The dress costs $66, plus $46 for the cape. It's the most expensive outfit I've ever owned, but I don't even hesitate. Screw my car—let it leak! Mark tells me how great I look, and that's all I need to hear. We discuss how I will make a grand entrance at the Sting, and be the envy of all the drag queens.

I return home after the shopping expedition, overjoyed with my first gown. I skipped the prom (not by choice, although I'd never admit that), and have never had another reason to wear a dress like this. I enter the kitchen where Mom is on the phone but still moving around. <u>Helen Reddy's "Ain't No Way to Treat a Lady"</u> plays quietly in the background as she opens cupboards, takes out dishes, checks the status of the formerly frozen vegetables in the saucepan on the stove and gossips about her love life. I duck under the long phone cord to get past her and go up the stairs to my room. I can't wait to get the dress on again, to feels its clingy silkiness, to show off. I slither into it and admire the hourglass shape it reveals, then clip on the cape and go to the top of the stairs. "Mom! I'm coming down. I have a new dress for New Year's Eve."

In the kitchen, Mom is still on the phone. She and Stan got back together in time for the holidays, and he's taking her to Puerto Rico the day after Christmas. She didn't say anything more to me than that, obviously not anxious for my opinion, or questions about why she's with someone she knows is wrong for her. She interrupts her lusty update to her friend, saying, "Oh, Karen wants to show me her new dress. She's coming down the stairs." I enter the kitchen. My mother stares, then narrates. "It's black and it seems to have feathers."

I hold out my arms and spread my cape, wordlessly asking, "Well? What do you think?"

"She wants to know what I think," Mom says, although not to me. "I think it's too mature for a teenager and I can't imagine where in the world she would wear it in the next five years." She pauses. "Yes, feathers! They look like they're from a turkey! Oh, and a matching cape!" She gives a little cackle.

I spin around and stalk out of the room. "Thanks for ruining my day!" When will I learn that she couldn't care less about me or anything that matters to me? I stomp back up the stairs where I remove the dress and cape and carefully hang them up on the inside of my closet door. Leaving the door open, I lie on my bed and look at them. I don't care what she said, they're beautiful. I try to imagine what New Year's Eve will be like. Other than last year, which was a fiasco, I've done nothing but babysit on that supposedly auspicious occasion, so at least I know I'll be raising the bar. I have to admit, I have a fascination with The Sting. It's different from anything else I've ever experienced and makes me wonder what else is out there in the world that might shake me to my core.

The next afternoon, New Year's Eve Eve, I head over to Gwen's.

The Cusp of Everything

We're going out to Tommy's Tavern on Garth Road that night to catch up with the drunks we haven't seen since the summer. Tommy's used to be our go-to place to drink and get laid our senior year of high school and right after graduation, but somehow, what with Playland and college, we haven't made the pilgrimage in months. It will be good to have some macho man attention after what seems like a very long time. But first I have to try on my dress and cape so her grandmother can pin it up and make it shorter in time for tomorrow night. The last thing I need is to trip and fall at The Sting—how humiliating that would be!

Gwen's mother peppers me with questions, trying to catch up since she hasn't seen me in ages, and trying to get a handle on what is going on in both my life and her daughter's. She has always claimed to have a psychic connection to Gwen, and certainly seemed to know more than she should, like she was reading a diary even though Gwen doesn't keep one. My own mother's oblivious self-absorption is a pleasure by comparison. Who wants their mother knowing what's going on in their life? I deflect the questions that indicate she's lost her psychic touch. The woman can be dangerous! She once broke all of Gwen's albums and threw them in the trash when she got a call from Scarsdale High about Gwen's cutting classes. Even her brand new Alice Cooper _Muscle of Love_ album.

It's close to 10:00 p.m. when we leave the oldsters to their sewing and Marcus Welby, M.D. and take my car over to Tommy's. Outside it fits into the whole Scarsdale brick Tudor theme, but inside it's dingy and dedicated to getting people drunk as quickly as possible. Still, it's a step up from the Candlelight, with its flimsy fake wood paneling and worn linoleum.

We sit at the tall round table closest to the door, the two of us and five guys. They seem as happy to see us as we are to be with them. We make small talk about the holidays, catch up on how a couple of the guys' baseball team, the Cunning Linguists, did during the baseball season, which seems like a million years ago. The jukebox plays countryish stuff like "Tush" by ZZ Top and old hits like Elvis' "Can't Help Falling in Love" from the time when the regulars were our age. It has two versions of Neil Sedaka's "Breaking Up Is Hard to Do," from then and now. It's like a big rainbow-shaped AM radio station/time machine.

One of the guys, someone I've never seen before, joins us at the table. We're all joking and tasting each other's drinks, and it seems to me he's surreptitiously smiling at me. When Gwen heads over to the bar to talk to Vincent, a construction worker she has a long-standing crush on, he comes over to take her place next to me, and we introduce ourselves. His name is Hal and he's 21, from Yonkers. He's not bad-looking, with shaggy brown hair and long eyelashes, but his kind expression and approachability make him seem more handsome than he really is. We start talking, about weather, drinking, typical stuff. Then we segue into sex and picking people up, like we're wise and witty observers rather than participants. It's funny, though: as we talk about how drinking leads to pick-ups and pick-ups lead to sex that is frequently regretted, I realize this isn't a sex thing. We're relating on the same level, not trying to seduce each other. I immediately feel comfortable with him.

I tell Hal I'm going to The Sting for their New Year's Eve event. "Have you ever heard of it?" I ask.

"Yes," Hal replies. "But I heard it was gay." This surprises me. I guess I thought Mark and I were the only straight people even aware of the Sting's existence.

"It is, but it's a nice place, and I'm going with a couple of friends including one who's gay. I think it will be a lot of fun and I can get all dressed up and dance. It will be a real New Year's Eve!" I pick up my pack of Marlboros and put one in my mouth.

"Sounds great," Hal replies, taking my lighter and lighting my cigarette. "I'm going to have a quiet night at home. My mom's really sick and won't be around much longer, so I want to spend as much time with her as I can. I leave on Thursday to go back to school."

Shit, I sure picked a terrible timing to light up. Let's hope she doesn't have lung cancer. "I'm sorry about your mother," I say, after my first smoky exhale.

"Yeah, it's hard. Watching someone die is about the worst thing you can imagine, especially your own mother," Hal says reflectively. "But it has its positive moments, too. We're talking about things we never talked about before. It probably sounds gruesome, but there's a positive side to having a chance to say goodbye, to say all the things you never felt you could before. And to ask all the questions you always wanted to know the answers to."

I don't know what to say to this. I can't imagine a time where I will want to tell my mother anything, and I don't think she has any answers for me. Of course, I don't want her to die either. Even thinking that someday she'll be dead is jarring. "What kinds of questions do you ask?"

"Oh, you know. 'How did you know Dad was the right one? Why did you have so many kids? What would you have done with your life if you hadn't had us? What did you and your mom say to each other when she was dying? Do you have any regrets?' That kind of thing."

"Wow, pretty heavy stuff. I'd never ask my mother any of those things. Although now that you mention it, I realize I don't know what her answers would be to any of them."

"Of course you don't. No one does. That's why they're called deathbed conversations. Somehow we never get around to them until it's almost too late. And sometimes not even then."

"But don't you think we *should* know those things about our parents? Maybe we should be having deathbed conversations without the deathbed."

"That's a nice thought, but I don't think parents and kids are made that way. They want to protect us and that's fine with us. We don't want to think of them as real people, falling in love, defying their own parents, having sex, making mistakes, regretting they'd ever had us."

"That's for sure," I agree. I know my mother defied her parents by marrying my father, and both sets of my grandparents eloped. Shunning parental advice seems to run in my family. Somehow that generational consistency never crossed my mind before. It occurs to me to ask, "How come you're not with her tonight?"

"She was in a lot of pain, so she took some pills. She'll sleep through till morning." Then he adds, "Let's talk about something else."

"OK," I agree, probably a little too quickly, happy to change the subject away from death and mothers. "Where do you go to school?" My heart is sinking a little bit as I realize he won't be around after the first of the year.

"University of Chicago. I'm in medical school there."

"Wow, medical school. I just finished my first semester at SUNY Purchase. Do you live in a dorm?"

"No, I did, but this year my girlfriend and I got a place off campus." Nope, he's definitely not trying to seduce me. Isn't relating on the same level great?

"That sounds…like fun," I say lamely. I can't even imagine living with a boyfriend. It sounds so modern and sexy. It's not what I want to talk about with him now. No death, no mothers, no other women.

I change the subject back to New Year's Eve, even though we'd already moved on. "I like The Sting. I never knew how to dance but I learned there and it's so much fun. And the people are so friendly. It doesn't make any difference that they're gay."

Hal says, "People are what they are, gay or straight, black or white, green or purple. If you're having fun and there's mutual respect, that's all that counts. Who is any one of us to judge what's right for someone else?"

OK, this is just unfair. He's perfect, and perfectly unavailable. I've been enjoying our connection, but now it's just depressing.

Gwen comes back to the table and tells me she has to be home by one o'clock, so Hal and I say goodbye and Gwen and I head for the dark and gravel-strewn parking lot. As we're getting in the car, Hal is suddenly by my side — at first my heart lifts thinking he wants my number, but it turns out I left my lighter on the table. He hands it to me with a warm smile. Damn. I've had just enough to drink that this makes me melancholy and self-pitying.

The car door is barely closed before Gwen is bitching that Vincent wasn't interested in talking to her. "Asshole. He says he's trying to make it work with his live-in girlfriend, so he doesn't want to hang out with me, but then he spent the whole night drooling all over this girl who was a year behind us—meaning she's still in high school! So I just flirted with his friend and ignored him."

"Mine has a girlfriend too," I say. "It's pretty depressing. I liked him. He's the kind of person I just know I could spend the rest of my life with."

"The rest of your life?" Gwen squawks. "That's ridiculous. You just met him! You need to lighten up. I'd say it's about time for another one-night stand."

"It's too cold and depressing for a one-night stand. Isn't there anything in between one night and forever?" I moan.

"Of course there is, but you're not going to find it at Tommy's Tavern," Gwen says. No, I think. I shouldn't even be doing this anymore. I should just be with Mark. I'm starting to get disheartened that he hasn't made a move when Gwen adds, "Just like we didn't find it in Times Square last New Year's Eve."

"God, don't remind me," I say, but at least she's taken my mind off Mark and his so-far platonic ways. Gwen and I ushered in 1975 by going to a Mountain concert at the Felt Forum, then wandering through Times Square in the rain getting grabbed and slobbered on by horny strangers. There was only one memorable moment: Just as we'd had about enough, I was grabbed by a ringer for the Marlboro Man, my eternal weakness. He enveloped me in his damp arms, tilted me back and kissed me deeply. I had visions of '40s movies and a tingle that felt like true love. I wanted it to go on forever but he raised me back up and strode off. "Wait!" I wanted to yell after him. "Let me give you my phone number!" If only I could have squeaked out a sound at that point, or remembered my phone number.

After that, Gwen and I had to run to Grand Central to get our sodden bodies on the train back to Scarsdale, which was delayed for more than an hour when a man died in one of the front cars. Gwen has no patience for tragedy and took his death as a personal affront. She knew that there would be no explaining her lateness to her mother. And sure enough, I dropped her home at 3:15 a.m. and when I got home at 3:30 my mother was sitting in the kitchen, cradling Gretchen. She said that Gwen's mother had called and would I please refrain from doing things that would bring on those calls. Hearing from Mrs. Gilbert upset her more than my practically being out all night! God, that all seems like a million years ago.

13
YEAR OF DECISION

My anticipation for The Sting tonight is almost unbearable. Goodbye, high school graduation year, hello exciting new adult life! For the first time ever, I have a date for New Year's Eve, and I can't wait for our first kiss, at midnight. Where will it all lead? Has he been falling for me these past months like I've been falling for him? I crave being with him. We have so much fun together and really share a lot about ourselves.

I put on my new ensemble, now the perfect length, just hitting the top of Mom's high heels. I apply makeup and curl my hair so it falls in soft waves to my shoulders. I head to Mark's house, where Loretta lets me in and has me do a fashion show in front of her and Mark's father, Steve. They tell me how beautiful I look, which I can almost believe, and send me down to the basement suite.

"Hello!" I call, as I descend the stairs.

"In here," calls Mark from the corner of his den where the birdcage used to be, in front of a new full-length mirror leaning against the wall. His new outfit is a Nehru-collared shirt, long jacket and pants, all black. He has a black scarf wrapped around his neck and has taken extra care with his hair, which he often has trouble taming. "What do you think?" he asks.

"Wow," I say. I'm not sure what to think. He looks...exotic. The outfit's a little strange, but I'm touched that he went to so much trouble for our special night. He cares so much about how he looks tonight that I'm convinced he's been waiting for New Year's Eve to declare his love.

"Are you sure?" he asks, like he's not convinced. "This may not be the right look for me. Maybe I shouldn't have let the salesgirl talk me into it." He twists the scarf in his hands. "It reminds me of something, I just can't put my finger on it."

"Well, I think it's very chic. And it is New Year's Eve, after all. What about me?" I ask, twirling.

"You look gorgeous!" Mark responds, looking away from the mirror.

I whirl around again. "Think I can hold my own against the drag queens?"

"They'll want to scratch your eyes out," Mark assures me, turning back to the mirror and twisting his scarf some more.

"Well, you'll have them eating out of your hand. You look so handsome."

"Why thank you!" He takes a small bow. "So are we picking up Craig?"

"Yes, and we should probably get going. Sorry I was a little late but 'gorgeous' doesn't just happen!"

"OK, I just want to grab a soda." We climb the stairs to the kitchen, where Mark's brother Dean, sick with the flu, sits drinking something out of a mug. Mark always says how mean he is, what cutting remarks he makes, but he's so handsome, so friendly to me. I have a crush on Mark, yes, but somehow I find his older brother even sexier. I would never tell Mark, though. I'm sure it would bother him if I said anything flattering about Dean. Instead, I just smile and say hi, and Dean smiles and says hi back.

As Mark opens the refrigerator, Dean gives us the once-over and asks, "Big night?"

"We're going to a club," I answer. The words sound unfamiliar but thrilling. I'm going to a club! On New Year's Eve! With someone I'm pretty sure is about to be my boyfriend!

"Well, you look great."

"Thanks," I say, swooning a little inside.

As we head for the door. Dean calls after us, "Bye, Karen. Have a good time. You too, Little Richard."

I look at Little Richard—I mean Mark. He practically does a Danny Thomas spit take all over the kitchen floor as his expression changes to one of horror. So *that's* what the outfit reminded him of! I can see his mind going through the calculations: there's no time to change so he'll have to de-Little Richard-ize himself on the run. He's already taking off his scarf in a panic before we get out the door. He spends most of the drive fixing his hair, which he seems to think was irreparably damaged by the scarf removal. This wouldn't be so bad, except that he's the one who's driving. A couple of times I almost have to grab the wheel as he adjusts himself in the rear-view mirror.

At Craig's split-level ranch in Murdock Woods, his sister Shelly answers the door. "Craig!" she yells. "Your friends are here!" From the living room I can hear Chicago singing "Old Days." The kids are watching "Dick Clark's New Year's Rockin' Eve." No parents are in sight, which must mean Craig's stepfather got his crazy mother out into the real world, at least for a few hours. Considering I have never known her to leave her darkened bedroom, this is quite an accomplishment. I wonder how he managed it.

We take off our coats so Craig can get the full effect of our fabulous outfits. We're standing there semi-posing when he strolls down the hall, wearing only briefs, his hair wet, his beefy thighs exposed.

"Hey," he says languidly. "I just got out of the shower. I still have to dry my hair. Make yourselves comfortable." He waves us into the living room, then heads back down the hall. I take a look down the couple of stairs into the sunken living room at the juvenile festivities but Mark, jaw dropped, looks after Craig as he heads back down the hall. We both remain frozen in place in the foyer. Mark has to be as furious as I am.

"I can't believe we're almost a half hour late and he's still in his underwear! We might miss the show," I snap. Not only am I outraged that Craig's not ready, I can't believe he didn't notice how great we both look. I turn and march after him, toward the sound of 1,000 watts of pure blow dryer power. It all comes back to me: how Craig at age 16 was obsessed with the mistaken perception that his hairline was receding, requiring hours in front of the mirror evaluating and treating his imaginary baldness. How often he missed the school bus because he took too long to get ready. How oblivious he is to schedules and deadlines and just about anything related to anyone other than himself. With Craig it's always the roller coaster of rising anticipation at seeing him, followed by a crashing infuriation at his selfishness and the wondering what you were looking forward to in the first place. I wish the hallway wasn't carpeted so my high heels would make angry clacking sounds. But the shag makes my passage silent, except for the swishing of polyester.

I lean into the spacious bathroom where Craig stands in his preferred position: looking into a mirror. In fact, the whole room is done up in panels of a smoky mirror with gold veins running through it. "Hey," I say. "Can you hurry it up?" Is that the best I can do? It doesn't begin to convey how pissed off I am. Sure enough, he pays no attention. After a brief glance in my direction he bends over, hangs his head upside down and blows his hair backwards: up from his neck and away from his forehead. I know this trick: when he throws his head back his silken shag will be puffed up. I try not to admire his hair. After all, I know it will be greasy by the end of the night, what with whatever he's got going on from genetics and the various potions he glops on. I'm starting to think it's possible to know someone too well. I don't want my familiarity with Craig to breed contempt, but he's not making it easy.

Finally he switches off the Conair and starts spraying and fluffing. As the last of the spray settles on the white shag rug, he makes a little kiss in the mirror and pushes past me to dress. A thin trickle of chest hair runs down the center of his ribcage. His nipples are hard, probably from seeing himself looking so gay. At 19 it's obvious he feels in the prime of his life with every fiber, cell, atom and whatever is smaller than an atom of his being.

I resist the urge to go sit on his bed and nag him as he slowly dresses. Instead I return to Mark, who has broken down and joined the Dick Clark watchers in the massive living room. Neil Sedaka is prattling on about the <u>Average White Band</u>, who must be about to perform, and talking about how they're counting down to 1976. Mark is slumped over like he's in pain. I give his arm a squeeze but he doesn't even look at me.

It's almost 11:00 when we pull away from Craig's, making it close to 11:15 by the time we reach the Sting. The drive is tense, what with Mark's constant fiddling with the radio, my silent fuming and occasional sarcastic remark, and Craig's oblivious chatter, mostly about his flyaway hair and the relative benefits of White Rain and Gillette's Dry Look. Not an auspicious start to the dawn of the Bicentennial.

At the entrance to the Sting, Craig is welcomed with hugs and kisses and waved inside for free. Mark and I are forced to pay the $10 cover charge. What blatant discrimination. I tell myself it's against straight people rather than the less attractive, but who knows? I'll bet if they could see my gown and cape rather than my boring wool coat they'd realize I'll be enhancing the place and let me in for free too…aah, who am I kidding?

Once inside, we check our coats by the door, then turn to face the music: K.C. and the Sunshine Band: "That's the Way (I Like It)" is blasting. I put my cape on over my gown and extend my arms to give the full effect. Naturally no one looks my way, except Mark who gives me a big smile. What a guy! This is the best I'm capable of looking, so if it doesn't win him over, I'm out of hope. He grabs me by the hand and pulls me into the crowd, chasing Craig who skipped the coat check and kept his leather jacket on.

The energy level is even higher tonight than it was the last time we were here. There are brightly colored Christmas lights strung along the walls and ceiling. The place is packed, the beat is thumping and I swear the crowd parts as Craig passes through. He occasionally gets grabbed and embraced. Mark and I bring up the rear like royal guards escorting the queen. Which I guess we are.

Waiters dressed in what look like silver gym shorts are passing champagne and Mark and I each grab a glass. It wouldn't be a first-choice drink for either of us, but we need to pace ourselves financially. Whatever's included with the admission price looks good, even to Mark who doesn't normally drink. We suck it down and stick close to each other.

"What happened to Craig?" Mark asks. Our friend has been swallowed up by the revelers; he never looked back to see if we were with him.

"Probably already on the dance floor," I yell back over the din. "Looks like we were just a ride to him." Mark grimaces. We've been used, no question.

"I guess the show hasn't started yet," I yell over the din.

"Guess not," Mark replies, a little sulkily. You'd think he'd be happy Craig's lateness didn't ruin our night.

"Shall we dance?" I ask. Unless we become total wallflowers, there's no place to stand, so I figure we might as well keep moving. Gloria Gaynor's "How High the Moon" has just started and I like it a lot. I'd rather he asked me, but I guess the end result is the same.

"Sure," Mark replies. Another waiter comes by. I grab another glass and Mark actually goes for one too. I've never even seen him drink any alcohol before so it's a little surprising, but I guess he's feeling festive. My heart jumps a little to think this could be the night everything changes between us. I smile at him as we hit the floor clinking our fresh glasses.

Men in suits mix with more than a few in gowns and high heels in sizes that definitely didn't come from any normal shoe store. Mark and I get positioned close to the stage and sway in place, drinking. There's no room for real dancing, but that's fine since we're not very good anyway. It's more a way to pass the time while we wait for the Diana Ross show to start. I try to catch his eye, to make it feel just a little like we're dancing, but he's scanning the room. "I wonder where Craig went," he says. He seems concerned that we might not all be together at midnight, but at this point I couldn't care less.

Around 11:30 the music cuts off and a voice announces the show's about to start. At midnight they'll do a countdown and we'll ring in 1976 together, one big happy, twisted family. All I care about is my kiss from Mark when the clock strikes 12:00. My reverie is interrupted by the announcer shouting, "Ladies, and…ladies! Please give a warm Sting welcome to Ophelia Cox!"

Ophelia Cox? Oh, I get it. Must be an opening act. And sure enough, out comes a very large drag queen who prances around in a gown that seems to have been designed to emphasize "her" rolls of fat. "*Mes chérs!*" she begins. "I am so glad to be here! It has been, how you say, touch and go." She touches her chest, which looks like a pair of sandbags. There is laughter and a little hooting. "Last week I went to see zee *docteur*. I say to him, '*Monsieur docteur*, I have zee bugs in zee bush. What should I do?' Zee *docteur*, he geev me a can and tell me, 'Go home, spray zees on your bush every day for three days and zee bugs will go away.'

"So I go home, I spray zee bush three times. I go back to zee office of zee *docteur*. I tell him, '*Docteur*, zee bugs they are gone! Zee bush it is gone! Et Pierre's moustache…pouf!'" It takes a moment but then there is a roar of laughter, and probably a great deal of sympathy for Pierre.

Ophelia tells a few more raunchy stories, strutting around the small stage and playing to the responsive crowd. She finesses hecklers: "Show us your tits!" "*Show* zem? I can *lend* zem to you! You obviously have teet envy!" She's great, and it's so much fun sharing the show with Mark. We laugh together and grab each other at the really funny parts.

The Cusp of Everything

At the end of her set, Ophelia announces that it's time to ring in 1976. "Grab whoever's closest!" she demands. Guys who already had their arms around each other squeeze tighter. I look up at Mark and give him a smile. He puts his arm around my shoulders as the announcer counts down: "10, 9, 8!" The crowd joins in. "7, 6, 5, 4, 3, 2, 1. Happy New Year!" I lift my face toward Mark's and he gives me a brief kiss, then quickly starts looking around the room again. Not quite as passionate as I would have liked for such an auspicious occasion, but it's our first kiss, and that makes it meaningful. I look up at him waiting for his attention to return to me just as someone nearby blasts a noisemaker and I jump. So much for our moment.

When Ophelia departs the stage, the announcer keeps the applause going for awhile. Then he says, "And now, ladies and gentlemen and everything in between…please welcome Diana Ross!"

"Diana," in a tight gold lamé gown and massive wig, steps out to the strains of "Reach Out and Touch (Somebody's Hand)," her first solo single. Immediately hands start reaching out toward the stage. I move closer to Mark. I'm hoping that the show is great, for his sake. After all, he's the Diana Ross fan. He's trained me, and I've been a willing student, but I'll never feel about any act the way he feels about Diana and the Supremes.

After her solo song, Diana gets into the Supremes material. She introduces it by saying how sorry she is that Mary and Cindy can't be there with her, how much she misses them. Suddenly two back-up singers in drag, each wearing silver lamé gowns and much smaller wigs strut onstage and they break into "Someday We'll Be Together." Mark's starting to get excited. They're all lip-synching, which I realize makes more sense than three guys try to hit the high notes.

Diana, Mary and Cindy start singing "Forever Came Today" and segueway into a medley that includes "Come See About Me," "Stop! In the Name of Love," "You Keep Me Hangin' On" and "I'm Living in Shame." When it ends the crowd noise is deafening. Diana take a deep bow, then looks back to see Mary and Cindy bowing left and right, blowing kisses, and just generally eating up the limelight. She raises her arms and silences the crowd. She turns around, faces "the girls" and starts to sing the theme from *Mahogany*, her recent hit. She walks toward them singing, "Do you know where you're going to?" and they squeal and scurry off the stage in mock terror. She then turns back to the audience and finishes the song. The lyrics are gloomy ("How sad the answers to those questions can be") but this drag

Diana turns it into a triumph for herself and sadness for her former sisters Supreme. It's a funny bit, and probably pretty accurate as well.

Of course the finale is "Ain't No Mountain High Enough." Mark's swaying and practically singing along, although I can't imagine him ever letting himself go to that degree. Diana squeezes out every last drop from the song and leaves the stage in triumph. I feel strangely emotional. The theme keep running through my head: "Nothing can keep me from you." I hug Mark and say, "That was great! I'm so glad we're here."

He hugs me back as the Three Degrees song "Year of Decision" begins. I hear the lyrics tell me it's time to get the things I need and that I shouldn't be shy. It's a sign. Yes, this is the year. I've been holding back, but it's time to make a New Year's resolution to get what I want. It's hard to think straight because there's a lot of jostling as people move off the dance floor or stay and start to dance, but I get the message.

Pushed ahead of me by the crowd Mark looks back and asks, "Do you want a drink?"

"Definitely," I reply. In fact, I'm desperate for a drink. I'm going to need some of Gwen's famed liquid courage since it looks like I might need to make the first move. I light a cigarette as we push our way toward the bar, along with what seems like everyone else in the building. At that moment Craig appears. As I predicted, his hair is greasy, its poufiness gone. I didn't predict the additional buttons open on his shirt, but I might as well have. He's pretty damn predictable.

"Happy New Year!" he slurs, falling into us. Apparently he beat the crowd to the bar. Or a beautiful stranger did it for him.

"Happy New Year," Mark and I say in unison. We all hug.

"Hey, I was looking for you guys," Craig says. He's so convincing, even though I know there's not a word of truth in what he just said. He disappeared as soon as we got here and now is pretending we were the missing parties. "Where were you?" I ask him. "Did you see the show?"

"Oh yeah, it was great!" he says. I give it 50-50 odds.

"We're going to get drinks. Want to come?" Mark asks him.

"Nah, I want to dance," he says. "The Hustle" is in full swing. It feels like it's from a previous decade, not last summer. "Oh, I ran into a friend so you don't have to take me home," he says as he takes an outstretched hand and hustles off. Mark looks after him, somewhat wistfully. He's probably wishing he could move like that.

"Do you want to dance?" I ask him.

"No, no," he says. "That's OK. Let's get you a drink."

"It could take a while to get to the bar," I point out.

"I'm not in a rush," he says.

I smile at him. "Me either." The night isn't even close to over and I'm already replaying it in my head. Do I know where I'm going to? Ain't no river wide enough to keep me from him. This is my year of decision. My new resolution. Our closeness. Our first kiss. It all feels so right. I just need a drink or two to get my nerve up and make the first move. To paraphrase the Three Degrees, there ain't no reason I should be shy. And to quote the fake Supremes, forever came today.

Mark makes it to the bar and orders. Armed with a Coke (him) and a sloe gin fizz (me), we find a pocket of air and stake it out. There's an obstructed view of the dance floor, where occasionally Craig's head bops past. We catch a glimpse and Mark asks, "Where do you think he goes when he disappears?"

"Honestly, I don't want to think about it," I say. "But I have to believe a car is involved."

"Not necessarily," Mark says. "In this weather, it's more likely the men's room. That's why I've been avoiding it."

"Oh, God, I hadn't thought of that. But thanks for the image of dicks on parade. I'm glad I have an iron bladder. Not that I'd have that problem in the ladies' room. Assuming they even have one here."

"You think you'd be safe in a ladies' room?" asks Mark. "Given this crowd, I'd say you could check out every stall and not find any flaps and folds." We look at each other, then down the rest of our drinks, trying to pretend we did not just have this conversation. "To Each His Own" by Faith, Hope & Charity starts up, and it seems fitting.

"What are you doing tomorrow?" I ask, desperate to change the subject.

"I never do much on New Year's Day," Mark replies. "It's a big football day, which means nothing to me. I'll probably go hang out with Sophia. I've only seen her once since she got home."

Sophia. I forgot about her. She's Mark's best friend from high school and is now a sophomore at Skidmore. We met briefly at his 1967-themed party but I doubt she remembers me. He told me he's mentioned me to her so often that she wants to hang out with me while she's home, but somehow I'm not anxious. In fact, I'm a little afraid of her. From everything I've heard and seen, she's prettier, smarter and nicer than I am, and her history with Mark means she probably knows him a lot better than I do. I can't help it, I feel a poisonous mixture of envy and insecurity whenever her name comes up. Time to change the subject again.

"Yeah, I haven't seen Gwen much either. She invited me to a party tonight but obviously I didn't go."

"Obviously."

"I think it's my turn to buy the drinks," I say. "The usual?"

"Sure, thanks. I'll hold onto our spot."

"Be careful!" I warn, smiling, and head to the bar.

* * *

It's two o'clock in the morning and I'm all liquored up. Good thing Mark drove. He's so big and strong. I'm a cheap drunk. Oh, except that I think maybe it was pretty expensive, I'm not sure. All I know is it's time to go.

I think I may be deaf. Mark's been trying to tell me something and I have no idea what he's talking about. Giving up, he leans me up against a post near the bar and makes an "I'll be right back" signal. I make a "Stop! in the Name of Love" signal back and crack myself up. I watch him walk away…oh, he was asking me about getting my coat! He's going to the coat check! What a guy. I forgot I even had a coat. I love my long black cape. I stand up straight and swing it around. It makes me feel so girly. At the Sting I guess that's not saying much.

Somehow Mark gets me into his car and we drive to Dunkin' Donuts for some coffee. Oh, and let's be honest: for some donuts too. It's the only place open for miles around, but with donuts and coffee you don't need anything else. Except cigarettes, and I have those already. I have everything I need! Isn't that wonderful? I am so happy. In another era, I might even have said I was gay.

We pick out our donuts from the wall behind the cash register. Mark knows exactly what he wants (plain). He gets that and a coffee and goes to pay. I sort of thought he might pay for me too, but that's OK. I'm liberated. I can pay my own way. What I can't do is decide on one donut. So I pick two: a glazed and an éclair. Seeing them together on two little squares of paper, they look pornographic, like the éclair wants to jump the donut, impale her. What is wrong with me? I ask for a bag and throw them in.

The Cusp of Everything

I join Mark at the counter. I'm debating showing him how my two donuts fit together but think better of it. That's a little raunchy, not the right tone for the evening. I'm supposed to be elegant! I'm wearing a gown with a matching cape. I spent the evening at a nightclub. It's New Year's Eve. I'm elegant, damn it! No donut sex. I shouldn't have even gotten two of them. That just makes me look like a pig! I'll leave them in the bag and pretend I'm not hungry. Yeah, we'll see how long that lasts. I pour a packet of sugar in my coffee and take a sip. Very ladylike. A small bite of donut won't hurt. I may even extend my pinkie.

I end up having both donuts, a cup of coffee and a cigarette while we relive the Supremes show and talk about how Craig shouldn't have used and abandoned us the way he did. I'm not really paying much attention. Mark seems deflated and I feel fat and gross in my slinky black dress and wrap my cape around me loosely. I still have to make my New Year's resolution come true: I have to get Mark to be my boyfriend. I'm going to tell him how I feel about him as soon as we get back in the car. It's not the most romantic place in the world, but it sure beats the glaring lights of Dunkin' Donuts. I have to move quickly, though, because I'm sobering up and that's not good for candor.

We get in the Bonneville. It's dead silent except for an occasional passing car, and Mark turns on the radio. Esther Phillips is singing "What a Diff'rence a Day Makes." It's not that dark because the lights from Dunkin' Donuts are coming through the windshield. And, to quote Gwen, it's cold as a witch's tit. God, where did that come from? But it is cold. Mark turns on the car and gets the heat going. He's about to put it in gear when I say, "Mark?"

He looks over at me, hand on the shift thing. "What?"

"Can we just stay here a minute?"

"Are you OK? You're not going to throw up, are you?"

Boy, there's a mood killer. "No, I'm fine. I just wanted to talk."

He takes his hand off the shift thing, still looking at me. Suddenly I feel incredibly sober. And I do think I could throw up.

"I don't know how to say this," I start, awkwardly. He doesn't say anything. I could use a little help here, but obviously none is coming. "I mean, I had a great time tonight."

"Yeah, it was fun."

Man, he's not making this easy! Does he not know where I'm heading? He's beyond shy, into the land of oblivion. I move closer to him on the seat. He's looking a little confused.

"I just need to tell you…I love you." There. It's out. Not exactly poetry, but I made my point. He still looks confused. He sucks in his lips, like he's trying to hide them from me, get them as far away from me as he can. Oh my God, he doesn't want to kiss me! I make him sick!

" Karen," he says. Yes? I think, but can't speak. "I love Craig."

What? What did he say? No. No. No. I pull back toward my side of the seat. It's never felt so wide, yet not wide enough. He loves Craig. I love Mark and Mark loves Craig. Jesus. If Craig loved me, we'd have a perfect circle of misery. But the love stops at Craig. He loves only himself. I should tell Mark that. I should tell him he's supposed to be my boyfriend, not in love with some guy. Especially Craig! Shit! Is this really happening?

I can't speak. I get out of the car, stagger to a trash can and vomit on top of discarded coffee cups and donut remains. I can still hear the disco beat of "What a Diff'rence a Day Makes," my new least favorite song. The sun hasn't even come up on the first day of the New Year and already it's a catastrophe. I'm a catastrophe. Craig was right to be smug, everyone *can* be had. I hate him. I hate the world.

I don't want to get back in the car but it's freezing. Plus it's too far to walk home and I'd never get a taxi and there's no one I can call. Except Gwen, but then I'd have to listen to what an idiot I am. How did she know? How did I not? I want to die. I may already be dead. This sure feels like hell.

Mark gets out of his car and comes over to me. Standing at a safe distance with his arms folded, he says, "I'm sorry. I thought you knew."

He thought I knew. He thought I knew! Jesus, who's oblivious now? Did he think I was playing matchmaker for him? If not hell, this must be Mars. This is not my planet. This is not my life.

"Can you get in the car?"

Can I? I don't know. Can I do anything? Can I breathe? Can I remember how happy I was an hour ago, even ten minutes ago? A lifetime ago? I stagger to the car and get in. Mark gets in on his side and turns off the radio. We sit there for a minute. I'm really stinking up the place and I couldn't care less. "I don't believe this," I say.

"Well, you told me he was crazy about me," Mark says.

"Craig?" I say. "I did?"

"Yeah, after we all went to the movies."

"You mean *Cuckoo's Nest?*"

"Yeah, he drove me home that night. We had a long talk and that's when I knew for sure. Then you confirmed it."

"But that was a month ago! Craig has the attention span of a gnat! Even if he felt it then, he's over you now." I'm not saying it to be mean, at least I don't think I am. I'm just speaking the truth.

"He said that?" Mark looks stricken, but it doesn't even slow me down.

"Does he have to? He didn't even spend five minutes with us tonight. I mean, it's pretty obvious he's moved on."

I can't believe this conversation. Mark's been carrying a flame for Craig since Thanksgiving? The past month flashes through my mind. He brought me a little flower when he came to pick me up once. He picked out an expensive necklace for me! I wouldn't have my slinky gown if not for him! We talk every day and are together almost constantly. And all this time, he's been pining for Craig, that flaming bastard. There are no words, for either one of us.

Mark stares out the windshield, into Dunkin' Donuts, then turns the key in the ignition. We drive in silence to his house, where, completely sober, I walk wordlessly to my car and drive off. Now I understand how Craig's mother feels, the forces that cause her to lie in the dark for years wallowing in regrets and what ifs. I don't know if I can ever face the world again. I am a zombie, dead but undead.

14

I HAD NO REASON TO BE OVEROPTIMISTIC

January first is officially the coldest, most anticlimactic, most depressing day of the year. This one is the Bicentennial, as Channel 2 has been reminding us every night for what seems like a year already, with its inane "Bicentennial Minutes." Big whoop, as Ruth would say. Two hundred years. How is that worth celebrating? I've been alive 18 and that feels like more than enough.

I wake up around 11:00 crying, after just a few hours sleep. My hair smells like the ruins of a torched building and my breath is surely even worse. I'm hacking away and probably look like I've been punched in the face. Not that it matters. No one's around to see me other than Gretchen, who's been sleeping on my bed while Mom is off with Stan and Ruth's at Dad's. I might as well get used to this feeling: I am alone, and will be forever.

My life is over. <u>My world is empty without you, babe.</u> <u>Please tell me, where do we go from here?</u> Oh God, is this what it's going to be like, lyrics defining my wretchedness? I cycle rapidly and masochistically through radio stations, the crying ebbing and flowing as different songs come on. <u>I've blown it all sky high.</u> <u>I honestly love you. If only you believed in miracles, so would I.</u> Shit, poor Patrick. Now I know how he felt to be rejected. Well, karma has certainly come home to roost.

I love Mark. Mark loves Craig. Craig loves himself. What a fucked-up situation. Why is the need to be loved so universal, and so futile? How is it possible for one to love so deeply and the other not give a shit? Why can't one damn thing ever work out? I just wonder what it will take to make me happy, or if anything ever will.

I guess Mark has convinced himself he's gay, which is utter bullshit because he's never had a meaningful sex or love relationship with anybody, male or female. He fell for Craig's pretty-boy charm hook, line and sinker. I'm sure that won't last long, but somehow I doubt that even when it ends he'll come running to me.

But I just had to say I loved him, didn't I? I'd thought about it before. Every now and then I felt a stirring for him, but something in the back of my mind always told me no, don't do it, you can't get any closer with him, you could only ruin what you have because he doesn't want that kind of relationship with you. God, I am so smart! And so fucking dumb.

And yesterday everything was normal. I did get very drunk last night, and it was like we were flirting with each other, which we always do and I guess means nothing. But at that moment everything seemed like a sign and I couldn't stand it anymore. How was I supposed to know he'd decided he was gay and in love with Craig, probably the only gay person he's ever even met?

When I go into the bathroom and look in the mirror, it takes my crying to a whole new level. I look like shit. Shit on a pile of rotten, puke-covered donuts. What have I done? Why can't I ever keep my big mouth shut?

I have to hold myself back from calling Mark, which has been my habit for months now, whenever I'm in my room with nothing going on. Instead I force myself to put on a record. I can't take the radio any more. "Our Day Will Come" almost did me in. I prefer to program my own despair. I play the heartbreaking "Second Avenue" by Tim Moore and the entire album *Late for the Sky* by Jackson Browne. "Fountain of Sorrow" reinforces the pertinent point that what I was seeing wasn't what was happening at all.

Next I pick *Tommy* by the Who, thinking that will mean a break from drawing parallels to my current situation. But even that reminds me of Mark. I hear the song "1921," about the dawning of a new year, as a conversation between us and 1976. What about the boy? What about the boy? Obviously nobody gives a shit about the girl.

Do I really love Mark? Maybe it's just the idea of being so close to a guy with nothing romantic. I don't think it's possible for me. Other than Craig, who at least made the occasional pass, I've never been friends with a guy. They just seem like alien creatures, and I can't think of them as anything but potential or rejected boyfriends. Even Mark, as close as we've been, I've never gotten past the fact that he's a guy, and that makes him different from my friends who are girls. That's just the way it is.

I try to piece it all together, figure out what made me make the biggest mistake of my life. I think it's partially because I felt so bad when I left Tommy's Tavern the other night after meeting Hal. Talking to him showed me how much I was missing in my life. So I started thinking, God, I need a boyfriend. Mark seemed like the perfect choice—we're close already, which saves having to get to know somebody new, and of course I care for him.

Is this true, or am I just rationalizing what I've done? I don't even know any more.

So where *do* we go from here? What can all this lead to? Why do I have so many questions? I do know I have to have Mark in my life. We have a bond, an understanding between us that I can't give up, even though I obviously wasn't grasping the situation accurately. My only hope is to convince him (and myself) that I was wrong, he's just very important to me, but I want him to be what he is, even if that means he's gay, which I don't believe he is. I just can't afford to have him always have in the back of his mind: she loves me—RUN! Oh, it's probably too late now anyway.

I can't handle this shit.

* * *

I'm grateful that Mom is in Puerto Rico and Ruth's with Dad. I couldn't possibly explain to them what I'm going through and don't need their prying eyes and questions. On the other hand, I find crying alone unbearable. Poor Gretchen—she hardly gets to go out since I have her trapped up in my room, hugging her and weeping. I view myself as a secondary character on some monotonous, uncreative soap opera, seeing how ridiculous I look, how ridiculous I am.

Jesus, enough already. I need to get a grip, or I'll drive myself completely around the bend. I need someone to lead me back to the path of normalcy, or at least toward it. Mark probably already told Sophia what a loser I am. The only person I can imagine telling my humiliating tale to is Gwen, although I'm not looking forward to her what-did-you-expect eye rolls. Her parents are away and she had some people over today. She was expecting me to join them, but there's no way I can handle that. I can't even call over there because I'm sure I'll burst into tears if she asks me why I didn't come. I wait until I know they're all gone, then drive to her house. It's going on twenty-four hours of abject misery and I can't take another minute alone.

Gwen lives in a classic suburban ranch house with newish furniture and a scattering of family heirlooms. It's fastidiously clean, no thanks to her. Tonight, all the lights are on and I can hear music blaring. Shit, that better just be her listening while she straightens up in her usual half-assed way. I ring the doorbell a few times before, shockingly, my classmate Barb answers it looking disheveled. Barb, as large and plain as I remember her from high school, seems annoyed to see me. How rude, just because I stopped returning her calls about two years ago! "Yes?" she asks brusquely.

"Hi, Barb. Is Gwen here?" I ask, faking a friendly smile.

"No. She went to take Candy home." She starts to close the door.

I stop it with my foot "Hey! What are you doing? I'm going to wait for her."

"Oh, all right, but stay out of the den."

She flounces off heavily, leaving me standing in the foyer. A door slam is heard, then music (the repulsive "Love Machine" by The Miracles) gets louder. I wander into the kitchen, make myself a screwdriver and collapse at the Formica table where I am alone and feeling it for twenty minutes that seem like twenty years. I gaze around, trying to distract myself, but there's nothing interesting in here except her mother's diet stuff: boxes of chocolate Ayds "reducing plan" candy and signs reminding her "Your body is a temple" and "Don't eat that!" Poor Gwen. Her mother is obsessed with staying thin and obviously wishes Gwen was too.

It gets a little less thumpy and a little more romantic in the den, with Linda Rondstadt's *Prisoner in Disguise* album now blasting. Visualizing Barb in a make-out session, I choke back my queasiness, replacing it with self-pity, and light a cigarette. I smoke my brains out and shuffle dirty glasses into one area near the sink until finally Gwen gets back.

She immediately picks up on the loud music (Linda wailing "I Will Always Love You") and my mood (miserable). "What the hell is going on?"

Looking up at her I exhale smoke and say, "Gwen, I am freaking out. Mark is *gay*!"

She lets out a big huffing sigh. "Well, duh! You know I'm not the 'I told you so' type, but you have to admit I saw this coming." I burst into tears and drop my head to the table, which luckily I have cleaned off, at least a little. "Oh, God," she says, throwing her keys on the counter. "I can tell this is going to be a long one! Can you make me a drink? And what the hell is that music?"

Through my crossed arms on the table I mumble, "That's your unsympathetic friend Barb." Suddenly pissed off, I sit up and add, "I come here looking for a shoulder and find Honeypot in your den heaving and moaning. Like I didn't feel like a big enough loser already, I now find out that even the queerest girl in high school is a man magnet compared to me."

"Oh, calm down. It's not like *you'd* want him. They just needed a place to be alone and talk about Star Trek and how they're saving themselves for something or other." She heads to the den. I hear doors slamming, muffled grumbling and music being turned off, then a car door slam and a peel-out. Barb and her mate have obviously left.

I get up and make us some drinks. Side two of *Exile on Main St.* starts up and Gwen returns to the kitchen. "Got to scrape the shit right off your shoes," her favorite line ever. Well, next to "Roll me over slowly, I've been drinking all night" from Deep Purple's *Burn* album.

"Now, she says, settling in with her rum and Tab and lighting a Kool. "What was your first clue? That he wanted to go to a gay club on New Year's Eve?"

"That was *my* idea," I remind her, shaking my head. "What the hell do I know? It's not like he has a lisp! He's just a normal guy. I never knew anyone who was gay until Craig came back from Israel drooling over his roommate!"

"Yeah, that must have been a shock," Gwen says sarcastically. She never liked Craig, so he might as well have been gay as far as she was concerned. "So give me all the gory details. Did you make a pass at Mark and he told you he only liked it in the butt—and only if he was on the receiving end?"

I shudder. "You know, my mother was right about one thing. You are coarse and vulgar."

"Is that what she calls me? That fucking bitch! Yeah, I'm a bad influence. Not like your butthole buddies from the Sting." She taps her cigarette against the overflowing ashtray, then looks up to see I am devastated. "Oh, I'm sorry. Sometimes I can't help myself. But sometimes you are *so* blind. I don't know which is worse!"

154

"It all sucks! I don't know why life has to be this way. I feel like everything around me is shifting, and I'm just standing in the middle of it all, crying."

"Yes, you're quite the cryer."

I ignore this. She knows me too well. "The most utterly, totally depressing thought is this: how much better does it get? Everyone's so wrapped up in their games. Even Mark—he has a shield up almost all the time."

"Wow. And I thought everything was going great!"

"It was! I mean, as it turns out, it wasn't. I was just having so much fun with him, shopping and talking and watching *All My Children* and taking his class, Supremes 101, and feeling like we understood each other completely…"

"Like you and I understand each other."

"Yeah, except there was never a chance that I would sleep with you."

"Like I said, just like you and me. Maybe more so."

I put my head in my hands. "Oh my God. I am such an idiot." I think about Mark having a crush on Craig and raise my head. "You know, I think he has a lot of nerve deciding he's gay without ever even having a girlfriend! How does he know he won't like it?"

"Oh my God, what are they teaching you at that school of yours? Gay is gay, you moron. Please don't tell me you think you're going to change him!"

"Well, maybe not me, but someone might, if he would open himself up to trying it."

"Have you suggested this to him?"

"I haven't spoken to him since last night. But I guess it's not too hopeful. The way he talks about women—'flaps and folds!'—like we're a complete turn-off to him…"

"That's because you are! Sorry to throw the cold water of reality on your little 'maybe he can learn to like it' dream, but dear Mark is *gay*, as I tried to tell you months ago. Accept it. He'll never be turned on by the flaps and folds. Which by the way I like a lot. I think that might be my new name for my little flower."

"What, no more hoohah?"

"Please! I haven't used hoohah in months! It's been Vulvacious since I moved to Boston."

"Maybe this is part of my problem. I call mine 'down there.'"

Gwen shakes her head. "And since it's so much less depressing to talk about your life than mine, how busy has Vulvacious been lately?"

"Wait, before I get into that sordid tale I need more music." She heads back to the den and puts on side one of Patti Smith's *Horses*. Jesus died for somebody's sins, but not hers. Gwen settles back in to give her rant, lighting another cigarette.

"Shit, my life's not much better. There are men, God knows, but they're all pretty much undependable jerks. Although at least they're straight, which I never even thought to include on the checklist!" She licks her finger and makes check marks in the air. "Cute, smart, generous, big dick, and now…straight!"

"Yeah, good luck with that list."

"Yeah, well I'm not quite ready to sign up as a fag hag, thanks just the same!"

I shudder. "Please don't use that expression!"

"OK, sorry, sorry. Listen, straight or gay, they'll destroy us, these men. In fact, I'm sort of in love with one now, but only because he makes me less miserable than any of the others. Hey, I think I'll write that down." She grabs a pen off the table and writes on a napkin: "Eddie Keenan. You make me less miserable than any other man makes me." She looks at it. "Does that sound like a love letter to you?"

"If it came from anyone other than you I'd say no. But I think that could be the nicest thing you've ever said about anyone! So what's so great about Eddie Keenan?"

"Not much. He's a grad student. He's poor, he drinks too much, he has a chip on his shoulder and he doesn't pay much attention to me. On the other hand, he's gorgeous and incredible in bed. Even if he does fall asleep immediately afterwards."

"Now *that's* a checklist! I'll fight you for him!"

"I know, it doesn't sound so great when I spell it out in cold hard facts. But really, most of them are better in the dark when you're half out of it anyway." Sadly, I know she's right about this. If only I didn't crave being with someone.

"Is he black?" I ask. Since sleeping with the Ethiopian exchange student at her graduation party in June, Gwen has quoted that "once you go black you'll never go back" line with increasing fervor.

"He is," she responds. "Let's just say I won't be bringing him home to meet the parents. Not that he'd want to come. We don't have that kind of relationship."

"Well, at least you have some kind of relationship." Now I'm depressed again, or make that still. But by the time I drive home I've gone a full day without talking to Mark, for the first time in months, and as hard as it was not to call him, I feel a little sense of triumph. A tiny, pathetic victory, over what I'm not sure.

* * *

It's Sunday afternoon, the fourth day of January. Through a combination of massive amounts of sleep, long talks with an increasingly impatient Gwen, excessive drinking at Tommy's Tavern and some babysitting, I've staggered through a series of days that start out seeming endless but wind up merely terminal. By bedtime I'm in the same miserable place I was when I got up, although slightly thinner (good) and crazier (bad). I've about doubled my smoking these past few days, and at seventy-five cents a pack that's one more way I need to get a grip.

Gwen returned to Boston yesterday and now I'm truly on my own. School doesn't start for a couple of weeks, but she'd rather be there than here and who could blame her? I'm sure I'm terrible company. I can bring on tears at will by telling myself nothing will be the same again—I'll always have the scars from these now-fresh wounds. I can't imagine Mark ever letting us get as close as we were because he's probably afraid of what I might do, now that he knows how I feel about him. I'm starting to wonder if I'll ever see him again. But I do understand his reaction on New Year's Eve: at this point even I wouldn't love me.

I've cycled through almost every depressing song in my collection and am now focusing on live performances. I don't know why, but the applause and spoken asides make them a little easier to take, giving me hope that I may be coming out of the darkness. It started when I heard a live performance of something called "The End of a Beautiful Friendship" by Carmen McRae on WBLS. I'd never heard of her or the song, which is about two long-time friends who one day look at each other and realize they are in love. I think it is my new favorite. What a masochist I am! After that ended, I switched to WNEW and they were playing a heartbreaking version of "Behind Blue Eyes" with just vocals and a guitar. That inspired me to pull out classic live albums and torture myself some more. Maybe music can help me get the obvious through my thick skull.

I'm relating to "You Don't Love Me," from Side 2 of the Allman

Brothers' _At Fillmore East,_ when Mark calls. "How are you?" he asks warily.

I'm thrilled he called but also scared it's to tell me we're through. I need to keep it light, but it feels heavy just to have him on the phone. I sit up straight and start running my fingers through my hair. Shit, what a greasy rat's nest. "Crappy. You?"

"The same. "

He sounds like death warmed over, and I'm sure I do too, unless my happiness that he called is coming through the line.

"Do you want to get together?" he asks.

"Sure," I say, probably a little too quickly. I glance around my room. God, it's a pigsty. Will I be able to clean it up by the time he makes it over?

"Can you come here?" he says. What a relief. Of course I can. What I can't do is get excited. I know he's not summoning me to say he's changed his mind. More likely he wants to tell me to back off, but doesn't want to contend with my stupid driveway. No, wait. He called me, so I have to assume he wants me in his life in some way.

"Sure," I agree. Mom and Ruth will be home any minute, so it's time for me to make my escape anyway. "I'll be there soon."

"Great. I miss you."

My heart flickers. "I miss you too."

"Hey, have you spoken to Craig?"

"No." Shit, he'd better not be calling me just to get in touch with Craig. "I called him a couple of days ago but he didn't bother calling back. He's an asshole."

"Yeah, well, I'll see you when you get here."

We say our goodbyes and I get out of bed to take a bath. (My antiquated bathroom doesn't have a shower, and the sloping ceiling over the tub wouldn't allow it anyway.) I throw on jeans and a sweater, nothing special, but do take a little extra time with my makeup, trying to hide those puffy eyes. Why I care about making myself more attractive to Mark, I have no idea. The dream never dies, I guess, despite Gwen's "gay is gay" curse. If I believed in praying, I'd pray that wasn't true.

I park in front of Mark's house and knock on the door to his den. He opens it instantly and I am taken aback by his appearance. He looks thinner than ever—and his cruel brother Dean recently called him "Biafra Boy," so it's not like he had a lot of extra meat on his bones to begin with. He's pale, with dark circles under his eyes. I don't say anything, since I'm sure makeup hasn't exactly solved all my problems either. It would be sickening to think he's lost all that weight pining for Craig rather than me, and I can't let myself believe that. Please, let it be me!

"Hi," he says, letting me in. "I just need to watch the girls on TV and then how about if we go to Cook's?"

This is so far from the way I expected the conversation to go that I'm baffled. "The girls? You mean the Supremes?"

"Yeah, they're on 'Sammy and Company,' that stupid Sammy Davis Jr. show."

Watching the Supremes is the last thing I want to do now, next to watching Sammy Davis Jr., but I don't have much choice. We go upstairs to the den and say hi to Loretta and Steve, who are both sitting there with their arms crossed. I'm sure they don't know about Craig and blame me for their son's misery. Everyone hates me, including me, although for different reasons.

Mark and I sit as far apart as possible in the narrow room. We smoke until the drapes need to be dry cleaned and my lungs are burning. The show sucks but I manage to hold my tongue. I should make that a habit.

Finally it's time for Cook's. I drive. The parking lot is packed, not surprising on a Sunday evening that's the last gasp of the Christmas-New Year's holiday. Kids run wild through the restaurant and game area while their parents smoke and suck down caffeinated beverages. Mark and I each get a coffee and find a filthy table, complete with overflowing ashtray. Right as we sit down, "You Are Everything," a duet by Diana Ross and Marvin Gaye starts. We shoot each other a look but I don't know what it means. A sign that we share something deep? Recognition of a message in the song that we are everything to each other? Or that he thinks Craig is his everything? Shit, I can't take this confusion.

"Are you OK?" I ask.

"I was going to ask you the same thing," Mark responds. "But you look like you're fine. You look good." Oh, stop. I don't want compliments! Well, maybe I do. God, I'm superficial.

"Thanks, so do you," I lie.

"Oh please," he waves my comment away. "I look like death warmed over. I haven't eaten since New Year's Eve, except when my mother forces soup on me."

"I'm sorry," I say, even though I don't think his misery is my fault. At least not completely. I wish it was because he now realizes that he made a terrible mistake not loving me too, but somehow I'm beginning to see that he's miserable because he's in love with Craig. He shrugs.

"So I guess I owe you an apology, " he says. I'm thrown but don't say anything. I have mixed feelings about learning what he's apologizing for, and I should probably be apologizing again myself, although I don't know how to describe my role in all this. "I guess I should have told you I was gay. But you have to realize, I had no idea how you felt about me. I guess I didn't think it mattered."

Uh, it matters! I stare at him.

"Our friendship is important to me. You know that, right?" he says.

"Well, sure. It's important to me too." God, so important.

"I'm just saying, I hope we can work it out."

"We have to." I hold back telling him I can't live without him.

He sighs. "I've been playing 'We Need You' a little too much lately." I look at him blankly.

"Diana, from the *Touch Me in the Morning* album. It's about feeling the absence of someone who's not there anymore." He fails to identify whose absence he's feeling so acutely but I can guess it's not me. Or not *just* me.

"Yeah, I know how that feels. Just with a different theme song." I don't detail my personal soundtrack; what's the point?

He gives a little half-smile. "So what happens now? Are we OK as friends?"

I look at him. He looks like he doesn't want to lose me. My heart wobbles. He'll never love me, but I know we have something together. Do I love him? Or was I just trying on that feeling for size? Can I love him like a friend? My brain is racing. I don't know how I can do it, but I'll have to at least pretend I can.

"Sure," I say, feeling like I'm lying and saving myself at the same time.

Mark smiles and reaches across the table to take my hand. I smile back, unsure how to adjust my emotions 180 degrees. I reassure myself that friendship is a more valuable and permanent role than lover. Love and sex ruin everything. Especially love, that despair-inducing mirage.

Something to my left catches my attention, some kid running by. I look up from our clasped hands and see Patrick, holding hands across a table of his own. With a girl. Her back is to me, but it's definitely a girl. At least the world hasn't spun that far out of control. He sees me and his head snaps to attention, his mouth opens and closes. I let go of Mark's hand and turn back to him, speechless.

"What's the matter?" he asks. "You look like you've seen a ghost."

I can't tell him. My past doesn't belong in our present, not while we're grappling with our shit. I shake it off and talk a gulp of weak, lukewarm coffee. "Nothing, nothing." I try to smile. "So what else is new?" I ask lightly.

"What else? You mean there's something else? I've thought about nothing but you and Craig since New Year's Eve." Ah, yes. Craig.

"Have you spoken to him?" I ask, willing myself not to look over at Patrick's table. I'm dying to see what the girl looks like, but it's none of my business and I don't want to give him any encouragement to come over and talk to me. Focus, must focus on Mark and his talk of Craig.

"Yeah, I called him a bunch of times and I finally got him yesterday. I asked him about getting together but he said he was tied up until he leaves for Syracuse again in a couple of days. I don't know if he's really that busy or if you were right and he's just not interested anymore."

"Well," I say, "he probably thinks of you as my friend, not a potential boyfriend." Saying that last word makes me shudder. I clutch my coffee with both hands, will myself not to look at Patrick again.

"That's what I figured, that's why I wanted to get together with him. He doesn't know how I feel."

I want to tell Mark that *he* didn't know how *I* felt until a few days ago, and it didn't make him feel the way I do. Why would he think it would be any different with Craig? Then I remember that, besides being gay, which gives him the edge over me, Craig's an egomaniac. He probably lives to hear that someone is in love with him. Rather than being horrified, as Mark obviously was with me, Craig would be flattered at Mark's declaration. He was flirting with Mark earlier, so this would be like proof that he's irresistible. Now he'll be even more insufferable. How can Mark not see this?

"Look," I say. "I've never noticed any great chemistry between you and Craig. What suddenly makes you think you're…" I can't say it. "…he's so great?"

"It's not sudden," he says. "I knew instantly, and the feeling's grown ever since then, especially since you told me he was attracted to me, too." Curse my big mouth! "And just so you know, I've known who I am since I was four."

"Who you are? You mean, gay?" I drop my voice for that last, disheartening, word.

"Yes. I've always been attracted to men." He drops his voice on that last word, too.

"Well, that's nice." I don't know what to say. I feel betrayed and insulted, but certainly Mark has never led me on, never hinted that we were anything other than friends. So why did I think we could be? And how will I adjust now that I know for sure we never will be? It's discouraging to think I have no one to blame but myself. Speaking of which, I turn almost involuntarily to look at Patrick, but he and the girl are gone, their table being taken over by another doomed couple. God, I didn't think I could get more cynical, but apparently there was still room to sink further. I turn back to Mark and ask, "So what happens now?"

"I just need to see him," Mark says, with a desperate tone to his voice. "I have to talk to him before he goes back to Syracuse."

How did this become my life? Sigh. "I'll see what I can do. But I don't have any special powers." That's for sure.

"Thank you," he says, and I know it's heartfelt. "All I'm asking is that you try and get us together." He runs his fingers through his thick black hair, which is looking a little wilder than usual. "I'm sorry about all this. I feel guilty that you've given up a lot in your life to spend so much time with me."

"Are you kidding? You kept me sane through my first miserable semester of college. I'll track him down," I promise. "You guys obviously need to talk."

"Thanks," Mark says. Cook's has quieted down since we got here. I can hear Harold Melvin and the Blue Notes singing about all the things that we've been through and how you should understand me like I understand you. I'm starting to hate music. Why does there have to be music everywhere?

It's a school night, although luckily not for us. We've still got some healing to do before we can face the real world again. We head back to Mark's, and it almost feels like it used to rather than an irrevocable, catastrophic, apocalyptic disaster.

* * *

The Cusp of Everything

And so I find a way to keep things between Mark and me basically the same as they were before: I channel that 10cc song, telling myself I'm not in love, that it was just a silly phase I was going through. Sure, I care for Mark, and do still love him in my own sick way. I think maybe I always will. But I have to force those feelings down or I'll lose him for real. Since he doesn't love me, at least I won't fall into the trap I did with Patrick, where I lost interest once he fell for me.

I wish Patrick better luck this time around, that she'll continue to find him fascinating for more than a couple of months. I know I should be happy he's found someone else, but I'm not a big enough person to feel anything other than a loser. I walked away from a straight guy who loved me to throw myself at a gay guy who doesn't. What the hell is wrong with me?

By devoting my entire life to Mark I've given up meaningful relationships with other people, and that's not healthy. I race home from school, where I talk to practically no one and have made no friends, to call him and hear his voice. Nothing means anything unless I share it with him. All that will stay true, I'm sure, unless I suddenly figure out how to make new friends, and I don't even want to do that. I just want Mark. Oops, almost forgot those feelings were just a silly phase. If I say it enough, maybe I can convince myself it's true.

He's so hung up on Craig, it's his only topic of conversation. It colors everything. Sure, I made an ass of myself on New Year's Eve. But now Mark's driving me up the wall. He's "so in love." It's all he talks about. He mopes and says he'll go crazy if he doesn't see Craig. He's worse than I ever was about anyone, except maybe him.

I have to talk myself back into wanting Craig as a friend after this debacle. His selfish and callous ways make it hard to think of him in any kind of positive way, but Mark organizes a campaign to sell me on him. He doesn't convince me that Craig will be thrilled to learn how he feels, but I do agree to set up a meeting between the two of them. Unfortunately, Craig is never around when I call, and despite my best efforts to get them together, Craig goes back to Syracuse without ever learning of Mark's adoration. I'm secretly relieved but know I need to commiserate.

Friday night, back at Cook's, we're talking about, duh, what else, when Mark gets the bright idea to make a trip up there. It's still another week before our classes start, so we have the time. We can share the driving and costs, which will be minimal anyway since we'll stay in the dorm with Craig. Despite my gut feeling that this is a terrible idea, ultimately Mark sells me on it as a big adventure. Long drives alone, just the two of us, to continue healing! A chance to be in a dorm, go to parties, live the real college life! His main reason is not the one I care to focus on: he'll have some quiet time with Craig to tell him he loves him. Of course, my main reason is that getting to know Craig will be the surest way for Mark to figure out he's made a terrible mistake. But I don't share that. I'm a supportive friend, after all.

I get swept up in the idea of going on a trip with Mark, regardless of its purpose. I'm so excited I can't wait to nail down the plans. We call Craig's dorm room from a payphone and talk to his roommate. Naturally he's out, but he'll get the message that will make his day: his dear friends might be coming to visit! We start making notes on napkins about how great it will be, like our coffee's laced with LSD. We're making up lyrics to the worst songs ever. Mark's contribution:

Oh men
I wish I could be with Craig
Up until 10, down until 5
Boy I'd take a dive
Karen would roara
For some mora

Nice one, Mark. And thanks for the mixed message! Then there's this, also by him:

Go to Cook's
With a schnook
All they offy
Is the coffee
Boink

Mine:

Hop in the car
Drive to a star
It's very far
From where we are.
Race to the sun
An awfully long run

But when you're done
I'll join you there, hon.

Good thing neither of us writes music.

We have gone completely goofy, caught up in the Craig fantasy. I feel a tickle of foreboding, a nagging reminder that Craig is a conceited prick who seems to have lost interest in Mark. But Mark finally seems happy so I want to believe this will be a great trip. Most of the time, Craig's a lot of fun. I figure we're going into this older (well, by two weeks, but it feels like much, much more) and wiser so we'll be prepared to deal with him if he gets out of hand. After all, we'll have each other and we won't put up with any of his shit.

We place another call before we leave Cook's, and this time Craig's there! I gush so much telling him about our plans that I'm incomprehensible. "What? What are you talking about?" he asks.

"We're coming to Syracuse! Can we stay with you?"

"You're coming here? When?"

Doesn't he get his messages? "We were thinking we'd come up next Wednesday and drive back Sunday."

"Next week? Why?"

"Why? What do you mean why? To see you! School doesn't start for another week, so it's not like you'll be busy."

"I'm always busy," Craig says, with a queenly tone. "And classes here start Monday. But I can make time for you guys. I just don't know about your staying here. I do have a roommate, you know."

"Yeah, we know." I whisper this nugget to Mark, who frowns. "Well, I guess we'll take our chances. We can sleep on the floor if we have to. Or stay up all night and sleep during the day when there are beds available."

"Yeah, OK, I guess so," Craig says. He doesn't sound as enthusiastic as we are, but I won't let Mark know this. I tell Craig we'll make our plans and get back to him, then hang up and say to Mark, "We're on!" He is so happy he almost hugs me. Almost. After all, he doesn't want me to get the wrong idea. I might roara for some mora or something.

We discuss transportation. Between Mark's Bonneville and my boat, it's a toss-up as to which is the most dependable, or I should say the least undependable. My odometer and speedometer have stopped working, so I don't even know my mileage—and won't be able to judge speed during the roughly six hundred miles we'll be driving round trip. The fact that the front passenger window doesn't go down seems pretty irrelevant given January temperatures in Syracuse. Mark, by contrast, thinks his entire engine is on borrowed time, and I'm pretty sure the boat's is solid. Mine it is.

15

THERE MUST BE 50 WAYS TO LEAVE YOUR LOVER

After getting my oil changed, I tell my mother I'm taking a trip up north with Mark. She strongly advises against it, emphasizing the winter temperatures in Syracuse and the age of my car. Ha! More likely it's because she doesn't like the idea of my traveling with a guy; she's as clueless as I used to be about Mark's alleged gayness. Part of me wants to tell her she doesn't have to worry about Mark defiling me, but on the other hand, if Mark doesn't change his mind about being gay, maybe I'll meet some cute Syracuse student. The bottom line is, it isn't her decision and my reasons are no business of hers. I'm doing this for Mark. He wants to be with Craig, and I want him to be happy. Of course, if I'm honest with myself, I don't think it's possible for him to be happy with Craig. But wanting him to be happy means I'm still a good friend, right?

Mark and I pack our warmest clothes. I pick him up at his house and somehow I'm not surprised that his suitcase is much larger than mine. It takes up half my trunk. I make the obligatory teasing remarks and we hit the road. I love grown-up road trips (*not* the family kind) and did a fun college scouting tour with my friend Susan last spring. We hit colleges in New England, including New England College where she ended up going. I earned the nickname "Stinky" on the trip to Boston when Gwen fell in love with B.U. and I forgot to pack deodorant. Those college visits made it harder than it already was for me to accept being a commuter.

The trip north to Syracuse is a brutal five hours, travelling at unknown speeds due to my broken speedometer. Damn, I wish I had a tape deck in the boat. We're totally at the mercy of what's on the radio, and since we left the range of New York's multitude of signals, it's been mostly static and Muzak. When we do find a "real" station, it's usually telling us there must be 50 ways to leave your lover. That song is a huge hit. It has a military feel to it, like you should be marching away from your rejected lover to the beat of a fife and drum. I resist supplying a missing line: "Don't love the shark, Mark." He's not finding a lot of Diana or the Supremes, despite relentless dial-twisting, but then there's not a lot of anything except dead air along this godforsaken route.

We talk, of course, but mostly about Craig. I try repeatedly to change the subject, but all roads lead to Craig's big brown eyes. Apparently they can lock in and make an instant connection with anybody unfortunate enough to look his way. According to Mark, "When we met, that night at the diner, he held my eyes just a second too long. I started to look away, but then I realized he was still looking at me. So I looked back, but I started to feel self-conscious. You were sitting right there and it just felt weird, like he was looking into my soul, like he knew my secrets. Plus of course he's so handsome."

Good thing I didn't just eat a donut or we might have a repeat of New Year's Eve, only without a trash can. Shit, they're just eyes! Windows on the soul, my ass. But Mark's just getting started. Everything about Craig is special, from his fluffy, tamable hair to his large feet, and everyone knows what that portends. Please save me. I want to be supportive, or at least I want Mark to think I'm supportive. I love him and need him in my life in any way possible. At this point I'm not sure what or why or how. I hope I don't veer off the road from boredom or churning emotions, from biting my tongue or just plain gay love overload. I'm going through a lot on this drive and the music isn't helping. Right now it's "Times of Your Life" by Paul Anka. I usually change the station when a commercial comes on, and this is a Kodak commercial masquerading as a song. But it's the only station on the dial right now.

What I really want to say to Mark is that it sounds psycho to hold someone's gaze too long, to pretend you're looking into his soul, to try and seduce him. Craig didn't know if I might have had a crush on Mark when they first met! What is wrong with someone who'd try to seduce someone else's crush? But I'm determined not to say a word against Craig on this trip. I want Mark to come to his own conclusion.

Of course I want his conclusion to be the right one: mine. But no tampering with the jury. He has to weigh the evidence and make his own decision.

Mark insists I put in my two cents, but I have to I think carefully before I answer. There's a lot to consider, like his fragile state and obsessive fervor about Craig, so charming, so undependable. I had no idea this was right beneath the surface; he seemed so together. Shy, yes, but sure of who he is in a way I'm not. Maybe he's as surprised as I was by his intense emotions. He does seem to need a lot of reassurance.

After this flashes through my mind I choose my words carefully. "The few times I've seen you and Craig together, it seemed like you didn't like him that much. You were sort of rude to him at the diner. You don't like his taste in music. He almost made us miss the Diana Ross show on New Year's Eve." I stop short of pointing out how selfish he is. "I guess I don't understand when you decided he was Mr. Wonderful."

"I know all about his flaws," Mark says. "He's attractive and charismatic and he uses his looks to get what he wants. I'd never do that, but I don't judge him for it."

"Why not? I judge him!" Again, I have to hold back from stating my assessment of Craig: megalomaniac user, boyfriend-stealing queen! "I mean, how are big feet enough to make up for even bigger character flaws?"

"It's the total package," Mark says. Then, in a voice imitating Groucho Marx he says, "And what a package."

Gag. "You know, I'm tired of driving," I say. If I can't change the subject, at least I can pause it. Besides, we're more than halfway there and I'm sick of the desolate highway, the smoke-filled car, the mediocre music. "Dream Weaver" is not enough to keep me awake with this whitely monotonous view. "Can you take over for awhile?"

"Sure. Let's get gas at the next rest stop and we can switch places."

I've had many classes I thought would never be over, lonely nights, even Allman Brothers jams. According to the laws of science, they all had to end, and so did this drive. But a January trek from Mamaroneck to Syracuse, in a rickety car with the man I love who loves a man redefines the concept of eternity. We've been driving for what feels like ten lifetimes and the sun is just starting to set as we pull up in front of Craig's dorm, a free-standing structure that looks like a penal colony. Considering who lives there, it's probably a penile colony. Yet another unshared thought. Hey, I'm getting good at holding back.

Even though the dorm is on the campus, it feels alienated, separate. It's huge and ugly, the kind of place where they'd be smart to post the suicide hotline number on every corner. Between the Soviet-style architecture and the brutal weather, the whole town seems to be screaming, "Get out while you still have a chance!"

It's not even dinner time but it might as well be midnight. I'm exhausted and cranky. Not Mark, though. He's psyched for what he's imagining will be the most romantic and life-changing days of his life. Let's just hope Craig isn't a total asshole but the outlook on that possibility is about as sunny as Syracuse in January.

We park next to a snowdrift and get out of the car. My winter coat—a tan-colored wool cape with slits for arms—feels like a bathing suit and I now truly comprehend the concept of wind chill. According to the radio it's 15 below zero. Factor in the wind and you get to the number where eyeballs freeze.

We carry our suitcases in past a distracted guard who doesn't even notice us and take an elevator to the twelfth floor. We find Craig's room and knock on the door, but nobody answers. Now what? Leaving our bags doesn't make a lot of sense, considering the lack of security we've already experienced, besides the fact that we don't know our way around and can't handle the cold. We don't know Craig's schedule, or his roommate's name…all in all, we're pretty damn ignorant. What are we doing here again?

We sink to the floor in the silent and abandoned hallway. We drop to the floor and lean up against a wall. There's an improvised ashtray of foil on the floor a few doors down and I get up and grab it.

"He knew when we were coming, right?" Mark asks, flicking his ever-present Supremes lighter as I return.

"Yeah, I told him Wednesday afternoon. But maybe he has a class." Or a horny stranger, I think.

"That's probably it." Mark is predisposed to grasp at straws and I'm still practicing keeping my mouth shut. I don't want to be the bummer, I want to be the consolation prize when, inevitably, it doesn't work out. Pathetic? Maybe. But as long as I have him, I'm happy.

When a girl with a big bush of hair and an even bigger stack of books slouches toward us down the hall, I ask, "Do you know Craig

Landon?" She looks at us, shakes her head and keeps going. I turn to Mark. "What a shock, girls don't know him."

Mark laughs. What a relief! My bitterness hasn't completely eclipsed my saucy humor, such as it is. I stand up to stretch as a nerdy-looking beanpole approaches. "Hey, do you know Craig Landon?" I ask. Removing a key from his pocket he answers, "Yeah, he's my roommate, why?"

"We came to visit him," I say. "I think I might have spoken to you on the phone. I'm Karen, and this is Mark."

Without responding, the guy comes right up to Craig's door, and inserts his key in the lock. Mark stubs out his cigarette and gets to his feet. As he's turning the key, Beanpole gives Mark the once over. Oh, great. Is he gay too? What happened to my old life, where guys weren't interested in me because I have small boobs, not because they're gay? "I'm Charlie," he says without making eye contact with either one of us.

Opening the door, Charlie waves us inside. "Come on in. I don't know when Craig will be back." I get the feeling Craig's schedule is a mystery his roomie has no interest in solving.

We grab our bags and follow him through a short, dark hall into a cramped room with a divider most of the way down the middle. There are two beds, two desks and two giant piles of laundry spilling out of two closets. In the mathematical equation that is this room, two extra bodies just don't add up. Mark and I shoot each other a look. Our trip is starting to feel like a terrible imposition, not so much on Craig but on us and his gawky roommate. I doubt this guy agreed to two extra lodgers in a space barely big enough for one person. Bad enough he has to deal with whatever Craig drags home on the average night. Where the hell are we going to sleep?

As if to answer my unspoken question, Charlie points to one of the messy piles of sheets and blankets and says, "That's Craig's bed." We put our stuff down next to it and Mark makes an attempt to smooth out the covers without actually looking anal enough to make the bed, even though I'm sure he'd like to. We sit down next to each other not knowing where to look or what to say, when Craig breezes in, followed closely by his familiar Jovan Musk scent. I leap to my feet and throw my arms around him, relieved that he showed up before midnight and determined to show his roommate, whose name I've already forgotten, that we're legitimate guests.

"Craig! We're here!" I turn to see that Mark is still sitting on the bed. I'd planned to leave them alone right away, but with Beanpole around, it's not like he can declare his love. So I don't feel any pressure to make myself scarce. Not that I have anywhere to go.

"Hey!" Craig exclaims. "You made it! How was the drive?" He flicks on a radio on his desk and "Convoy," that CB radio novelty hit we've already endured twice today, blasts out. I quickly reach over and turn it down.

"Pure hell," I say. "But it's worth it to see you." What is wrong with me that I feel like I have to tell everyone what they want to hear? In this case, maybe survival instinct. We don't know anyone else for more than 300 miles.

Craig looks past me. "Hi, Mark. How are you?" He reaches over and they shake hands. Mark remains mute, but he gives a little head bob.

Turning back to me, Craig asks, "So what's up? Do you guys have any plans?" Boy, do we, I think, but instead say, "Just seeing you. Whatever you feel like doing works for us."

"Well, I feel like going out tonight. Three days into the new semester and I'm already sick of the whole thing." He takes off several layers of outerwear as he talks and throws it on top of our puny single layers on the back of his desk chair/clothes rack. Mark gets up and speaks for the first time.

"I need a shower," he croaks out.

"Go right ahead," Craig replies, looking at him steadily, probably delving into his soul again and turning him even gayer. Mark grabs his massive suitcase and bangs his way into the bathroom. I'm sure it hasn't been cleaned since September, and I feel a twinge for him. After figuring out where to put a suitcase that takes up half the room, he'll likely spend most his time in there trying to wipe up pubes and loogies without actually focusing his eyes on them. At least I can take out my contacts and spare myself the brain-searing image. Ignorance is bliss and I already know way too much for my own good.

Painfully aware that Craig's roommate is behind the skimpy divider, I speak carefully as Craig's radio plays Neil Young's old song "Only Love Can Break Your Heart." "It's great to see you, but I'm a little concerned about where we're going to sleep."

"Yeah, I'm wondering about that too," Craig responds. "I can probably find another place to stay, and you and Mark can take my bed."

What a great idea! I can't wait to tell Mark and watch him suck in his lips again. "I don't think that's the best solution. You know that Mark and I are just friends, right?" I say to Craig.

"Oh, I know," he says, with a smug smile that makes me feel especially dickless. Yes, he probably does know he's so irresistible that Mark chose him over me. It's all over but the humiliation of me sleeping sitting up in the hallway while the two of them do whatever gay guys do which, like pubes and loogies, I refuse to visualize. I think I need a nap since there doesn't seem any other way of leaving this situation. I shrink myself into a corner of Craig's rumpled bed and close my eyes.

When I wake up I'm alone and sweaty. Damn, it's hot in here, probably overcompensation for the tundra outside. A desk lamp illuminates the piles of crap that fill the tiny space and a digital clock reads 7:16. The radio is off and voices pass by in the hall outside. I know I should get up and shower but I can't bear the thought of taking off my clothes in this place. The waistband of my jeans is cutting into my stomach and probably leaving an unsightly red line. But it's obvious no one in Syracuse is going to see me naked, so who gives a shit. I'll just open the button and unzip a little bit and wait for the boys to come back. They better not have gone to dinner without me. I haven't eaten anything today except Kit Kats and Ruffles and I desperately need a real meal. And a bigger pair of jeans if this menu plan keeps up.

I get up to pee, in a bathroom that looks like it has been recently cleaned. Thank you, Mark! The sink and shelves are lined with grooming products: creams, roll-ons, sprays. I don't have anywhere near this number or variety of potions. While I'm sitting on the toilet reading labels, I hear the door open and quickly finish up. Mark and Craig have returned. Craig reports that they went downstairs to the lounge and bought some crap from the vending machines, but I can't tell if they've had a chance to have "the talk."

They both toss their chips and cookies on the bed and we start getting ready to face the wind chill. I take a heavy sweater out of my suitcase and throw it on so my cape won't be my only protection against the Syracuse winter. There's a knock at the door and a short, angry-looking girl enters. Craig introduces me to her: Michelle. They ran into her in the lounge and Craig invited her to join us. Her grandfather is some big Broadway producer, which is nice for her, but did I really need to learn that within 30 seconds of meeting her? Normally I give people the benefit of the doubt, but Michelle rubs me the wrong way from the moment I lay eyes on her, with her troweled-on make-up and her big fur coat. I feel like telling her, "*I'm* the token girl here, so we won't be needing *you*," but apparently I don't get a say.

Craig has a little green Fiat with a backseat that's practically nonexistent. Michelle and I get to wedge ourselves back there for the drive to DJ's, the bar/restaurant Craig has selected. I consider trying to make conversation, but asking "Where are you from?" is gratuitous when her first syllable told me "I'm from Long Island" with a hard G in the middle. I don't get what she's doing here. Is this some kind of twisted double date? I make a couple of comments about the weather and how small the back seat is and leave it at that. Michelle does a little whining of her own, and Craig fills any conversational vacuum with chatter about himself.

At DJ's, everyone jockeys for position, ending up with Mark and Michelle on either side of Craig in the booth while I take a chair. Fine with me. I'm already sensing that Michelle feels territorial about Craig. How deluded can she be? Wait, she has a crush on a gay guy. Maybe I should try empathy rather than contempt. Nah, if she has a crush on Craig, she's toast anyway. Mark, as usual, is quiet. Like me, he's probably wondering what we've gotten ourselves into.

Since it's the beginning of a new semester, Craig's flush with cash from his parents and tells us he's picking up the tab. I plan to enjoy it while I can, and order greedily. Who cares if my jeans are turning into sausage casings? No one at this table, that's for sure. Craig holds court, telling long but admittedly funny stories about how he squeaked through last semester by sucking up to his professors—I assume not literally, but can't be too sure. He would have failed two out of five classes, but visits to the teachers' offices with sob stories and hastily pulled-together make-up work bought their sympathy and took him to a C+ average. He's charming, I'll give him that. It's just that charm is about one step away from phoniness, and phoniness makes me sick. Unless I'm the one employing it, naturally.

After we finish dinner, we're walking past the bar when Craig hears the tail end of "Right Back Where We Started From" by Maxine Nightingale. "I love this song!" he shouts and reaches around Michelle to grab my hand. He pulls me close and starts doing his moves while I try to look like I have even the slightest sense of rhythm. The song is a Supremes rip-off, which makes it even more awkward. It ends quickly, though, and Natalie Cole's "Inseparable" starts. Craig puts his arm around my waist and pulls me close. "It's so wonderful to know you'll always be around," he sings along, locking eyes with me, damn him. Now *I'm* probably going to be gay! I peek over at the sidelines to see Mark and Michelle standing there. He looks despondent, she pissed off. Luckily it's also a short song so I don't have to be resented for long. And I have to admit, it feels good to be held, even by Craig. Life is so damn complicated.

Michelle and I compress ourselves into the back of the Fiat again and our merry band returns to the dorm. As we're going up the elevator, Mark shoots me a desperate look. I turn to Michelle and ask her to give me a tour of the building. It's massive, so that ought to kill some time. The doors open on Craig's floor, and I ask her, "Isn't there a student lounge somewhere?"

"Yeah," she admits grudgingly as Mark and Craig get off the elevator and I stay on. She looks after them, but neither of them says anything so she follows me back on and presses 2 a little harder than is necessary. The doors close on Mark heading to his destiny and, yet again, I feel nauseous.

I manage to stretch the tour into more than a half-hour, but ultimately we have to head back. I knock loudly on Craig's door and Beanpole answers. This throws me, since I had forgotten he existed just as I'd forgotten his name. Michelle and I go into the room, where Craig is on the phone and Mark is sitting on the bed looking like a zombie. It's almost 11:00 o'clock and he obviously hasn't made any progress. Now what? Where are we going to sleep and when is Mark going to confess his love and how will we all survive whatever happens then?

Beanpole has made himself scarce on his side of the divider, but the other three of us wait for Craig to hang up. He takes his sweet time, stretching languidly as he discusses people I've never heard of and makes plans for the weekend. I hope Mark grasps the ramifications; he's staring straight ahead and doesn't seem to realize I'm even here. But if Craig's making plans that don't include us, that doesn't exactly validate our decision to come up here, or to stay past tomorrow.

By the time Craig finally hangs up, I've thought up a brilliant plan. I don't even run it by anyone, since that would entail an awkward "Can I speak to you privately?"-type situation. I just blurt it out: "Hey, how about if I sleep in Michelle's room and Mark stays here?"

Craig glances over at Mark, who looks startled. I'm sorry I caught him off guard, but he must see that this is the only way he'll have any time alone with Craig. "Sure, whatever works," Craig says with a shrug. "There sure isn't enough room for everyone in here."

Michelle has looked pissed off all night, but that was just a warm-up for her current expression. She glares at me. I can just imagine my mother saying about her: "She'd better watch out or her face will stick like that." She's got real atty-tude, as Mark would call it, and it's as plain as the scowl lines at the top of her nose. I bet she and her mother get mistaken for sisters, but not in a way that's flattering to either of them. Craig picks up the phone again and dials while he says, without even looking at her, "OK with you, Michelle?"

Trapped like a rat, Michelle has no choice but to pretend I'm her new best friend. I give Mark's shoulder a little squeeze, grab my suitcase and head for the door. I can't bring myself to look back.

* * *

It's not one of my better nights. Michelle's roommate is even Jappier than she is and their place looks like a bordello. They've added a bunch of floor lamps and draped what look like flammable scarves over them. The beds have animal-print linens and enough throw pillows to make Patrick's mother jealous. Michelle gives me some towels and one itchy blanket to use as a bed on the floor. Good thing I learned to sleep without a pillow. I manage to make a little Craig-oriented chit chat—after all, I've known him longer than Michelle has, so as much as she may despise me, she does take the opportunity to do some brain-picking. I tell her as little as possible and ask her if I can take a shower. It means repurposing some of my "bed," but it's worth it to get the stench of today off me and remove myself from her presence.

I brush my teeth, then stand under the hot water until my fingers go pruny. When I finally emerge from the bathroom in my flannel nightgown, the lights are out. I stumble to my remaining towels and wrap up in the itchy blanket. It's like lying on a slab in the morgue, but still beats pressing up against Michelle in her leopard-print twin bed. My discomfort, combined with my earlier nap and the repetitive mental challenge of trying not to think about what's going on two flights up, keeps me wide-eyed until well after 2:00 a.m.

The next morning the sound of knocking wakes me up. I come to unsure of where I am but as soon as I try to move, my stiffness clears it all up: I just spent the night in the room of someone I don't like who isn't even a guy. Michelle and her roommate are obviously gone. My contacts are nailed to my dry eyes and I try blinking to stave off permanent blindness. More knocking. I get to my feet and, holding the wall, make my way to the door. "Who's there?" I ask. I don't know anyone in the dorm, so I'm hoping I won't have to open up and show off my morning hangover face. And I slept on wet hair, all the more reason to keep the door closed tight.

"It's Mark." Mark! I throw open the door. He's alone.

"What time is it?" I ask.

"Eleven."

"You're kidding! I can't believe it." Suddenly it all comes back to me. "What happened last night?" Mark comes in and closes the door. "Did you tell him?"

"No," he says. "I didn't get a chance. His roommate was there. And he never stopped talking. He even talks in his sleep!"

"Figures," I say, moving toward the window. I open the Venetian blinds and let in some gray light, even though I'm sure it's not doing me any favors. "So now what?"

"I don't know, but I'm starving," Mark says. "Do you know where we can get some food?"

"Well, there's no cafeteria in this building," I tell him. "Believe me, I had the full tour last night. The only food around is in those vending machines downstairs."

"I can't eat that crap anymore," Mark says. "Why don't you get dressed and we'll go out and find a restaurant? I got the feeling from Craig that he'll be gone all day. But at least he gave me a key."

"Does he have classes?"

"Who the hell knows? I don't know if he's avoiding me or if his life is really that busy, but I can't even get him to have a real conversation. You didn't say anything to him, did you?"

"What? Of course not! I can't believe you'd even ask me that." What does he think, I have a big mouth or something?

"Sorry, I just don't know what's changed. I thought I had everything all figured out but nothing is the way I expected it to be. And I'm so hungry that I can't even think straight."

This is like a nightmare. "All right, give me a minute and I'll pee and get dressed. But I need to take my suitcase back up to Craig's because if I leave it here I can't get back in. Not that I want to. God, I hate that bitch!"

"I know, she's so tie-ud," Mark says, imitating Michelle's accent perfectly. Hell, his parents grew up in the Bronx and they don't sound like that. Does she have any idea how awful her voice is?

I dress in the same basic outfit I wore yesterday since it's the warmest thing I brought and who cares what I look like anyway. I don't even bother putting on makeup, other than mascara. When I ran away from home in high school I took a twenty-dollar bill and mascara—it's the fourth necessity: water, air, money and Maybelline Great Lash. I dump my suitcase back in Craig's room and head out with Mark. Damn, it's cold! I don't care how babushka-like I look, I wrap a scarf around my head and face. Mark's looking all macho with his overcoat and no scarf or hat, but he won't last long in these temperatures. We stand in front of the dorm and look around. No restaurant in sight. "Should we drive somewhere?" I ask.

"Do you know where anything is?"

"Of course not! Do you?"

"Hell, no," he says.

"Well, I don't want to get lost in this godforsaken place. Once we start driving we may never find our way back." I have my car key, but frankly I'm afraid it might snap off in the lock from the sub-zero temperatures.

"Are you kidding? You can probably see this tower for miles around," he points out.

"OK, so you want to drive around and look for something?" I ask.

"Well, we have such a great parking space…"

"Jesus Christ! Make up your mind!" I try to wrap my scarf more tightly around my face. "Are we going anywhere or not? It's freezing out here!"

"I thought there'd be some place nearby," he says, looking panicky. "I don't want to drive around aimlessly. Craig could be back any minute."

"Screw it, we're going to live out of vending machines." I stalk back inside with Mark right behind. We pass the security guard like he's seen us a thousand times and take the elevator to the second floor where we stock up on pretzels, chips, cookies and sugar-laced drinks. We carry our armfuls of junk food up to the twelfth floor and start devouring them. Mark switches on the TV to drown out "50 Ways to Leave Your Lover" coming from down the hall. There are soap operas on all three channels, none of them "All My Children," and each understated compared to the drama we're living.

Hours pass. We each doze off at different points. I'm lying on the floor, this time with a pillow, trying to read <u>Kurt Vonnegut's *Breakfast of Champions*</u>, but it's not making much sense so I close my eyes. When I wake up, I see Craig getting something off his dresser. Some skeavy-looking guy is licking his ear and grabbing his crotch. I start to sit up and open my mouth to speak, but Craig puts a finger to his lips and the two of them tiptoe out of the room. I get up and look over to find Mark lying upside down on the bed with his head hanging off the edge and his mouth open. I quickly look away so if he wakes up he won't know I've seen him that way. He'd be horrified. I lie back down. What the hell was that, Craig tricking with some neighbor? It's so damn hot in here, I think I may be delirious. I pass out again.

Around 6:00 o'clock Mark and I are both awake at the same time. It's dark out; the whole day is shot. I haven't wasted time like this since I was a kid whining about having nothing to do. This is insane. I want to throw Mark against a wall and beat some sense into him. "Wake up, man!" I want to yell. "Get out and don't look back!" Instead, with his fragile state, I ask, "What do you want to do?"

He gets to his feet and looks outside. "Shit, what time is it?"

"Around 6:00."

"Any sign of Craig?"

"I think he passed through at some point, but I might have been dreaming." No way am I telling him what I saw. Things are bad enough already.

Mark runs his fingers through his hair and tilts his chin back, considering. He looks at me. "It's not going to happen, is it."

"I don't know what the hell is going on here. Seriously. This whole experience is surreal."

"It is, isn't it?" We reflect on the surrealness of it all. The insane temperatures. The endless waiting around. The hideous buildings. The even more hideous Michelle. Craig and his depravity. Surely Mark will have to acknowledge this has all been a terrible mistake, that Craig couldn't care less about him.

He lets out a long sigh. I've never heard a death rattle, but this has to be what it sounds like: the end of everything, condensed into a single, carbon dioxide-laden groan that leaves nothing behind.

Finally he says those magic words: "Let's get the hell out of here." I get up and grab my suitcase and coat.

"Whatever you want," I say.

16
LEAVE ME AS YOU FOUND ME,
EMPTY LIKE BEFORE

It's starting to snow as we exit the dorm. This time the cold feels bracing, tastes like freedom and making the right choices. I unlock my trunk and we put our bags in. There are already snowflakes on them as I close it up. When they melt, whether tonight, tomorrow or in the spring thaw, it will be the last trace of Syracuse that I ever have in my life. Like Scarlett O'Hara swearing she'll never go hungry again, I swear I'll never come back here, never go through anything like this again.

I turn on the car and let it warm up. Mark fiddles with the radio and <u>David Ruffin's "Walk Away From Love"</u> comes on, right at the beginning where he says he's leaving, walking away from love before it breaks his heart. Jesus, you couldn't ask for a clearer sign than that: Walk away! Better yet, drive away! We just sit there listening to the song play and the engine rev. Mark leans his head against the door. I know this has to be agony for him. If anything, he's in worse shape now than he was before, and he was a mess before. That fucking Craig. He's lucky I'm not armed. How dare he treat people like they're disposable? He has to know we didn't just show up to say hi, and he chose to leave Mark hanging. His assholishness has attained a level I'm sure no one else I ever meet will be able to equal.

The song ends and a commercial comes on. I switch off the radio. Mark turns to me. "I can't go home," he says, pleadingly.

"What? Where do you want to go?" It had better be south, I think. The only thing north is Santa's workshop.

"I want to see Sophia, at Skidmore," he says. There's a catch in his throat. Oh God, please don't let him cry. I'll take him wherever he wants to go, just please, no crying. I can't stand to see him so miserable.

"Where's Skidmore?" I ask.

"I don't think it's far," he says. "I'm sure we can make it tonight." He opens the car door. "I'm going to call her and let her know we're coming. I'll get directions." He jumps out and jogs back to the dorm. Shit. Is there no end to this hell? I'm trying to be a good friend! Does he need a *better* friend, an older friend, a friend he doesn't have to worry is going to try to jump his bones? After everything we've been through, is she still his best friend? Why aren't I enough for him?

I look out the window and see Craig about to walk past the car in a coat that looks like a down comforter and checked scarf. I leap out and confront him. "Where the hell have you been?" I demand, pushing him in his chest as hard as I can. God, I wish I could knock him over and jump up and down on him until he's flattened like a worm on a highway!

"Hey, stop it! What's wrong? What are you doing?" He tries to fend me off but in his big puffy coat he doesn't have full movement of his arms.

"We're leaving, you jerk!" I push him again. Snow is coming down hard now. I should be freezing but my fiery rage keeps me heated.

"What the hell did I do?"

"You ignored us! You avoided us! You screwed us over, just like you screw everyone—in the ass!" I yell. A couple of people look our way. OK, that was a little over the top, but I don't care. I'm never showing my face around here again anyway. And Craig can consider it free advertising.

"You're crazy!" he yells back, probably for the audience since he knows damn well I'm a hell of a lot saner than he is. "I had to go to class!"

"Liar! I saw you with your little trick! You treated us like shit and you broke Mark's heart." Oops, how'd I let that slip out?

"What the hell are you talking about? I didn't ask you to come here!"

"You're right, you didn't. Thanks for the hospitality! We'll be going now! Have a nice life!"

Furiously I turn my back and return to the car, slamming the door. Have a nice life? Thanks for the hospitality? I sure hope he recognizes sarcasm when he hears it! I'm about to get out of the car to hammer home my point when Mark comes out of the dorm and runs right into Craig. I can see them talking as snow falls on them, but I can't hear what they're saying. Craig's pointing at the car, probably telling Mark to watch out for my psycho mood swings. I'd put down the passenger window to eavesdrop but the damn thing hasn't worked for months.

I turn on the radio and encounter <u>"Fanny (Be Tender With My Love)" by the Bee Gees</u>, an arrow hitting the bullseye of the current situation: you don't want my love, but if you do take it, you'd better be tender with it because I'm easily hurt. Who the hell is programming tonight? It's like they're sending special gay messages directly to Mark. They might as well be singing, "Be tender with my fanny!" I can't let him hear this. Combined with "Walk Away from Love," it just might kill him.

I turn off the radio and look out the window. They're still talking. Will Mark get up the nerve to declare his love? Will I have to unload the car and be stuck here another hellish night? Jesus, I pray Craig doesn't tell Mark I said he broke his heart. What the hell is wrong with me? Wait, what the hell is wrong with Craig, making me think there's something wrong with me? He's the bad guy here! That son of a bitch. I open the door and start to get out. The phrase "loaded for bear" pops into my head. Craig looks my way, yells goodbye to Mark and takes off into the dorm. I get back in the driver's seat.

Mark gets into the car and closes his door and says, "What the hell did you say to him? He said you totally lost it. I think you freaked him out!"

"Good! Fuck him!" I say—it's an insult, not a suggestion. "Let's get out of here. Where are we going?"

"There was no answer at Sophia's. But I got directions from the girl at the desk. It's about 150 miles, so if we go over sixty the whole way we'll be there by nine."

Mark asked a stranger for directions! My little boy is growing up. But the concept of schlepping to yet another college where we know only one person and haven't been invited is sickening. Now it's my turn to give a death rattle; with great restraint I swallow it. "Fine. Which way?"

"You want to get on the 81. Go up to Van Buren and take a left."

I put the car in gear and start to drive. Neither one of us touches the radio. Barely a word is spoken, other than directions, for almost an hour as we decompress in snowy silence.

* * *

Right around Utica, the vending machine lunch wears off and we decide to stop at a House of Pancakes. I discovered the tuna melt on rye at an IHOP last year and it is officially my favorite food. I order one and Mark gets a burger. Our feelings are stormy, swerving crazily in a thousand directions. We're not through this thing yet. It's too soon even to be shell-shocked, but I'm looking forward to the day. That will mean it's all over except the permanent psychological damage.

It feels like we're in the middle of a war, like we just survived combat and have fresh memories of live ammo whizzing past our ears. Normal life feels, well, lifeless. We're surrounded by civilians, people with no understanding of what it's like to bond on the battlefield or face down an enemy and emerge injured but not destroyed. Lucky bastards. Their lives are so simple compared to ours.

When we get back to the car, I ask Mark if he'll drive, but he just looks at me like he's still the walking wounded. Fine, I'll keep going. I get back on I-90 and get the speed up to what feels like 70 but could be 80 or 90. We're ready for a little music but there aren't any stations. Mark's turning the dial when he notices that the heat isn't coming out like it had been. It used to be blasting, and now it's barely whispering. He tries turning it up, but it just gets weaker and soon we're seeing our breath when we exhale. I get off at the next exit and we pull into a service station that unfortunately is closed. I open the hood and Mark and I peer at the car's innards. He turns to me. "Who are we kidding?" he asks.

Shit. I could check the oil, but that's about the extent of my knowledge. The snow is still coming down and it's around zero degrees. Skidmore must be at least an hour away. What the hell do we do now? Mark looks around and spots a payphone. "I'll call Sophia," he says, trotting toward it. Great. Who is she, Glinda the Good Witch or something? How can she help us? I have to admit, I'm getting pretty damn good at holding my tongue. So why doesn't that give me any sense of satisfaction?

The Cusp of Everything

I bang down the hood and open the trunk. There are still Syracuse snowflakes on my suitcase, and more joining them every second from wherever the hell we are now. I brush off the snow, open my bag and take out another sweater. I've been driving in just one, but now I get back in the car and add on a second, plus my coat and gloves. Mark returns, shivering, as I'm wrapping my scarf around my head. I want everything covered except my eyes for seeing and my mouth for bitching and smoking.

"Still no answer," Mark reports. "I even called her mother in Mamaroneck. No one's around."

He must be out of his mind. Why call them? They can't help us! We're on our own. At least we have our driver's licenses. Whoever comes across our frozen bodies will be able to contact our next of kin, and that's not "best friend" Sophia or her mother.

I share none of this, however. Instead I tell Mark, "I got an extra sweater out of the trunk. Do you want to get anything? If we're going to drive without heat, you're going to have to dress more warmly than that." I hold out the key. Mutely he takes it and heads toward the trunk. He comes back with a sweater, sport coat and scarf, hands me the key and starts throwing on the layers. I turn on the car and get back on the Thruway. After awhile Mark says, "Route 30! That's our exit! You want to go north."

North? Oh, no I don't! Damn it! I should have known this would get worse before it got better. North! And on some kind of a country road no less. We're going about thirty mph, half the sixty we need to keep to our schedule, and with the road conditions we'll probably have to slow down even more. We lost almost an hour at IHOP but I've been hoping we can still make it by 10:00. Forget that.

This road hasn't been plowed and it's icy. I'm sliding all over the place on my bald retreads. If only I'd kept the studded snow tires that were on the car when I first bought it. I'm so cold I'm starting to shake and even under optimal road conditions I wouldn't be able to hold the wheel steady. I'm just about to ask Mark to drive when I go into a skid and slide right off the side of the road into a snowbank. I rev the engine but the car won't move. I throw it into reverse. Nothing. I start to cry. "We're going to die!" I wail.

Mark reaches over and puts the car in Park. He touches my shoulder. "We're going to be fine," he says shakily. I know he doesn't believe it, and he's not convincing me either. I cry louder.

"My tears are going to freeze!" I moan melodramatically, my

teeth chattering. Even if this were true, it would be the least of our problems. I just can't think of anything else to say. I've crossed some line and I'm done with his misery. I care only about myself now and I know something's seriously wrong. Frozen tears are my code for what I really want to say: "Save me! I don't want to die here!" Oh, and with a dash of "It's time for *you* to take care of *me* now!"

Mark can't get his door open because it's up against a snowbank, and he can't climb out the window because it doesn't work. After a few claustrophobic seconds during which I am of no use at all, he climbs over the seat and gets out on the driver's side. He opens my door and, reaching in, turns off the headlights and the ignition. He half-lifts, half-drags me out, grabbing my purse as well. I'm still crying. I already hated my life. Who'd have thought it could get worse? Why oh why did we have to take this disaster on the road? If I live through this, I seriously have to question everything about myself: my ability to see the world clearly, my ability to make intelligent decisions, my ability to choose friends and boyfriends and lovers and the right clothes for a winter outing...Waah!

Mark puts his arm around me and turns me gently. "Look!" he says. "A house. We'll go ask them for help. You can warm up inside. It'll be fine."

The house looks like a glorified trailer but at least the lights are on. I'm shaking like I have palsy, from my teeth to my toes. I can't talk. I can't feel my butt. Mark guides me through the snow to the house with his arm around me and rings the doorbell. A grandmotherly woman answers and Mark explains that we're stuck in a snowbank in her front yard and his friend here can't seem to stop shaking because we didn't have any heat in the car, and...

"Come in!" she says, reaching for his arm. "No heat! That's dangerous. What's your name, honey?"

"I'm Mark, and this is Karen."

She looks at me. I can't stand up straight, my head is tilted to the side and I'm still twitching and shaking. I've never been so cold. Even inside the house I feel enveloped in my own weather system: it's still snowing, but just on me. I say nothing as she takes my elbow and pulls me toward a wall heater. "Honey, I'm Mildred. We're going to take care of you." She stands there with me, still holding my elbow. I should probably feel heat—otherwise what are we doing here?—but I don't. I just hear "The Waltons" playing on her TV across the room.

"Here, come stand with her. I'm going to make a call." She

passes my elbow off to Mark and leaves the room. We hear water running, then her voice, presumably talking on the phone. "snowbank...no heat...hypothermia...truck." A sound like a kettle whistling. Soon she comes back with two mugs of tea. I can't bend my fingers to hold a handle. Mark takes one mug and tries to get me to drink. He knows I hate tea. I hold my lips together tightly, like he did when he was afraid I might kiss him. I'm not drinking that. But then I am. It's hot and utterly flavorless, or maybe my tastebuds froze off. I feel the heat spreading through my body. Before long I feel heat coming out of the wall. I can bend my fingers a little, although I doubt I could hold anything. My teeth are still chattering as I wheeze, "Thank you." I'm coming back from my near-death experience.

There's a knock and Mildred opens a door that goes to the garage. She lets in a man in his 40s. "Hi, Harry. Thanks for coming. This is Mark." She motions him over, leaving me standing by myself, pressed up against the wall heater. "Mark, tell Harry what happened."

Mark describes how we lost heat gradually, then slid off the road. Harry nods sagely and says, "Let's go take a look. Are the keys still in her?"

Mark nods. "I figured nobody was going to steal it."

They head outside. After a few more minutes I feel almost back to normal and I walk over to Mildred's picture window just in time to see Mark make a vertical leap the height of the car onto the snowbank as the boat is pulled back onto the road. What was that move? Now Harry has the hood open. Mark's hugging himself and jumping around, and I guess Harry tells him to get inside because he comes jogging back toward the house. He opens the storm door and Mildred meets him, opening the front door.

"Everything all right?" she asks.

"He got it back on the road in about thirty seconds," Mark reports. What a lifesaver! Thank you so much! Now he's trying to figure out what happened with the heater. He thinks there must be a leak." Of course! We probably trailed fluid all the way from Syracuse to here—and by the way, where's here? I ask Mildred.

"You're in Amsterdam, honey," she says.

"Amsterdam? Is that in New York?" I ask. For a moment I think we must have traveled through to another, European, dimension, and I wonder briefly why everyone is speaking English.

She laughs. "Of course! Now come and sit down." I sit on her chintz couch. Amsterdam, New York. Who knew? She picks up my mug from the coffee table and heads back toward the kitchen to get me a refill.

"Did I just see you do some kind of Superman leap?" I ask Mark.

"Did you see that? I wasn't even going to tell you because I knew you wouldn't believe me."

"You're right about that. I saw it and I still don't believe it. What happened?

"I was standing behind the car, between the car and the tow truck. When the truck started to move, I had maybe a split second to get out of the way. Somehow I just took off and cleared the car before it ran me over. I couldn't do it again in a million years." I shake my head. Another near-death experience survived. That's a good sign, right?

Harry comes in through the door from the garage. Shaking off snow he says to Mark, "Yup, you've got a leak, and it looks like your water pump is shot. I'm going to give you some coolant and some antifreeze, and you're going to have to stop every ten miles or so to replenish her fluids. I'll show you where they go." Mark looks over at me with fear in his eyes. I think the combination of "her" and "fluids" has paralyzed him.

"I'd like to see, too." I say. "It's my car."

"Oh, sure," says Harry, seemingly thrown by this fact. "Well, come on out."

"She's not ready to go back out," Mildred says as she enters the room with my mug.

"I'm fine," I say. "I can't thank you enough for taking care of us. Honestly, I think you might have saved my life."

"Oh, honey, you just needed to warm up." She hands me the mug and I sip the tea. I can now taste it and I try not to let on how disgusting I think it is. "Where are you kids headed?"

"Skidmore," Mark and I both say simultaneously.

"Oh, Skidmore. That's only about 25 miles from here. You'll be there in about an hour." An hour to go 25 miles? Jesus! We should have just taken a bus to Syracuse and back. Wait, what am I thinking? We shouldn't have made this doomed trip at all!

"We're ready to go," I say. "Thank you again." I feel choked up. What would I have done without her? She let two strangers into her house! Doesn't she watch the news? I give her a hug and she pats my back. I blink tears from my eyes.

"I'm going to give you a phone number to call tomorrow," Harry says. "Frank's a friend of mine. He's got a service station in Saratoga Springs and he'll fix you right up. Tell him I sent you." He scrawls on a scrap of paper and hands it to Mark, who thanks him. Mark's not much of a hugger, and I'm sure Harry isn't either, but I hope he knows how grateful we are.

"How much do I owe you?" I ask. Those fluids aren't cheap and I'm dreading his answer.

"Oh, twenty bucks ought to do it," Harry says. "The tow's on me." Too bad for him if he's not a hugger. Neither am I but I'm hugging him anyway. I pull a twenty from my wallet and hand it over. If he'd said forty...well, if he'd said forty I it would practically wipe me out, but I wouldn't think he was ripping me off, either. Mark offers me money but I wave him off. I got off cheap and I know he's a strapped for cash as I am.

"Come on out through the garage, you two," Mildred says. As we're walking out the door and down the few steps into the garage, I turn to thank her again, trip and take a tumble right into a giant box sitting next to the stairs. I'm trapped, with my legs sticking up and my head out of sight. What a klutz! Mark rushes over and looks in, his face contorted with suppressed hysteria. I peer up at him quizzically and he explodes with laughter. He reaches to take my hand but he's laughing so hard he doesn't have the strength to pull me out. Mildred comes down the stairs.

"Oh dear! Are you all right? I've been meaning to get this box out of here for weeks but it just keeps snowing. That's my new dryer!" she says proudly. For some reason this sets Mark off anew. Seeing me in a dryer delivery box has cheered him right up. Goodbye angst, hello joy at the expense of another's pain!

"Would you get me out of here?" I snarl. Still laughing, Mark dumps the box over on its side so I'm lying on the garage floor folded in half with my feet over my head. He goes around to the bottom and lifts it so I slide out. Yes, he's still laughing. I am outraged. Sore and humiliated and outraged. I refuse to look at him as I head out to get my lesson in fluids from Harry. Mark's going to drive now, that's for damn sure. As soon as he can stop laughing.

* * *

Despite stopping every five miles to replenish the car's fluids, the heat never comes back on and before long I'm shaking again. I can't talk and I can't cry. Mark has to figure out the directions on his own and I can tell he's trying not to freak out. I can't help him anymore. I'm starting to think I'll never get home, never live to fight with my mother again. It's hard to admit she was right about this trip. The first thing I'll do when I get to a phone is call her and tell her. I don't know why, but I feel an intense need to talk to her. She'd never understand what I've been through on this trip—hell, I'm not sure I will either— but I still need to let her know I'm OK. Maybe I'm just thinking about her so much because my life is passing before my eyes. Maybe this is it for me and my pathetic existence.

Mark manages to get us to Saratoga Springs and Sophia's dorm. He parks by a hydrant, rushes around to my side of the car and somehow drags me inside. He asks at the reception desk where her room is and heads that way, supporting me. It seems to me that he should take me to a hospital, but he doesn't suggest it and I still can't talk. It's like that nightmare I had as a kid when the mean dachshunds Mom left me with started to attack me and I tried to scream but nothing came out. Crap, this really *could* be my life passing before my eyes. I haven't thought about that dream in years.

Mark knocks on a door but no one answers. Is she even back from vacation, I want to ask? Why did that never occur to me before? If I had use of my extremities, I'd tie a string around my finger to remind myself to strangle him later for not thinking things through, the theme of this misadventure. If either one of us had a fully functioning brain, we'd be sitting in Cook's right now making fun of people and writing godawful lyrics.

I'm feeling nostalgic for Cook's? Please, someone call a doctor!

There's a lobby area on Sophia's floor and Mark deposits me in a big chair where I sit quaking. He sits on the ottoman and rubs my arms and shoulders, trying to get blood flowing. After a little while, it starts to work. I'm still shaking but I can rub my own arms, and my legs, too. I'm going to live! I grab Mark's hand. "I think I'm going to be OK," I gasp, twitching.

"Oh, thank God," Mark says, practically collapsing onto the floor. "You scared the shit out of me."

"You know, the hospital might have been a good idea," I rasp. "Just for future reference."

"If you didn't stop shaking I was going to," he tells me.

"Mark?" A group of girls is walking across the lobby. Sophia pulls away from them and rushes over to Mark. Her dark beauty once made me jealous, but now it's reassuringly irrelevant. "What are you doing here?"

I smile at her and sit up slightly. I still feel tingly.

"We just came from Syracuse," Mark tells her, not introducing me. I guess it's pretty obvious who I am.

"Oh!" she says, grasping the implication.

"Hey," he continues. "I parked by a hydrant and our bags are still in the car. Is it OK if we stay over? Karen's car is just about dead and we have to take it in tomorrow." He doesn't mention that I was almost dead, too, but I suppose I'm over needing attention. I'm just glad to be alive.

"Sure. There's a guest room for visitors. Come with me and we'll move the car and get you a key."

God, I want to be her. She's so much nicer than I am. So calm and competent. I have to change my whole demeanor to be more like her. One more thing to add to the list of major life changes I need to get started on.

"Is there a phone I can use?" I ask. "I need to call my mother. I'll call collect." I stand up, wobbly but alive.

"Don't be silly," Sophia says. "Here, come to my room." She opens the unlocked door and lets me in. Now this is a dorm room! No piles of laundry, no unmade bed, no creepily mysterious roommate, no bordello lamps. Just a neat and homey space for two. "I'm going to go help Mark. Make yourself at home. It's nice to finally meet you."

"I'm so glad to meet you too," I tell her. "I can't thank you enough."

"Don't worry about it. You guys look like you've been through a lot."

I roll my eyes and reach for the phone.

* * *

Mom sounds so happy to hear my voice that I start to cry. I tell her we had a fight with Craig and decided to drive across upstate New York in a snowstorm in a nine-year-old car with no heat and bald tires. I make sure to tell her I had hypothermia because it sounds so medical. The more I describe our road trip, the stupider I feel. What the hell were we thinking? We put our lives in jeopardy to spend time with an arrogant creep who didn't even want us there.

The Cusp of Everything

To her credit, Mom doesn't criticize my series of terrible decisions. Instead, she tells me she had a feeling something was wrong and was desperate to hear from me. Shades of Gwen's mom and her maternal ESP! She asks about getting the car fixed so we can get home. I tell her I'm sure it's going to be at least $100 and I'm down to about $22.

"When you get to the repair place, give the man my number," she says. "Hopefully he can take a credit card over the phone. If not, I can send you money through Western Union. And don't worry about paying me back. I'm just glad you're OK." I cry a little more. I can't believe she's there for me this way. I'm so touched and relieved that I call her "Mommy" as I hang up. I have to admit she's not so bad. She still annoys the crap out of me most of the time, though.

Mark and I sleep in the dorm's nondescript guest room. I crash as soon as we get in there, but he stays up almost all night talking things through with Sophia. I wake up Friday morning refreshed from, among other things, not having heard Craig's name for twelve hours.

Sophia's classes haven't started yet so she's free to go with us to Frank's car repair place that morning. I have never felt such intense gratitude as I feel for her, for Mom, for Mildred and Harry and especially for Mark. Despite laughing at my mortifying fall and not calling an ambulance, he really stepped up and took care of me. Just a day ago I saw the world as filled with selfish assholes, but now I think it's possible they're the exceptions rather than the rule.

The car is fixed by 5:00 o'clock. As anticipated, it costs about $100, plus I buy a couple of new tires after Frank said the ones I had wouldn't get us farther than Albany. Since I didn't even know we were near Albany, I decide to throw a map on Mom's tab. Never again do I want to feel as helpless and lost as I did yesterday, when I wasn't even sure what continent I was on.

Mark and I decide to stay one more night so we don't have to drive in the dark. It's quiet in the dorm, with winter break not over until Monday. We hang out with a group of great girls, the kind I used to read about in Nancy Drew books: smart, funny, self-confident. I'm comfortable with them, although I do feel like the outsider I am. I don't think I'll ever be part of such a together team, always just one of a ragtag group of incompatible friends. We futz around and listen to records; I particularly like one by Henry Gross, with a great logo: the two s's of his last name dripping all the way down the front of the yellow album cover. I can't get his song "Simone" out of my head.

The Cusp of Everything

Saturday morning Mark and I say our goodbyes and get ready to head for home. Sophia tells us she's sorry to see our pity party come to an end, but I think she's relieved not to see have to deal with our drama anymore. I let the boat warm up to make sure the heat works, then head to the Thruway and south at last. I had no idea New York was so big. People from the city call Westchester "upstate," but they have no idea. I had no idea. There's a lot up here. A lot I'll never need to see again.

Mark and I haven't spoken about Craig since leaving Syracuse. Sophia took over as his sympathetic ear once we arrived, and I can't say I've missed the extended rehash of a visit that defines the notion of unfulfilled fantasies. As we drive, we chat superficially, to a static-y version of Labelle's "Lady Marmalade," about the weather, road conditions, arrival time, second-semester classes, anything but the elephant in the boat. I don't think he could handle my blunt analysis of Craig's miserable treatment of him. He doesn't ask for my insights, and I don't volunteer them. It's a quiet drive, toasty and anticlimactic. Mark seems calm, if numb.

Past Albany, we're driving through a grove of snow-covered trees listening to "My Little Town," and talking hopefully about getting away from our own towns and into the city soon. The signal fades out again. Mark starts looking for something new but turns up only static, from 88 to 108 on the dial. He turns off the radio.

"We're back in no man's land," I comment.

"Yeah, there's nothing," he replies. We drive in silence for awhile. Suddenly he reaches over and switches the radio back on, like he just got one of his psychic deejay messages. There's still static, but he starts turning the dial and is rewarded when a note breaks through the white noise. He hones in on it: some sort of dentist's office music, all overwrought string and horns. He sticks with it. I'm about to tell him I'd rather listen to nothing than that crap when I realize: the song is a Muzak version of "Touch Me in the Morning." I look over and he's contorted up against the door, face turned out the window. Mentally, i provide the lyrics. Right when I get to "leave me as you found me, empty like before," the static overtakes the music. Mark doesn't move. I reach over, turn off the radio and continue south.

17
SHAME, SHAME, SHAME

Winter break ended about a month ago and my life is pretty much back to the way it used to be: on-campus anonymity and seeing Mark whenever I'm not working. Mom and I aren't fighting as much, but otherwise it almost feels like Syracuse never happened. I'm not quite over Mark, but I've figured out how to suppress any real yearnings so I can keep him in my life. It's not optimal, but it will have to do.

I'm taking Abnormal Psych this semester, and man is it hitting home. I am questioning who gets to define "abnormal." Society wants to be able to predict how people will act and react, and if they don't meet expectations they're considered abnormal. Do my bouts of depression put me in that category? My severe procrastination or sluttiness? Craig and Mark's gayness? Where do we draw the line? And who gets to make those decisions? It's my favorite class and should come in handy in my writing, not to mention understanding what the hell happened between the twisted trio that is me, Mark and Craig.

I'm not over Mark and Mark isn't over Craig but we both know we should be and that's a start. My feelings are almost completely sublimated and at least he's not going on and on about Craig anymore. Mark and I drove out to see the Supremes (Scherrie, Mary and Cindy edition) at a club called Jupiter's on Long Island at the end of January. I'd had all four of my wisdom teeth out a couple of days earlier and despite painkillers I was in agony the whole time. Not to mention I looked like an unhappy chipmunk hoarding rotten nuts. Mark was very solicitous and even date-like—right up until I slipped on some ice the way back to his car and he had to grab me before I fell on my ass. I almost started crying at how pathetic I was. Gone, my kind and caring pseudo-boyfriend, replaced by a sadistic fan of slapstick pratfalls. He threw in a chipmunk comment at that point too, and of course a reference to my fall into Mildred's dryer box. He laughed so hard he almost wiped out on the ice too.

Valentine's Day passed last week without the slightest acknowledgement on either of our parts. We're getting back to normal—whatever that is! Maybe it's just the absence of all those things that define abnormality.

When the Syracuse trip comes up—as it still does—Mark starts to wallow again, reliving how Craig ignored him and what a loser the whole trip made him feel like. I try to move the focus to non-tragic elements, like his leap over tall snowdrifts in a single bound and the sainted Sophia. We listen to records together and I turn him on to a great Harold Melvin & The Blue Notes song, "I'm Searching for a Love." The lead singer is Sharon Paige instead of Teddy Pendergrass and it doesn't sound like anything else on the Wake Up Everybody album. The message: Search for someone new! Let's move on!

We're spending more time together than ever. This weekend is a good example: Friday evening I visited him at Korvettes. We reshuffled Supremes albums and watched a group of kids dancing to Archie Bell and the Drells' "Let's Groove" while their mothers shopped. We spent Saturday in the city, wandering around and imagining our NYU future. We should hear back from the Admissions Office within a month and the tension is killing us both. That night we watched the Grammy Awards. The Paul Simon album with "50 Ways to Leave Your Lover" on it won for Album of the Year. Hearing that song is jarring.

Sunday we worked on papers together at his house, then went to Cook's. By Monday, after spending almost every waking hour together for three days, we're finally having a break, but in the afternoon he calls, distraught. Florence Ballard has died of a heart attack. I rush over to console him.

"I heard it on the radio as I was driving to Iona to take my English final," he tells me, choking up. I'd been helping him study for it, so I knew how nervous he was even before the Flo news. "I cried all the way to school. She was the underdog! She had fallen so far—a Supreme on welfare! She was crawling back and now this. They'll never be together again." He's seems near tears. I'd go hug him but we're not really huggers. The best I can do is sit and let him talk, get it out of his system. Hopefully it won't take as long as Craig.

"After my final I couldn't stay for the rest of my classes," he continues. "I got in the car and started playing with the radio. I went all the way down to the end of the dial, to stations I never listen to, and I got one, very faint, from North Carolina. They played all eight number one hits that Florence sang on. And each one was more intense than the other, especially when they came to 'Back in My Arms Again,' with 'Flo, she don't know.'" He gasps. "It was devastating. Then I put on other stations and they would say, 'As you know, Florence Ballard of the Supremes passed away.' I cried all the way home."

Mark always held out hope that "Someday We'll Be Together" was an implied promise—even though, as he informed me, neither Mary nor Cindy actually sang on the song. Now a real reunion can never happen. "Mary, Flo and Diana will never get on the same stage," he says despondently.

We walk over to Florence Park, just a few blocks from Mark's house, now forever identified in our minds as Florence Ballard Park. It's freezing, though, so we don't stay long, returning to my graduate school classes on the Supremes. I learn that Florence sang lead on only three Supremes releases: the embarrassing "Buttered Popcorn," "Ain't That Good News," from the extremely minor *We Remember Sam Cooke* album, and something from the even more esoteric *The Supremes Sing Country, Western and Pop*. Her voice is good, but not as unique as Diana. She must not have been as ambitious, either. Naturally I don't share my personal review with Mark.

Up and down the dial are tributes to Flo. I burst into tears at "I Hear a Symphony" and the overwhelming sadness of our lives. I know when the song was released (1965), that it hit number one, that it was written by Motown songwriters Holland-Dozier-Holland. Why don't I know this much about Physics or something useful?

I still can't completely accept that I've absorbed all this Supremes trivia, but I'd rather he talk about that than Craig. Unfortunately, it's not an either-or situation. Flo's death has thrown Mark off track during what had been his Craig ramp-down time and he's back to obsessing. He explains that no one but Craig holds any interest for him, despite his awareness that Craig's a "Player"—an explanation he makes with a song by First Choice underscoring that Craig's a cold-blooded son of a gun—but addictive.

Mark also thinks that maybe too much dependence on each other is unhealthy. To my horror, he tells me, "Remember how you thought I was so together last year? That's because I spent a lot of time by myself." He leaves it hanging in the air so I can draw the inevitable conclusion: he needs his space.

"You know, you call me as much as I call you," I remind him, trying not to sound too defensive or hurt. "I'm not forcing you to be with me every day."

"I'm not saying you are. I just think that not spending any time alone is making me lose touch with myself. I need to regroup. I still can't believe I sat around waiting for him in Syracuse. I need to get my self-respect back." So the reason he spends so much time talking about himself, he says as he continues to talk about himself, is that I'm around too much.

I have walked in on Mark enough to know he used to have a daily ritual of listening to the Supremes and Diana—usually "Ain't No Mountain High Enough"—by standing in front of his stereo and playing the same lines over and over. Maybe he hasn't been able to do it as much lately and he's suffering from the loss of whatever calming effect doing it has on him. Maybe he needs to be alone to play his records in his own weird way, and to get a break from me.

The thought that spending time with me is killing Mark's self-esteem hurts my own. I'm panicked about the idea of seeing him less since I want to share everything with him. But considering we don't go to the same school or live in the same town, that we aren't related or romantically involved, our dependence on each other does seem a little compulsive. If I look at it that way, I have to accept that it's time for us to decouple a bit. That means I'd better get comfortable being by myself, or find someone else to hang out with while he's fixated on Craig and playing those healing Supremes mantras.

Being alone is not my first choice, but who else is there for me? He and Gwen are my two closest friends, despite their being so different from each other. Gwen's attitude is "have a good time and damn the consequences." Mark and I, on the other hand, seem to live by the creed of "have a crappy time and dissect it forever." We philosophize and analyze for hours, going over things that weren't fun to begin with, rarely finding any deeper meaning. There has to be some middle ground, and I guess this enforced freedom is my time to find it.

So who do I reach out to first? Even I don't believe it, but it's

Craig. Not to spend time with him, obviously, since he's still in the hinterlands, but out of guilt. With a month's hindsight, I'm questioning how I handled Syracuse and I think I overreacted to Craig's dismissive attitude toward us. What he said to me on the street has finally sunk in: he didn't invite us up there. We built up our own expectations, but he never knew about them or owed us a specific outcome to our visit. He's unquestionably a dirtbag, but I feel like one too, hitting him and screaming at him in public. How tacky! And to think that *I* might have been out of line! It's almost unbearable.

Without telling Mark, I call Craig several times until I finally reach him. "Craig? It's Karen."

There's a pause. "Karen who?"

"Karen the crappy, uninvited guest. I've been thinking about our visit and I wanted to apologize to you."

"Really! After attacking me and cursing me in the street, you're now admitting you were wrong?"

"I was wrong to get so crazy. I was wrong to blame you for not being available at our beck and call. I'm sorry. We inflicted ourselves on your life and then gave you a hard time for living it."

There is silence on the other end of the phone.

"Craig?"

"I'm here. I'm just trying to figure out how to react. You were one crazy bitch and I didn't expect to talk to you again."

"Oh, you know you're going to forgive me. We've been friends for years and we can't stop now, so let's just cut to the chase."

He chuckles. "All right, what the hell. We all make mistakes."

"That's for damn sure," I agree.

"But I hope you know how lucky you are that I'm taking you back. I'd written you off after that scene."

"I know, I appreciate your forgiveness," I say. Gag. I didn't plan to grovel. I hope I'm not making a terrible mistake.

"So what are you and Mark up to these days?" he asks.

Damn, I don't want Mark's name dragged into this. Can't I just make peace and hang up? "Oh, the same," I say, vaguely.

"Does he miss me?" he asks.

That son of a bitch. "Miss you?" I say innocently.

"Yeah. Didn't you say I broke his heart?"

Damn it, damn it, damn it! After being so careful and supportive, my one slip of the tongue destroys everything! I try to throw him off. "Oh, please. Don't flatter yourself! I also thanked you for your hospitality, so you know I was delirious."

"Karen, don't bullshit a bullshitter. You think I can't tell how Mark feels about me? I knew why you were here—he can't resist me. But he's not my type. I was trying to spare both of you. I'm not a total monster, you know."

I don't know.

"Hello?" he says.

"I'm here. I'm just trying to figure out what the hell happened up there, then. We came all that way! Why didn't you just talk to him? You told me you thought he was hot! Why'd you bring a trick back to the room when you knew he was there?"

"I didn't *want* to talk to him. What would I say? 'Leave me alone'? I like to be admired, not obsessed about."

"So you don't see a future for you and Mark?" Who am I, some kind of twisted matchmaker? "I thought you were crazy about him!" I add.

"Aah, just for a moment. Mark's not my type physically," Craig says. "I like lots of muscles and a giant bulging crotch. And a mouth big enough to fit a Conair 1750.

"Oh my God, you are *disgusting*!" My gag reflex is about to go into overdrive.

"No I'm not. I'm just not looking for love. I'm looking for fun, and dealing with someone who's obsessed with you *and* not your type just isn't fun. I've been there. I know."

I guess I know, too. "But what do I do about Mark?"

"What do you mean, what do *you* do? Why is he your responsibility?"

"He's not, I just don't want to see him in pain. It's been pretty awful."

"Really fell for me, did he?" Craig chuckles a little.

"Please! Only because you led him on! If you didn't like him why'd you tell me you did? You know my big mouth—you must have known I'd say something to him! Was this all just a sick game?" I ask.

"What's wrong with games? Why does everything have to be so serious?" Man, he really doesn't understand how life works. At least I didn't toy with Patrick's emotions on purpose. At least I feel bad I hurt him.

"You're talking about somebody's heart! Do you even have one?"

"Are you seriously asking me that?" Craig asks, sounding more insulted than pained. "You know I have a heart! How was I supposed to know he'd feel like this? No matter what I did, he never let on he was succumbing to my charms, never flirted back." He sighs. "Maybe I went too far. Do you think it would help if I call him?"

"I don't know if it would help or make things worse. I guess it depends on what you say. What would you say?"

Craig sighs. "I don't know, maybe just try to be friends."

I snort derisively. "Yeah, because being friends instead of lovers is always so satisfying." At least there's one aspect of breaking up I'm an expert on.

"Well, you have all the answers, what do you think I should say?" Craig asks.

"I don't think you should call him! If you can't be the person he thinks you are, then what's the point?"

"Who the hell does he think I am? He has to know I'm no choirboy!"

"The entire state of New York knows that. Word may even have spread to Jersey."

"Ha ha. So what does he want from me?"

"I don't know, maybe just some validation of his gayness. I don't think he'd ever acknowledged he was gay before he met you."

"He's not the first one I've brought into the fold."

"God, you are so arrogant! I didn't say he wasn't gay before, I just said he didn't talk about it." Those sure seem like the good old days now.

"All right, well, I guess I'll just see you guys when I come home again. That'll be spring break, if I make it that long."

"What do you mean? Why wouldn't you?"

"Let's just say my mind hasn't been on school lately. I'm failing everything. One class I haven't even been to once."

"Why? What's wrong?"

"Nothing, I just don't feel like going. School's a bore."

"Jesus, Craig, you don't want to get kicked out of college! What the hell would you do then?" He's definitely not the burger-flipping type. And his father's a real hardass who scares the crap out of him. That alone should keep him on the straight and narrow.

"Oh, I have plenty of offers," he says.

I sure don't want to hear about them. "All right, it's your life. Just let me know what's going on."

"I will. And Karen?"

"Yes?"

"Thanks for calling. It means a lot. I can't imagine my life without you in it."

"Me either," I say. It's true, although I don't know why.

"OK, we'll talk soon. Bye."

"Bye."

I hang up. I feel better clearing the air with Craig, but I'm concerned I've said too much about Mark. I hope I haven't completely betrayed him. I hadn't planned to tell Craig anything, but I console myself with the fact that he pretty much knew it anyway—until I realize that he knew because of my original slip of the tongue. I'm guilty any way you look at it, but on the other hand, if Mark doesn't deal with Craig directly his problems could fester for years. It's not about me anymore; I really want him to get over Craig, period. Once he finally grasps what a superficial slut Craig is, he'll have to be turned off. It's just a matter of breaking through the cute, fun-loving, gay-inspiring façade and seeing there's nothing underneath. No, he's not a monster, but he is dangerous. I'll have to handle this carefully. Certainly I can't let them be alone together; that's how all the trouble started.

* * *

Once Mark told me he needed more space, we cut our time together in half. It wasn't easy but I've adjusted, and have learned not to call him every time I'm alone. Instead, I'm spending more time studying (well, a little) and more on the phone and writing letters to other, neglected friends. I've added a new babysitting client, the Bernsteins, but my heart isn't really in it. I hardly invade their privacy at all. I'm only doing it for the money, not to discover the dark underbelly of boring rich people. Craig's name hasn't come up for a couple of weeks. Already I'm regretting my conversation with Craig and dreading his return.

I think the change in our relationship has been worthwhile, because Mark's feeling a lot better these days. Or maybe he was cheered up by something his mother told him. She ran into Eric's mother at the supermarket who said Eric brought home a girlfriend from Georgetown over Christmas but she broke up with him on New Year's Eve. I don't wish Eric ill; in fact I had forgotten all about him. But the thought of that pompous ass doing the countdown alone is entertaining. Of course, he'd be equally amused by my own misery that night, with the bonus that he'd find out his lifelong neighbor, the one who stole me away from him, is gay. What a kick in the teeth.

A couple of weeks into my Mark reduction, realizing I need a time-filler, I head to Tommy's Tavern where there's always a bunch of Cunning Linguists hanging out at the bar. After I say hi to the team, Vincent, the construction worker who blew off Gwen the night I met Hal, starts pursuing me. I never paid much attention to him because Gwen liked him, but it turns out he's sweet and charming. He has great, thick hair and his wire-frame glasses give him an air of vulnerability. His friends have cool names like Bullets and Baf. With "December, 1963 (Oh, What a Night)" by the Four Seasons playing on the jukebox, he tells me I'm beautiful and interesting. He says he likes the song because it's about losing your virginity and he also lost his in December 1963. Wow. I was in first grade then! We listen to the lyrics and both laugh at "as I recall, it ended much too soon." Shades of Patrick, and probably every other guy's first time.

Vincent's a fan of the blues, and I try not to let on that I'm not sure what that is. His favorite artist is Jimmy Reed, whom I have never heard of. He likes some of the same music I do, though, like the Allman Brothers and Clapton. He works for his father's company and seems to have a lot of free time. At one point, he takes my hand in his, raises it to his mouth and kisses it gently, then turns it to the side and bites off the top of my thumbnail. "Hey!" I say. He just laughs and spits the nail off to the side. I want to scream "What's wrong with you?" and run for the door, but with nowhere else to go, I order another drink instead.

After a couple of weeks of talking about music and Scarsdale, smoking and drinking at a feverish pace, Vincent makes his move. "You know," he tells me, to "Dream On" by Aerosmith, "the first time I saw you, I knew we would be together." I've had second thoughts about getting involved with Gwen's crush, not to mention an older guy who might be an alcoholic, but once he says this, all bets are off. She has someone up in Boston anyway. He's fair game.

I follow Vincent's pickup truck back to his place in White Plains, listening to WBLS. They're playing a long and sexy song by the Temptations called "Mary Ann." I get caught up in the song until I suddenly realize we're in a dead end and Vincent's pulling into the driveway of a rambling two-story house. It looks like an old farmhouse, but it's across from a massive apartment buildings, and I can only assume its days are numbered. The parallels to my own weird residence are astounding. I feel comfortable immediately, or at least as comfortable as is possible when I'm about to do the deed with a relative stranger.

We go straight to the bedroom, where the bed is unmade and a stale body odor is in the air. He embraces me. "You are the most special woman I've ever met," he whispers, undressing me slowly. I'm melting. I'm a woman, I'm special and I'm melting. God, he is so sexy! Sure, he has a pot belly, but that just makes mine look smaller.

Vincent is the first man I've ever been completely naked with. I feel self-conscious but not in an overpowering way. He doesn't pay much attention to my body anyway. We make out for ages. He sucks my bottom lip, which makes me swoon, gives a gentle kiss to my nose, a slow lick down my chin, a lingering exploration of my neck. Then he heads straight down to the bottom of the bed.

The name of his baseball team pops into my head. This must be his specialty. I've never had it done to me before and it's a weird sensation. He goes down on me so long that I try to check my watch to see what time it is, but it's too dark to see. It feels like hours. I think I may even have conked out for a few minutes. Is this fun for him? I don't get the appeal of the whole oral sex thing, giving or receiving. In fact, sex in general just seems like a hurdle to get over. Speed it up, man! I need my sleep! Like I could fall asleep with someone lying next to me. What if I make funny noises or drool? I can't even pee if I know someone can hear it hit the water.

I try to reach for him, to distract him with a hand job, but he's squished down by the foot of the bed, toiling away. Somewhere before dawn I realize that if I don't fake some moaning I might be trapped here for days. That seems to do the trick and Vincent finally lifts his head, grunts and moves up toward the rest of me. Jesus! Why didn't I think of that before? Please, don't kiss me! He may be willing to dig around down there but I'm not.

Now that the tedious part has ended, I figure we'll move on, but he just throws his arm over me and passes out. He starts snoring like he's having trouble catching his breath: huge, gasping reverberations. Now what? Escape is certainly my first choice, but I'd probably have to wake him up and that would be too awkward. Plus I have no idea where I left my purse. I've never spent a whole night with a man and hadn't anticipated doing so tonight. What the hell happens in the morning? What will I tell Mom, assuming she notices I didn't make it home?

Somehow, while debating my move and listening to Vincent's wheezing snores, I fall asleep, too. I wake to blinding sunlight through his curtainless and apparently east-facing window. I check my watch: it's not quite 7:00 a.m. and he's gone. I don't know whether to be relieved or insulted. I get up and throw on my clothes. I'm just about to make a much-needed bathroom visit when he walks into the room with two cups of coffee.

"Good morning," he says, kissing me carelessly and handing me a cup.

"Good morning!" I reply. "I thought you'd left."

"I'd never leave you, babe," he says, and kisses me again. As hyperbolic as this sounds, it's still pretty flattering. "I have about ten minutes before I have to hit the road," he adds. So much for hyperbole.

"Oh, OK. I have a class so I should probably be going anyway." He smiles at me as I sip black coffee for the first time in my life. I'd kill myself before I'd ask if he has any milk or sugar, but Jesus, this tastes disgusting. I put the cup down on his dresser, next to a half-empty bottle of Aramis, and look around for my purse. I find it lying on the floor at the end of the bed with my cigarettes, keys and a mangled tampon spilling out. I quickly shove everything back inside and put the strap over my shoulder.

"Well, thanks for the coffee and…everything," I say lamely.

"My pleasure," he replies with an exaggerated wink. Really? Well, to each his own.

Vincent walks me to the front door, past a black velvet painting behind a wet bar on the right. I take a quick peek to the left, into a bright, homey living room, with overstuffed furniture and lots of hanging plants in macramé holders. "Bye," he says, giving me a quick peck. "I'll call you later." As I am rushing home to pee, I realize he doesn't know my last name, doesn't have my phone number, didn't even ask for it.

My first class isn't until 10:30, giving me time to shower and mull over the situation. It isn't making much sense to me, but I don't know who to talk to. Mark's aware I have "a past," but somehow I can't ask his advice about my messy present. My whole fantasy would fall apart with one simple question, like "When are you seeing him again?" And Gwen might think I'm rubbing her nose in it, since she never got anywhere with Vincent despite prodigious efforts. I go back and forth all day, but that evening, listening to "Over My Head" by Fleetwood

Mac, I decide to call her anyway. She's spent a lot of time with him and his friends and surely knows things about him that will be useful in helping me figure him out.

I call her in Boston and tell her I went home with him. She goes apoplectic. Even though she's still with Eddie, and Vincent has always ignored her, she's furious I'd go after someone she likes.

"I didn't go after him, he came after me," I tell her, but that hardly helps.

"Oh, bullshit. You knew I liked him and you went home with him. Some friend you are! You know, he has a girlfriend he's lived with for ten years."

"Oh, really? I didn't see anyone in bed with us," I tell her bitchily.

"That's probably because she was off getting another abortion," Gwen snaps back. I feel my blood stop circulating, drop about 10 degrees, then move in the opposite direction.

"What do you mean?" I choke.

"She's had about three of them. Back a few years ago, when it was illegal, he flew her down to Puerto Rico. Didn't even go with her. Now it's easier. Good thing, too, since she seems to be pretty damn good at getting knocked up." She pauses and I can hear her light a cigarette.

"Jesus," I say. Abortion is everyone's back-up plan, but only in the abstract. And having three couldn't have been any kind of plan. "If he's so awful why are you interested in him?"

"Damned if I know," she says. "The mysteries of attraction, I guess. All I can tell you is don't get involved with Vincent."

"Look, I'm already involved. I don't know why I'm so attracted to him either, and I'm sorry you like him too, but it's not like you guys were ever together. And don't forget, you do have someone else."

"That's irrelevant. Besides, Eddie's sort of a jerk."

"Only 'sort of'? That's better than being a total jerk, like most of them."

"Even grading on the curve, he's still damn close to failing." She's apparently glad to change the subject, as am I. "We have these philosophical discussions that make me want to scream. Everything is an object to him, even people. Last night he asked what a 'right' is. He said, 'All objects have equal value, so if I have the right to break a glass, why shouldn't I also have the right kill somebody?' I mean, I sort of understand what he's saying, but I draw the line at him thinking I'm an object too, or that he has the right to do whatever he wants to me. You should have heard us at the bar. I was yelling, 'Am I just another *glass* to you?'"

"Wow, he sure sounds like a total jerk to me."

"No, it's more complicated than I'm making it sound. He's exploring new ways of thinking, testing boundaries. Plus I'm sure part of it is just trying to get a rise out of me."

"If that's how he wants to get a rise out of you, I wouldn't do anything to get a rise out of him, if you know what I mean."

"Yeah, you're about as subtle as a hard-on in a leotard. I don't need your two cents. *I* didn't call *you* for advice, remember? At least he's better than Vincent."

"You may be right, but I still want to see how it plays out. I really like him, Gwen. Can't you just put aside any unfulfilled feelings you have for him?"

"Oh, fine, what the hell. It's not like it makes a big difference in my life anyway. So is he good in bed?"

"I'm not sure yet."

"What? I thought you went to bed with him!"

"Well, sort of. But we didn't have sex."

"How do you go to bed with someone and not have sex? Was he too drunk to fuck?"

I consider this. "You know, I think maybe he was. All he did was go down on me for what felt like forever, and then he passed out."

"Really! Well, at least some good came out of it."

"Good? I think that's bizarre!"

"Bizarre! The only thing bizarre is not appreciating head."

"Yeah, well, then I'm bizarre. I think it's gross."

"Oh, you poor thing. You are the opposite of uninhibited!"

"Wouldn't that be inhibited?"

"Well, that sounds better than frigid."

"Frigid! What are you saying?"

"I'm saying if you enjoy sex so little, why are you such a slut?"

"I'm not a slut! I'm just looking for love!"

"Don't kid yourself. I've been there, remember? You're eighteen and you've already run out of fingers to count all the guys you've slept with."

"You are completely wrong. I still have one finger left, and I'm saving it for you."

"Go ahead, live in denial. But you're missing out on the real thrill of sex."

"Fine, I accept that. What the hell, at least I won't get knocked up! I just called to see if you have any advice."

"I already gave you my advice. Stay away from Vincent. Unless you change your mind about not liking head, that is."

"Thanks a lot."

"You're welcome. Listen, I have to go, but I'll see you over spring break."

"That's not until April!"

"I know, I'll talk to you before then. Just not about Vincent."

"OK, I get it. Bye."

"Goodbye and good luck."

We hang up. So much for useful advice. I'm on my own again, so I'll go to Tommy's tonight and try to figure it out myself. I put on my newest album, _I Want You_ by Marvin Gaye, and imagine Vincent watching me and getting turned on while I freshen my makeup. But when I get there, he's nowhere in sight. Home again, to my lonely garret. I'm dangerously close to why-bother-getting-out-of-bed depression. What's the point of it all?

The next day Mark calls me practically incoherent, babbling about mail and "the letter" until I figure out he got into NYU. I hang up and jump in the car. I drive to the mailbox at the end of the driveway and I have the same package! Just in time, I have been saved from despair! I keep driving until I get to Mark's and we celebrate by going to Tung Hoy in Larchmont. We stuff ourselves with sweet and sour pork and blather on and on about what our new lives will be like. Will we be dormmates? Find true love? Take interesting classes that will lead us down the pathway to success? It's like a light has come on and illuminated a new, previously off-limits road leading away from our suburban hell and into a bright urban future.

* * *

Since our NYU acceptance, I've gone by Tommy's a couple of times but Vincent hasn't been there, which for some sick reason only stokes my interest in him. Mark and I start spending more time together; there doesn't seem to be any reason not to. Getting into NYU has been better medicine than all the "Ain't No Mountain High Enough" a boy can consume.

These days, Mark and I have swapped obsessive places: he rarely mentions Craig but I'm tortured wondering when I'm going to see

Vincent again. I still can't bring myself to tell Mark the whole sordid tale of Vincent, but I do say I met somebody at Tommy's that I like. And I finally let him know that Craig and I are back in touch and that the three of us will get together when he comes home. I warn him that Craig isn't interested, but he says he doesn't care, he just thinks it will be fun to do stuff together. Having a gay friend isn't quite the same for him as for me, but I guess it makes sense. He doesn't exactly say he's over Craig, but the news that he'll see him again doesn't seem to faze him either. Maybe I'll dodge the bullet my big mouth shot.

But Craig surprises us: he doesn't come home for spring break. Oh, he comes back to Westchester, but he's dropped out of school and isn't welcome in Murdock Woods. His parents are getting divorced and everything is in turmoil. He moves in with an older guy, Roger, an elementary school teacher he met at the Playroom, a gay bar in Yonkers. Roger—and now Craig—lives in an incredible duplex apartment in White Plains. He has wicker throne chairs and a giant vase filled with ostrich feathers. He has a modular sofa upholstered in Ultrasuede and glass nesting tables and fluffy white flotaki rugs on top of wall-to-wall carpeting. He has a spiral staircase, the biggest bed I've ever seen and vertical blinds that operate with a remote control. It's like a gay indoor Playland.

The most amazing thing of all about the apartment is that it's directly across the street from Vincent's house. Mark and I race over there after getting the call from Craig, and I almost faint when we make the turn off Lake Street. Could this be a sign that Vincent and I are meant to be together?

Our reunion is a happy one, like Syracuse never happened. We talk for hours in Roger's apartment, although Roger, who's well into his thirties, is so quiet it's hard to get him to join the conversation. He just sits there smiling, for some reason entertained by what must sound to him like inane chatter. Craig describes how he ended up failing out of Syracuse his freshman year and Mark talks about going to NYU while I spy on Vincent's house from Roger's balcony. There's absolutely nothing going on over there.

The next day, Mark, Craig and I go into the city. It's hard for me to believe it, but we're all friends now. Mark's time alone has paid off: he seems comfortable around Craig, not clingy. He tells me he did a lot of thinking since Syracuse and willed himself out of love. That sounds way too simplistic, but I don't press him for details. I don't want to test whether he's really pulled it off. But if he has, I need him to teach me his secrets.

Craig has changed, too. He seems less jumpy, comfortable with Mark, not running the other direction. He's excited about our move to NYU, even talking about moving to Manhattan himself to be nearby when the next school year starts. Apparently Roger is only a temporary solution to his homelessness.

We visit Colony Records on Broadway so Mark can look through the Supremes section. I browse and find a Jimmy Reed album, _T'Aint No Big Thing But He Is..._ I buy it even though it's $17 so I can learn about what Vincent likes. When we get back to Craig and Roger's place, I ask if I can play it; I don't want to wait until I get home. The first song on side one is called "Shame, Shame, Shame," and Craig says he knows it. He places the needle on the disc and immediately falls on the floor laughing hysterically. It turns out the blues are simplistic, repetitive melodies sung by a drunk guy who occasionally switches from slurring his words to playing the harmonica. The song is unlistenable. Craig takes it off and gets another record. He puts on the "Shame, Shame, Shame" he knows, a disco song by Shirley and Company that bears no resemblance to the blues, and starts dancing.

18
I HAVE BEEN REMOVED

It's a freakishly warm Easter Sunday and I have reluctantly agreed to go to church with Dad and Ruth. The three of us are dressed up and heading to St. Pius X. I spent years of Wednesdays at CCD classes there, and even more Sundays parroting the Missal at Mass. St. Pius. I even got confirmed there, with Dad as my only guest. I've pretty much avoided the place ever since. There's nothing about this bland building or its mind-numbing services that encourages me to believe in God, or that if He exists this is where He'd choose to hang out. I haven't been to church in more than a year and don't even feel guilty about it. I'm only doing this for Dad.

"Crazy" by Patsy Cline, Dad's favorite song, plays on a cassette in his car. As she croons, Dad says, "I'm glad you girls were able to come to church today. I know your mother doesn't take you."

Ruth pipes up, "And Karen never wants to drive me."

I turn around to see her in the back seat since I called shotgun.

"Oh yeah? When was the last time you asked?" To Dad I say, "The little angel."

Dad says, "Well, church is an important part of life. And it's important to me that you continue to go even if your mother doesn't approve. You girls are Catholic and you should be going to church every week."

"Sorry, Dad," I say, meaning I'm sorry it means so much to him. He started too late with my indoctrination. Maybe if I'd been baptized Catholic and had it pounded into me from the beginning, I'd be on board. But he reclaimed his faith after I'd already been accompanying Mom on her quest for the perfect congregation, and at this point I've seen enough different churches to know that one's no better than the next. I'd never say it to Dad, but all of them are more concerned with keeping congregants in line and collecting cash than getting us closer to God.

"Your mother never understood why it was so important to me that you be raised Catholic. She has done nothing but undermine me on the subject," Dad says.

I respond, "Dad, you and Mom are divorced now, so you don't have to let her bug you anymore. I'm sorry we haven't done better at going to church. We're not trying to pick Mom over you—we don't go to her church either."

Ruth says, "I do, sometimes. But I don't like it."

With a bitter laugh, Dad says, "Ruth, honey, I'm not asking you not to like church. Just to try and go to your real church if you can. Karen will take you, I'm sure."

"Sure, Dad," I say, knowing I am making an empty promise. Ruth won't ask and I won't be around. I'm counting the days until I'm gone for good.

"I mean, I know you're not seeing Patrick any more, and he was Catholic. But I hate to think of you as an atheist."

"I'm not an atheist," I say, surprised that this is his impression of me, and that he remembers Patrick, whom he never even met.

"Oh, I thought you were. I know you don't consider yourself Catholic anymore."

"That doesn't mean I don't believe in God."

Dad shrugs noncommittally. "Hmm." Jesus, I think he cares more about my being Catholic than whether I believe in God.

Poor Dad. He tries so hard but he's always disappointed. When I was in fifth grade, our first year living in New York, he coached the girls' softball team. It's hard to imagine there was a time when we all thought we might fit in in Scarsdale, but if there was, those early days were it. I guess he and Mom wanted to believe they'd made the right move, leaving the home and schools we were so comfortable in for a new place with alien customs.

Some of the girls on the team were getting their first bras, which we called brassieres around our house, but I used that word once at a game and was ridiculed for weeks. Still, that wasn't as bad as when I found out that no one outside my house seemed to know the word tilliewacker, just as I had never heard "penis" at age ten. Anyway, these girls were snooty and obnoxious (the most overused word of that time) and definitely not interested in sports of any kind. Basically they didn't like to perspire because they felt it wasn't feminine. Getting the team to show up for practice and games was a weekly challenge, except for Barb and a couple of other jock types.

Well, somehow—probably due to Dad's coaching since he was about the only one expending real effort—our team made it to the finals. We were going to have to forfeit the championship game, though, because not enough girls committed to playing in it. Mom got on the phone and went through the entire Quaker Ridge directory. Practically every girl in fifth grade came, some for the first time ever. Man, were they pissed that they'd been drafted. Girls don't play sports! they huffed indignantly. I felt the same way, but my father was the coach so my loyalties were divided. We ended up having enough girls to play two teams. Many didn't even get to play, which was fine by them, although they still bitched about being there.

We won the championship, and Mom ran out and bought tiny little plastic trophies for everyone, including the ones who had only shown up once and never even played. She wrote a name on each base in magic marker and I had to hand them out in school that Monday. A lot of the girls didn't even want one. They were so mean and dismissive. It's not like I could reuse them since they were personalized. I wanted to yell, "Just take it!" But I could feel myself turning red from top to bottom so I just walked away and threw the unwanted ones in the trash. I didn't tell Mom. She was so sure they would be excited and proud, I couldn't tell her so many of them thought the whole thing was a joke. I never played on another team. And Dad never coached again either.

Dad has tried to be a good father and he's always believed in me. In fact, when I called him from Gwen's to say we'd been arrested in White Plains that first time, he said he would come right over. He sounded completely supportive, more worried than mad. This was a huge contrast to Gwen's parents: her mother was already plotting which punishment would hurt her the most and her father tried to hit her when he was driving us home from the police station. "Don't just sit there like a bloody plum pudding!" he yelled at her in his English accent. It was hard not to let out a belly laugh from the safety of the back seat, where I sat poking her with my foot.

When Dad showed up at Gwen's house, Mrs. Gilbert practically knocked him down asking, "Do you know what these girls have been up to? Stealing! They were arrested for shoplifting!" He gasped, truly shocked. Turns out he thought I'd been caught jaywalking. I started crying when he said that. He doesn't know me at all, and thinks I'm such a good girl. Letting Dad down was harder than the actual arrest. Living by the rules is important to him, and stealing means I broke a commandment, a super-rule.

The service at St. Pius is just as I remember it: tedious and repetitive. Everyone just reads along in the Missal, so there's no real thought involved. Reading doesn't equal faith. Even memorization doesn't equal faith. I know that because I've repeated everything so often that I've memorized it, but it still leaves me cold. The only thing to look forward to is all the s'es in "forgive us our trespasses as we forgive those who trespass against us." For some reason I always find the hissing amusing. One of Mom's churches replaced "trespasses" with "debts," which is a lot less sibilant and not entertaining at all. The recently added "offer each other the sign of peace" does add a little amusement, as congregants shake hands, hug and say, "Peace be with you." Very hippie dippy.

Because it's Easter there are more flowers than usual, but otherwise it's the same old thing. I get my religion from music, not church. And so I drift into a fantasy, imagining a scenario played out to <u>Aretha Franklin's version of Elton John's "Border Song."</u> In my mind a gospel choir appears on one side of the altar and I picture the priest conducting a wedding ceremony between me and Mark. I lose control of my own fantasy when an altar boy stands up and is revealed to be Craig right as the song hits the line "Holy Moses, I have been removed." I back away in shock, then slowly levitate up to the ceiling, watching as the new couple's wedding proceeds below. The wind has changed direction and the two grooms kiss as I look on.

Holy Moses, I am really losing it. This is the closest I've had to a religious experience, and even though it's not what Dad would have envisioned, it's a revelation. I mean, it's not revealing anything I didn't already know—like the fact that Mark felt for Craig something he'll never feel for me—but somehow I see everything more clearly now. Gwen was right all along, gay is gay. Maybe this should make me sad, but it feels cathartic. I'm truly over Mark. If anything, I love him more now, accept who he is and what he wants.

When Dad takes us home after the service, Mom is still out at hers. She's trying the Methodist Church in Mamaroneck these days since that's where Stan goes. She's even started working there, as a secretary in the office. Dad would never let her work when they were married, but once she didn't have to do what he told her anymore, she couldn't wait to get a job. I don't think she makes much, but I guess she gets some satisfaction from it. I hope Dad doesn't find out she's working for a non-Catholic church. Oy vey, twist the knife.

By the time we get home from St. Pius, the temperature is around ninety degrees. I remember it snowing on Easter not too long ago. Maybe growing up means getting used to living in a world of the unexpected, where the weather is out of control and guys like other guys instead of you. Maybe it means seeing yourself for the first time as you really are—a complete idiot—but also knowing you might be turning a corner and leaving loserville. This feels perceptive. I think I'm starting to understand how the world works. Maybe, unlike my mother, I won't have to go through life being wrong about every damn thing.

My room is an oven so I bring a few albums downstairs to play. I sit in the den sweating, reading the *New York Times* and listening to a Paul Simon album from a few years ago, _There Goes Rhymin' Simon_. Mom walks into the house and joins me in the den, fanning herself with the Methodist bulletin. She looks pretty and festive in her pink dress with a matching hat. She rarely wears hats even though she looks great in them.

"How was church?" she asks, stepping over to the stereo and turning down the volume.

"Terrible, as usual. How was yours?"

"Oh fine. It's nice to see everyone, and I love the Easter hymns, like "Christ the Lord Is Risen Today." She starts humming, but she's competing with a subdued "Was a Sunny Day" from *Rhymin' Simon*. "Stan and I went out to lunch after the service." She pauses, looks up from the album cover. "How's your father?"

"Well, I don't think he'll ever get over my leaving the Catholic Church. He blames you, you know."

"I'm used to that. He blames me for everything."

A few months ago, hearing her say that would have bothered me. But I'm starting to see that her life with Dad wasn't a happy one. He blames her, she blames him. It didn't work for either of them, but she was the one who cut their losses. I don't know whether he never recognized their marriage was hopeless, or whether he'd never even think that way because, to him at least, their vows were sacred. Maybe he loved her more than she loved him. Regardless of how it used to be, he sure seems to hate her more now.

I start to light a cigarette. "Please don't smoke in the house," she says. She lived with a smoker for eighteen years and couldn't get him to stop, at least not for long. Fine with me, I'm moving out soon anyway. My days of living by her rules are as numbered as were hers living by Dad's. I put the cigarette away.

"I talked to Dad about helping pay for NYU," I tell her. "I haven't heard back from the Financial Aid people yet and my Regents Scholarship is only going to go so far. I don't know how much I'm going to need, but I'm afraid it's going to be a lot."

"What did he say?"

"Well, he didn't exactly commit to covering everything."

"That's because he can't afford to. You'll probably have to take out a loan." She sighs. "Maybe we could ask your grandmother to make a contribution. I know it would never occur to her to offer."

Her relationship with her mother is distant. Mimi disapproved of Mom's marriage to Dad, and apparently now she disapproves of the divorce. There's just no pleasing some people. I'd rather not call her for money, but I will if I have to. I've come this far, I'm not going to miss out on NYU and the city. Besides, Dad already sent in the deposit and I've told SUNY Purchase this semester will be my last—not that I'll be missed there. I'm somewhat panicked about the money thing, switching from a public to private college and tacking on room and board, but I'm not going to have a breakdown.

"Don't worry, we'll find a way," Mom says. "Are you going back to Playland this summer?"

"God no, I can't go back there," I say. "I need to find something else."

"Well, maybe there's something at the church nursery school. I think they have a day camp and they might need someone."

"Thanks," I say. That doesn't sound like the job for me, but it's nice of her to suggest it. Time to end this conversation while I'm ahead. "I can't take this heat! I'm going to go swimming at Gwen's and maybe see a movie."

"Have fun," Mom says. I leave her sitting in the den, reading the Arts & Leisure section and listening to "Loves Me Like a Rock." She likes this album, too.

I take a bath and walk out to my car to drive to Gwen's air-conditioned house. Just my luck, I have a flat tire. The damn car continues to bleed me dry. For a few months after Skidmore, nothing went wrong. I'd almost gotten used to trouble-free drives, but sure enough, it didn't last. I won't need a car come September, but there are still a few months to go and it's failing a little more every day. The driver's-side door no longer opens, so I have to slide in from the passenger side. This month I had to replace the muffler, and now the flat.

I change the tire myself—Mom made me take an Auto Mechanics at an adult class at Scarsdale High, much as I resented it. As I tighten the lug nuts and consider a third bath of the day, I think about how she's spent my whole life trying to make me capable enough to stand on my own two feet. She says that's her only real responsibility as a parent: to raise kids who don't need her. I get that—believe me, I don't want to rely on her, or Dad. But I can't help it, I wish her tactics and timing had been better. "Building independence" is a convenient excuse when what's really going on is that her own life is now more interesting to her than being a mother. Those parental moments like the one we just had don't happen often anymore; we're rarely even in the same room, and soon I won't see her for months at a time.

I'm on the precipice of independence, at the launch of my real life. She laid the groundwork, and I can't wait to leave her, and my past, behind.

* * *

At Roger's one night in May, he, Craig, Mark and I cut up construction paper for a school project to help Roger's second-grade class get ready for the summer. To the bass tones of <u>Barry White singing "Let the Music Play,"</u> we make flowers and umbrellas, flags and strawberries. Roger is so nice, it's a pleasure to help him. He's a gentle soul, a little boring but I'm sure a wonderful teacher.

Craig shares a little bottle he calls poppers. Mark refuses, but I take a sniff and feel my heart racing and my body heating up. It's intense and scary and I tell him I'd rather drink than try that again. He says all the boys are doing it, but he doesn't care whether I like it or not. More for him, I guess. He breaks out a bottle of something called B&B. It's the first time I've had a drink that didn't involve a mixer, and it's strong but smooth. It's not liquor, he says, it's *liqueur*. What a difference a French accent makes! I get giddy as I grow more used to the taste.

After three B&Bs I decide to check and see if Vincent's home. It's been a couple of months since I spent the night at his house and I still think about him every day. Why hasn't he been at Tommy's? Why hasn't he tried to contact me? He could have found out my number somehow. I go out on the balcony and look across the street. The lights are on and there's a car in the driveway.

I get a pen and a piece of Roger's construction paper and write out some words cribbed from Marvin Gaye: I want you, but I want you to want me too. I sign the paper and fold it in half. "Goodbye," I yell to my gay friends. "I'm going to visit Vincent."

Mark leaps to his feet and comes after me. "Wait! What are you doing?"

"Vincent's home and I'm going to go tell him how I feel."

"Are you kidding? You're wasted!"

"I know what I'm doing. He'll be happy to see me."

"Karen, it's my duty as your friend to refuse to let you leave this apartment."

"It's your duty as my friend to get out of my way," I say, trying to push him aside.

"Watch out, Mark," Craig yells from across the living room. "She gets violent when she's mad."

"I'm not mad, I'm leaving," I say. "And you can't stop me." I have it all figured out. I'll knock on his door and when he opens it I'll give him the paper. He'll read the quote, tell me he wants me too, and we'll fall into each others' arms. I'm not telling these guys my plan, though. They have no appreciation for the written word.

Mark looks at me. "Are you sure this is what you want?"

"I'm sure."

He moves away from the door. "Then all I can do is wish you luck."

"She's going to need it!" yells Craig.

I lurch across the street to Vincent's house and knock on the door. Step one complete—my plan is underway! I stand clutching my piece of paper. I hear movement inside, and then someone walking toward the door. My heart pounds like I just sniffed more poppers. The door opens, to a woman. She's thirtyish, with a friendly smile. Normal looking, like maybe she does macramé for a hobby. She wipes her hands on a dishtowel. "Can I help you?" she asks.

I stare at her like she's an orangutan in a zoo. My mind is blank.

"Yes?" she asks. I have to think fast. I know "Is Vincent home?"

is definitely out. I look down at my folded construction paper, then back up at her.

"I'm here in your neighborhood wondering if you want to make a donation," I manage to squeak.

"A donation? A donation to what?" she asks. Damned if I know! I'm making this up as I go along and I can tell she's getting suspicious. Who wouldn't be?

"Um, to our president," I say. Who the hell is that again? I know Nixon's out. Why can't I remember who took his place? Oh, right, Gerald Ford! "To re-elect President Ford," I add.

"Are you kidding?" she says, scowling and shaking her head. "I wouldn't give a nickel to a Republican!"

"Yeah, that's probably smart," I agree as I start backing away. She looks at me with a confused expression. I turn and start to run.

Back at Craig and Roger's apartment, I pound on the door. Mark opens it, looking at his watch.

"Damn, I was off by five minutes! Hey Craig, you win!"

"Shut up."

"You seem a little out of breath," Craig says, laughing at me.

"Shut up!" I tell him, too. "Don't let me drink anymore. I just made such an idiot out of myself."

"Good thing it was the booze and not you," Craig says.

I turn on him. "I hit you once, don't think I won't do it again."

Mark puts his arm around me. "I tried to stop you. Come in and sit down. Tell us what happened."

"Did you have time for a quickie?" asks Craig, then brays like a donkey at his great wit. I suppress the urge to jump out of my corduroy club chair and pummel him to death.

"His *girlfriend* answered the door," I tell them, as Mark lights my cigarette with his Supremes lighter. "I guess it's over."

"It's over," agrees Mark, but the way he says it, it sounds comforting, a relief rather than a tragedy.

"You don't miss a trick!" screeches Craig, and I start to get up. Mark pulls me down.

"Why don't you go lie down for a little while and sober up," he says. "We'll finish this, then I'll wake you up and we can go."

I look over at Roger, sitting quietly on the couch gluing cut-out shapes onto posterboard. He must think I'm dumber than his second graders. This is so embarrassing. I don't want to leave with his project unfinished, but I can't be any help to him now. "OK," I say.

The Cusp of Everything

I finish my cigarette and go upstairs, choosing the den rather than the bedroom. No way am I getting on that bed! I lie on the couch and, spinning, think about Vincent. I'm expecting to feel a sense of loss and hurt, but I don't. That woman seemed so at home there. What the hell was he doing trawling Tommy's for teenagers? What did I ever see in him? How could I have been so desperate that I built up a one-night stand into a great love affair? I've never behaved this stupidly about any guy, and that's saying something. What happened to all my big plans for self-improvement?

Patrick was the last person I had "real" sex with, and that was last summer. Almost a year ago. That's the last time anyone loved me, too. All my pining for love, and here I lie, in an apartment with three gay guys. By my own standards, I'm a big fat failure. I want to be loved and no one loves me.

And yet, I don't feel like a failure. Even more surprisingly, I don't feel like crying. I've experienced enough of love this year to know it's not the solution to my problems. If anything, it's a problem-generator. Friends are more caring, more dependable, more available, more fun. They stick around longer than lovers and are less annoying than family. I pledge to myself to become a better friend and a nicer person, to appreciate my friends more and obsess over loser men less. I pledge to be more discriminating, not to like someone just because he pays attention to me. I still want somebody, but not so badly that I'll settle for the wrong guy just because he's in the right place. While I'm at it, I figure I should cut back on the smoking and drinking. I hope I remember all this when I come to. No one else can do it for me. As Stevie points out, <u>I'm the only one to see the changes I take myself through</u>.

19

I WOULDN'T CHANGE A THING

One Saturday in the middle of June, Mark and I take the train in to see Diana Ross at the Palace Theatre. The concert opens with a mime, which is a little unsettling, but after his hand turns into a butterfly, Diana comes out singing "Here I Am/I Wouldn't Change a Thing" in a white dress. Then dancers unravel her dress, which becomes a movie screen showing scenes from *Mahogany*. It's brilliant! She blends the *Mahogany* theme with "Ain't No Mountain High Enough" and the crowd goes wild. Apparently Mark isn't the only one who relates to it, although he may be the only one who plays little bits of it like mantras every day.

Diana has a current hit with "Love Hangover"—Mark pulls the car over whenever it comes on—so it's not just an oldies show, although she does plenty of those. There's also a tribute to Ethel Waters, Josephine Baker, Bessie Smith and of course Billie Holiday, since Diana was nominated for an Oscar for playing her in *Lady Sings the Blues* a few years back. We have a great time, and I'm sure Mark will slide his program into a plastic bag the minute he gets home so he can save it forever. Of course, I'll save mine too. I have quite a collection thanks to all those shows Dad took me to after the divorce.

We head back to the Mamaroneck train station on a Diana Ross high, then to the diner for coffee and an in-depth appraisal of the evening. Mark, naturally, wants to go over every detail.

I'm finally heading home late, pumped full of caffeine and Diana Ross, when the boat dies. Climbing a hill on Old White Plains Road, suddenly I'm rolling backwards. The brakes don't work and the power steering is out. Somehow I maneuver it across the street, off the road and into some bushes. My gas gauge hasn't worked for months, so it's possible I'm out of gas, but then again, it could be anything. Furious, I trudge back down the hill to a payphone, ironically located outside a car repair place. I call home and wake up Mom. She's not happy, but she has no choice but to come and get me. When I get home I go straight to bed and sleep for ten hours. By the time I wake up and stumble to the kitchen, Mom's had the car towed and stripped. She hands me the radio, ripped from the body of my beloved/detested boat. Multicolored wires extend in all directions, like veins bled dry. This is all that's left. I collapse in a chair and start to wail.

"Oh, stop," she says unsympathetically. "You're lucky they accepted the car as payment for the tow. What a hunk of junk."

"Hunk of junk? Half the parts in that thing were new!" I say through my tears. "They'll make a fortune selling it off in pieces! You had no right to make that decision! It might have just been out of gas."

"Oh, please," Mom snorts. "Don't kid yourself. Get over it." This is her response to everything. "You're going to the city soon. You don't need a car. You should be grateful I dealt with it."

She's infuriating. She wants me to be independent, but still acts like she has the right to make decisions on my behalf. But there's nothing I can do. Now I have to figure out how to get through the summer with no transportation except my old bicycle, abandoned since I got my driver's license. September can't come soon enough.

But Mom's not done killing off things that mean something to me. "By the way," she says, as I'm trying to absorb the blow of being car-less. "We're moving, maybe as early as next month." She heads out to the refrigerator porch as she says this.

"What?" I sputter. "Moving to where?"

"To Armonk. It's a lovely town, right by Purchase," she says, returning with a can of store-brand dog food.

If only I had the strength to jump up and choke her. No jury of daughters would convict me. "I know where Armonk is! What the hell are you talking about?"

"Watch your language," she says, with maddening calm. She spoons food into Gretchen's bowl and puts it on the floor while I seethe, finally turning to me and putting her hands on her hips. "I just feel in my bones it's time to go. We've been here month-to-month for years now, and the landlord could give us the word at any time. Somehow I know it's now."

"What, you had like a vision or something? Are you kidding?"

She goes to the sink to wash her hands. "I can't explain how I know, but I do. I've been checking the ads and I've found the perfect place. I've seen it already and I'm taking you and Ruth to look at it today." Well, she knows I can't get anywhere on my own, so I guess that makes me a captive audience. Besides, part of me is curious.

"What's so perfect about it?" I ask grumpily.

She ignores my attitude and responds brightly, "It's a house for rent, but it was in the 'for sale' section of the real estate ads. I don't know what possessed me to look at that section. God knows we can't buy anything. But this ad was misplaced so I'm the only one who called. It's a sign that it was there just for us."

Possessed? A sign? What the hell has come over her? It's like she fancies herself some sort of clairvoyant. Speechless, I gape at her, trying to convey anger and disdain, not easy to do while wearing jammies.

"Stan's already seen it and agrees it's a great bargain," she adds, pushing her hair off her face and turning to the dishes in the sink. As if this seal of approval would win me over! Unable to consider eating, I stamp up the stairs to my garret, with a fresh appreciation for its quirkiness, its quiet. How lucky I've been to have my own floor, to live on what's practically an estate all these years! How did I lose sight of my home's unique beauty? How could Mom be so heartless as to throw it all away?

A resurgence of love for Prince Willow Lane washes over me. The solitude! The decade of memories! Even the driveway suddenly seems eccentric instead of shameful.

I don't want to leave home from a place that's not home! I don't want to pack up everything I own! Moving means changing Ruth's school and a much longer drive for Dad to come and visit her. It could be years before we need to move, so why now? I'm speechless.

I go back to bed and try to pretend I'm already gone, but an hour later Mom wakes me up and makes me get in the hideous red Ford station wagon with her and Ruth and drive to Armonk to see her psychic find. I sulk the whole way and even Ruth seems subdued. We arrive at a long gravelly driveway—without potholes, at least—ending at some kind of plantation house, white with lots of columns. Mom says it reminds her of Tara. *Gone with the Wind* is her favorite movie, almost to the point of being an obsession. How many times I've heard her say "I'll never go hungry again!" or "Frankly my dear, I don't give a damn," typically aimed at me. The house is on several acres on King Street, right across from American Can's park-like corporate headquarters in Greenwich, Connecticut. American Can owns the property, which presumably they will develop someday. How are there so many places like this in otherwise normal neighborhoods? And how do they keep popping up in my far-from-normal life?

Mom has me and Ruth wait in the car while she goes inside to talk to somebody about moving in. We're sitting there listening to the appalling "Afternoon Delight" on the radio because I feel so drained thinking about how my life is not my own that I don't have the strength to reach over from the back seat and turn it off. Suddenly there's a movement up on the roof. Some guy comes up over the peak and stands there looking down at us. Ruth points. "Look! There's a man on the roof!"

"I see him. What the hell is he doing?"

The guy goes back over the peak. Ruth gets out of the car and I follow her. What is this place? Several spaced-out looking quasi-adults are wandering around, but I don't want to talk to them and the feeling seems to be mutual, except for one excessively grinning man.

"Come on," I say to Ruth, taking her hand and leading her in the opposite direction.

"Where are we going?" she asks.

"I don't know, let's just explore." I try to make it sound fun instead of disturbing. There's an open field to the left of the house and we start walking across it.

"Hey!" yells Ruth as she starts running. "It's a swimming pool!"

The pool is about the size of four side-by-side bathtubs, set into the field. A couple of lawn chairs with shredded woven seats are strewn about. Ruth pulls off her sneakers and sticks her foot in. "It feels great! I wish we could go swimming."

"Me too," I lie. "Come one, put your shoes on and let's go see what else is around." Reluctantly she does.

There's a barnyard with horses and pigs, a barn on one side and a freestanding garage on the other. Ruth wants to jump the fence and pet the animals, but I hold her back. This place isn't really that bad, except for all the other people and the fact that it could, like Prince Willow Lane, vanish any time. I don't know what to think as we head back to the car where Mom stands looking around for us. Ruth runs to her. "Are we going to live on a farm?" she asks hopefully.

"We sure are!" she says. "I paid the deposit and we move in July 15!" Today is June 15, what would have been Mom and Dad's twentieth anniversary if they'd managed to stick it out. I briefly wonder if the date registers with her at all. Then I snap back to thinking we'll be uprooted and dropped down in alien territory in one month. Ruth is jumping around whooping, but I feel nauseous.

"That's it?" I ask. "Do we pick rooms in this place? Is it some kind of commune? More importantly, don't I get a say?"

"No, you have no say. You'll only be here a month or so before you go to NYU anyway." She starts walking toward the barnyard. "We're not going to be in the big house, we're renting the apartment over the garage." Next to the pigs. Above where the cars park. Nausea gives way to shock. "Come on, don't you want to see it?"

"Have *you* even seen it?"

"Yes, when I was here with Stan. It's nice; you'll like it."

I am one hundred percent sure she is wrong about this, as she is with everything else, but actually, for a garage apartment on some corporate hippie estate/farm/future something, it's not bad, even though it's about half the size of where we are now. We each have our own room, me for the summer and those few times I come home during the school year. Of course, without a car I'll be spending a lot more time here than I'd like before I make it to the city, and little to none once I start school. I'm sure I'll be damn sick of the place by the time I leave. I just keep telling myself once I go, I don't have to come back. Christmas at Dad's hovel in the Bronx—now there's a festive plan.

We head home to start sifting through the past decade of our lives.

* * *

Turns out Mom's psychic vision was on target. The day after she signed the lease on the Amonk house she got a letter from the Prince Willow landlord. It's spooky. After nine years, we have ninety days to clear out. Won't they be surprised when we're gone in thirty! I wish we could take the bathtub with the feet, or maybe a doorknob. There isn't much worth saving, but what the hell, the house is coming down so why not grab a souvenir? But Mom says no. There's no room at the new place.

The Cusp of Everything

Moving for the first time since we left Maryland is agonizing. I take a tour around the property that has been my home since I was nine, half a lifetime ago. I was a naïve kid with blue horn rims riding my bike down the driveway to explore the neighborhood with my first New York friend, Vicki. We'd ride for hours, then go to her house to play records like _Bridge Over Troubled Water_. She and I aren't friends any more—we have nothing in common except those memories and the street where we live, and now one of those is ending, at least for me.

It's my home, part of my identity. For at least half the time we've been here I've despised it, welcomed its looming deadline. But now that we're leaving I can't bear it. Scenes run through my mind like a silent movie: playing with Ruth and our mingled friends in the vast front yard and fields, reading in a hammock, swinging on a tire, walking back from my paper route through the fields between Stonewall Lane and our house. Sitting on the roof outside my attic window, looking at the stars and trying to come up with profound thoughts. Slumber parties and Twister in the living room. The Christmas when I got white go go boots and a red record player. All our dogs and my one secret cat.

Then there are the not-so-silent scenes: Watching _Tom Jones_ and _Glen Campbell_ and _Ed Sullivan_ and _Laugh-In_ and the moon landing, gathered around the black-and-white TV in the den. Hearing the siren for the Mamaroneck Fire Department echo through the trees. Playing records with Ruth and dancing like idiots. Mom and Dad telling us—twice—that they were getting divorced.

I don't know what the hell happened to our family or how things might have turned out better. Even before the divorce there was never enough money in New York. In Maryland I went to private schools and rode horses and my parents designed and built a brick house on a wooded acre. It was modeled after the house in Washington where Mom grew up and Mimi still lives. I've seen the sales sheet for it, so I know it sold for $27,500 in 1967. I used to study the real estate ads in the _Scarsdale Inquirer_ religiously, determined to find a real house for us, and remember when, around 1969, the six-figure mark was reached.

Obviously it's a huge spread between $27,500 and $100,000, so I understand why we didn't buy here. But we never had to live in Scarsdale—or even Mamaroneck. Dad's then-new job was in the Bronx, after all, and there are plenty of cheaper places. At this point it looks like neither of my parents will ever own a house again, and that just makes no sense to me. If we moved here because Dad got a better job, why are we living so much worse than we did before? It's so frustrating not to know the truth. Dad always complained it was because Mom's math skills were so pathetic that she couldn't figure out which of two different-sized items was cheaper by weight. But after they got divorced she hinted that he was the bad money manager, spending without a budget but lambasting her over a five-cent difference on a can of tuna. One more reason never to marry: avoiding blame for someone else's failings and disappointments.

I have to admit, this property is magnificent. When we first arrived, Mom turned what had resembled a wheat field into a sweeping lawn and a place for badminton and croquet. Before she started mowing, you could just run out and squat somewhere in the tall grass and weeds and no one could find you until you stood up. She liked it better manicured, though, despite the fact that it's a lot of work for her. I realize now I never once offered to help, even though Ruth and I benefited from a yard more than an acre of weeds. Once it was done, Dad took over, but since he left she's been the official mower again. Bet she won't miss that job.

The property had been a nursery at some point long before our arrival and still has plantings that show off its glory days: massive forsythia bushes, daffodils surrounding the bases of oak trees, lilacs that overwhelm with scent and droop with pastel enormity, an abandoned apple orchard whose small, sour, worm-filled apples have to be some kind of metaphor.

Behind the house is an ancient gas pump. There also used to be an office, with peeling paint and termites. It's in ruins now, its broken glass, splintered wood and disintegrating roofing shingles mingling on the floor with decayed seed catalogs and invoices, pulpy from age and elements. Before it fell, maybe five years ago, the office always had a moldy scent of decomposition and damp lumber that I found both foul and intoxicating. Dad used to park in the garage about 100 feet away, next to that gas pump. In time he abandoned this sagging structure, which collapsed about a year before his marriage did. Anyway, I don't know why I'm even thinking about those buildings. They don't exist anymore; they're just a pile of rubble I hadn't visited in years. I see it now and mourn. It's depressing and yet I don't want it to be gone.

When we were younger, our friends alternated between reveling in all our space to run around and pitying us for not being able to afford a bright new house on a crisply defined lot. Now that I'm past the age of going outside to play, there are only disadvantages, only pity. Certainly there's plenty of self-pity too, which seems to be my new forte. How can I hate a place so much yet hate the thought of leaving it?

Packing up is a long process of getting sidetracked by school papers, magazines, photos and letters, crying at the thought that my memories are being packed up and their long-time home destroyed. My nostalgia for my past feels phony, but I can't control it: I'll miss this crazy place. It won't exist in the real world anymore, so I need to keep it alive in my head.

Bring on the bulldozers, but I'm not leaving without a doorknob.

20

I DON'T KNOW A SOUL WHO'S NOT BEEN BATTERED

July fourth is the Bicentennial, the two hundredth anniversary of the signing of the Declaration of Independence. It's been so overhyped that I got sick of the whole thing long ago. I hadn't seen it as anything to get excited about, but strangely as the day approaches I start to feel differently. I'm especially excited to see the Tall Ships.

The Tall Ships are reproduction sailing vessels from around the world that have been heading toward New York Harbor to join others like them for a Bicentennial celebration called Op Sail. They've been the big topic for weeks, their progress tracked in newspapers and on TV. Christopher Columbus discovered America with ships like these. I'm no history buff, but I want to see them, and I want to be in Manhattan, my new home. I like the idea of having a vision from the past to counter the newness of my New York experience. Plus, I am drawn to the city any day; how can I not be there on one of its biggest days?

Mark has a theory that after the Fourth of July, summer's basically over: a couple of beach trips and it's September. This year, that's a good thing: summer means riding my bike three miles to do ticketing at the Allegheny Airlines counter in Westchester County Airport. There are some cute Air National Guard guys based there, but they're not around much and I can tell I'm in for some tedious times ahead. Mark's going to be working for his parents' insurance company. September and NYU can't come fast enough. The end of summer is when our real lives begin.

Mark and Sophia have a friend from high school who invited the two of them to a July Fourth party in Manhattan. The apartment, with a view of the passing ships on the Hudson River, belongs to someone's sister's boss or something, I can't really follow the connections. But it's an open house so they can bring other people. Mark invites me and I invite Gwen, who is home from her first year at B.U. Having broken up with Eddie, she's looking to stay as busy as possible. I also call Craig to join us. He says Roger wants him to go to a party on a boat in Connecticut, but that's with "a bunch of old queens" and he'd rather come with us. I hope for Roger's sake he's not getting too attached. Mom's taking Ruth to fireworks in Mamaroneck Harbor with Stan, and I'm sure I won't be missed.

Getting ready for our city adventure this hazy Bicentennial morning, listening to Lou Rawls' wonderful <u>"You'll Never Find Another Love Like Mine."</u> I'm suddenly struck by the thought that there might be something going on between Craig and Mark. How did this not occur to me before? Mark's explanation that he got over his Craig obsession through pure strength of will never quite added up for me. What if he's been covering up so I don't suspect the truth: that he and Craig are secret lovers, that he's finally content because he's consummated his greatest crush?

I have to sit down. I feel sick just thinking about the two of them getting together behind my back. Intellectually, I know it's none of my business. But emotionally I can't help feeling it is. I'm not even thinking about their actual physical coming together—seeing two guys kiss was jarring at the Sting and not something I care to repeat. But that's not what's bothering me; it's the idea that Mark might have taken such a momentous step and not told me.

He really does seem different since going through the Syracuse drama, and I shouldn't care whether it's because he cured himself or because he's finally getting some (or giving some—I really don't want to know how it works). But I do care about not being trusted. Could he be afraid I'm still carrying a torch for him?

Fuck it, I have to know. I dial his number on the pretense of discussing travel logistics, like what train we're taking, Then I blurt out, "Is there anything I should know about you and Craig?"

"What do you mean?" he asks, sounding either confused or defensive, I can't tell which. Shit, what am I doing? I don't want him to think I'm nosy or feeling left out, even though both are true.

"Sorry, I didn't mean for it to come out like that," I say quickly. "I just meant that you and Craig have been so comfortable together and I don't really understand how that's possible after everything that happened."

"And you think the only option is that we're getting it on?" he asks, a little coldly.

"No, of course not. I mean, it's none of my business even if you are. I guess it's just been driving me crazy that I can't figure out how you can be friends with him. You offered him your heart and he stomped all over it."

"Yeah, that pretty much sums it up," he says. "But you know what? I got my dignity back. I spent a lot of time alone after we got back from Syracuse, and after Flo." He pauses after her name, and somehow I picture him making the sign of the cross, even though he's given up the Catholic church, too. "I know now that Craig isn't anyone I want to be with romantically. His sexual habits are just disgusting—trust me, you don't want details." I believe him. "But he's fun, you have to give him that."

"Poor Roger," I say, thinking, What a relief.

"That's for sure. Craig's cheated on him all over town. He even came on to me again. We fooled around a little, but sex is obviously so meaningless to him that I shut it down."

So something did happen. "Was there a reason you didn't tell me any of this before? You're not afraid I'm still in love with you, are you?"

He laughs. "No, it's pretty clear you're past that."

"Okay, good. Because I don't want you to feel you can't talk to me about anything," I say. "I know I have a big mouth, but I would never share your secrets with anyone."

"Well, you did tell Craig I was hung up on him. That was a little hard to hear."

I knew it. I knew Craig wouldn't be able to stand not lording it over Mark that he was so damn irresistible, and that I was such a crappy friend. "That just slipped out when I was hitting him outside his dorm. I thought maybe he didn't hear me, but no such luck. I'm really sorry. I've been working on keeping my mouth shut. You can trust me with anything now."

"That's good to know," Mark replies. "Look, I'm over Craig, and he was never that into me to begin with. So let's enjoy the Bicentennial. No tension. No drama. No wondering if you're missing something, because you're not. Relax. You're my dear friend and I love you, OK?"

Hearing this makes me as happy as it would have if he'd said it on New Year's Eve. We're truly friends, the most permanent and least fraught of relationships. "OK," I laugh. "Thanks for understanding. I feel less neurotic already."

"You wish," he chuckles. "I'll see you at noon."

* * *

Rather than drive into what is sure to be chaos, Mark, Sophia, Gwen, Craig and I are meeting at Mark's to take the train to Grand Central, then the subway to the Upper West Side. Gwen and I head over to Mark's. Sophia is already there, but naturally we end up waiting for Craig's appearance. We listen to <u>the Supremes' latest album, <i>High Energy</i></u>, with the upbeat <u>"I'm Gonna Let My Heart Do the Walking."</u> I hope it gets a lot of play at The Sting and elsewhere, but somehow I'm not optimistic.

We're about to leave without Craig when he hits the hour-late mark, but he shows up just as Mark's turning off the stereo and we cram into his father's Lincoln and head for the Mamaroneck station. The train ride is festive and fun, with a rowdy crowd, led by Craig. A lot of people are wearing red, white and blue; some are carrying little flags. The occasional noisemaker squawks, and for a change it's not irritating. We arrive after two o'clock, later than I'd wanted but still in plenty of time to catch the Tall Ships and be a part of history.

The party is in a huge apartment on Riverside Drive. There's actually a man in a uniform operating the wood-paneled elevator that takes us to the twelfth floor. I'm sure he'd rather be out celebrating, but he doesn't let on. I make a mental note never to have another job where I have to wear a uniform. I don't want to miss holidays!

We try to fit in, talking to other guests as we get drinks, but they're strangers, and much older than we are. We go out on the balcony to look down at the Hudson River. Craig makes some embarrassing loud remarks about throwing things off the balcony and we get some cold looks.

We must have missed most of the Tall Ships because there are hundreds of little motorboats, but only a couple of historic-looking ones. From up here they look like tiny specks. The music isn't terrible, but it's way too mellow for the mood of the day. Right now I'm hearing America's "Today's the Day" which could actually be more boring than their "Horse with No Name," and that set the standard for boring songs.

Old coot music makes it feel like we're very distant from the real party and the kind of New York experience we came for. I grab Mark's arm. "We have to get out of here." The five of us aren't a cohesive group, but luckily we do all agree on one thing: we'd rather be outside, where the action is. We scarf down a few *hors d'ouevres*, take the elevator back down and start walking south.

We make our way down streets swarming with what look like ad hoc parades and street festivals. Thousands, maybe millions of people are celebrating together, and it feels welcoming and joyous. Even those who didn't plan ahead have run inside and brought out boomboxes. As we move through the city, they blast different tunes: Gwen's favorite "Tear the Roof Off the Sucker." The overplayed "Turn the Beat Around." One that makes me welcome my love-free life, "Young Hearts Run Free." A bunch of cute guys walk by with a boombox blasting "I'm Gonna Let My Heart Do the Walking." Mark and I exchange smiles.

The revelers wear tinfoil hats and bang drums made out of cups and spoons. Anything to join the celebration, to be one with the city and a part of this giant, shared birthday party. Even when it rains briefly, everyone keeps smiling, especially me.

I have never been in such large crowds, never felt a part of something so powerful and positive. Once we get south of Fourteenth Street, we see more Tall Ships on the Hudson and we gaze in awe, as much as we can see them over the heads of the throngs who took earlier trains. It sounds hokey, but I am so glad to be an American, so glad to be moving to New York, so glad to be young, with my whole life ahead of me. I can't picture my future but I know it's going to be better than my past. Whatever happens, good and bad, I can't wait to experience it all. I'm so full of emotion that I feel dizzy. I could even be on the verge of a heart attack; it wouldn't surprise me if this is what it feels like when a heart bursts. I love everyone and everything. At least, I will until tomorrow, when I'm back packing boxes on Prince Willow Lane.

By the time the sun sets, the four of us have made it all the way down to the southernmost tip of Manhattan. We sit on a curb with the hulking World Trade Center behind us and the Statue of Liberty—that Fourth of July icon—ahead in the distance. The Tall Ships are scattered about, along with all those little boats, and fireworks burst overhead. As we ooh and ah, I am deeply moved. I feel fortunate and grown up: I love my friends, can tolerate my family and know I won't starve. My new life is about to start, here in this city. I know I can't depend on happy endings, but at least I finally feel like I can have my happy beginning.

Paul Simon's "American Tune" plays in my head. It's pretty negative (I don't know a soul who's not been battered) but it invokes the Statue of Liberty, which I can see right now, and it does have the somewhat soothing message that "it's alright." And I actually believe it is. I believe life sucks, but there's hope. I believe that despite all that's gone wrong, despite our crazy world, our wounded country, our personal failings and overwhelming uncertainty, it's all right. We're all right. Everything's going to be OK. Because it's in a song, I know it's true.

The Cusp of Everything

ACKNOWLEDGMENTS

It took me so damn long to write this book that I have to give a blanket thank you to those who hung in over the years and believed in me when I was sure I would be forever stalled in my Playland Summer. Special thanks to the woman who drove into me in a Pacific Coast Highway crosswalk and forced me to imagine dying unpublished. She was very motivating!

For moral support above and beyond the call of even familial duty, my sister Lisa Gualdino and my sister-friends Laurie Sale, Sarina Simon and Liesje Stoett.

Love and thanks to Aunt Geri and Uncle Ken Buttke and the rest of the Foti-Buttke-Wilkinson family.

A special thank you to my talented and motivational writing group: Asaad Kelada, Vicki Shapiro and the brilliant Denise Nicholas.

For getting the word out and being a rock solid friend over the decades, Sharon Weisz.

For thoughtful commentary, Tim Braseth, Suzanne Rosenblatt Buhai, Cynthia Comsky, Tom Dean, Amy Friedman, Linda Epstein Graval, Carole Kramer, Fay and Tom McGrew, Frank O'Halloran, Kris Sofley and Leslie Wintner.

For keeping me accurate with the music, as well as for other much-appreciated insights, Chart Watch-er (and friend) extraordinaire Paul Grein.

My friends who helped in infinite ways: Bambi Alperson Christie, June Bilgore, Sue Billet, Robert Carter, Ted Cohen (yes, Ted, I mentioned you!), Mark Fine, Pamela Giddon Freedman, Jane Gilman, Myrna Robin Gintel, Marcia Golden and David Dukes, Hope Heyman, Sunta Izzicuppo, Laurie Hersch, Juliana Koranteng, Vicki Lynn, Dorene and John Martin, Jim and Nina Stern McCullaugh, Eileen Millan, Lenore Ruben, Marsha Shoushtari, Adam Somers, Diane Stanley, Tere Tereba, Christine and Clive Toye, Lois Whitman and Jeffrey Zink. A special thank you to Mary Wilson.

Paul Schwarz, my brilliant eighth-grade English teacher at Quaker Ridge School, who first told me I was a writer and taught me how to spell "accelerator." He was my first publisher (the 1971 yearbook) and still encourages me today.

My brother Paul, the inspiration for a future volume. Don't worry, Paul...well, maybe worry a little.

* * *

Credit for the terrific '70s-evoking cover goes to NorthSouth Studios (northsouthstudios.com).

Thanks to Mark J. Bonislawsky (astigmatic.com) for the great title font, Spicy Rice.

Thanks to Nancy Casolaro for making me look as good as possible in the author photo.

The Soundtrack

Six-digit numbers are dates (month-day-year) indicating when a song first appeared in the top 40. If the song never made the top 40, or if it was not contemporary to the timeframe of the book, only the year of release is given.
Artists mentioned without reference to a specific song are in **bold**.
Books and movies referenced in the book are also included.

CHAPTER 1
One of These Nights
1. Love Will Keep Us Together–Captain & Tennille–052475
2. Philadelphia Freedom –Elton John–031575
3. One of These Nights–Eagles–061475
4. Carnival music–The Red, White and Blue
5. **Eric Clapton**
6. **The Who**
7. **Bonnie Raitt**
8. San Francisco (Be Sure to Wear Flowers in Your Hair)–Scott McKenzie–1967
9. That's the Way of the World–Earth, Wind & Fire–072675
10. **Jackson 5**

CHAPTER 2
Don't You Want Somebody to Love
11. Paint It, Black–Rolling Stones–1966
12. *Riot on Sunset Strip* (movie)–1967
13. **The Supremes**
14. Somebody to Love–Jefferson Airplane–1967
15. Carney–Leon Russell–1972
16. **Gentle Giant**
17. Reflections–The Supremes–1967
18. **Diana Ross**
19. Lodi–Creedence Clearwater Revival–1969
20. Stand!–Sly and the Family Stone–1969
21. **Ray Conniff Singers**
22. **Marvin Gaye**
23. **Aretha Franklin**
24. **Jackson Browne**

CHAPTER 5
Summer Madness
57. *The Happy Hooker* (book)–Xaviera Hollander–1972
58. I Am Woman–Helen Reddy–1972
59. *Hotel* (book)– Arthur Hailey–1965
60. Rhinestone Cowboy–Glen Campbell–090675
61. The Hustle–Van McCoy–053175
62. Delilah–Tom Jones–1968
63. You Can't Always Get What You Want–Rolling Stones–1969
64. Is That All There Is?–Peggy Lee–1969
65. Burl Ives children's song
66. Summer Madness–Kool & the Gang–062875
67. How Sweet It Is (To Be Loved By You)–James Taylor–071975
68. Sweet Emotion–Aerosmith–071275

CHAPTER 6
The Solid Time of Change
69. O'Jays
70. Spinners
71. TSOP (The Sound of Philadelphia)–MFSB featuring the Three Degrees–1974
72. Harold Melvin and the Blue Notes
73. A Horse With No Name–America–1972
74. All Around My Hat–Steeleye Span–1975
75. *Master of Reality* (album)–Black Sabbath–1971
76. *Close to the Edge* (album)–Yes–1972

CHAPTER 7
Feelings
77. Holdin' Onto Yesterday–Ambrosia–071975
78. Thank God I'm a Country Boy–John Denver–060675
79. Remember Me–Diana Ross–1971
80. Crosby Stills Nash and Young
81. Feelings–Morris Albert–082375
82. Dancing Machine–Jackson 5–1974
83. Just a Little Bit of You–Michael Jackson–071275
84. Bad Luck (Part 1)–Harold Melvin and the Blue Notes–050375
85. Hey There–Rosemary Clooney–1954
86. How Long (Betcha Got a Chick on the Side)–Pointer Sisters–082375

CHAPTER 10
You Haven't Done Nothin'
112. Haydn: Sonata in E-flat Major for Piano, Hob. XVI:49: I. Allegro–
    Vladimir Horowitz
113. *Fulfillingness' First Finale* (album)–Stevie Wonder–1974
114. You Haven't Done Nothin'–Stevie Wonder–1974
115. Born to Run–Bruce Springsteen–101175
116. Who Loves You–The 4 Seasons–092075
117. *One Flew Over the Cuckoo's Nest* (soundtrack album)–1975
118. Dreaming a Dream–Crown Heights Affair–1975
119. (Are You Ready) Do The Bus Stop–Fatback Band–1975
120. I'll Always Love My Mama–The Intruders–1973
121. I Love Music–The O'Jays–111575
122. Find My Way–Cameo–1975
123. Baby Face–The Wing and a Prayer Fife & Drum Corps.–122075
124. Love Rollercoaster–Ohio Players–112275
125. Forever Came Today–Jackson 5–070575
126. Forever Came Today–Diana Ross & the Supremes–1968

CHAPTER 11
Our Day Will Come
127. *The Sunshine Boys* (movie)–1975
128. Help Me–Joni Mitchell–1974
129. Our Day Will Come–Frankie Valli–110875
130. Doctor's Orders–Carol Douglas–1974
131. Fly, Robin, Fly–Silver Convention–102575
132. You Can't Hurry Love–The Supremes–1966
133. Neil Young
134. Johnny Mathis
135. Bad Blood–Neil Sedaka–092075

CHAPTER 12
He's My Man
136. He's My Man–The Supremes–1975
137. Love Child–Diana Ross & the Supremes–1968
138. *Love to Love You Baby* (album)–Donna Summer–1975
139. In-a-Gadda-da-Vida–Iron Butterfly–1968
140. Love to Love You Baby–Donna Summer–122075
141. Ain't No Way to Treat a Lady–Helen Reddy–083075
142. *Muscle of Love* (album) –Alice Cooper–1973

176. 1921–The Who–1968
177. Love Machine (Part 1)–The Miracles–121375
178. *Prisoner in Disguise* (album)–Linda Rondstadt–1975
179. I Will Always Love You–Linda Rondstadt–1975
180. *Exile on Main Street* (album)–Rolling Stones–1972
181. Sweet Virginia–Rolling Stones–1972
182. What's Goin' On Here–Deep Purple–1974
183. *Horses* (album)–Patti Smith–1975
184. Gloria–Patti Smith–1975
185. The End of a Beautiful Friendship–Carmen McRae
186. Behind Blue Eyes (Live)–The Who
187. You Don't Love Me (Live)–The Allman Brothers Band–1971
188. The Supremes
189. Sammy Davis Jr.
190. You Are Everything–Diana Ross & Marvin Gaye–1974
191. We Need You–Diana Ross–1973
192. If You Don't Know Me By Now–Harold Melvin & The Blue Notes–1972
193. I'm Not in Love–10cc (see 53)

CHAPTER 15
There Must Be 50 Ways To Leave Your Lover
194. 50 Ways To Leave Your Lover–Paul Simon–010376
195. Times of Your Life–Paul Anka–112975
196. Dream Weaver–Gary Wright–013176
197. Convoy–C. W. McCall–121375
198. Only Love Can Break Your Heart–Neil Young–1970
199. Right Back Where We Started From–Maxine Nightingale–031376
200. Inseparable–Natalie Cole–022876
201. 50 Ways to Leave Your Lover (see 194)
202. *Breakfast of Champions*–Kurt Vonnegut–1973 0385334206

CHAPTER 16
Leave Me As You Found Me, Empty Like Before
203. Walk Away From Love–David Ruffin–112975
204. Fanny (Be Tender With My Love)–Bee Gees–011776
205. Theme from *The Waltons* (composed by Jerry Goldsmith)
206. *Nancy Drew*–Carolyn Keene
207. *Henry Gross* (album)–1973
208. Simone–Henry Gross–1973

209. Lady Marmalade–Labelle–032975
210. My Little Town–Paul Simon with Art Garfunkel–110175
211. Touch Me in the Morning (instrumental)–Mantovani

CHAPTER 17
Shame, Shame, Shame
212. The Supremes (Scherrie, Mary and Cindy edition)
213. I'm Searching For A Love–Harold Melvin & The Blue Notes–1975
214. *Wake Up Everybody* (album)–Harold Melvin & The Blue Notes–1975
215. Let's Groove–Archie Bell and the Drells–1975
216. *Still Crazy After All These Years* (album)–Paul Simon–1975
217. Back in My Arms Again–Diana Ross and the Supremes–1965
218. Someday We'll Be Together (see 154)
219. Buttered Popcorn–The Supremes–1961
220. Ain't That Good News– The Supremes–1965
221. *The Supremes Sing Country, Western and Pop* (album)–The Supremes–1965
222. I Hear a Symphony–The Supremes–1965
223. The Player–First Choice–1973
224. December, 1963 (Oh, What A Night)–The 4 Seasons–013176
225. Jimmy Reed
226. Allman Brothers
227. Eric Clapton
228. Dream On–Aerosmith–021476
229. Mary Ann–Temptations–1976
230. Over My Head–Fleetwood Mac–121375
231. *I Want You* (album)–Marvin Gaye–1976
232. *T'Aint No Big Thing But He Is…* (album)–Jimmy Reed–1963
233. Shame, Shame, Shame–Jimmy Reed–1963
234. Shame, Shame, Shame–Shirley & Company–022275

CHAPTER 18
I Have Been Removed
235. Crazy–Patsy Cline–1961
236. Border Song–Aretha Franklin –1972
237. *There Goes Rhymin' Simon* (album)–Paul Simon–1973
238. Christ the Lord Is Risen Today–Hymn
239. Was a Sunny Day–Paul Simon–1973

240. Loves Me Like a Rock–Paul Simon–1973
241. Let the Music Play–Barry White–012476
242. I Want You–Marvin Gaye–050676
243. Don't You Worry 'Bout a Thing–Stevie Wonder–1974

CHAPTER 19
I Wouldn't Change a Thing
244. Here I Am/I Wouldn't Change a Thing–Diana Ross–1976
245. Theme From *Mahogany* (see 160)
246. Ain't No Mountain High Enough (see 111)
247. Love Hangover–Diana Ross–042476
248. You Keep Me Hangin' On (see 158)
249. **Ethel Waters**
250. **Josephine Baker**
251. **Bessie Smith**
252. **Billie Holiday**
253. *Lady Sings the Blues* (movie)
254. *Gone with the Wind* (movie)–1939
255. Afternoon Delight–Starland Vocal Band–060576
256. *Bridge Over Troubled Water*–Simon & Garfunkel–1970
257. **Tom Jones**
258. **Glen Campbell**
259. *The Ed Sullivan Show* (TV series)
260. *Laugh-In* (TV series)

CHAPTER 20
I Don't Know a Soul Who's Not Been Battered
261. You'll Never Find Another Love Like Mine–Lou Rawls–071076
262. *High Energy*–The Supremes–1976
263. I'm Gonna Let My Heart Do the Walking–The Supremes–080776
264. Today's the Day–America–061276
265. Tear the Roof Off the Sucker (Give Up the Funk)–Parliament–061276
266. Turn the Beat Around–Vicki Sue Robinson–061976
267. Young Hearts Run Free–Candi Staton–062676
268. I'm Gonna Let My Heart Do the Walking (see 263)
269. American Tune–Paul Simon–1973

The Cusp of Everything

About the Author

Laura Huntt Foti grew up in Westchester County and has lived in Los Angeles for more than 20 years. Following a successful career in journalism, the music business and the interactive world pre-web, she now works as a freelance writer, editor and consultant. Laura has a teenage son, two dogs and two cats. *The Cusp of Everything* is her first book, and she can't wait to get it published as an ebook with a real-time soundtrack. She is currently working on a sequel.